BREWER

AND

THE BLACK ROSE

BREWER
AND
THE BLACK ROSE

BY

JAMES KEFFER

www.penmorepress.com

DEDICATION

To Emma Rose,
may you grow to love books and reading as much as I do

CHAPTER ONE

Captain William Brewer had never been in a position like this before. Soft cooing wafted to his ears, and beautiful blue eyes sparkled with unconditional love and joy. He reached down to brush the cheek of the babe in his arms, only to have her squeal with delight and catch his pinky in her tiny hand. He looked up and met eyes even bluer and more lustrous-- those of his wife, who was sitting on the settee beside them.

"What shall we name her?" he asked.

"I wanted to wait for you before making a decision. Father has taken to calling her, 'You', but she can't use that for a name. Have you any suggestions?"

They played with the baby for a while, until suddenly he looked up at Elizabeth again. "I don't believe I've ever asked, but what was your mother's name?"

She studied his face, surprised by his question. "Anne," she said.

"Anne," he repeated softly. "I think that's a wonderful name. Shall we call her Anne?"

He saw tears well up in her eyes, and he thought for a moment he had said something wrong. Elizabeth rarely spoke of her mother; in fact, the sum total of Brewer's knowledge of her was that she had died giving birth to Elizabeth. He breathed a silent sigh of relief when she nodded her head. "Oh, yes, I think that will do very well."

She rested her head on his shoulder, and he felt her tears fall on his shirt. "Hello, Anne," she whispered.

Brewer looked down at his daughter. "Anne," he said. "It fits her nicely. And heaven help the first officer who tries to court her!" They laughed, and little Anne began to fuss.

"And what do you have to complain about, my darling Anne?" Brewer asked. He tried bouncing her gently in his arms, but that did nothing to pacify the infant.

"Here," Elizabeth said, reaching for the child, "she may be hungry or need changing. If you will excuse us, Daddy?"

Brewer looked up at the name and smiled. He handed the babe to her mother and rose as they left the room. He walked to the table under the window and poured himself a drink. Then he looked around the room. He was in the library of her father's house on St. Kitts. Elizabeth stayed here while he was at sea. He turned to see his father-in-law, Governor Henry Danforth, enter the room, and he bowed. "May I pour you a drink, sir?" he asked.

"No, thank you," the governor said. "Sit down, won't you, William? I want to talk to you. Do you have a moment?"

"Of course. What can I do for you?"

"There are a couple things I wish to discuss. First, were you briefed at all when you returned, regarding the situation in the Caribbean?"

"No, sir. My ship was put in dock for repairs and a quick refit as soon as we arrived, and I was granted leave to come and see Elizabeth and... Anne."

The Governor's eyes brightened at the child's name. "Yes, Elizabeth told me you'd named her, when I saw them in the hallway. That was good of you. My Anne would have been so proud! Elizabeth bears a great resemblance to her mother, and I think the child is the very image of her mother at that age."

"Believe me, sir," Brewer said, "it would not bother me at all if the child inherited every bit of her looks from her mother."

The governor sighed. "Yes, well, on to the subject of the Caribbean. You took out El Diabolito and Roberto Cofresi when you had command of HMS *Revenge*, but it seems that piracy is again on the rise in the last six or seven months."

"Indeed? Do they have any idea who is responsible?"

"No, but I understand that after each attack, the pirates leave behind a black rose."

Brewer started. "A black rose? Do they say anything or leave a message to go along with it?"

The governor replied, "Not to my knowledge. One thing I have heard, and from more than one source, is that many suspect this pirate captain may be a woman."

Brewer's eyes went wide. "*A woman?*" he exclaimed. "*Are there women pirates?*"

"Not many," the governor said. "The last one known was Anne Bonney, who sailed with Jack Rackham, and that was more than a hundred years ago."

"Wasn't she hung when he was?"

"No. She was sentenced to death by hanging for piracy, but the sentence was delayed on her plea of pregnancy. She escaped shortly thereafter and was never apprehended."

Brewer shook his head in wonder. *Of all things,* he thought, *now we may have a woman raiding shipping in the Caribbean*. He looked to his father-in-law. "What was the other matter?"

"Oh, yes. You need to be aware that my term as governor will come to an end on December 31st. I shall be returning to England to enjoy my retirement and my grandchildren."

This was news to Brewer. He wondered why Elizabeth had not mentioned it before. "I see."

The governor continued, "Naturally, Elizabeth and Anne are welcome to stay with me while you are at sea. I would consider it an honor to look after them. But you may want to think about where you both would like to settle down."

"Yes," Brewer answered. He would definitely have to talk with his wife. The end of the year was still ten months away, but all of a sudden ten months did not seem like a very long time.

"Well," the governor said as he rose, "let me know what you and Elizabeth decide, won't you? I shall see you at dinner." He bowed and left the room.

Brewer went looking for Elizabeth, and he found her nursing the baby in their bedroom.

She looked up as he came in. "Turns out she was hungry."

"So, I see," he said. He sat beside her on the bed. "I just spoke with your father. Why didn't you tell me he was leaving at the end of the year?"

"I'm sorry," she said quietly. "I was going to, and then I got your letter saying you were on your way home, and I decided to wait until I saw you again."

"Do you know where he intends to retire?"

She shook her head as she watched the baby nurse. She looked at her husband and said, "I believe he intends to go to London first, but after that I have no idea. His people come from Northumberland, so perhaps he will go there."

"And where would you like to go?" he asked. "I know we haven't discussed that, but events have forced our hand."

She thought about it while she switched the baby to the other breast, then looked back to her husband.

"I don't really know," she said. "I've lived my whole life with my father, but I'm not sure about living in London. Throughout his postings in the foreign office, we never lived in a big city. In fact, St. Kitts is the most prestigious appointment of his career."

Brewer stroked Anne's head with the back of his fingers.

"You have no other family in England."

"No," she agreed.

"And I don't think I can send you to mine," he added, "not until my father finally forgives me."

"I'm sure he will, William," she said hopefully. "Perhaps when you write them and tell them about Anne?"

He smiled reassuringly. "Perhaps."

At dinner, the governor laid out his plans. "I shall go to London and rent a house for several months while I make enquiries. My family has an ancestral home, such as it is, in Northumberland, but I do not know whether my eldest brother is still in residence there. We had a falling out, and haven't been in contact for years. If the house is available, I shall most likely retire there."

Brewer noticed a shiver in his wife's shoulder. Apparently, the prospect of following her father to the North Country did not appeal to her. From what he'd heard about the climate, he didn't blame her.

Elizabeth said to her father, "Perhaps Anne and I could stay with you in London while I look around for a situation that suits William and me."

Her father smiled. "Every day with you and my granddaughter is a treasure to me," he said.

She turned to her husband. "What do you think, William?"

His reply was forestalled by a frantic knocking at the door, and in burst Randall, one of the governor's servants.

"Governor! Governor!" he cried. "There's a man from the port office downstairs. He said a ship has just entered the harbor, and she looks like she's been attacked!"

"What?" the governor exclaimed.

Brewer rose immediately and went down to the entrance, where a man was standing.

"You are the man from the port office?" he asked.

"Yes, sir," the man said.

"I am Captain Brewer of His Majesty's frigate *Phoebe*. Tell me what's happened."

"Sir, twenty minutes ago, a brig was sighted drifting into the harbor. We rushed a pilot out to her, and the pilot reported back that the ship looked like it had been attacked and that there were many dead and wounded people on board. I was sent to tell the Governor."

"Quite right," Brewer said. "Is there a wharf berth open?"

"Aye, Captain."

"Move the ship there, and put a guard on board," he said. "See that they treated by a doctor, but nobody else goes aboard until the governor or I say so. Hold the pilot there as well; the governor will most likely have questions for him."

"As you say, sir. I'll see to it at once."

"Thank you. The governor and I will be down directly."

"Right." The man put his cap on his head and left.

Brewer made his way back upstairs. He found Elizabeth and her father outside the dining room.

"I'm having the ship brought in to a wharf so we can go aboard," he told the Governor. "I also gave orders for the wounded to be seen by a doctor, and for no man to go aboard until you and I arrive, sir."

"Right," he said. "Let me get my hat."

He left, and Brewer saw the worried look on his wife's face.

"Pirates?" she whispered.

"I don't know," he answered. "I hope to find out the truth." Her father returned, and both men left for the waterfront.

They arrived at the wharf just as the last of the wounded were being removed to a large room at the back of the port office that had been converted into a makeshift hospital. Brewer and the governor stood aside and allowed the stretcher to pass before proceeding down the wharf and up the gangway to the ship. Brewer was pleased to note the presence of a guard at the bottom of the gangway.

The ship was a brigantine, named *Zephyr*. Everything Brewer saw as he stepped onto the deck confirmed the report that she had been attacked. Judging by the amount of damage and the size of the holes in the side of the ship, the captain estimated the attacker was armed with 8-pounders.

He heard a gasp and turned to see the governor staring wide-eyed at the death and destruction before him. His hand covered his mouth. Brewer moved to stand in front of him and block his view.

"Sir," he said, quietly but firmly, "perhaps you should visit the wounded and see how they fare? Perhaps some of them could tell you what happened here. I will assess the damage aboard and report to you."

His father-in-law caught his eye and blinked as he regained control. "Yes, if you think so, Captain. I shall await your report."

Brewer watched as the governor retreated down the gangway and made his way up the wharf before turning to the business at hand. He counted twelve dead scattered around the deck. Some had been killed by swords or daggers while others had been shot. The savagery evident in two or three killings seemed to confirm his suspicion that pirates were the culprits.

He made his way below deck to examine the hold. What he found solidified his suspicions. Whatever the cargo had been, most of it was missing. He also found none of a ship's usual supplies—casks of meat, spirits, bread, and the like. He made his way aft to the master's cabin to look for the ship's manifest. The cabin had been completely wrecked, no doubt by someone searching for a cash box or gold. Brewer looked around him and sighed. He would detail one of the port office men to collect every paper strewn about the cabin, and he would inspect them later. *Well,* he thought, *perhaps the governor will discover the cargo.*

He went back on deck and made a cursory search of the dead. He found one body, which had fallen near the wheel, that had had his hat dropped onto his head after death. Brewer stooped to lift the man's hat when his attention was captured by something else.

Across the man's chest lay a single black rose.

Brewer picked up the rose and left the ship. He found the governor talking to the doctor.

"Ah, Brewer," the governor said. "Doctor, may I introduce my son-in-law, Captain William Brewer of the frigate HMS *Phoebe.* Captain, this is Dr. Christopher." The two men shook hands.

"Doctor," Brewer asked, "what can you tell us about their injuries?"

"Cuts and slashes, mostly, Captain," the doctor said, "although there are one or two that look like they were made with a whip. Eleven wounded total, two serious enough that I'm not sure they'll see the morning."

"What did you find on board, Captain?" the governor asked.

"I counted twelve dead, all on the deck. The cargo's missing. One of the attackers made a shambles out of the master's cabin. Can you detail someone from the port office to collect all the papers in the cabin and bring them to you? I want to look them over."

"Certainly. I'll see to it right away."

"One more thing. I found this lying on one of the dead by the wheel." He held up the rose.

The two men stared at the flower in his fingers. The Governor's face turned dark, and Brewer saw the doctor swallow hard.

"So, it's true?" the doctor whispered. "Pirates?"

"So it would appear."

The governor took the black rose and inspected it closely. "Come, Captain. We have reports to write for your admiral and the foreign secretary. Doctor, we shall return tomorrow to interview these survivors."

Brewer's first interview the next morning was with the brigantine's third mate, Daniel Sheldon, the only officer to survive the attack.

"They took us by surprise, sir," he said, in reply to Brewer's question. "Pretended to be a merchant ship, and when they were close enough, they ran out their guns and fired! Broadside after broadside, with no warning or demand to surrender, either! The master was killed in the first volley, and the mate fell soon afterward. I hauled down the colors as fast as I could, but it made no difference. They fired two more broadsides and then boarded us.

"We didn't resist at first. My thought was to let them take what they wanted and leave. Some of them went below while the rest gathered the watch on deck in a group. Soon them that went below returned, driving the rest of the crew up on deck. Their leader called out that our ship and cargo was theirs, and we were dead men. That's when they began to slaughter us. A few of us managed to get hold of swords to try to defend ourselves, but we never stood a chance. I went down with a bad gash in my side. I guess it bled bad enough that they thought I was a goner and left me for dead."

Brewer took notes as fast as he could. "You said you saw their leader? What did he look like?"

Sheldon frowned. "He was a small man; I would say no more than the middle of my chest or so tall. Thin, with a high voice almost like a woman's. Wore a black kerchief on his face. Cursed like a sailor, whoever he was."

"Did you get his name?" Brewer asked.

Sheldon shook his head. "He never said, and I didn't hear anyone address him. Don't you have any idea who attacked us?"

"I have a very good idea," Brewer said, still scribbling furiously. "Was the master the man on the deck by the wheel?"

Sheldon thought for a moment, then nodded. "I think that's where he fell. Why?"

Brewer stopped writing and looked at the wounded man. "Because dropped on his chest we found a single black rose."

Sheldon's eyes went wide with fear, then he squeezed them shut and turned his head away from Brewer and refused to say another word.

Brewer spoke to several other survivors but learned no additional information. He reviewed his notes and returned to the governor's house.

The governor was occupied with meetings all morning, so after checking on Elizabeth and Anne, Brewer went to the library to review the papers collected from the brigantine. He sorted through them until he found the cargo manifest. The ship was carrying foodstuffs and wine out of Martinique, bound for St. Kitts. That explained why the cargo was taken; pirates never passed up food and drink. Brewer frowned; it would help if they knew when and where the pirates had fallen upon the ship. Unfortunately, word of the black rose had effectively silenced the survivors for now. He would have to question them again in a day or two.

None of the other papers gave him any worthwhile information; perhaps the log had been thrown overboard. Brewer set them aside and went to find Elizabeth. He found her in the baby's room, watching her sleep. He came up behind her and put his arms around her, and she leaned back into his chest.

"So, was it pirates?" she asked.

"What did your father say?"

"Nothing. I think he didn't want to worry me." She looked up at him. "Was it?"

He hesitated, then finally nodded. "I believe so. We found a black rose on the captain's body."

She turned back to watch the baby, and he felt her shiver.

"Shall I arrange passage back to England for you and Anne?"

"Where would we go?" she asked. "I have no family in England."

"You could go to Smallbridge until your father arrives."

She leaned her head back onto his chest and closed her eyes. "No," she said quietly. "We shall stay."

He knew better than to argue with her. Maybe later, once he knew more, he could convince her it was safer to leave. He steered her quietly out of the room and eased the door shut behind them.

"If only we knew who this Black Rose was," Elizabeth said as they walked down the hall. "Apparently the leader leaves it as his calling card after each attack. Do we know what he looks like?"

Brewer held the library door for her and closed it behind them. They sat on the sofa.

"The survivors I questioned gave a similar description to what we already knew: small build, high, womanly voice. Other reports say he has long dark hair, but the men I questioned did not confirm that."

She sighed. "Not much to go on, is it?"

"No," her husband agreed.

* * * * *

Diego looked over the new recruits with a discerning eye. He liked what he saw. None of the eleven brought back by their sloop looked like a spy, and Diego had a reputation for being able to spot a traitor.

"You all know the code," he said to them. "Make sure you stick to it. There will be no mercy; do not give any, and do not expect any. Do your work well. Obey orders, and we shall all be rich!" He saw several of them grin at the prospect. He motioned to the pirate next to him. "Go with José. He will show you where you will sleep."

Diego watched them go, then turned his attention to the ship. The crew was already at work making the usual small repairs that were always necessary after a voyage. At the moment, they attended to the rigging; after that, they would service the guns. The ship would be provisioned and ready to sail again by tomorrow night.

He walked back to their little encampment. It was a half-mile trek through thick woods, keeping the camp well hidden from the sea. He emerged from the woods to the sounds of construction. Recruiting efforts had been unusually successful lately, so it was necessary to build more huts for additional sleeping space. The new hands would join in the efforts, which should speed completion considerably. Soon there would be a dozen huts surrounding the meeting lodge.

He stopped at the door of the first hut and hesitated before entering. He took a deep breath to steel his nerves and stepped inside. As he expected, he found her still seated at the table, exactly as he had left her, playing with a knife, her food untouched in front of her.

"You must eat," he begged her. "Starving yourself will not bring him back."

Her eyes darted to him, and he thought for a moment he had gone too far, but she resumed toying with the knife and ignored him. He shook his head and went to the cupboard. He pulled out a loaf of bread and cut himself a thick slice. He slathered it with butter—an unexpected treat, taken from a fluyt they'd raided and then sunk last week—and sat down across from her. He took a bite and watched her as he chewed, but she continued to ignore him.

"How long do you think you can keep this up?" he asked. "You've hardly eaten for days."

The knife stopped its twisting, and her eyes went to him again. He took another bite and waited.

"How can you expect me to eat," she asked quietly, "now that we know what happened?"

Diego munched quietly on his bread. Everything had changed last week when one of the recruits had turned out to be a survivor of the British attack on El Diabolito's ship. Until he turned up, they had thought the entire crew had perished in the attack and subsequent explosion, which rumors said had destroyed the ship. Captives that the British claimed were taken from the ship before it exploded were all hung for piracy. Now they had a man in camp who claimed to know the truth of what had happened. His assertions had been verified by questions about El Diabolito, Roberto Cofresi, and others that only someone who had been present would be able to answer. That was enough for her; she had brought him to their hut and demanded to know what had happened.

He'd spared no detail, telling his tale slowly and deliberately, ending with a description of the British captain, Brewer, killing El Diabolito. The recruit had been taken off the ship with the other captives before the ship blew up, and had managed to slip away unnoticed when they anchored in an island harbour to make repairs. Three days later, an unsuspecting ship stopped there for water and rescued him.

"And what about Cofresi?" she had asked.

"He was shot," he said, "by a little man from the British ship."

"A little man?"

"Short," he added, and held his hand less than five feet from the floor. "Perhaps this tall."

Her eyes grew angry. "Tell me."

He told the entire story, claiming he saw the two fight a duel below decks. He remarked that the little Britisher was very good with a sword. But the fight had ended when the little man shot Cofresi in the head.

"And you do not remember the name of the ship?" she demanded.

"No. I'm sorry."

She had sat there, staring at nothing through hooded eyes. Diego had motioned for the recruit to leave.

She had hardly spoken or eaten in the days since. Cofresi had promised to marry her when he returned, but now all that had been ripped from her. She brooded relentlessly, and when they went out on raids, her savagery exceeded anything Diego had seen from her before.

Now she let the knife fall to the table. She rose and silently began to wander around the hut.

"What do you intend to do?" he asked.

She walked over to a vase by a window. She withdrew a single black rose from the many it contained and held it up to her nose. She sniffed, her eyes staring into space.

"Rose?" he prodded.

She blinked and glanced in his direction. She took the rose with her as she resumed her wandering.

"We must find this little man," she said. "And when we do, I shall have my revenge."

CHAPTER TWO

Brewer packed his bag for the trip back to Jamaica. He had arranged for a berth on a mail packet that was leaving on the morning ride. He heard a sigh coming from the doorway behind and turned to see his beautiful wife leaning against the jamb.

"Lady Barbara was right. "I don't think I shall ever get used to you leaving us," she lamented. She sat down on the bed and placed her hand on his arm. "How long will it be?"

"Hopefully not more than a few months," he told her. "I must ask you to be brave." He moved his kit to the floor so he could sit beside her and take her hand in his.

She turned to look out the window. "I just didn't think it would be so hard."

He pulled her to him and wrapped his arms around her.

"I'll be back as soon as I can."

"I know you will." She wiped her tears on her handkerchief.

He said goodbye to them at the bottom of the staircase near the front door. He kissed Anne on her forehead before kissing Elizabeth and hugging them both. She smiled as he let them go. He could see she was fighting back tears but didn't comment on it. He turned to his father-in-law.

"Don't worry," the older man said as they shook hands, "I'll take care of them until you return."

"I'm in your debt." He turned to his wife and daughter one last time, trying to memorize their faces. "I love you both. Goodbye." He left the house without looking back.

He walked to the wharf, already feeling the pang of missing them. He hated saying goodbye this way, but Elizabeth had insisted. She said she couldn't bear to watch him sail away. He shook his head and sighed, hoping one day she would change her mind.

He found the mail packet and went aboard. He was taken below deck to a cabin aft, next to the master's cabin, which was barely long enough for him to lie down in, with a hammock slung from the deck beams above. The low ceiling forced him to bend nearly double. There was no furniture in the small space. He tossed his bag in the corner and went up on deck.

The voyage passed without incident. The cramped confines of his cabin encouraged Brewer to spend every waking moment on deck. He quite enjoyed the warmth of the winter Caribbean sun and the cool breezes of the evenings, but his watchful eyes would scan the horizons. He knew Black Rose was out there somewhere.

When they came into the harbor at Port Royal, he arranged to be transferred to HMS *Phoebe* immediately. He found her anchored in the bay, her need of the dockyard over. He asked the master to signal the frigate to send a boat for him.

He was greeted by Mr. Greene as he stepped up on to the deck. The two men saluted and shook hands.

"Welcome home, sir," Greene said.

"How'd the refit go?" Brewer asked.

"We were able to get the copper cleaned, sir," Greene replied. "Fortunately it was all intact. Judging from the amount of stuff they cleaned off, Mr. Sweeney estimates we may get as much as an extra three knots from the old girl."

"Good. What's left to do?"

"The bosun and his mates are almost done replacing the rigging, and we're scheduled for the lighters to top off our water supply the day after tomorrow. Alfred and Winfield want to accompany the purser ashore tomorrow to make their final purchases. Alfred will no doubt wish to go over the list with you before he leaves. We should be ready for sea in forty-eight hours."

"Good." Brewer made to go below, but Greene stopped him.

"There's a packet for you, sir, from the new admiral. I put it on the desk in your cabin. The label says you are to open it when you return."

"Thank you, Benjamin."

He made his way below and entered his cabin. It struck him as strange that he should feel at home here. As much as he missed Elizabeth and Anne, when he was with them, he always felt a distinct pull in the back of his mind that said he should be here. He ran his hand across the back of his chair and looked around the cabin. He was indeed home.

He heard a squeak behind him and turned to find Pudge standing there, his knuckles pressed to his forehead. Brewer smiled. Pudge was one of the ship's boys who happened to be in Mac's mess, and he had taken a shine to the big Cornishman. Pudge's ambition was to take over from Mac one day as the captain's coxswain. For now he was assigned as the captain's cabin boy.

"Hello, Pudge," he said. "We don't salute indoors."

"Sorry, sir." The arm dropped to his side.

"That's better. Now, what may I do for you?"

"Alfred sent me to see if you would like anything, sir."

"Not at this time, thank you," the captain replied. "I'm fine. Tell me, Pudge, how's your training going?"

"Well, sir, Alfred's teaching me how to polish your sword, and last week Mac took me out and started teaching me 'n Skimp how to sail the launch." The lad nodded his head vigorously. "Don't you worry, Captain, when Mac retires, I'll be ready!" The boy paused and frowned. "I *hope* I'm ready in time. Mac's getting old, you know!"

Brewer could hardly keep from bursting into laughter. "In that case, Pudge, perhaps you should speak to him about teaching you faster."

The boy beamed at the suggestion. "Good-O!" he crowed. He went to salute and caught himself, and Brewer smiled at the confusion on the boy's face.

"You come to attention," he said, coming to the rescue, "and then you may leave."

"Oh! Aye, sir." Pudge came to attention and ran back to the pantry.

Brewer was still smiling as he turned his attention to his desk and the packet thereupon. It bore the seal of the Commander-in-chief, West Indies Squadron. He sat down and picked up the packet, studying it for a moment before breaking the seal. The packet contained only one page bearing a single sentence in tightly written script, inviting him to appear at Admiral's House at his earliest convenience. It was signed Admiral Sir David Cartwright, Commander-in-Chief, West Indies Squadron. Brewer gazed at the signature. Admiral Simpson, Hornblower's successor as squadron commander, had died suddenly while Brewer and HMS *Phoebe* were in the South Atlantic. Cartwright had not yet arrived to take up his post when Brewer went on leave to St. Kitts.

Brewer raised his head to call for Alfred, but then thought of a better idea.

"Pudge!" he called, and the boy came running out of the pantry, skidding to a halt in front of his captain and snapping to attention.

"First off, don't run," he said. "Second, please find Lieutenant Greene. Give him my compliments and ask him to join me. Then I want you to find Mac and ask him to get the gig ready to take me ashore."

"Aye, aye, Captain!" Pudge started to salute and caught himself. Then he turned to run for the door and nearly fell when he stopped himself. He ended up walking out of the cabin as fast as he could. Brewer chuckled after he was gone. A moment later Alfred appeared in the pantry door.

"Too bad we can't bottle that energy and sell it, Alfred. We'd have no more need of prize money, I can tell you that!

My best uniform, if you please. Time to meet the new admiral."

Brewer was escorted to the library at Admiral's House, where he found Admiral Cartwright warming himself before a fire. A large portrait of the king hung over the hearth.

"Captain Brewer, sir," his aide announced.

The Admiral turned at the announcement. He walked over and shook his guest's hand.

"Brewer, of course. A pleasure to meet you," the Admiral said. He was a petite man, barely five and a half feet tall and thin. White hair cut short, clean shaven, with bright grey piercing eyes, Cartwright gave the impression of intelligence and control.

"Come over to the fire and warm yourself. Jenkins! Two glasses of port, if you please. Come, Captain."

The two men sat in comfortable chairs before the fire, and Brewer toasted the king's health when their port arrived. Cartwright set his glass down and stretched out his hands to the fire.

"I've just had time to finish your report on the pirate attack. Is there anything you can add?"

"I'm afraid not, sir," Brewer replied. "Every survivor I questioned refused to say another word when they found out about the black rose."

Cartwright frowned. "Whoever this Black Rose is, he is getting more brazen and deadly with each attack. If we can't stop him, soon we shall have to convoy ships in and out of the Caribbean, or else the merchant crews may refuse to sail. From the reports I am seeing, the ship that made it into St. Kitts was the first in which every member of the crew was either wounded or killed, but not the last. No passengers, were aboard, I take it?"

"None."

Cartwright grunted. "Small mercy. Did the survivors at least describe what sort of ship attacked them?"

"A large sloop, by all accounts. One of the survivors identified the guns as being 8-pounders. He said the sloop carried twelve to sixteen."

The Admiral chewed on his bottom lip while he rubbed his hands before the fire.

"When will *Phoebe* be provisioned for sea?" Cartwright asked.

"Forty-eight hours, sir."

Cartwright nodded, not taking his eyes—or his hands—from the fire. "I'm sending you out again. Your mission is to find this Black Rose and put an end to his ravages. Either bring him back for trial and punishment, or else blow him out of the water. I suggest you start your search along the Lesser Antilles and Windward Islands. Unfortunately, the attacks have been so spread out that we have no idea where his base of operations is located. Report in as you can. Let me know of your intentions, in case some information comes to me that may assist you." The Admiral rose. Brewer followed suit.

Cartwright escorted him to the door. "Your orders will be sent to you tomorrow. A pleasure to meet you, Captain. Good luck, and good hunting."

Brewer came to attention. "Thank you, Admiral."

HMS *Phoebe* put to sea on schedule. Her course was ESE toward the Lesser Antilles.

Early in his captaincy, Brewer had developed the habit of entertaining his officers on the first or second night at sea so that they might become reacquainted and he might acquaint them with their orders. So, on the second night of their new commission, Brewer hosted a supper. He sat at the head of the table, quietly observing his guests. Mr. Greene sat to his right, fully recovered from his wounds received during their battle with the Brazilians. He was in an animated conversation with Lieutenant Rivkins, who was now confirmed as *Phoebe's* second lieutenant. Both men were speaking in such hushed tones as they could manage amongst the din of the table, but they were gesturing so emphatically that Brewer made a mental note to ask Greene about the conversation later. Beyond Rivkins sat Lieutenant Reed, similarly confirmed in his rank. Reed was trying his best to make polite conversation with the officer to his right, the newly-commissioned Lieutenant Cromwell. He'd come aboard at Port Royal as *Phoebe's* new fourth lieutenant. Thus far, Brewer thought Reed's efforts a failure, as the new lieutenant merely sipped his wine and nodded his head occasionally.

On Brewer's left was Dr. Spinelli, energetically taking part in a three-way debate with the two men to his left, Mr. Sweeney, the sailing master, and Captain Enfield of the Royal Marines. Brewer could not quite make out what the argument was about, but he thought the principals to be Spinelli and Enfield, with Sweeney caught in the middle and doing his best to keep the peace. Last but not least, on Enfield's left sat Mr. Murdy, Phoebe's senior midshipman. He was keeping to himself while trying to listen in on Mr. Reed's remarks to Lieutenant Cromwell.

The captain rose from his seat, and the room grew quiet.

"Thank you all for coming," Brewer said, "and let me say that I am glad to see you." He gestured to the new face at the table. "For those who may not have met him yet, let me introduce Lieutenant John Cromwell, our new fourth lieutenant." There was a spattering of applause. "Make sure you make him feel welcome. Alfred is busy working his usual magic for us; supper should be ready soon. After the meal, I shall announce our orders, and we will discuss plans for working the ship up to standards."

As if on cue, Alfred, Mac, and the stewards began carrying in delights to tempt the saints to defect. For a first course, they placed bowls of steaming, aromatic turtle soup before each man. Brewer amused himself by counting the number of times one of his guests was unduly hasty and winced or muttered "Ouch!" as he burned his tongue. The empty bowls were cleared away and the main attraction was brought: a meat pie which was set before the captain. This was followed by Welsh Rabbit: slabs of toasted bread covered in melted cheese with a fried egg on top. Pease pudding was served, as was fresh, hot bread instead of the usual ship's biscuit. Last but not least, two large apple pies were placed in the center of the table. Brewer was pleased to see Pudge bringing food to the table.

"Bless my soul," Rivkins said, "I think I've died and gone to Heaven."

They lost no time in helping themselves, passing platters around until each man's plate could hold no more.

"I'll say this, Captain," remarked Enfield, "if we had Alfred cooking for us at Waterloo, we'd have whipped Boney sooner, so we could enjoy our breakfast in peace!"

"Should have joined the Navy, Captain," Rivkins chided him.

Sweeney pointed with his fork, a piece of rabbit still stuck on the tines. "I hope you realize how lucky you are to have Alfred," he said. "I can assure you that on some ships, the lads wish they'd joined the Army for better food. Wouldn't you agree, Captain?"

Brewer nodded emphatically as he chewed. "Bad cooks are bad for morale, and have probably caused more desertions than the threat of immanent battle."

"What I don't understand," Reed chipped in, "is how Alfred can be such a wizard in the galley and still handle a sword like he does. Captain, I know you practice with Alfred; have you ever beat him?"

"No," Brewer answered frankly, "I never have. But what I've learned from him has saved my life more than once." Brewer set his fork on his plate and leaned back in his chair. "When I took command of HMS *Defiant* after the captain was lost overboard, the captain's servant was a man by the name of Jenkins. Mr. Greene, the doctor, and Mr. Sweeney may remember him." The men nodded vigorously as their captain continued. "He worked miracles in the galley, let me tell you. The governor of Jamaica offered him a position cooking for him, and Jenkins took it. Can't say I blame him. He was kind enough to make sure it was all right with me before he left. It was through him that Alfred came to us. God watching over us, that's all I can say." He picked up his fork and resumed eating.

"Why did he leave?" Mr. Murdy asked.

Brewer tried to remember. "I seem to recall that he was very attached to the previous captain, and it hit him hard when he was lost. I guess being on the ship afterward was uncomfortable for him. Am I correct, Mr. Sweeney?"

"Aye, Captain. I believe Jenkins had been with Captain Norman for years."

Brewer looked to Murdy with a "there-you-have-it" gesture of his fork.

Sweeney swallowed and sat back. "I remember a bad cook we had once. I was sailing on a big merchantman just after the outbreak of the French revolution, and the cook we had was absolutely terrible. Didn't bother him one bit either! It got so bad that the complaints reached the captain's ears. He didn't listen—until his own cook caught a fever and died. He ate with the crew for two days, and that was all he could stand. He brought the man to his cabin and told him to improve his cooking, or else! Well, the food improved, but only marginally. What he didn't burn, he curdled. Then somebody found out that one of the quartermaster's mates had been a cook for a county squire in Berkshire before he was pressed at the end of the Napoleonic wars. Just a day or two later, we pull in to an island looking for fresh water. The captain calls out the list of men to go ashore in the boats, and the cook's name is heard loud and clear.

"Now the captain does something I'd never seen him do before or since. He leaves the quarterdeck while we were in a strange harbor and goes to his cabin. The boats go ashore with the empty water barrels and bring them back full, but they returned without the cook! At the time, they said he ran off, deserted; but I found out later that they marooned him on the island. We sailed without him, and the next day the mate was reassigned as the new cook. Both food quality and crew morale improved significantly."

Greene stared in astonishment at the sailing master. "Why didn't the captain just take the mate to be *his* new servant?"

Sweeney eyed the first lieutenant as he finished chewing a mouthful of meat pie. He swallowed and pointed at the premier with his fork. "Well now, I didn't ask him, Mr. Greene, but offhand I'd say he didn't want to be marooned on that island with the cook."

The table erupted with laughter. Rivkins hooted and slapped Greene on the back. Greene shrugged and took another forkful of pudding.

"At the battle of Quatre Bras," Captain Enfield said, "my unit took a French soldier prisoner. This was just before Waterloo. We soon discovered he had no particular love for Bonaparte and so had no interest in escaping. That evening, when our mess was sent up to us, we duly gave him a portion. He takes one bite, screws up his face, and asks if what he was served had been intended for the camp dog. We asked if he could do better, and he said 'Yes.' So we let him try. We took him to the field kitchen and left him to inventory the supplies. A short time later, we found him walking back into camp with his arms loaded with plants and herbs he'd foraged. He made the best food I ever ate in the army; I can tell you." He shook his head sadly. "Too bad for us, General Maitland heard about him and took him as his own chef. I think today he owns a famous French restaurant in London."

Several of the men chuckled. Brewer was glad to see them in such good spirits. He waited while the stewards cleared the table and refilled the glasses before standing. Conversation died as all eyes turned to him.

"The time has come for me to inform you of our orders," he said. "In short, we are commanded to hunt down and capture or kill the pirate known popularly as the Black Rose."

Several sets of eyebrows rose at the news, and Mr. Sweeney pursed his lips and let out a soft whistle.

"Unfortunately," Brewer continued, "we have only the barest description to go on. We are looking for a relatively small man of slight build with a high, almost womanly voice. Some thought they saw black hair under his hat. He wore a kerchief over his face. Black, of course."

"Someone like that could hide pretty easily," Sweeney said.

"That's not the most interesting aspect to the story," Brewer went on. "The governor of St. Kitts told me he has heard, from several quarters, the idea that Black Rose may be a woman."

"*What?*"

"*A woman?*"

A commotion arose. Finally, Mr. Reed turned to the captain.

"Is there even such a thing as women pirates, sir?" he asked.

"I know of none today, Mr. Reed, but a hundred years ago, Anne Bonney was one of the fiercest pirates in the Caribbean."

"What happened to her, sir?" Reed asked.

Brewer told them of her capture and escape. His officers listened raptly.

"Even if Black Rose does turn out to be a woman," Brewer said, "don't lower your guard, even for a second. She will kill you if you let her. Never forget that."

A more somber mood seemed to settle in around the table. Brewer continued. "We have been ordered to the Lesser Antilles and the Windward Islands. We'll start our search there. Any questions?"

"Do we know what they are sailing?" Enfield asked.

"Survivors said that the pirates sailed ad a sloop," Brewer replied, "but we have no idea if that is their only ship. Other than El Diabolito, pirates have traditionally stayed with smaller, quicker ships like sloops or brigs. Their strategy is to frighten and board, rather than get into a gun battle. There is one thing you should know, however." He paused to make sure he had their attention. "In his, or her, latest attacks, Black Rose's pirates have killed or wounded every man aboard. The pirates are escalating the ferocity of their attacks, and they are spreading terror among merchant crews in the area. We need to find this pirate and put an end to the terror quickly."

"Aye, sir," Greene said, answering for them all.

After this, there was general discussion of training schedules. Brewer was pleased by what he heard, and approved the plans his officers evolved. He thanked them, and after a final toast to the success of their mission, he bade them good night.

They rose and filed out of the cabin, except for the doctor, who had not moved from his seat.

"Well?" Brewer asked.

Spinelli tapped on the table with his finger. "More pirates. Seems that's all we do in these waters."

Brewer shrugged. "What can I say? You should have seen the looks on the faces of those survivors when I told them about the black rose I found. Adam, it was sheer terror."

"I believe you," the doctor replied. "Sailors haven't feared a pirate like this since Blackbeard."

"Hence our orders." Brewer sighed. "I find it hard to believe that a woman could be behind this ferocity."

The doctor had no such trouble. "You haven't been around women driven to an extremity of rage or terror; I have. Who knows what caused this particular reign of terror? Perhaps we shall find out when we catch her, if indeed Black Rose *is* a woman." He looked off into space, searching his memory. "What's the old saying? *Hell hath no fury...?*"

Brewer considered this, and wondered if Spinelli had intuited something about the Black Rose. Then he replied, "Well, we shall have to be ready for anything. Perhaps Alfred should begin giving the crew training at close combat. Pirates aren't known for long-range gun battles."

Pudge sat on a stool in the pantry, helping Alfred polish the captain's silver.

"Not like that," Alfred said. "Use a circular motion to buff the plate."

"Right." The boy changed his motion.

"That's better. See how it shines now?" Alfred picked up a fork to polish. "How goes your training with Mac?"

"Well enough," the lad replied. "Sometimes it seems a little slow. I wish he would teach me more."

"Remember that Mac has many responsibilities besides training you. I'm sure he's doing the best he can."

"I suppose," Pudge said as he picked up another plate. "I just wish I could help him more. I mean, he looks after me, and I want to look after him, too. Only I don't know enough yet."

Alfred smiled. "It will come, young Pudge. I'm sure Mac appreciates that you try to look after him. I believe everyone needs a friend."

"Yes," Pudge agreed. He turned the plate over and started on the back. "So, who's your friend, Alfred?"

The servant hesitated, startled by the unexpected question, but quickly began buffing again. "Well, I have Mac as a friend, and the captain has been very kind to me. And now I have you as a friend, too."

Pudge looked up and smiled. "I was hoping that I could be your friend, Alfred. Will you teach me to fight with a sword?"

"You're a bit young for that, I think. How old are you, anyway?"

The boy frowned. "I'm not sure. Mac and me talked about that once, when we were trying to stay warm down by the South Pole, remember? We decided that I must be eight or nine."

"Well, which is it? Eight or nine?"

Pudge considered. "I think I like eight better."

"I don't blame you," Alfred said. "I liked eight, too."

"Does that mean I can learn to use a sword?" the boy pleaded. "Even just the wooden one?"

Alfred grinned. "We'll see."

Captain Brewer came on deck to enjoy the Caribbean sun, but he was disappointed. The afternoon was overcast, and he thought the threat was in the air for a squall in the next watch. He began pacing the quarterdeck. Not that he needed to think; this was purely for exercise. Even with the cloudy conditions, he soon felt a trickle of sweat roll down his back.

He stopped pacing and stood by the larboard rail, looking out towards the horizon. He couldn't stop his mind from straying to St. Kitts and wondering how his wife and daughter were getting along. Unfortunately, he had no leisure to find out.

"Mr. Sweeney," he said, "make your course for Curacao. If we don't find Black Rose there, we shall head east to Grenada and work our way north."

"Aye, sir."

Brewer turned to find Lieutenant Rivkins approaching. The lieutenant touched his hat.

"Begging your pardon, Captain, but I didn't realize you had finished your walk."

"Quite all right, Mr. Rivkins," Brewer replied. "Tell me, what do you think of young Mr. Cromwell?"

"Hard to say, sir," Rivkins replied. "He doesn't talk much."

"What do we know of him?"

Rivkins shrugged. "Not much, Captain. He was the senior midshipman on HMS *Dreadnought*, which was at Port Royal when we returned from South America. He had already passed his boards, so when we reported being down a lieutenant, he was promoted and assigned to us. He reported aboard about three days before you returned, but he has refused to be drawn out, sir."

Brewer decided to remedy the situation. "Ask the doctor to join me in my cabin, if you please. Five minutes after that, pass the word for Mr. Cromwell to join me there."

Rivkins touched his hat and went off on his errand, and Brewer made his way below to his cabin. He had barely removed his hat when the sentry admitted the doctor.

"You sent for me, Captain?" Spinelli asked.

"Yes, Doctor. Just a moment." He opened the door and spoke to the sentry. He closed the door and turned to his guest. "I think it's time we got acquainted with our new lieutenant, don't you?"

Spinelli smiled. "A capital idea, sir." He followed Brewer to the day cabin and sat down on the settee. "Mr. Greene won't be joining us?"

Brewer shook his head. "He just got off watch, so I decided to let him sleep."

There was a knock at the door, and the sentry announced the fourth lieutenant.

Ah, Mr. Cromwell," Brewer said as he rose. "Come in, sit here beside me. Will you join us in a glass of wine?"

"Thank you, sir." He took the indicated seat on the captain's right.

"Alfred! Refreshments for three. Thank you." The captain resumed his seat. "Lieutenant, I believe you know our good doctor. I have called you here, Mr. Cromwell, because I have not yet had the chance to become acquainted with you. Oh, thank you, Alfred." The servant presented his silver tray so the officers could help themselves before withdrawing. Brewer raised his glass. "A toast! To Lieutenant John Cromwell! May he enjoy a long and glorious career in His Majesty's Navy!" "Here! Here!" said the doctor.

"Thank you, sir," Cromwell said.

"Tell me about yourself, Lieutenant," Brewer said. "Where do your people come from?"

"Cornwall, sir," he said. "My mother still has a house in Falmouth. My father was a lieutenant in the navy. He was killed at Trafalgar when I was three. Fortunately, he had done well in the matter of prize money before he died, so my mother and I were able to get along."

"I'm sorry to hear about your father," Brewer said. "Is his example the reason you joined the navy?"

"More or less, sir. It is something of a family tradition. My grandfather fought with St. Vincent."

Brewer took a drink of his wine. "And what ships have you served on?"

"I was ship's boy on HMS *Shannon* and midshipman on HMS *Dreadnought*, sir. I passed my boards at Valparaiso, and when *Phoebe* came in and needed a lieutenant, I was offered the commission."

"And I am glad you accepted," Brewer said. "At what age did you go aboard HMS *Shannon*?"

"I was ten, sir. It was just before she sailed to fight in the second American war."

"Were you there when she defeated *Chesapeake*?"

"Aye, sir," Cromwell replied. "I was a powder monkey serving a carronade in the larboard quarterdeck battery."

"Indeed! Then you are no stranger to action," Brewer said.

"What do you do in your leisure time, Lieutenant?" Spinelli inquired.

"Leisure time, sir? I read, and I try to write my mother every day. That way I have something to send to her any time they call for mail."

Spinelli leaned forward and came to the point. "Do you play chess, Mr. Cromwell?"

"Chess? Yes, sir, but not very well. The chaplain on HMS *Dreadnought* taught me."

Spinelli sat back with a satisfied smile. Cromwell looked inquiringly at the captain.

"The doctor is always looking for a new opponent," Brewer said.

"Ah!" Cromwell acknowledged. He took another small sip of wine.

"I hope you don't mind, Lieutenant," the doctor said, "but I can't help but ask, are you related to the Lord Protector?"

"Yes, sir. He was a distant uncle, I think."

Spinelli looked at the captain and laughed. "We are on a ship of famous relations, Captain!"

Cromwell looked confused.

"Lieutenant Rivkins' uncle was Viscount Nelson," Brewer explained.

Cromwell looked unimpressed and took a swallow of wine. "I say, sir," he said, "do you think it's really possible? For Black Rose to be a woman, I mean."

Brewer shrugged. "Entirely possible. We'll find out for sure when we catch her. Or him."

"Yes, sir." Cromwell finished his drink and set the glass on the table. He waited to see if the captain had any other questions.

Brewer drained his glass and rose. His guests did likewise.

"This is a good ship, Lieutenant," he said, "with a good crew. I would encourage you to learn all you can from everyone you can. That's what makes us a better crew, a better family. And that's why we'll win. Welcome aboard." He shook the young lieutenant's hand. Cromwell came to attention and left the cabin. His captain watched him go and sat down again.

"Well? What do you think?" the doctor asked.

Brewer sighed. "Lieutenant Rivkins was right. He doesn't say much."

Spinelli eyed the cabin door. "Do you think he's hiding something?"

"If he is, it'll come out soon enough. Keep your eye on him. Play chess with him."

Spinelli smiled. "You may count on it."

*　　　　　　　　　　　* * *

*

Diego hesitated before knocking on the door. He was not sure which way she would turn, and he disliked uncertainty.

He knocked and she bade him enter. He closed the door behind him and stood still to allow his eyes to adjust. Of late she kept the hut dark; whether to match her mood or encourage it, Diego did not know.

His eyes adjusted, and he saw her huddled in the back corner. It bothered him that he could not see her eyes. Reading them was the surest way to gauge her mood.

"The sloop is provisioned and ready for sea," he said. "We can leave whenever you like." She said nothing.

"One of the new recruits had information on two fat merchantmen that are scheduled to sail from Havana soon." He hoped she would rise to the attraction, but she didn't.

He sighed loudly. "Let me know when you make your decision." He turned to go. He had laid his hand on the door when she stirred.

"We must find him, Diego."

He turned back to the darkness. "Who?" he asked, knowing the answer.

"The little man," she said. "The one who killed Cofresi."

He crossed his arms and leaned his back against the door. "And how do you expect to find him?"

He heard her rise and move toward the table in the center of the hut. There was a sound of something being moved, and he heard her strike a match. She applied the flame to a new candle, which she put in the holder on the table. She leaned on the table with her hands spread far apart. Her head and shoulders were visible in the dim halo of candle light.

"Diego," she said, "do you remember what that recruit said? When he escaped from the British ship at San Andres, he said there was another ship there. A French frigate that had also fought against the pirate ships. He also told us that the two ships left together. Where would a French ship go for repairs but Martinique? Search our men for two spies who can ask questions at Martinique without attracting attention. I want to know the name of the French frigate, but more than that, I want to know the name of the British ship that helped the Frenchman against the pirates."

Diego considered. "I think I know just the men."

She stood upright, lifting her face out of the candle's aura. "Good. When you have prepared them, we shall sail for Martinique. They can be put ashore during the night and picked up a few days later. Go. Speak to these men. See if they will accept the mission. If they bring me the information, they will be richly rewarded."

She leaned down again and blew the candle out.

CHAPTER THREE

Lieutenant Percy Rivkins turned over the deck to Lieutenant Reed at the end of his shift and went below to the gunroom for a bite to eat. He entered and was about to call for Winfield, the gunroom steward, when he saw Mr. Cromwell sitting at the table, reading and nursing a glass of wine. Rivkins walked up to the newcomer.

"Mr. Cromwell," he said, "good to see you." He held out his hand.

Cromwell eyed the hand with suspicion but shook it firmly. "Lieutenant."

Rivkins held the hand until the other met his eyes. "In here, call me Percy," he said with a smile.

Cromwell managed a forced smile and a nod. "John."

"Winfield!" Rivkins called as he took a seat a couple down from Cromwell. The servant appeared. "I'd like my supper, please, and a glass of wine."

The servant bowed. "Very good, sir."

"So, John," Rivkins said, "how are you settling in? I wager it's quite a change from a seventy-four. Anything I can do to help?"

Cromwell set his book down. "I don't think so, Percy. Everyone has been very gracious thus far. I think from now it will just mean getting used to my division and the new routine."

Rivkins paused as Winfield arrived with his meal. It was lobscouse, a stew made of whatever leftovers happened to be lying around, but seasoned with the spices purchased ashore on the islands. It was one of Rivkins' favorites, and he scooped up a huge spoonful and chewed meditatively. "I'm curious; I know you haven't been here long, but I've never served on anything larger than a frigate. Which do you prefer, a frigate or a seventy-four?"

Cromwell took a drink of his wine as he considered the question. "To tell the truth, I'm not sure. Frigates are smaller, but they're also less crowded." He shrugged. "I haven't had enough experience on a frigate yet to form a reasoned opinion."

Rivkins dug into his lobscouse and told Cromwell about the ship's adventures in the South Atlantic, although he was careful not to mention anything about the ship's history before the current command.

"One good thing about frigates," he remarked, "is you've still got a chance for prize money, even today." He tapped his nose with his finger. "The captain's got a nose for it."

"I shall look forward to spending mine," Cromwell said. "I say, is it true that Nelson was your uncle?"

Rivkins looked up from his food. "Yes, I'm afraid it is," he answered. "He was my mother's brother."

"Interesting. Did you know him? You must have been quite young when he died."

Rivkins shrugged as he chewed. "I don't really remember him. He was this mythical colossus I had to live up to. And for a long time I didn't do a very good job."

Cromwell closed his book. "May I ask what made you change?"

Rivkins motioned with his head toward the deck above. "The captain. He was my division lieutenant when I was a midshipman on the old *Lydia.* Kind of took me under his wing, you might say." He put his elbow on the table and pointed at the fourth lieutenant with his spoon. "He was the first one who ever talked to me like I was a person, if you know what I mean, and not as someone who owed it to my family to emulate my famous uncle. Nobody had ever said to me the things that he said. And what he said made sense."

"I see," Cromwell said. His eyes stared unfocused at his book, and Rivkins wondered what he was thinking.

"Have you ever fought pirates?" Cromwell asked.

"Certainly! *Lydia's* last commission was fighting Barbary pirates in the Med."

"And that's where you served with the captain?"

Rivkins nodded and dug out another spoonful.

Cromwell's eyes danced now, darting from place to place as his eyes narrowed, grew wide, and then narrowed again. "I wonder if they're any different from the ones here?"

Rivkins considered as he chewed, then swallowed and shrugged. "I guess they're basically the same. In it for the money, don't care who they hurt—or kill. The major difference, from what I can gather, is that the Barbary pirates liked to take captives and hold them for ransom. The ones here don't bother. If they take you, they kill you when they're done amusing themselves with you."

Cromwell's brows nearly flew off his head. "I shall keep that in mind."

Rivkins stifled a laugh with another spoonful of his lobscouse. When his mouth was empty, he pointed at the other man again.

"Is it true that one of your ancestors was the Lord Protector?" he asked.

"Yes," Cromwell answered as he picked up his book again. "He's a distant uncle on my father's side."

Rivkins' head bobbed as he chewed. "Something to be proud of."

Cromwell snorted. "That depends on who you ask."

"What do you mean?"

"I've had several men—lesser nobility mostly—tell me that my entire family should be sent to the block for the killing of Charles I." Rivkins watched him closely, but his face remained an austere blank. "And that included some officers of His Majesty's Navy."

"Well," Rivkins assured him, "you won't find any of those on *this* ship. Do your duty and obey orders, and you'll get along fine."

"I was told once that my ever-so-great Uncle Oliver was nothing more than an opportunist who managed to convince those around him to murder the rightful king. *'Just wanted to kill one of his betters'* was how he put it."

Rivkins lowered his spoon and sat up. "You don't believe that, do you?"

Cromwell shrugged. He rose and made to go.

"Just a minute," Rivkins said. "Sit down, John, please. Now, I read a book on Oliver Cromwell once, although, I admit, it happened some years ago. The one detail I do remember from that book was that Oliver Cromwell was a man of principle. Most everything he ever did was in obedience to his guiding principle. It wasn't because of blood lust or petty jealousy, and certainly not for greed. He led the war against the king out of principle. That was also the reason he dissolved Parliament later on. One may disagree with his principles, but one has to concede that he held to a code of rules that he lived by."

Cromwell stared. "Thank you, Percy. I've never heard it put that way before."

"You are welcome. Say, the captain told me about a good bookstore in Boston in the United States. If we pull in there some day, we should try to find it. Perhaps they have that book."

Cromwell rose. "Thank you. I'd like that. Bur now I need to get some sleep before I go on watch. Good night, Percy."

"Good night, John."

HMS *Phoebe* made her way southeast across the Caribbean, hailing every ship she encountered to see if they had any recent news on the whereabouts of Black Rose. No one did. Brewer actually chuckled when one captain told him, *"No, and I hope I never do."* They continued toward their first stop, at Curacao, training as they went. Not only were sail and gun drills done over and over again, but strong emphasis was placed on boarding and repelling boarders. Plans were also developed to put carronades into two of the ship's boats, in case they needed to attack pirate pinnaces in shallow waters.

Alfred was asked to instruct the crew in swordsmanship. He met with groups of twenty men and their officers at a time on the fo'c'sle. On the third day of the training, Captain Brewer spoke with the diminutive instructor prior to his lesson.

"Who do you have this morning?" he asked.

"Twenty men from Lieutenant Cromwell's division, sir," Alfred replied. "Some new men in the group, as I understand."

"Will the lieutenant be attending?"

"I'm not sure, sir."

"If he is," Brewer said quietly, "choose him as your first opponent."

Alfred gave him an inquisitive look.

Brewer shrugged. "I want to see what he can do. That's all."

"Of course, sir," Alfred said.

The men assembled at the appointed hour, and Brewer was there to observe. Alfred stood before the assemblage with Pudge beside him, carrying the teacher's wooden practice swords.

"Men," Alfred addressed them, "the captain has asked me to instruct you in the art of sword fighting. Listen to me, learn what I am going to show you, and you will stay alive." He paced back and forth, looking them over. "First question: does anyone feel they don't need to be here?"

A big tar stepped through the ranks from the back and faced Alfred. The servant did not even come up to the middle of the man's chest. Standing off to the side, Brewer looked on with amusement. He remembered what Alfred had done to Mac, and he looked forward to seeing how he would deal with this rebellious student.

"I don't think there's anything you can teach me about fighting," the man said menacingly.

"We shall see," Alfred said. He took the wooden swords from Pudge and tossed one to the tar. "If you pass this test, you may leave with my blessing."

"Test?" the man asked warily.

"Yes," Alfred swung the sword around to loosen his joints. "The first man to score five hits on the other wins." He assumed the *en-garde* position. His opponent smiled and did the same.

"Keep score, Pudge," Alfred said.

The tar launched three violent attacks in swift succession. Alfred parried the first two and sidestepped the third, taking the opportunity to bring his sword down sharply on the man's forearm.

"One!" Pudge cried.

"Lucky blow, that was," the tar grumbled, as he resumed his position. Alfred smiled and said nothing.

Alfred made what seemed to Brewer to be two slow strikes, easily parried by the tar, before stepping back. Emboldened, the tar gave a cry and raised his sword for a crushing blow.

He never got the chance. Alfred dashed in quicker than the eye could follow and planted the end of his sword in the man's gullet.

"Oof!" the man cried as he doubled over.

"Two!" cried Pudge.

The captain smiled.

The tar growled as he prepared for round three. Alfred said nothing, but his smile was gone, and Brewer knew he was getting serious.

The tar roared and charged. Alfred parried thrust after slash after stab as he gave ground slowly. His opponent missed a backhand slash when Alfred ducked under it, which gave the teacher an opportunity to deliver a hard whack to the man's thigh.

"Hey!" he cried. "Isn't that against the rules?"

"What rules?" Alfred demanded. He looked to the group and raised his voice for all to hear. "The only rule in this is, *Do unto him before he does unto you!*"

"Three!" Pudge announced.

"Alfred?" Brewer said. "End this, please."

"Aye, sir," the servant answered. He assumed the position again.

His opponent seemed confused. "Didn't the captain just tell us to stop?"

"Oh, no, my friend," Alfred replied somberly. "He told me to end this fight!"

The man looked angry and charged. Alfred ducked a thrust and stabbed the man in the ribs.

"Four!"

The tar was breathing heavy, and Brewer wondered from the pained look in his eyes whether Alfred had fractured his rib. The man gamely stood ready. When he attacked this time, he was more cautious, ready to pull back and block any counterstroke. Brewer shook his head; he remembered when he'd thought that might work against Alfred. It hadn't.

Alfred made a feint at his opponent's lower abdomen. When the tar moved swiftly to block, Alfred switched the sword to his other hand and swiftly laid a stiff blow to the side of the man's head, felling him to the deck.

"Five!" Pudge cried. "Alfred wins!"

The teacher handed his sword to Pudge and retrieved his opponent's from the deck where he'd dropped it. "I hoped you were all watching," he said to the group, "because this man made just about every mistake we need to learn to avoid." He helped the man up. "You two," he said, pointing to two spectators, "kindly take this man to the doctor. Mind his ribs, now." The two men hefted the man between them and guided him below deck to the sick bay.

"Lieutenant?" Alfred said, holding out the sword, "care for a try?"

Cromwell was caught off guard by the invitation, but he recovered quickly.

"Very well," he said. He took the wooden weapon and swung it, gauging its weight and balance. Brewer nodded when he saw Alfred's eyebrow rise slightly. The lieutenant assumed the position. "Ready when you are, sir."

The two crossed swords in the formal manner. Cromwell launched a couple light thrusts, feeling his opponent out, as it were, and Alfred parried them with ease. The two men circled each other, each man's eyes never leaving his opponent. Alfred attacked with a combination that Brewer knew had proved effective in the past against experienced swordsmen, but Cromwell parried it. The teacher slashed high and advanced in behind it, but his opponent expertly sidestepped the assault and made a stab at Alfred's thigh that was barely avoided. Alfred backed off a couple steps and smiled.

"You've had some training, Lieutenant," he said.

Cromwell nodded once.

"Very well," Alfred said. "Let's see what you've got."

Alfred charged in, feinting high before landing a blow to his opponent's thigh.

"One!" Pudge announced with glee.

Cromwell saluted with his sword and readied himself. Alfred came in again, but this time Cromwell pinned his sword with his own between their bodies and, reaching up with his free hand, slapped his opponent on the side of his head. He backed off quickly, leaving his teacher standing there in surprise. Brewer gasped, astonished at what he had witnessed. Even Pudge was so surprised by the point that he had to be reminded to announce it.

"Oh, one," he said with no joy.

"Lieutenant," Alfred said, "my congratulations. You are the first to score a point on me."

"Thank you, sir," Cromwell said.

The two men went to war. Alfred held nothing back, quickly scoring two more points to go up three to one. Cromwell scored the next point by taking advantage of Alfred's one weakness: his small size became a detriment if the opponent could work in close. He was able to throw the teacher off balance just long enough to score a touch on his exposed ribs. Alfred scored his fourth point by dashing quickly to the side and stabbing at Cromwell's thigh.

Cromwell charged his opponent, raining down several powerful blows in a row, throwing his opponent thoroughly on the defensive. Suddenly, he dropped down and kicked Alfred's legs out from under him. The teacher fell to the deck and bounced up again.

"Well done!" he cried.

"I say," came a voice from the crowd, "isn't that against the rules?"

"What rules?" Alfred shouted as he faced the group. "The only rule is to survive. You do anything you can to win. I guarantee your opponent will."

He faced the young officer again. To the surprise of all, Alfred gave a great shout and threw his sword at Cromwell's head. The lieutenant blocked the missile with ease, but it left his chest area exposed. Alfred came charging in right behind his sword and leapt onto Cromwell, grabbing his shirt with one hand and making a gesture with the other of plunging a dagger into the unfortunate man's chest, earning his fifth point and the victory.

"Excellent move, sir," Cromwell said by way of congratulations. "You took me by surprise with that last attack."

"I'm glad it worked. I was running out of ideas on how to best you. Where did you learn to fight like that?"

"My father insisted," Cromwell explained. "I must say, I've never used wooden swords such as these; they make excellent training weapons. The weight and balance are similar to a cutlass."

"It took me several tries to get it right. Mac was a great help. Lieutenant, if you don't mind, I would like to practice with you. You are the only real challenge on this ship."

"It would be an honor and my pleasure, sir."

"All right!" Alfred turned back to the crowd. "Who's next?"

At this point, Brewer, who had been watching from the rail, walked away, wondering what other surprises lurked inside his newest lieutenant.

* * * * *

Diego was disgusted. The two men he had selected to go on the special mission to Martinique showed up drunk for their interview with Rose, and she promptly threw them out. Privately, Diego thought they were lucky to escape with their lives. At her insistence, he had not been present for the interview. He began to suspect something was wrong when he walked into the hut an hour later and found her wearing a colorful dress and applying some rouge to her cheeks. He paused, eyes wide, as he watched her from across the room.

She looked like one of those fortune tellers he had seen on Tortuga or one of the French islands.

"Rose?"

Her eyes met his briefly in the mirror, and she went back to applying color to her face. When she was finished, she turned in a whirl and presented herself for his inspection.

"Well?" she said. "What do you think?"

"Beautiful," he answered, still confused. "Rose, what's going on here?"

She pulled out a chair and sat down. "Those two imbeciles you sent me both showed up so drunk they didn't know their own names. So I have decided to go myself."

Diego blanched. "You?"

"And why not me?" she demanded. "It is only right that I should have a hand in the vengeance to be had on Cofresi's murderer." She paused to see if he would challenge her statement; wisely, he did not. She continued, "The brig can sneak me into Martinique and pick me up again when I have the information we seek. Hopefully, I shall be back within the week."

CHAPTER FOUR

Brewer paced up and down the lee side of the quarterdeck, wracking his brain, trying to think of some way to narrow his search. Black Rose's known strikes were too spread out to allow him to comb a single area intensively. That left patrolling the shipping lanes and hoping they got lucky—a strategy that up to this point had been a dismal failure.

They had put in briefly at Curacao and learned nothing. They had headed west toward Trinidad, only to learn that no pirate attacks had been reported in the vicinity for nearly a year. Brewer had then turned his ship north, making way up the west side of the Windward Islands and hoping for a miracle.

He stopped pacing and gazed out over the empty sea. *Where are you?* his voice raged within his head. *You must be out there somewhere! I will find you, Black Rose—whoever you are—and I will end your butchery, one way or the other. I swear it.*

Mr. Greene stepped up to him. "Begging your pardon, sir, but the purser reports that we are getting low on some supplies. We shall need to put in to a port to replenish soon."

Brewer sighed. "Do we have enough to complete our search of the Windwards and get back to Port Royal without rationing?"

"I don't believe so, sir," Greene admitted.

"What does that leave us, Benjamin?" Brewer began to pace again, and Greene fell into step beside him. "Where can we put in?"

"I believe we can make St. Kitts, sir," Greene ventured.

Brewer's eyes darted to his right, but Greene was staring at the deck. Brewer shook his head. "Perhaps. After all, we know Black Rose has been active in the area. Benjamin, I think the crew could use a day of shore leave while the purser is ashore, don't you? Where in this part of the world would you recommend?"

Greene looked up and grinned. "Martinique, sir."

Brewer ceased his pacing. "My thought exactly, Mr. Greene. See to it, if you please. Report to me in my cabin afterward."

"Aye, sir."

Contrary winds meant it was the third day before HMS *Phoebe* slid into one of the beautiful harbors of the island of Martinique. They dropped anchor off the capital, Fort-de-France. Across the bay lay the nearly 200-year-old Fort Saint-Louis, now used by the French as their main naval base in the Caribbean.

A pilot came aboard and guided the ship to its berth in the harbor. After he departed, Brewer called for a conference of all officers in his cabin.

Standing at the head of the table, he looked over the assembly before saying, "Gentlemen, Mr. Franks will go ashore to provide us with sufficient supplies for sixty days at sea. How's our water, Mr. Greene?"

"We have sufficient for sixty days, sir."

"Good. Alfred and Whitfield may wish to go ashore as well," Brewer said. "Now, about shore leave. I shall go ashore immediately to visit the governor and request his permission. I suggest we allow two divisions per day to go ashore, one each during the forenoon and afternoon watches. Providing the ship is correct in all respects, shore leave may commence tomorrow morning. Mr. Greene will determine the rotation. Thank you, gentlemen."

Alfred came in and began to set out his captain's best uniform for his meeting with the governor. Just as he finished, the door opened and the sentry admitted the doctor.

"I heard you're going ashore to see the governor?" he asked.

"That's right," Brewer said, as Alfred helped him into his coat.

"Mind if I tag along?"

"Why?"

Spinelli shrugged. "There's a nice little tavern on the waterfront I know of. I was hoping to visit it again. I can buy you a drink once your interview with the governor is finished."

Brewer buckled the hanger of his sword around his waist and pulled his vest down over it. "Very well, Doctor, let's go."

The trip ashore was pleasantly uneventful. The two men paused at the end of the wharf. Spinelli pointed down the road to their right.

"Do you see the blue sign? That's the tavern. I will be there, nursing a cognac. Join me when you are free."

"I shall."

Brewer made his way to the governor's house. A steward answered the door and directed him to wait in a parlor off the foyer while he was announced. It was only a matter of minutes before the steward was back.

"The governor will see you now, Captain Brewer. If you will follow me?"

The steward knocked twice on the door at the end of the hallway, opened the door, and stepped inside.

"Captain William Brewer, Governor."

"Send him in."

The steward stood to the side, and Brewer strode into the office and stopped dead in his tracks. The governor rose and stepped around his desk.

"It's good to see you again, Captain. How is my dear friend Alfred these days?"

"A—Admiral Roussin!" Brewer stammered. "What is this? How did you come to be governor of Martinique?"

The two men shook hands. Roussin indicated two overstuffed chairs before the hearth.

Please, Captain, let us sit." He turned to the steward. "Henri, refreshments for two, please."

The steward departed.

"So," Brewer said, "what is it like being governor?"

Roussin shrugged. "Between us, Captain, I had more authority on the quarterdeck of my ship."

The steward returned and placed two glasses of wine on the small table between the chairs. He bowed and withdrew. The two men picked up their glasses, and the governor raised his.

"A toast," he said. "To old friends."

Brewer raised his as well. "Old friends."

They drank and set the glasses down, then Brewer waited to hear his host's story.

"After we parted in the South Atlantic," Roussin began, "we sailed for Martinique. When we arrived, we were informed that the previous governor, Monsieur le Comte de Donzelot, was dead. Due to my rank, I took over as acting governor until a permanent replacement arrived from Paris. I sent Captain de Robespierre on to Paris with an updated report. Three days ago, the reply arrived from Paris: I have been officially appointed as governor."

"Congratulations, Governor."

"Thank you, Captain. So, tell me, to what do I owe the pleasure of this visit?"

"We are on the hunt," Brewer said, "for the pirate known as Black Rose. My ship needs provisions. I also wanted to ask for shore leave privileges. I estimate we'll be here three days."

"I see," the governor said. "The provisions should be no problem, Captain; the Royal Navy's money is always good with the merchants of Martinique." He shook his head in an I'm-not-sure gesture. "As for the shore leave…"

"Oh," Brewer said, as though recalling a message, "I also came to invite you to supper aboard HMS *Phoebe* tomorrow night at sundown."

"Thank you." Roussin nodded graciously and rose. "Shore leave is granted. Until supper tomorrow, Captain."

Brewer rose. "I look forward to it, Governor."

The doctor stepped into the tavern and inhaled deeply. It had been many years since he'd last crossed that threshold. He looked around and was pleased to discover that very little had changed. The familiar tables and benches were in their accustomed places, the smell of smoke and spilled ale were much as he remembered. He made his way to his favorite table, in the back of the room to the left of the bar. He sat with his back to the wall so he could see the room. A barmaid came over and asked what he wanted, and he ordered a cognac.

He surveyed the room again. He'd always liked the décor of this place and the atmosphere it created. He felt... comfortable here. It wasn't very big: only a dozen or so small tables and booths, just right for the room. He studied his hands on the table and wondered idly how long the captain would be.

"You ordered cognac, Señor?"

He looked up to find a small woman with long black hair holding his drink. "What happened to the other girl?"

"She was doing me a favor by taking your order," she said as she set the glass on the table. Spinelli fished a coin from his pocket and placed it on the table. The barmaid scooped it up.

"Stranger in town?" she asked. "I do not remember seeing you before."

The doctor took a gulp and set the glass down. The barmaid smiled at him. She was beautiful, he decided. Raven hair past her shoulders, dark eyes set far apart and a generous mouth. She was not tall, but she had a good figure and a sultry voice. The doctor smiled.

"Yes," he replied. "My ship just pulled in."

She studied him and shook her head. "You do not look like a sailor."

"I'm not. I'm a doctor."

"Truly? What is your ship?"

"HMS *Phoebe*."

"Aha!" she cooed. "So, the Royal Navy has arrived. And who are you protecting us from this time?"

"Actually," Spinelli said as he drained his glass, "we are hunting pirates."

"Pirates! Truly?" she looked surprised. "And which pirates would that be."

Spinelli held up his empty glass. "Bring me another, and I'll tell you."

She took the glass and was back in a minute. This time, she sat down next to him.

"So, who is it you are hunting?"

Spinelli saluted her with his glass. "Black Rose."

The doctor did not see her eyes flash wide as he took a drink.

"Oh, my!" she cried. "Black Rose has killed many men, seized many ships! Are you sure you can catch him?"

"Yes, my dear. We are old hats when it comes to this sort of work."

Her eyes narrowed briefly, and she reached out to begin drawing on the back of his hand with her fingernail. "You have hunted pirates before?"

"Yes."

"And which pirates have you caught?"

"Most famously, El Diabolito."

Her nail paused for the barest moment before she forced it to trace a bird. "I have heard of him. Very famous, very dangerous. Did you kill him?"

"No, my captain did that."

She took his hand in hers. "Many merchant masters are in his debt. Were any other pirates killed?"

Spinelli looked up and lost himself in her eyes. "Of course. Most of his crew was killed in the action. We did bring back some prisoners."

"Was anyone else famous killed?"

"Why, yes," Spinelli said. "Roberto Cofresi."

Her eyes went wide, but not for the reason the doctor thought.

"I have heard of this one, too! Very dangerous! Did your captain kill him as well?"

"No, it was his servant."

"His servant? You mean a cook? A cook killed Cofresi?"

"Yes. Not just any cook, mind you. Alfred is a swordsman."

"And your ship is in the harbor? HMS *Phoebe*?"

"Yes, but all happened before, on my old ship. A sloop-of-war named HMS *Revenge*. Yes, she was well named, and it was certainly a name that Alfred lived up to," He rose. "Is the privy still out back?"

"But of course." She released his hand and watched him head for the back door. As soon as it closed behind him, she jumped up and headed out the front.

* * * * *

Brewer and the doctor returned to the ship just before dusk, and early the next morning Alfred was dispatched ashore to purchase what he needed to prepare for the governor's impending visit. Brewer spent much of the day on deck, enjoying the cool sea breeze and playing chess with the doctor.

"So, Roussin is now the governor of Martinique?" Spinelli asked. He moved a rook. "Will wonders never cease?"

Brewer countered the move by taking a pawn with his knight. "We may need him before this is over. It never hurts to have friends in high places."

"True enough." The doctor studied the board before moving his queen. "Check. Have you heard anything from our men ashore?"

Brewer moved his king. "Nothing yet. Mr. Cromwell is ashore with his division; he knows to keep his ears open. What about you? Did you learn anything last night?"

The doctor sat back and sighed. "No, nothing. I did get to talk with a pretty barmaid, but she disappeared while I was in the privy."

The captain laughed. "It seems you've been at sea too long, my good doctor, if barmaids are deserting you!"

Spinelli's only reply was to purse his lips and make a *tsk-tsk* sound. He moved his rook again. "Checkmate."

The turn of the first dog watch found Captain Brewer and his officers standing at the entry port to welcome Admiral Roussin. The admiral stepped aboard and salutes were exchanged before he shook the captain's hand warmly. He turned to Lt. Greene and shook his as well.

"Good to see you again, Lieutenant," the governor said. "I say, Captain de Robespierre is going to be very disappointed when I write him about tonight. How he loved meals prepared by Mr. Alfred! Many was the night that Robespierre decried the fact that we did not kidnap your servant." He leaned in close and lowered his voice. "It may come as a surprise to you both, but not all Frenchmen can cook."

Captain Brewer led his first lieutenant and the governor below to his cabin. A steward took the governor's hat and cloak, and the three men retreated to the day cabin. Pudge entered with three goblets of wine on a tray, pausing so each man could take one.

"Thank you, Pudge," Brewer said. The lad bowed silently and retreated.

"So, Captain," Roussin said, "Black Rose, eh? How goes your search?"

Brewer cringed slightly as he set his drink down. "I'm afraid it goes *nowhere*, Governor. We have not come across any new information in weeks."

Roussin gazed at the captain over his drink. "Are you sure it was Black Rose who attacked the *Zephyr*?"

Brewer's brow rose. "You know about that?"

The governor shrugged. "A French ship was in the harbor at the time. She brought rumors back to Martinique." The two Englishmen shared a look.

It was Greene who answered. "The black rose found aboard seems conclusive."

"I see." Roussin took a drink of his wine.

"Black Rose seems responsible for attacks that are growing in violence," Brewer said. "My orders are to track him down and end the threat to shipping in the Caribbean."

The governor raised his glass in mock salute. "I wish you luck."

"Yes, well," Greene said, "I hope we can count on your help, Governor. You will let us know if you hear anything?"

"But of course, Lieutenant."

Pudge entered the room and announced that supper was served. The three men made their way to the table. The governor sat on Brewer's right, and Mac brought the first course, a wonderfully aromatic soup. This was followed by a neat's tongue, roasted leg of mutton, young carrots, fresh bread with butter and marmalade, and a rich plum duff.

"Ah, Captain," the governor cooed as he cut into the mutton, "I torture myself every time I indulge in your generosity. Where is Alfred? I must try to woo him again!"

"Alfred!" Brewer called, and the man appeared.

Roussin rose and bowed. "I salute your talent, my dear Alfred! Is there no way I can convince you to desert your slavery on this English barge? I would shower you with jewels! A gold-plated stove! Anything!"

Behind him, Brewer and Greene were trying their best to maintain control. Greene put his hand over his mouth to keep from laughing, while the captain was squeezing his mouth shut and looking at the deck.

Alfred made a short bow. "Governor, I thank you for your compliments. I am honored, as always, by your praise. However, I must once again decline your gracious offer. The truth is, Governor, I am needed here."

"Yes, my friend," Roussin deadpanned, "I can well understand that."

"Captain," Greene whispered, "I'm not sure, but I think we've been insulted."

"I'm sure," the captain replied.

**

It was three weeks before she returned. Diego was alerted by the sounds of revelry that followed her up from the cove. She smiled like a cat as she walked past him into the hut. He followed her and closed the door behind him.

"Why the celebration?" he asked.

She pulled the bandana from her head and shook her long, raven hair free. "We took two prizes on the way home. One was filled with spices and gold coins." She stepped behind a screen and began to change.

"And your mission?" he asked, trying to sound patient.

Her head and bare shoulders appeared at the edge of the screen. Her smile was one Diego knew well. It always meant trouble for someone. "His name is Alfred, and he is a captain's steward." She disappeared behind the screen again. "I had trouble believing that. Who would think a mere *cook* could best my Cofresi? But my source was confident of his information." She appeared, sporting the loose pants and tunic she usually wore in port. She went to the cupboard and fetched two wooden goblets, which she set on the table as she sat down. Diego fetched the bottle of rum. He poured them each a generous portion before putting the cork back into the bottle and setting it on the table. He sat and raised his glass to her.

"And where do we find this Alfred?"

She raised her goblet. "He is assigned to a sloop. HMS *Revenge*."

HMS *Phoebe* sailed with the morning tide. Captain Brewer stood in his usual spot by the lee rail, watching as one of the junior lieutenants—Mr. Cromwell, in this case— conned the ship out of the harbor to resume her northerly course. Lieutenant Greene stood beside him, hoping that Mr. Cromwell performed well enough to draw a word of praise from his captain. When the maneuver was complete and the ship had resumed her search, Cromwell reported to the first lieutenant.

"Ship on course, sir," he said after his salute. "One point west of north under all plain sail."

"Very good, Mr. Cromwell," Greene replied. "The deck is yours."

"Aye, sir." Cromwell saluted and moved to the wheel. Greene glanced over his shoulder at his captain.

"He's getting better, Benjamin," Brewer said softly. "Get him to work on being confident in his decisions. Part of that is simply practice, of course. You may tell him I've seen great improvement in his skills since he came aboard."

Greene touched his hat. "Thank you, Captain."

"I'm going below," Brewer said. "Don't forget our little surprise this afternoon."

Greene grinned. "Been looking forward to it all day, sir. Four bells of the afternoon watch?"

"Right," Brewer said. "I hope he likes it."

Pudge sighed as he sat in the pantry and polished yet another plate. This job never seemed to end! He polished spoons and forks, plates and goblets, over and over again. He remembered the day before, when Alfred showed him how to polish the captain's sword. Now *that* was a task he would never tire of!

Alfred came into the pantry and Pudge went back to his polishing.

"How goes it, Pudge?" he asked.

The boy sighed. "Do we ever finish with the polishing?"

Alfred smiled. "Every day, there is work to be done. We have to do the jobs we don't want to do before we get to polish the captain's sword. Right now, I have a job for us both. Will you help me bake a cake for the captain?"

The boy's eyes lit up. "What do we do first?"

"That's the spirit," Alfred replied. "First, let me show you how to crack an egg."

The boy jumped from his perch, and for the next three hours Alfred taught—and re-taught, in the case of a couple eggs that ended up shattered rather than cracked—his young apprentice the art of baking a cake aboard ship. To his surprise, Alfred realized that he enjoyed working with the lad, and he found it much easier to tolerate Pudge's mistakes than he thought he would. He rather enjoyed seeing the smile on Pudge's face and the feeling he got from helping the lad succeed.

They finished the cake and moved on to the icing. Both of them laughed heartily when they discovered they had to make a second batch of icing—their "taste testing" in search of perfection had consumed most of the first! The second batch was quickly made, and Alfred demonstrated how to spread it smoothly on the cake. Mac stopped by and whispered something in Alfred's ear, then nearly lost his life when he dared to try to scoop a little icing off the side of the cake with his finger. Pudge shoved the big Cornishman away from the cake, then grabbed the bowl that held the icing and slammed into Mac's belly.

"Here!" he growled. "Stick your fingers in this! But leave my cake alone!"

Mac chuckled and dutifully cleaned the remaining frosting from the bowl. He handed the bowl back to Alfred.

"That's a mighty good looking cake you boys have made," he said. He looked to Pudge. "Are you ready to show it to the captain?"

"Now?" Pudge was surprised. "It's not suppertime yet."

Mac smiled and winked at Alfred. "I think the captain wants you to bring it out so he can see it."

Pudge picked up the platter carefully and looked the cake over. "Do you think he'll like it, Mac?"

"Aye," the other said. "I think he'll love it. After you." He opened the door.

Pudge carried the cake carefully from the pantry. He was surprised to find not only the captain, but also all the lieutenants (except Mr. Reed, who had the deck), Mr. Sweeney, the doctor and Captain Enfield.

"Well, Pudge," the captain said, "that's a mighty fine looking cake you have there."

"Thank you, sir," the boy answered proudly as he set it down on the table. "Alfred helped me."

"Yes, I'm sure he did. But, you know, Pudge, there's still one thing missing. Mr. Greene?"

Pudge watched in confusion as the first lieutenant approached and placed a single candle in the middle of the cake.

"What's that for, sir?" he asked.

Greene smiled. "Because, my young friend, this is a *birthday* cake!"

The lad's face lit up. "Really? Whose birthday is it?"

Captain Brewer stepped beside him and smiled. "Yours, Pudge."

Pudge's face screwed up in confusion. Mac went down on one knee beside him and put his arm around the boy's shoulder.

"Pudge," he said, "do you remember when your birthday is?"

"Well, no."

"Then how do you know it's not today?"

Pudge looked at the coxswain with eyes so wide it was hard not to laugh. "Are you sure, Mac?"

The big man nodded. "Trust me, Pudge. It's the perfect day for a birthday. Happy birthday."

"Here! Here!" echoed throughout the room. Pudge threw his arms around Mac and hugged his neck, then he leapt on Alfred and did the same.

"Happy birthday, lad," the servant whispered in his ear, and Pudge gave him another squeeze before letting him go.

Alfred retreated to the pantry and reappeared carrying his silver tray loaded with glasses of wine—and one glass of water for Pudge. The captain cleared his throat and the room went quiet as he raised his glass.

"As captain of His Majesty's Frigate *Phoebe*, I hereby declare that today is Pudge's birthday! Today, young man, you are officially…" He paused, lost in thought. "How old are you, anyway?"

Pudge didn't know what to answer, so he darted a quick look at Mac.

"Nine," the Coxswain whispered loudly.

Pudge nodded vigorously and turned back to the captain. "Nine, sir!"

"Right. Today, I declare, by the authority vested in me by His Britannic Majesty, King George IV, Pudge is officially *nine* years old!"

Cheers erupted as the men drank the toast and congratulated the boy. When the noise quieted down, Brewer again cleared his throat.

"Alfred, if you will be so kind as to cut the cake, we will get on with the festivities. Follow me, gentlemen, if you please."

Brewer led the way aft to the day cabin. He sat on the settee beneath the great stern windows and patted the seat beside him for Pudge to sit there. The lad positively glowed as he took the seat of honor.

"All right," Brewer announced to the room at large, "who's first?"

"I'll go first, if you don't mind, sir." Mr. Greene stepped up and went to one knee so he could look Pudge eye-to-eye. "Captain, I believe that, now that he is nine, Pudge is old enough to carry this." He reached into his pocket and pulled out a small dirk with a six-inch blade and handed it to Pudge. A bit of laughter rose at the look of astonishment and joy on the lad's face. He took the dirk and held it with the reverence due a holy icon.

"Thank you, Mr. Greene," he said.

Greene patted him on the knee and rose. "Perhaps Alfred or Mac can show you how to use it and take care of it. Happy birthday, Pudge."

Greene stepped back, and the captain spoke up. "Next!"

Mac stepped forward. He held out a leather scabbard. "You'll need this to carry that dirk that Mr. Greene gave you." Pudge thanked him as he took the scabbard and slid the dirk into it. It was a perfect fit, and the boy looked with tears of joy in his eyes at Mac, who said, "There's still one thing missing. Stand up, Pudge." The lad did so, and Mac pointed to the cord around his waist that held up his britches. "A proper coxswain doesn't carry a dirk on a line tied around his waist." Mac reached out and untied the cord, pulling it off and handing it to Mr. Greene.

"But Mac!" Pudge protested, "My pants will fall down!"

The Cornishman grinned. "Not with this around your middle." He pulled out a leather belt and showed the boy how to put it on. Then he took the scabbard and knife and attached them to the belt. "Now you're ready for anything."

Pudge hugged him. "Thank you." He resumed his seat next to the captain.

Mr. Rivkins was next. He also went to one knee as he pulled a folded handkerchief from his coat pocket. "Every gentleman needs a proper handkerchief, Pudge, so I wanted to give you this one." He turned it over and showed an H embroidered in the corner. "My mother told me that it belonged to her brother, Lord Nelson, when he was a boy. I want you to have it."

Pudge looked up at the captain, obviously confused by the name.

"Lord Nelson was a famous admiral," Brewer explained, "who won many battles against the French during the wars. He was Mr. Rivkins' uncle."

"Oh!" Pudge whispered. "Thank you, Mr. Rivkins, sir! I will take good care of it."

Rivkins stuck his hand out. Pudge looked confused by the gesture.

"Gentlemen shake hands, Pudge," Rivkins explained.

Pudge grinned and gave a hearty handshake.

"Does this mean I'm a gentleman now?" he asked.

"Well," Brewer said, "it means you have started your training to become one."

The boy nodded enthusiastically as he set the kerchief on the seat beside him.

The doctor was next. He handed the lad a thin book. Pudge took it and looked at him.

"What do I do with this?" he asked.

"You read it, of course," came the reply.

Pudge handed it back to the doctor. "I can't read."

Spinelli pushed it back. "Well, young sir, you are going to learn."

"I am?"

"Of course!" Spinelli motioned to Mr. Rivkins, standing off to the side. "Pudge, not only do gentlemen shake hands, they also read."

"Really?" The boy looked astonished. He looked to the captain beside him. "Did you learn to read, Captain?"

"Why, yes, Pudge, I did."

"Who taught you?"

"Well," Brewer said as he searched his memory, "my mother taught me first, and then I went to school to learn the rest."

Pudge looked at the book in his hands. "I wish I could go to school."

Spinelli spoke up. "Ah, but you can! Mr. Sweeney and I will be your teachers, and the sick bay and the quarterdeck will be your schoolhouse. I shall work out a time with Alfred when you will come to school every day to learn not only reading, but also how to write and do your sums."

"Thank you, Doctor!" Pudge said as the doctor stepped back. He set the book gently beside the kerchief.

Mr. Cromwell approached and knelt as those before him had. "Pudge, another thing a gentleman needs is a coin." He pulled a coin from his pocket and handed it to the boy. Looking over his shoulder, Brewer was surprised to see the coin looked like it was very old.

"This coin has been in my family for over a hundred years, Pudge," Cromwell explained. "Now I'm giving it to you to keep. Don't spend it on anything—it's very special and very old. Keep it, and it will bring you luck."

"I shall. Thank you, Mr. Cromwell." Pudge set the coin on the kerchief beside him. Cromwell nodded and rose.

Rivkins leaned over to him after he had stepped aside.

"An old coin, John?"

Cromwell shrugged. "As I said, a gentleman needs a keepsake. That coin has been handed down in my family for over a century. Family legend says it is the coin that Charles I gave to his executioner."

Rivkins stared at his friend. "Egad!" was all he could whisper.

"Your turn, Captain," Mr. Greene announced.

"Right you are, Mr. Greene." Brewer reached behind him and brought out his present, which he placed in Pudge's hands. The boy looked baffled, for the present appeared to be a long string with a loop at one end and a square patch of cloth set in the middle.

"What is it, sir?" Pudge asked.

"It's called a sling, Pudge." Brewer took it back and showed him how it worked. "In the cloth is where you put a projectile—usually a rock or something similar. Then you whirl it over your head and let go of the end. The projectile shoots out and hits your target!"

Pudge was speechless with astonishment.

"Understand, Pudge," Brewer continued, "it takes practice to aim a sling correctly. But when you learn, you will be as dangerous as if you had a brace of pistols."

"Really?"

"Oh, yes," Brewer assured him. "When you learn to read, I will show you in my Bible a story about a shepherd boy named David. He killed a giant named Goliath with one rock out of his sling. Alfred will teach you how to use it."

Captain Enfield stepped up. "You'll need some ammunition to go with that sling, laddie." He handed Pudge a small bag containing three balls of twine about an inch in diameter and seven musket balls. "The twine ones are for you to practice with, and the musket balls are for you to use after you learn."

"Thank you, Captain," Pudge said. He stuck out his hand as Rivkins had shown him. Enfield shook it and stepped back.

Now the group parted, and Alfred stepped up. His hands were behind his back. Pudge looked at him expectantly. Alfred smiled and handed the boy one of his wooden practice swords.

"For me?" Pudge asked.

"No," Alfred replied, "but you will need it. My present to you is the lessons you have been asking for. After you've learned with that, we shall look at getting you a proper sword, suitable for your size."

"Thank you!" Pudge cried as he thrust the wooden sword in the air in celebration, nearly hitting the captain in the head in the process.

Alfred retrieved the sword. "Yes, well, I see we have work to do. Your lessons begin tomorrow. In the meantime, gentlemen, the cake has been cut and awaits you. Captain?"

Brewer led them back to the table, where Alfred served each man in turn. Pudge was called to the head of the line, and he downed his slice in all of three bites.

Brewer stood off to the side next to his coxswain.

"Thank you, Mac," Brewer said as he leaned in close. "This was the best idea you've ever had."

"Thank you, sir."

CHAPTER FIVE

The knock on the cabin door was followed by the sentry admitting Mr. Dye. The midshipman removed his hat and came to attention.

"Mr. Reed's respects, sir," he said. "There's a sail approaching from the nor'west."

Brewer raised his eyebrow and set his pen on the desk.

"I'll come at once."

On deck, Brewer accepted a glass from Skimpy with a nod of thanks. Lieutenant Reed saluted and said, "Lookout reports she's a brig, sir, flying British colors."

Brewer considered his options. His curiosity was warring with his caution; he was not about to be fooled again by another pirate flying false colors.

"Beat to quarters, Mr. Reed."

"Aye, sir!"

The drum roll began, and men sprang to their stations.

Brewer walked to the waist. "Mr. Greene!"

The premier appeared. "Sir?"

"Load and run out. Stand by to fire."

"Aye, sir!"

Brewer turned. "Mr. Cromwell! Load with grape. Stand by to fire. Mr. Dye, my compliments to Lieutenant Reed; please give him the same instructions."

"Aye, sir!"

Brewer looked through the glass again, to satisfy himself the brig was indeed coming their way.

"Mr. Sweeney, bring us about. Intercept course. Stand by to maneuver."

"Aye, Captain."

The brig hove to and lowered a boat.

"Heave to, Mr. Sweeney," he said. "Turn three points to starboard; I want them under our broadside." To the midshipman of the watch: "Pass the word for the first lieutenant."

"Aye, sir."

Greene joined him at the rail. The approaching boat was still fifty yards away. A lieutenant in a British uniform was sitting in the stern sheets.

"What do you think, sir?" Greene asked. "A message? Perhaps Black Rose has been sighted or captured?"

"We'll know in a minute," the captain replied. "Meet the lieutenant, if you please."

Greene touched his hat. "Aye, sir," he said, and moved to the entry port to await their visitor.

Brewer stayed on the quarterdeck and watched as his first lieutenant received the newcomer. He saw Greene nod and lead the visitor his direction.

The two lieutenants saluted. "Captain," Greene said, "may I present Lieutenant Morris of HMS *Serpent*? Lieutenant, Captain Brewer."

Morris held out a sealed packet. "Captain, we were sent by Admiral Cartwright to find you and give you this."

Brewer accepted the packet. "Thank you, Lieutenant. What are your orders now?"

"We are to take over the search for Black Rose, sir."

Brewer frowned. "Thank you, Lieutenant."

Morris saluted and disembarked. Brewer looked at Greene and said, "Mr. Greene, brief the lieutenant on the particulars of our search. When you are finished, please come to my quarters." He turned to Cromwell. "You have the deck, Lieutenant. I'll be back shortly."

The captain retreated to his cabin. He wasted no time sitting at his desk and opening the packet. He removed the single page it contained and read it.

Return to Port Royal with all dispatch.

Signed,

James Cartwright

Admiral Commanding West Indies Squadron

When the first lieutenant arrived, he found his captain sitting at the table with a paper in his hand. Without a word, Brewer handed over the missive and Greene read it. He read it a second time, just to make sure he wasn't missing anything. Greene looked up. "Sir?"

Brewer's face was set hard. He didn't like the lack of information. "Return to the deck, Benjamin. Dismiss the hands from quarters. Have Mr. Sweeney set course for Port Royal. All sail. Then come back, and bring the doctor with you, if you please."

Greene handed the letter back and came to attention. "Aye, sir."

Alone with his thoughts, Brewer tortured himself wondering what the summons might mean. Were they at war again? Perhaps with France, or maybe the Americans wanted to try a third go-round? His mind was] racing in circles until a knock at the cabin door heralded the return of Mr. Greene, with the good doctor in tow. He handed the doctor the note from the admiral and left Mr. Greene to answer any questions while he placed an order for wine for three with Alfred. He stepped back to hear Benjamin doing his best.

"I'm afraid that's all we know, Doctor," the first lieutenant was saying. "The lieutenant from HMS *Serpent* dropped off a sealed packet for the captain and left. No explanation. We are now on course for Port Royal."

Spinelli looked incredulous as he read the note yet again. Brewer smiled at the absurdity of the situation and wondered if his own face had had the same look.

"Well, Doctor," he asked, "what do you think?"

"What do I think?" Spinelli repeated as he dropped the page on the table. "You ask me what I think, Captain? I think the good admiral has either lost his mind or is trying to make us lose ours! That's what I think!" He fumed for a moment before picking the letter up again. "Why on earth would he not give us any sort of explanation at all?" He shook his head in frustration, then looked up at the others. "You don't think Black Rose has been found, do you?"

"Sir?"

Brewer turned to see Pudge standing behind him holding Alfred's silver tray with three glasses of wine on it. "Thank you, Pudge," he said. He handed glasses out to the others before taking the last one for himself. "Let's talk in the day cabin, gentlemen."

They made their way aft. Brewer and Greene sat on the settee, and the doctor took a chair opposite them. Several of the stern windows were open, and the Caribbean winds were cooling nicely as the sun descended.

"To answer your question, Adam," Brewer said, "no, I don't think Black Rose has been found. Lieutenant Morris said that *Serpent* was ordered to take over the search from us. Why would Cartwright do that if Black Rose had been found somewhere else? And why not just tell us where she was and send us directly there? No, Adam, I think something else is going on, something that has nothing to do with Black Rose, and for some reason, the admiral thinks *Phoebe* is the ship for the job."

Spinelli took a lgenerous swallow of his wine and sighed. "So, we fly to Port Royal?"

Brewer's eyes had a strange light in them. "Just as fast as we can."

The doctor thought for a moment before jumping to his feet and rubbing his hands together. "So!" he exclaimed. "What's it to be? Shall I send for a fourth for cards, or are you going to get the chess set out?"

Brewer and Greene laughed, but neither man said a word. "Right!" Spinelli said. "Chess it is!" He headed for the desk where the captain stored his prized set. The others laughed again, and Greene rose.

"With your permission, sir," he said to Brewer, "I shall check our course, and then I shall get some sleep. I shall leave word on the deck to wake me first if anything happens."

"Very well," Brewer said. "Thank you, Benjamin. Good night."

"Good night, sir. Doctor, good night. Go easy on him; you know how grumpy he gets when he loses." Greene looked at his captain and grinned.

"Get out, Benjamin," Brewer joked.

"Aye, sir." Greene picked up his hat and left.

"Well," Spinelli said wryly, "at least he's doing something productive." He placed the set on the table between them, and they set up the pieces. Brewer won the draw and chose black. The doctor frowned; he hated when the captain made him go first. He sat down and moved his king's pawn. Neither man spoke for several moves, then Brewer moved his knight but kept his finger on it while he checked for threats.

"Why us?" he asked, removing his finger.

"What do you mean?" Spinelli said. He moved a pawn.

"Why did the admiral send for us?" Brewer took the pawn with a bishop.

The doctor castled to his queen's side. "I'm sure he has his reasons."

The captain advanced a rook. "Such as?"

"How am I supposed to know?" Spinelli advanced his knight, and Brewer immediately took it with his queen. Spinelli pushed his rook to the farthest rank. "Check."

Brewer frowned and moved his king around a pawn for protection. "I don't know. You usually have some clever insight at times like this."

The doctor advanced a bishop, neatly boxing his opponent's king. Brewer frowned and moved his queen to threaten white's king. It was the move the doctor had been waiting for. He moved his knight and sat back in his chair.

"Sorry to disappoint you, dear Captain," he said. "We shall have to wait and ask the man himself. Checkmate." Brewer frowned. This was going to be a long trip.

* * * * *

Brewer was shown into Admiral Cartwright's office to find the commander of the West Indies Squadron seated behind his desk with his head in his hands. The admiral stood and nodded a greeting to his guest.

"Yes, Captain Brewer," he mumbled, "thank you for coming so quickly."

"We came as soon as *Serpent* found us, sir," Brewer said. He sat in the chair indicated by the admiral in front of the desk.

"The impossible has happened, Brewer," Cartwright exclaimed, "or what I would have thought impossible until now. A Royal Navy crew has mutinied and taken over one of our ships."

Brewer stared at him, completely dumbfounded. He had heard of such things, but they were so extremely rare as to be considered, as the admiral had said, impossible.

"What happened, sir?" Brewer asked.

Cartwright drew a deep breath to steel himself. "Two weeks ago, a luggar sailed into the harbor. She carried fifteen officers and men from a British ship. The ranking officer, who was the third lieutenant, came to me immediately and reported the mutiny. I sent *Serpent* to look for you the same day."

"Why, sir?"

Cartwright held his eyes. "HMS *Phoebe* is the nearest frigate." He shuddered a moment, then regained control of himself. "There is an additional reason: Because you used to command the ship."

Brewer stared, aghast. *"Revenge?"* he asked in a whisper. The admiral nodded silently. Brewer shook his head in disbelief, then asked, "Does that mean Gerard is dead?"

"I don't know," Cartwright said. "The third lieutenant, whose name is Smythe, said that the captain came down with a mysterious illness. Smythe did not know if the cause was malaria or a poison of some sort; according to him, the doctor did not know either. The captain retired to his cabin, violently ill, and the first lieutenant, a man named Stetson, assumed command. Stetson was one of the officers transferred from *Phoebe* to *Revenge* when you assumed command of the frigate. According to Smythe, floggings had been a regular part of life aboard ship, but *torture* began that very night. That is Smythe's word, not mine." Cartwright looked miserable. He rose and began to pace. "Apparently, Stetson approved of his former captain's method of discipline. According to Smythe, the captain was far too ill by this time to intervene, and Stetson refused to return to Port Royal, despite the doctor's recommendation to do so."

The admiral returned to his desk and sat. He folded his hands on the desk and continued. "Smythe tried to see the captain, but Stetson forbade it. He posted an additional sentry at the captain's door to make sure he was not disturbed. Smythe said he threatened to flog Smythe if he tried to see the captain again."

Brewer's eyes went wide at that. "Stetson threatened to flog an *officer?!* Is the man insane?"

Cartwright shrugged. "So it would seem. At any rate, the harsh disciplined continued. After two weeks of daily floggings, the crew of the *Revenge*, led apparently by the hands who had previously suffered the same treatment aboard *Phoebe*, mutinied during the night. Stetson was drug from his bed and flogged. He died under the punishment. The bosun, let me see, his name was..." Cartwright looked at the report on his desk. "Brumby. He led the mutineers, and he was the one who flogged the first lieutenant to death. Smythe and the others who stayed loyal were forced to watch. The second lieutenant, Kirby, was next. He was still alive after six dozen lashes. Brumby declared himself too tired to continue with the flogging, so he threw Kirby overboard! Brumby turned to find his next victim, but others among the mutineers refused to murder anyone who had not participated in Stetson's abuse. They forced Brumby to let go of those who wished to leave. They were put out in a boat without food or water. After two days of drifting at sea, the luggar rescued them and made her way here."

Cartwright's head lowered as he finished his tale, and Brewer could hear him sobbing quietly. "I'm sorry," he said as he regained control of himself. "I've never had anything like this happen under my command before. I'll be ruined. The Admiralty will put me on the beach after this."

Brewer was outraged by what he heard. *A ship of the Royal Navy has mutinied,* he thought. *Men I knew and commanded may well be dead, and all this fool cares about is his own career? I have a good mind to....* Brewer caught himself and clamped his mouth shut. He held on to his control with all his might.

"What are my orders, sir?"

"Go to sea at the earliest opportunity," Cartwright said, oblivious to the captain's fury. "Orders have been issued to give *Phoebe* priority in whatever you need. Your sailing orders are with my lieutenant outside. Find *Revenge* and take her back."

Brewer rose. "Aye, sir." He turned and left the room before he said anything he would regret. When he got to the door, he paused for a quick look back. Cartwright's head was on the desk, rolling slowly from side to side. Brewer bit his tongue and left.

Outside he found the lieutenant and accepted his orders. The lieutenant looked a bit sheepish as he handed over the packet, and Brewer realized that he was embarrassed by his admiral's behavior.

"Where can I find Lieutenant Smythe?" Brewer asked.

"The admiral ordered all those from HMS *Revenge* held in isolation in the naval hospital," came the answer. "They are not allowed to speak to anyone. They are to be sent to England when the mail ship leaves in three days."

Brewer wrote out a note to be sent to *Phoebe*, ordering Lieutenant Greene to provision the ship for sea immediately and informing him of Admiral Cartwright's order that they be given every priority. He obtained a note from the admiral allowing him to interview the men from *Revenge* and left to find them.

He made his way to the hospital, walking slowly in order to calm himself. Obviously, mistakes had been made in transferring crew to *Revenge*, but apparently Stetson had given no indication of being an adherent to the methods of Captain Judah.

Brewer entered the naval hospital and made his way to the ward where the men from HMS *Revenge* were being kept. As he approached the door, a sentry stepped forward.

"I'm sorry, sir," he said, "but no-one is allowed to enter."

"Sergeant," Brewer said, "I have been ordered by Admiral Cartwright to go out after the *Revenge*, and I need to talk to these men before I do." He handed the sergeant the admiral's note.

The sergeant stepped aside, and Brewer entered the ward. He stood inside the door for a moment to allow his eyes to adjust to the darkness. The shades were drawn on every window. Brewer wandered into the room slowly, looking around.

Suddenly, a familiar voice stopped him in his tracks.

"Blimey!" it said. "It's the captain!"

He turned and saw two forms rise from the floor where they were seated and make their way toward him. As they neared, he recognized them as Kelly and Jones, two hands from *Revenge*. They knuckled their foreheads, and Brewer saluted in return.

"Kelly, Jones," he said, "I'm glad to see you."

"Not half as glad as we are to see you, Captain," Kelly replied. "How's Mr. Reed these days?"

"Still breathing, thanks to you two." Brewer said, and the two men nodded. One of the hands on *Revenge* had tried to have Reed killed, but the attempt had failed. Brewer had assigned Kelly and Jones to act as his bodyguards to discourage further attempts on the then midshipman's life.

"Where's Lieutenant Smythe?" he asked them.

"Gone, sir," Kelly answered. "He went crackers, and they took him away a couple of hours ago."

Brewer stepped in close and lowered his voice. "Is there someplace we can talk?"

Kelly and Jones shared a quick look, and Kelly nodded once. Jones looked to his former captain. "This way, sir."

Brewer followed them to a table back in the corner of the ward. Two men were already seated there.

"Scat, you blokes," Jones snarled.

"Scat yourself," one of those seated growled back. "We were here first."

Kelly stepped up, and the two stood. Brewer feared they were going to fight, so he shouldered his way past Kelly.

"I would appreciate the use of this table, gentlemen," he said.

The two men's eyes widened when they recognized him. "Captain Brewer! Lord, it's good to see you, sir! Come to get us out, are you, Captain?"

"Not quite yet. Sorry." Brewer apologized. "But right now I need to talk to Kelly and Jones."

"The table's yours, Captain," the second one said. The two saluted and moved off.

Brewer sat opposite his companions. "Admiral Cartwright has ordered me to take *Phoebe* out and retake *Revenge*. I have questions that need answered first. Tell me what happened."

He heard the two men sigh. Kelly leaned forward and took a deep breath.

"Things changed after you left, Captain," he said softly. "Captain Gerard seemed like a good man, and if we'd still had the old crew, I think he would have been fine. The trouble was, they brought a good number of troublemakers over from *Phoebe*, including the first and second lieutenants."

"They was no good, Captain," Jones said. "Evil, they was. Kelly, what was that word Peg-leg used?"

"Sadistic."

"Aye! That's the word—sadistic! They seemed to enjoy flogging people."

Brewer looked at them incredulously. "And Captain Gerard let them do it?"

"I don't think the captain realized what was going on," Kelly explained. "They was good, Captain. Those two knew how to get a man angry enough to do the wrong thing, and then they would go to the captain about it and demand the man be flogged. Since they was technically right in the charges they brought, I guess the captain felt he had to go along. He tried to keep the number of lashes down, but they added up. They even went after the midshipmen! Mr. Short spent a watch seized up to the mizzen shrouds!"

"Mr. Short?!" Brewer said in disbelief. "Whatever for?"

Jones winced at the memory. "He tried to shield a hand from the second lieutenant, and the way Mr. Kirby—he were the second lieutenant—told the story to the captain, he made Mr. Short out to be belligerent and disrespectful. But he weren't, Captain! I'd swear he weren't!"

"Did you hear what he said?" Brewer asked.

Jones looked miserable. "No, sir. I was too far forward. I could see what was going on, but the wind was gusting too hard for me to hear. It looked like Mr. Short was trying to explain something to the lieutenant. The sergeant-at-arms was standing right behind the lieutenant; I guess he thought he might need him, so he brought him along. Anyway, the lieutenant stands aside and motions for the sergeant to take both Mr. Short and the hand into custody! The next thing we knows, Mr. Short's seized up on the mizzen shrouds."

Brewer stared off into the darkness, trying to process what he learned. Obviously, the two officers had retained all the worst from the hellhole that was HMS *Phoebe* before Brewer took command. What he could not understand was, why had Gerard allowed the situation to get so bad?

"Go on," he said.

"After the captain got sick," Kelly said quietly, "Stetson took command—he was the first lieutenant—and the floggings got worse. Minor offenses, or even no offense at all, got a dozen or two. The men began to gripe about it, and Stetson brought us all on deck and said that if the griping continued, he would flog every third man to teach all of us a lesson. The last month we were on the ship, he turned up every hand twice a watch!" He shook his head miserably. "Even the best of us lost hope, sir."

"And that was when Brumby stepped forward?" Brewer asked.

"Aye, sir," Jones said. "He went from mess to mess. Said that with the captain down, we had to protect ourselves from the first lieutenant's insanity. We told him to get lost at first, sir, but eventually some of the lads came around to his position."

Brewer nodded. Sadly, he could understand. He remembered how Captain Norman had done something similar on HMS *Defiant*. Even a good man could only take such mindless abuse for so long before being turned into a rabid animal, with self-preservation his only goal.

"After Stetson threatened to flog every third man," Kelly took up the tale, "Brumby made a lot more headway. The lads started growling and griping below deck, and soon it began to affect their work. Once *that* happened, Stetson had them right where he wanted them. Then, all Brumby had to do was to put the match to the powder, so to speak."

"The admiral told me everything Lieutenant Smythe said," Brewer told him.

Jones leaned in close. "Smythe's a good man, Captain, but he's young. He only got his commission six months ago, and I think all this was just too much for him. Thought it was his fault somehow, or maybe he felt guilty for abandoning Captain Gerard. He had no choice, sir; Brumby said to get in the boat or face the cat. We already saw him, what he did to the first and second lieutenants with it, so we dragged Mr. Smythe into the boat and shoved off."

Brewer looked at Kelly. "What happened to Captain Gerard?"

"Brumby said he was too sick. Wouldn't let him leave. The doctor decided to stay and take care of him, and Brumby forced one man to leave the boat to be his nurse."

"Who?" Brewer asked.

Jones paled. "Mr. Short."

CHAPTER SIX

Brewer left the hospital and headed for the wharf. Neither Kelly nor Jones could give him any help when it came to *Revenge's* whereabouts. The mutiny had taken place just west of the Cayman Islands, twenty-eight days ago. *Revenge* was on course for the Gulf of Honduras at the time. They could be anywhere by now.

Brewer's plan was simple. He would make for the Cayman Islands and try to pick up a lead on where Brumby might be heading. He was the key to the whole thing, Brewer was convinced of that. Kelly and Jones told him that the bosun was one of those who had come over from *Phoebe*, and they didn't know him very well. Maybe someone on the Caymans did.

When Brewer returned to the *Phoebe*, he was met at the entry port by his premier.

"Mr. Greene," Brewer said, "are we ready for sea?"

"Aye, Captain."

"All crew account for?"

"Yes, sir," Greene said. "Alfred and Mr. Franks have returned within the last hour. Winfield returned earlier."

"Very good." Brewer looked about the deck before turning to Mr. Greene. "We sail at once. Warp the ship out of harbor, and set course for the Cayman Islands once we are clear. I shall be in my cabin."

"Aye, sir." Greene watched his captain disappear below deck. He turned to Mr. Sweeney, who was standing by the wheel. "What do you make of that?"

Sweeney looked to the companionway with concern in his eyes. "Something's got him bothered, that's for sure." He looked to Greene. "What should we do?"

Greene picked up a speaking trumpet. "We get under way. Give me a course for the Caymans, if you please." He raised the trumpet and began giving orders.

Brewer entered his cabin and tossed his hat and his coat on the table. He walked aft to the day cabin and sat down on the settee, elbows on his knees and his head in his hands. His mind was spinning, and his spirit was being torn in several directions due to what he had learned in the last few hours. He was having trouble putting the disgust he felt at Admiral Cartwright's behavior behind him. His skin crawled as he replayed in his mind Cartwright's whining about his career. He could not for the life of him imagine Hornblower, Pellew, or Cornwallis doing anything of the sort. He squeezed his eyes shut to banish the vision from his mind. He sat up and overcame the urge to scream at the top of his lungs, settling instead for a deep breath. He held it a moment before exhaling in a long, slow manner meant to drain the tension as well as the air from his body. He rested his head in his hands again and thought.

He had no idea how much time had elapsed when the motion of the ship told him they had cleared the harbor and were in the open sea. He opened his eyes and saw Alfred standing in the doorway.

"Can I get you anything, Captain?" he asked softly.

"No, Alfred, thank you," Brewer said. "Pass the word for Mr. Greene and the doctor, would you please?"

"Aye, Captain." The servant paused for just a moment before going; Brewer noted the concern in his eyes.

Brewer let his head fall back, and he blew a sigh toward the ceiling. He couldn't help wondering whether Gerard was still alive. How could Gerard have allowed Stetson and the second lieutenant to stir up so much trouble? Brewer shook his head. *What a first command,* he thought. *Well, whoever gave him a crew made up of malcontents must have thought he would be able to handle it. Apparently, they were mistaken.*

There was a knock at the door, and a moment later Alfred led the first lieutenant and the doctor into the cabin. Brewer saw care and concern in their eyes, and he knew he had to get hold of himself. He had to be the captain now; he could hurt later.

"Gentlemen," he stood and said, "thank you for coming. Alfred, Madeira for three, if you please. Thank you. Please, gentlemen, be seated." He waited while Alfred served each man a glass and silently retreated. "As you know, I went to see the admiral. To be blunt, he informed me that there has been a mutiny on a Royal Navy ship here in the Caribbean." He took a breath before continuing. "That ship was HMS *Revenge.*"

Greene's glass stopped halfway to his lips while the doctor stared wide-eyed at the news.

"Gerard?" Greene asked.

"Alive, as far as we know," Brewer said.

He spent the next hour telling them the story, from his interview with Admiral Cartwright (but leaving out the admiral's behavior and remarks about his career) through his lengthy interview with Kelly and Jones in the hospital ward. Greene and the doctor listened without comment. The doctor closed his eyes as Brewer told of the mutineers' execution of the first and second lieutenants, while there grew a cold fury in Greene's eyes at the news.

"So, you never actually spoke to Smythe?" Spinelli asked.

Brewer shook his head, his eyes staring blankly at the deck.

Greene swallowed hard and tried to keep his anger in check. "What are your plans, sir?"

Brewer stirred and sighed. "We are on the way to the Cayman Islands. I hope to pick up some information there that might give us a clue where Brumby was going. I'm hoping that he put Gerard and Short ashore there, but I admit it's a slim chance."

"What will happen to Kelly, Jones, and the rest?" the doctor asked.

"I don't know," the captain replied. "Admiral Cartwright is sending them back to London. It's entirely possible that the admiralty will send them on a long voyage —Australia or somewhere similar —just to keep the news from breaking for a little longer."

"Well," Greene said as he crossed his arms over his chest and leaned back in resignation, "one thing's for sure—there's no going back for Brumby and the others."

"No," agreed Brewer.

"How's that?" Spinelli asked.

Greene looked at him in disbelief. "They executed two of the king's officers, Doctor. No matter what the reason, the only punishment awaiting them is the gallows."

"He's right," the captain said.

"Even if they were driven to it?" Spinelli winced under the hard glares thrown his way by his fellows. "For argument's sake, I mean."

Brewer shrugged. "Even so. Doctor, these men deliberately took the life of two officers of the Royal Navy. There can be no consequence for that but death. Had the mutineers imprisoned them, the officers might have gone before a court martial and be tried for their behavior, but once they took the law into their own hands—or allowed Brumby to do it for them—their fates were sealed." He thought for a moment. "Mac!"

It was Alfred who appeared in the door.

"I'm afraid your coxswain isn't here, sir."

"Please pass the word for him, Alfred."

"Yes, sir."

"So," the doctor said, "our job is to hunt the renegades down."

"Exactly so," Brewer replied. "Is there something you don't understand, Doctor?"

"Unfortunately, no. It just seems incredibly harsh to punish all of them for the actions of one man."

"The law is very plain, Doctor," Greene informed him. "Every man who elected to stay on that ship rather than leaving with Lieutenant Smythe and his group—with the exceptions of the captain and Mr. Short, of course—would be charged equally with mutiny, and they would share equally in any other crime committed on board." He paused. "Although I can't imagine any stain will be attached to the doctor for remaining behind to tend Gerard." Brewer nodded his head in agreement.

Spinelli looked rueful. "It just seems unfair somehow."

"Remember back in '97," Brewer said, "when the Channel Fleet mutinied at Spithead? They had a list of legitimate grievances that were presented to Lord Hood. No officers were harmed, and his lordship agreed to the mutineers' demands."

Mac appeared in the doorway. "You sent for me, sir?"

"Yes, Mac. I want you to go below and see if you can find anyone of the old *Phoebe* hands who can tell me about a bosun named Brumby. Quick as you can, Mac."

"Aye, sir." Mac departed to set about his task.

Spinelli watched him leave and turned to his captain. "Do you think that will help?"

Brewer shrugged. "Can't hurt. I need to know who I'm up against." He rose. "Thank you, gentlemen. Please keep this information confidential for the time being."

The two men rose. "Aye, sir," Greene answered for them both. They came to attention and made their way from the room. Brewer watched them go before picking up his glass of wine and draining what little remained inside.

He looked around the room and sighed. It was times like this he hated. He was never able to copy Hornblower's ability —Bush had it, too—to set his face like a stone so nobody could tell his mood or what he was thinking. The crew most likely already suspected something was in the wind, if only because of their rapid provisioning and warping out of the harbor. If he stepped up on deck now, every hand who saw his face would know that something was very wrong.

He wandered aimlessly around the cabin. He paused before his bookshelf, but he could not bring himself to read. His eyes fastened on his writing desk. He pulled out paper, ink, and quill in an effort to calm his mind through a letter to Elizabeth. He wrote of his love for her, and how he wished to be at her side. He informed her of a new, unexpected mission he had been handed by the admiral and how it might delay his return. He wrote of their coming move to England at the end of the year and how his only request was that he be allowed a study or library where he could retreat to write or work from time to time. Other than that, he wrote, she had his blessing to choose their house in whatever village she pleased. His only desire was to come home to her.

It was just after the turn of the watch that a knock at the door preceded the sentry's announcement that his coxswain had returned. Brewer set down his quill and turned to see the big Cornishman standing in the doorway. Beside him was a short, older hand the captain had seen on deck but never had an occasion to speak to.

"Yes, Mac?"

"Captain, this here's Michaels." Mac indicated his fellow. "He's a bosun's mate, and he says he worked with Brumby on the old *Phoebe*."

Brewer looked at the newcomer. It was difficult to guess his age. His body bore the look of years at sea, with leathery, tanned skin and ropy muscles. The captain also suspected that, were he to look, Michaels' back would also show scars from a flogging or two, given the harsh standards of *Phoebe's* former captain.

"Michaels?" he said. "Is this true?"

"Aye, sir," the man replied. Brewer noted the man's voice was deep and confident, with a self-assurance born of hardships endured and bested.

"What can you tell me about Brumby?" Brewer asked.

"A schemer, Captain," came the reply. "Not a man I'd want in my mess, if you know what I mean. Not one I'd turn me back on, neither."

Brewer's head tilted to the side. "Go on."

"He came aboard, let me see," the old man's eyes narrowed in recollection, "must be nearly two years before you took command, sir. Captain Judah had been in command for, oh, six months or so by that time. Brumby signed on at Kingston. We had just lost our bosun to a sickness—he died while we were at sea—and the captain and first lieutenant had decided by the time we got back to Port Royal that none of his mates was up to the job, so the captain sent the third lieutenant ashore to scout out a replacement. He came back three days later with this Brumby."

"I see. Mac, bring a chair, if you please. Sit down, Michaels. Go on with your story."

The mate sat and shot a tentative look to Mac, who winked at him and smiled reassuringly. Michaels turned back to the captain. "Well, it didn't take too long for those of us who were his mates to realize he didn't know near as much as he said he did. He was able to hide it from the captain and first lieutenant while we was in the harbor, mostly by bullying the younger mates into doing his work for him. Oh, he could put on a good show when the captain was around, but otherwise he was his own man with no caring for the ship or crew."

Brewer didn't like the picture that was taking shape. "How did he get along with Captain Judah and the first lieutenant?"

Michaels studied the deck beams above, as if searching for the right words before answering. "At first they treated him just as any other captain or first lieutenant would treat the bosun. Then the first lieutenant caught on to one or two of Brumby's schemes and, instead of reporting him to the captain, demanded a cut of the take. Brumby refused, and Mr. Stetson started making his life a living hell. Brumby's got a nasty temper, Captain; if you push him hard enough, he'll eventually lose control and react. Lieutenant Stetson got real good and getting him to react on deck, and then he'd go to the captain and have Brumby flogged. Lieutenant Kirby got in on it, too. After a while, it got to where they didn't care about the schemes or the money, they just enjoyed torturing Brumby. I'm surprised Brumby never tried to sneak up on either of them in the dead of night and slit their throats. He's that kind of man."

Brewer had heard enough. He rose, and Michaels followed. "Thank you, Michaels," Brewer said. "I must ask you to speak of this to no-one. Dismissed."

"Aye, sir." The old tar came to attention and walked towards the door.

"One second, Michaels," Brewer called after him. Michaels stopped and turned back to his captain.

"How old are you, if I may ask?"

The tar's face betrayed his surprised at the question. "Let me see... I'm thirty-seven, Captain."

Brewer could only stare as the tar left the cabin.

Mac felt an extraordinary sense of pride, and he wondered if this was what it was like to be a father. Pudge was standing in front him, unnecessarily holding his arms over his head while Mac put his belt and scabbard around his waist. He buckled it snugly and gave the pants legs a tug to make sure they stayed in place. He was looking at the scabbard, secured on the boy's belt on the left side, when a strange thought occurred.

"Pudge," he asked, "which hand are you?"

The lad looked confused as he lowered his hands. "I dunno, Mac. How can I tell?"

Mac looked around and spotted a small block of wood on a mess table. He picked it up and turned to Pudge.

"Back up a couple steps," he instructed the boy. "Now, I'm going to toss this to you, and you have to catch it, but you can only use one hand. Got it?"

"I suppose, but which hand do I use?"

"Doesn't matter. Just use *one*."

"But how do I know..."

"Pudge!" Mac yelled as he tossed the block.

The boy was startled by Mac's voice and reacted by sheer instinct. He reached out with his left hand and snatched the block from the air.

Mac was shocked. "Pudge, you're *left*-handed?"

For a moment, the boy thought he'd done something wrong. "I'm sorry, Mac! I was startled and...."

Mac scooped the boy up, hugged him and tussled his hair. "It's fine, Pudge! I wanted you to catch it without thinking. So, you're a leftie, are you? We'll have to remember that when we teach you to write. We ought to tell Alfred, too. Here, stand up."

Mac set the boy on his feet and proceeded to unbuckle his belt. Pudge threw his arms in the air, and Mac chuckled.

"You don't have to do that, Pudge," he said.

"Why are you taking it off when you just put it on?"

The coxswain took the belt off and attached the scabbard to the other side. "Well, seeing's how your left-handed, Pudge, the scabbard goes on the other side, so it's under your right arm."

"What if Alfred doesn't like it there?"

"Then he can move it later." Mac buckled the belt again and tugged the pants legs. Satisfied, he sat back on his heels and surveyed his work.

"Now you look like a real tar, Pudge," he said proudly. "There's only one thing missing."

He reached around the boy and picked up the knife off the blanket. He held it up in front of him. "You need to put this where it goes."

Pudge grinned as he took the knife and very deliberately guided it to the scabbard. He looked back to Mac.

"Right," Mac said. "Let's go see Alfred."

Pudge could barely contain himself as he followed Alfred to the gun deck. Since Alfred had said he would give Pudge his first lesson as soon as he finished his chores, he'd worked hard and got them done early. Alfred had anticipated this and was ready.

As they stepped out on to the gun deck, they came upon Lieutenant Cromwell supervising a crew that was working on one of the aft 18-pounders.

"Something I can do for you, Alfred?" he asked.

"No, Lieutenant. If you don't mind, Pudge and I will go to the other end of the deck. He's receiving his first lesson in weapons."

Cromwell's eyebrows rose, but he nodded. "I see. Good luck, Pudge."

"Thanks, Mr. Cromwell!" Pudge called as he followed Alfred forward.

Alfred stopped by the Number Two 18-pounder and set down two wooden training swords, the sling, and a bag containing the practice ammunition. He turned to find Pudge fidgeting like a cat on a hot plate.

"Now, Pudge," he said, "first let's lay down some rules."

That brought the fidgeting to an abrupt halt. "Rules?"

"Yes." Alfred picked up the sling and a wooden sword and squatted, his back against the breech of the 18-pounder. "These are *not* toys. This sling, this sword—well, when you get a real one—you can kill people with these. Remember the story the captain told you about? The one from his Bible about David and Goliath? David killed Goliath with a sling just like this one, so you've got to be careful. You must remember this one thing, Pudge: 'I'm sorry' doesn't make up for killing someone by accident. You *never* play with these or any other weapons. Do you understand?"

"Yes, sir," the boy replied seriously. "But how do I get good at them if I'm not allowed to play with them?"

Alfred smiled. "There's a difference between *practicing* and *playing*. We need to practice so we are proficient if we are ever called upon to fight pirates or enemies of the king. Practice is done on purpose, to make us better, whereas playing is done just to have fun. See the difference?"

"Aye, sir!" Pudge stood to attention and knuckled his forehead. Hard.

"Ouch!" he whispered.

Alfred smiled and tussled his hair. "Easy does it, rascal! So, which one first?"

Pudge eyed each piece on the deck. Alfred suppressed a smile at the way the boy's eyes went back and forth from sword to sling to the dirk on his belt and back again. The boy chewed on his lip as he tried to make a decision.

"Well?" Alfred asked.

"The sling," Pudge pointed. "The sling first, please."

"Hm," Alfred said. "I was afraid you would say that."

"Is something wrong?"

"Not exactly." He sighed. "It's just that Mac says you're left-handed. I'm right-handed. I'll have to teach you backwards, so to speak. Let me think about this for a minute."

Alfred rubbed his mouth as he tried to think of an easy way to teach a left-hander how to use the sling. He came up with nothing.

"Well, Pudge," he said at last, "we're just going to give it a try and see how it goes. Let me demonstrate how to use the sling. Watch carefully."

He demonstrated twice how to use the sling, then he handed it to his student.

Pudge held it like a relic before slipping his hand in the loop and giving it a try. Alfred frowned.

"Not quite," he said. "Watch me again."

Demonstration followed demonstration, but still Pudge seemed unable to make the transition from Alfred's right-handed teaching. Alfred sighed at the lad's frustration.

"Never mind," he said. "We'll try it again tomorrow, Pudge. Let's move on to the sword."

Pudge quickly scooped up one of the practice swords and touched Alfred in the chest with it.

"One!" he crowed and laughed.

"Very funny," Alfred said dryly. "Come stand beside me and do what I do."

The lad learned quickly and copied every move his teacher made. He was doing well until he got a little overenthusiastic and hit a gun carriage at the end of a slashing attack.

"Control yourself, Pudge!" Alfred said. "If you do that with a real sword and the blade gets stuck in the wood, you've lost! Your opponent can do whatever he wants to you. You must always keep control of your blade."

"I'm sorry, Alfred."

"This is why we practice. Now, let's try again."

Pudge curbed his enthusiasm as best he could. He did well, Alfred had to admit; the lad was quick to pick up the basic attacks and defensive postures. The teacher took the swords and set them down beside the sling, then he held his hand out for Pudge's dagger. The lad handed it over.

"I'm going to teach you two things with the knife," he said. "How to use it in battle, and how to throw it."

"Wow!" Pudge said. "You can throw a knife, Alfred?"

The teacher responded by flipping the knife in the air, grabbing it by the tip of the blade, and burying it in the side of the ship, ten feet away. His pupil was astonished.

"May I try?" he asked.

Alfred retrieved the dagger from the wall and handed it to Pudge. "Hold the tip between your thumb and forefinger, and throw it at the wall as I did."

Pudge did his best, only to have the dagger hit the deck halfway to the wall. He ran and retrieved it. The second attempt hit high above the gun ports—hilt-first. Pudge retrieved the blade again.

"This is hard!" he said.

Alfred took the blade. "This is why we practice, Pudge. How many times do you think I had to practice before I could throw the way I just did? Thousands, I'd say."

The boy's jaw dropped. *"Thousands?!?!"* he wailed. "I can't even count that high!"

Alfred took the dagger. "Mastery comes in stages. Do you know how many times I had to practice before I first got the knife blade to stick in the tree—I was throwing at a tree at our home. Care to guess? No? Then I will tell you—*thirty-seven times*. I speak the truth, Pudge; I actually counted, because my father said he wanted to know."

Pudge looked at Alfred with a combination of amazement and dawning hope. Finally, he said, "So it may take me ... thousands of throws to become as good as you are, but It may only take me thirty-seven throws to hit something point first?

"Maybe more, maybe less," Alfred said, holding out the knife. "Let's see if your count improves on mine. The trick is to find the release point when you let go so the blade will land where you want it to land, point-first. On your first throw, you held it too long, and it went down. On the second, you let go too early, and it went too high. See what I mean?"

"I think so."

"Good. Give it another try." He handed over the dagger. "Pay attention to when you let go. Aim for the wall, even with the muzzle of the gun. Your eyes do the aiming for you. Look where you want it to go."

Pudge took the blade and stared at the wall. He raised the dagger and let fly. The blade struck flat and high, but only half as high as the previous attempt.

"Better, Pudge, much better!" Alfred said. "Try it again. This time try to hold on a pinch longer."

Pudge tried again, and the knife struck hilt-first halfway between his mark and the deck."

"Good!" Alfred said. "Keep trying, you're getting there."

Pudge retrieved the knife and went to work. He tried over and over again. He cried out in triumph when the knife stuck in the wall, even though it was three feet above his mark. When Alfred pointed out that it was too high, the boy indignantly announced that he was pretending he was fighting Goliath from the captain's Bible.

Finally, the throw came where the blade stuck in the wall very close to the aiming point.

"Yes!" Pudge cried, throwing his arms in the air.

"Well done, sir!" Alfred said. "Do you know what number throw that was?"

Pudge's eyes went wide. "Oh, no! I forgot to count!"

Alfred smiled. "I was counting. That throw was number *thirty-five!*"

"Really? I beat you?"

Alfred walked up to the wall and put his finger on it. "Pudge, keep your eye on that spot." He took the knife and threw it. The tip hit right on the spot he'd marked. He looked at his student. "What does that tell you?"

Pudge swallowed. "I need to practice. Lots."

Alfred nodded and handed him back the dagger. Three of Pudge's next five throws stuck in the wall, but none were closer than two feet from the aiming point. The ship's bell tolled, and Alfred ended the lesson.

"That's enough for today, Pudge," he said as he gathered up their equipment. "Time to get the captain's meal ready. We'll practice more tomorrow."

"Can we try to sling again?" Pudge asked.

"Oh, yes," Alfred reassured him. "We're not giving up, I promise you. I just have to figure out a way to teach you better, so you can do it yourself."

"Hurrah!" Pudge exclaimed, as he skipped along in Alfred's wake,

Later that night, Alfred and Mac were in the pantry cleaning up from supper and talking over the day's training. Pudge was already in his cot below, fast asleep.

"You should have seen him, Mac," Alfred said as he washed the last few glasses and set them aside to be dried. "You'd have been so proud of him, especially at how fast he took to throwing his knife."

"I'm sure," Mac agreed as he dried. "Did he really do it in thirty-five throws?"

Alfred looked up from his washing, his face an unreadable mask, but Mac thought he could make out just a bit of mischief in his eye.

"Of course," Alfred deadpanned.

Mac gave an exaggerated nod. "I see. A compliment to your instruction, I'm sure. Or at least how well you can count."

Alfred shrugged. "Something like that. I wish I could figure out a better way to explain the sling to him. I hoped he could watch me and then do it backwards for himself, sort of like looking in a mirror, but it's too confusing for the lad. Got any ideas?"

"Humph," Mac grunted. "Too bad you're not left-handed."

Alfred stopped his washing and stared at the big coxswain. "What did you say?"

Mac looked confused; had he said something wrong? "You mean, 'Too bad you're not left-handed'?"

Alfred threw his rag into the dish water and pointed at his friend. "That's it! Mac, you are a genius!"

"What's it?"

"*Left-handed!*" Alfred cried. "I just need to teach Pudge left-handed!"

Mac frowned. "But you're not left-handed."

"No," Alfred admitted, "but I can teach myself to do it with my left hand! And at the same time, I will teach Pudge! It'll be a contest—which of us can learn first!"

Mac shook his head in an I'm-not-so-sure sort of way. "*Can* you teach yourself and the boy at the same time?"

"I don't see why not. It might even help the lad to pay attention, trying to find out mistakes that I make and fix them for himself."

"We'll see," Mac said, and went back to his drying. The Cornishman mulled it over. *He may have something there,* he thought. *Might be a good idea to be able to do things with both hands, just in case you get hit in your good arm, say?* He nodded; the more he thought about it, the better he liked the idea. To be able to use a sword, throw a knife, shoot a pistol, or even use a sling, equally well with either hand would go a long way towards saving a man's life. *I wonder if Alfred would teach me, too?*

It was two days later before Alfred could find the time for Pudge's next lesson. They gathered again at the front of the gun deck. Pudge tried not to show his disappointment when Alfred picked up the swords. They repeated the same moves as before, the same thrusts, slashes, and stabs, the same blocks and parries. Pudge learned quickly not to let his mind wander, for Alfred was quick to remind him by a smack on the arm or thigh.

Before they began knife-throwing practice, Alfred picked up a small can from the floor and moved to the wall.

"What's that, Alfred?" Pudge asked.

"Whitewash," Alfred said as he painted a circle on the wall about as big across as two pieces of ship's biscuit. "Now each of us can see where the other was aiming."

Alfred went first and put his knife inside the circle. When Pudge tried, his knife hit the wall flat about three feet above.

"Not bad," Alfred was quick to compliment him. "Not a bad throw at all for only your second practice. Try it again."

It took four more throws for the knife to stick, and twenty after that before Pudge was able to land a good throw inside the circle. His arms went up in the air again in triumph.

"Well done, sir!" Alfred said. "A good throw to end today's practice."

"End the practice?" Pudge could not hide his disappointment. "Aren't we going to try the sling again?"

"I meant *knife-throwing practice*," Alfred stressed. "Now we go to the sling. Pudge, you and I are going to have a contest."

The boy looked at him. "What kind of contest?" he asked warily.

Alfred picked up the sling and held it out. "We are going to see which of us can learn to use the sling first left-handed."

"But you told me you're not left-handed."

"As my father used to say, *Right you are, me ol' boy!*" Alfred said as he put his left wrist through the loop. "But we are both going to learn to use the sling with our left hands. I'll try it first, with the sling empty."

Alfred took the other end of the sling and held it between his thumb and forefinger, then he began to twirl the sling in a clockwise motion over his head, faster and faster, until he let go of the end of sling and flung his imaginary ammunition. He handed it to Pudge, who did a creditable imitation of Alfred's motion.

"Good," he said. "Now we'll try it with the practice ammunition that Captain Enfield gave us." He took one from the bag on the deck and put it into the cloth on the sling. He twirled it slowly over his head. "Aim is more important than power at the beginning. It doesn't matter how hard you throw it if you miss the target. I can feel where the weight is as it is going around, Pudge; when it gets even with your shoulder on the outside, that's the time to let it go."

Alfred spun the sling above his head a couple more times before making his cast. The twine ball bounced off the wall about three feet to the right and below the circle.

"You missed!" Pudge exclaimed as he bounded forward to retrieve the ball. "My turn!"

Alfred handed him the sling and moved to stand about ten feet behind the boy and to his right so he could see the wall clearly. Pudge carefully placed the ball in the cloth pouch and began to twirl it over his head. However, unlike Alfred, he spun the sling as hard as he could. He let go of the line to release the ball, which promptly struck Alfred right in the chest.

"Oh, Alfred!" Pudge said, as he ran to retrieve the missile. "Are you hurt?"

"No, but let's try it again. Slowly, this time, as I showed you. Try to feel where the weight is as the ball moves around in the sling. Wait for it to come around to outside your shoulder, then let go of the end. *Slowly*, now."

Pudge put the sling in motion, twirling it slowly over his head.

"Do you feel the weight going around and around?" Alfred asked.

"I think so," Pudge said. He increased his speed just a fraction. "Yes, I do now."

"Then let it go when you're ready."

Pudge slung it around a couple more times and let go.

The ball hit the wall about four feet to the left of the target.

"See?" Alfred said. "You can do it."

CHAPTER SEVEN

The sun was barely above the horizon when Captain Brewer stepped up on deck. He had breakfasted early with the express purpose of getting some exercise in the early morning breeze before the sun made the deck uncomfortable. Mr. Rivkins had the morning watch; he saluted as his captain approached.

"Good morning, Captain," he said. "Up early?"

"Good morning, Lieutenant. And yes, I am."

Rivkins nodded toward the lee rail and the captain's usual pacing area. "It's ready for you, sir."

"Thank you, Mr. Rivkins." Brewer began pacing. The fresh air cleared his mind, and the sounds of the deck reassured him that, here and now, all was well. Before his first turn, his chin was on his breast, his eyes focused on the deck two steps in front of him. His mind was racing.

First, we are sent out after Black Rose, the fiercest pirate in recent years, he thought, *and now we're pulled off that and sent out after our old ship! The worst part is, we don't even know whether Gerard is dead or alive!* He made the turn and headed aft. *What happened on that ship? How could Gerard allow something like this to happen?* He frowned at the thought and tried to remember how many and who of *Revenge's* crew had remained aboard when he'd departed to take command of *Phoebe.* The administrative staff of the admiral's office had taken the transfer; the only crew he had requested beside his officers had been Alfred and Mac.

What happened, Gerard? he wondered as he made another turn. *How could you let things get that far?*

Obviously, getting sick must have.... How did you get so sick, anyway? And why did it incapacitate you so long? Nobody I talked to said anything about your doctor being incompetent. So, if your care was beyond him, something he'd never seen before, why didn't your first lieutenant make for the naval hospital at Port Royal under all the sail she'd carry?

Brewer stopped his pacing and watched his ship's wake streaming out behind him until it was lost in the endless sea. That tiny voice in the back of his head was screaming again, and he didn't like that. It always meant trouble. But it was there, nonetheless, repeating the same warning over and over again.

Something's not right.

He heard the ship's bell toll four times and decided to return to this cabin and write letters. He turned to say something to Mr. Rivkins before he went below, but the lieutenant was nowhere in sight. Instead, he saw Mr. Cromwell standing by the wheel.

The lieutenant touched his hat as his captain approached. "Good morning, sir,"

"Good morning, Mr. Cromwell," Brewer said as nonchalantly as possible. "Where's Mr. Rivkins?"

"Mr. Rivkins went below at the end of his watch, sir," Cromwell replied. "Shall I pass the word for him?"

Brewer stared at him for a moment before coming to the realization that he had been pacing for more than four hours! He blinked and said, "No, thank you. I shall be in my cabin, Mr. Cromwell."

"Aye, sir."

He turned to head toward the companionway when a call came from above.

"Deck ho! Sail on the starboard bow!"

"Where away?"

A gust of wind prevented the captain from hearing the man's reply, but the lookout signaled the direction. Brewer grabbed a glass and went to the rail to see for himself. He soon spotted the ship—still a speck of white, barely visible on the horizon. He thought for a moment before turning to Cromwell.

"Alter course to intercept, Mr. Cromwell."

"Aye, sir!" The lieutenant picked up a speaking trumpet and began bellowing orders. The ship swung around smartly and steadied up on her new heading.

Brewer saw Skimpy come up on deck and pointed to him with his glass. "Skimp! You're with me."

"Aye, sir!" The boy followed hot on his captain's heels.

The captain's destination was the forward carronade on the starboard side. He braced himself against the gun and raised the glass again. The hint of white on the horizon was growing slowly. Brewer judged the ship would be hull-up in less than twenty minutes. He lowered his glass and turned to Skimpy.

"Skimpy, I have a job for you. I want you to climb up to the lookout in the foretop and be ready to run messages from him to me. If it seems like I can't understand him, you bring me his report."

"Aye, sir!" The lad knuckled his forehead and jumped for the lower shrouds. He had neared the lookout nest when Lieutenant Greene appeared and touched his hat.

"Something, sir?" he asked.

Brewer handed him the spyglass and Greene moved to the other side of the deck for a better view. The ship surged forward with an unexpected gust of wind.

"Captain!"

Skimpy leapt off the shrouds and came to a halt with his knuckles on his forehead. "Sir! The lookout says he thinks it's a sloop, sir!"

Greene frowned. "Didn't the survivors you interviewed say Black Rose sailed a brig?"

Brewer nodded silently. His head tilted to the side as an unlikely thought crept in. *Could it be?*

He turned to Greene. "You have the deck, Benjamin. I shall stay here. Beat to quarters and lay on all sail. Marine sharpshooters to the tops."

"Aye, sir." Greene returned the glass, touched his hat, and went aft.

"Skimpy, get back aloft. I want to know as soon as the lookout can identify that ship."

"Aye, sir."

Brewer concentrated on the horizon. He could now pick out a sliver of brown below the cloud of white. Behind him he heard the activity that would turn his ship into a machine of war. Eleven minutes later, Greene was back.

"We're ready, sir," he said.

"Thank you, Mr. Greene," Brewer answered. He did not lower the glass. He muttered to himself, "Any minute now...."

"Deck there!" the lookout cried. "I think it's *Revenge*!"

"Just as I thought!" Brewer said. "What's she doing, lookout?"

The lookout yelled, "She's running, sir!"

Sure enough, the ship was crowding on sail and turning to run. Brewer frowned and closed his glass. "Let's go, Benjamin."

The two men headed aft to find Mr. Sweeney at his place on the quarterdeck.

"Morning, Captain," the sailing master greeted them. "So, it's *Revenge,* is it?"

"So it would seem, Mr. Sweeney," Brewer replied. He turned to include Greene in the conversation. "We have the advantage in that we are already under full sail, and I believe we have a two- or three-knot speed advantage in any case. Am I correct?"

"Possibly a knot or two more, Captain," Sweeney said. "I don't think those mutineers are still keeping to the standards you instilled when the ship was yours."

Brewer nodded at the compliment and turned to Greene. "Given what Mr. Sweeney says, what do you estimate the time to overtake?"

Greene considered a moment. "Possibly as much as five hours, sir. It depends on how well they handle the sails."

"That is my assessment as well," Brewer agreed. "Let's get to it. Mr. Sweeney, I want that ship."

Sweeney grinned. "Aye, sir."

He turned to Greene. "Mr. Cromwell has the deck. I am to be called if *Revenge* changes course or if we come within range of the long nines."

"Aye, sir."

"And pass the word for the doctor to join me in my cabin."

"Aye, sir."

Brewer surrendered his glass. "Mr. Greene, I would very much appreciate it if you and Mr. Sweeney would join me in my cabin for a simple meal at midday. Shall we say, two bells of the afternoon watch?"

"Thank you, sir."

Salutes were exchanged, and Brewer made his way below to his cabin. He found the doctor waiting for him. The two men entered, and the sentry closed the door behind them.

"So," Spinelli said, "looks like we found them, eh?"

Brewer was annoyed. "Is there a rag newspaper on this ship?"

"May as well be," Spinelli said, ignoring his captain's mood. "Do you think Gerard and Short are still alive?"

"I don't know," Brewer conceded. "They're running right now, but we should catch them long before dark. That's when the trouble starts. Chess?"

Brewer got his chess set from his desk and brought it to the table, and the two men set up the board. The doctor drew white and made the first move.

"Any idea what we're going to find aboard Revenge?" he asked.

"I have concerns and fears, no certainties," Brewer replied. He answered the pawn move by bringing out his queen's knight.

"It would be easier if we knew they were dead," Spinelli said. "That way, if they refuse to surrender, we could just blow the ship out of the water and leave those mutineers who survived to the sharks."

Brewer glanced up at his opponent with one eye. "You can be very cold-blooded for a doctor."

"Yes," Spinelli said as he took a bishop with a pawn, "I've heard that a few times."

Brewer moved his rook across the board. "Check. Well, I doubt they would ever admit their hostages were dead, if only for that very reason. That is why I intend to send Mr. Greene across to their ship when we finally catch them. He will demand to see the hostages. If Brumby refuses, then we shall blow them out of the water, hostages or no hostages."

The doctor glanced up at that. "And Gerard?"

The captain never took his eyes from the game. "Gerard would understand."

Spinelli sat back and studied his captain. It wasn't often that Brewer allowed these cold, black moods to come over him, but when he did, the consequences were usually dire for someone. He allowed a smile to creep into the corners of his mouth as a thought came to him: *Poor Brumby.*

At the end of the third game—all won by the doctor—a knock at the door announced the arrival of Lieutenant Greene and Mr. Sweeney. The table was cleared and the men sat down.

"Thank you for coming," Brewer said. "While we are awaiting whatever Alfred has readied for us, tell me, how close are we now?"

Greene replied, "I estimate two hours will bring us within range of the long nines. But they won't do us any good until we get close enough to have a shot at their beam."

"Why not?" Spinelli asked.

"Last we heard, Doctor," Brewer said, "the hostages were in the captain's cabin. We don't want to take a chance on hitting them."

"Shall I alter course one point to larboard?" Sweeney suggested. "That way, when we reach them, a sharp twenty or twenty-five degree turn to starboard may give the long nines a chance at the bow."

"An excellent idea, Mr. Sweeney." Brewer rose and opened the door. "Pass the word for the midshipman of the watch," he told the sentry.

"Aye, sir."

Not loing after, there was a knock at the door and Mr. Henry entered. He pulled off his hat and came to attention.

"You sent for me, sir?"

"Yes, Mr. Henry," the captain replied. "My compliments to Mr. Reed, and will he please alter our course one point to larboard."

The midshipman blinked. "One point to larboard, sir?"

"That's correct, Mr. Henry."

"Aye, sir. One point to larboard. Aye, sir!" the confused lad came to attention and left the cabin. A muffled chuckle followed his departure.

"Shall I explain it to him later?" Sweeney asked his captain.

Brewer grinned. "Only if he asks about it."

Dinner was served. The main course was stewed albatross, shot the day before by a marine at target practice, and acquired by Alfred for an unspecified amount of tobacco. Normally, the dish was not a favorite of Brewer's, but he loved Alfred's version. The little man had revealed his secret recipe once, but the captain could not remember what he'd said. Perhaps it was better that way. ON the side were carrots and a cauliflower, along with bread—not ship's biscuit—and marmalade. The men dug in appreciatively.

"Let me ask you gentlemen a question," Brewer said between mouthfuls. "What do you think of steam power applied to warships?"

"Interesting idea," Greene replied, "but has anyone actually done it yet?"

"It can't work," Sweeney interrupted.

"Why not?" the doctor asked.

Sweeney swallowed his mouthful and pointed at the doctor with his spoon. "They're powered by these huge paddle wheels on either side of the ship, although I understand some in the United States have a single one in the rear. Either way, the paddle wheels will be too easily shot up in a battle. Believe me, a shot in a hot steam engine will be as devastating as one hitting a magazine."

"Ah!"

"Actually," Brewer said, "the United States has already done it."

Sweeney sat bolt-upright. "The devil you say!"

"I found out when we made our first visit to Martinique in HMS *Revenge*," Brewer explained. "The governor told me, and I asked an American officer I later met when he was visiting my father-in-law on St. Kitts. They built a steam-powered ship during their last war with us, and it was designed to defend New York Harbor. It was called... let me see... *Demologos*, I believe."

"How did they solve the paddle-wheel problem?" Sweeney asked.

Brewer swallowed and said, "The ship was a twin-hulled design, I was told, with the engine below the water line on one side. The single paddle wheel was put in between the hulls."

"Ingenious!" Spinelli said.

Brewer helped himself to the carrots. "The ship was armed with thirty 32-pounders along with two 100-pounders designed to hole enemy ships below their water line." Greene and Sweeney were impressed by the armament. Brewer continued. "Remember, this ship was for harbor defense. She had a rudder at both ends; they only had to reverse the engine to go the other way. No turning around!"

"Backwards?" Greene was mystified.

"Let me back up," Brewer said. "No pun intended. As I said, she was for harbor defense, so she did not need a standard hull configuration; I understand she's more of a floating battery than a seagoing ship. The twin hulls gave the ship a sort of rectangular shape." He drew a rectangle in the air with his finger. "Her gun deck had eight big guns on each side, and two on either end." The unusual layout stunned his guests. "Not only that, the outer hull was *five feet thick all the way around!* I understand she could make five knots in a good seaway."

"Did she make it into the war?" the doctor asked.

Brewer shook his head. "She wasn't completed until after the treaty was signed."

"I wonder if they'll try to make a steam frigate?" Greene asked.

"Not with that design," Sweeney opined. "Frigate's built for speed; eyes of the fleet and all that. Five knots won't cut it."

"So," Brewer said, "we are waiting for the next breakthrough, the next new technology, the one that will allow us to make more efficient use of steam power to get fourteen or fifteen knots out of a steam frigate." He took a bite of bread and chewed meditatively. "I wonder how long that will take?"

"Are you sure it will happen?" Sweeney asked.

"I am," the captain affirmed. "It's only a matter of time."

Dinner ended, and Brewer led his guests aft to the day cabin. No sooner were they seated than Pudge appeared with a tray containing four cups of hot coffee. Each man helped himself, and the boy bowed and retreated.

"He's coming along fine, Captain," Spinelli said. "Do you think we might be able to put him through some schooling? Skimpy, too, along with any others who wish to attend. I think anyone nowadays who can't read or write, and do sums, is asking to be taken advantage of."

"We can look into that, Doctor," Brewer said. "Sounds like a good idea."

Brewer sipped his coffee and sighed; good as always. He sat forward and set his cup down. "Once we catch up with *Revenge,* I want to make her heave to."

"And if she doesn't?" the doctor asked.

"Then I will take it that the hostages are no longer alive," the captain replied coldly, "and I will blow the ship out of the water."

Nobody commented, so he continued. "When they heave to, I intend to send you, Mr. Greene, across with a boarding party. Benjamin, your mission will be to see the hostages and speak to them. If they refuse to allow you to see the hostages, return to the ship, and we shall open fire. If the boarding party is taken prisoner, in fact, if I even hear a gun go off—*no matter whose*—I will blow that ship out of the water, even with you aboard. Make sure Brumby understands that I am deadly serious."

"Understood, sir."

A knock at the door heralded the entrance of Mr. Murdy, the senior midshipman. He came to attention and said, "Mr. Rivkins' respects, sir, and would you please come on deck? He says we shall soon be in range of the long-nines."

"Thank you, Mr. Murdy," the captain said as he rose. "My compliments to Mr. Rivkins. Please tell him we shall be right up."

"Aye, sir." Murdy came to attention and retreated from the cabin.

They stepped up on deck and were greeted by Lieutenant Rivkins.

"Won't be long now, sir," he said. "We need another fifteen minutes or so before we can make the turn to starboard and open fire safely."

"Thank you, Mr. Rivkins," Brewer said. He studied the chase for a moment before lifting his voice. "I have the deck! Mr. Greene!"

Greene stepped forward, and Brewer led him to the starboard rail.

"Benjamin," he said privately, "do you think we can make a turn to port and use the forward 18-pounder to put a ball off her bow? That would certainly get their attention. Then if they don't heave to, we can pull over to starboard and put two shots with the long-nines into her bow."

Greene studied the scene for a moment before turning to his captain, his eyes ablaze. "Let's do it, sir!"

"Good! Get down to the forward 18-pounder and make ready. I will give you the word to fire."

Greene touched his hat and departed, and Brewer stepped over to Mr. Sweeney and the quartermaster to explain his plan. Then he called Rivkins over to the starboard rail.

"Percy," he said, "I want you to take command of the long-nines. In a moment, we are going to turn to port, and Mr. Greene is going to try to put an 18-pound ball off her bow. If she doesn't heave to, we shall come around to starboard again for you to put two balls in her bows. Understand?"

Rivkins nodded. "Aye, sir!"

"Good! Go!"

Rivkins went forward, and Brewer called for a glass and studied the stern of the ship ahead. He realized he would be doing them a favor by simply blowing them to kingdom come; the penalty for mutiny is death by hanging, but this way their families could be told they were lost at sea. He shook his head.

"Pardon me, sir."

Brewer turned to see Mr. Tyler. "Yes, Mr. Tyler?"

"Sir, Mr. Greene sends his respects and says to tell you he is ready when you are."

"Good. My compliments to Mr. Greene. Please tell him that after we make the turn to port, he is to fire as his gun bears."

"Aye, sir!" Tyler saluted and sprinted off for the stairs.

Brewer stepped over to the wheel. "Ready, Mr. Sweeney?"

"Ready, Captain!"

"You may make your turn."

"Aye, sir!" He turned to the wheel. "Three points to larboard!"

The quartermaster's mates put the wheel over, and the ship came around in obedience. Immediately when they steadied up, the number one gun fired. The ship quickly outran the smoke.

"Lookout!" Rivkins called.

"Beautiful, sir!" the lookout replied. "Water spout fine off the larboard bow! Sir! She's heaving to!"

"Thank God!" Rivkins heard his captain say beneath his breath. The two men headed aft and were met by Lieutenant Greene on the quarterdeck.

"Well done, Benjamin," Brewer said. "Get your boat's crew ready. Take Mac with you; he looks big and ugly. He may help keep the mutineers at bay."

"Aye, sir." Greene saluted and went forward, shouting for McCleary as he went.

Lieutenant Greene fought to control his rising anger and indignation as he sat in the stern sheets of the launch and approached HMS *Revenge.* The 12-pounders of her main battery were run out, along with her carronades, not that this worried Greene. At this very minute, *Phoebe* was running out the 18-pounder long guns on her gun deck and 32-pounder carronades on the fo'c'sle and quarterdeck of her starboard battery.

"Mac," he said quietly to the coxswain beside him, "you'll board with me. The rest of you will stay in the launch for now. Johnson," he said to the leading hand on the oar before him, "if anyone starts shooting, get away from *Revenge* and stand off to safety. Try to make your way back to *Phoebe,* but you may have to wait a bit."

Johnson nodded to acknowledge the order. "We'll enjoy the front row seat, sir."

"Good man," Greene said.

They hooked on at the entry port of the sloop, and Greene rose to ascend. Mac grabbed his arm.

"Pardon me, sir," he said. "I think I should go first."

Greene made to argue, but the look into the coxswain's eyes dissuaded him.

"Very well, Mac."

The big Cornishman scrambled up to the deck. Not hearing any scuffle, Greene followed. He stepped onto the deck and stood beside the coxswain. They were surrounded by a semicircle of about twenty-five or thirty men. Greene was disagreeably surprised to find that he recognized some of them. A few of them avoided his eyes and moved to the back of the crowd.

"I am Lieutenant Greene of His Majesty's Frigate *Phoebe!*" he said loudly. "Which of you speaks for the others?"

Off to his right, the crowd parted and a short, dark-haired man stepped forward.

"I don't reckon we've got anyone exactly like that," he said. "But you can talk to me."

"Your name?" Greene asked.

The man smiled. "I'd imagined you already knew," he said. "It's Brumby."

"The only thing I have to say to you, *Bosun*," Greene said coldly, "is that you are ordered to surrender."

"Not likely," Brumby replied. "If that's all, Lieutenant?"

"I want to see your hostages, if you please," Greene said.

"What's to stop me killing you and your pet gorilla," Brumby pointed at Mac with his chin, "and leaving with my hostages?"

Greene gestured towards the frigate behind them. "If they see either of us fall, or hear a shot, or if we're not back aboard within..." he pulled out his watch, "forty-eight minutes from now, Captain Brewer will will open fire."

"With you on board?"

"With me on board."

Brumby noticed several of the others looking at him and moving closer, fists clenching. "All right, then, Lieutenant. But only you. The ape stays where he is."

"Fine by me," Mac said. He stood still with one hand on the hilt of his sword and the other on the butt of the pistol in his belt.

"Agreed," Greene said. "Take me to them."

Brumby turned without a word and led Greene below.

Mac stood where he was, his glare telling all what he thought of them. One of the men off to his left stepped forward.

"I wouldn't," Mac said.

"Give up your arms," the hand said.

"No," Mac replied.

"You can't beat us all," the mutineer sneered.

Mac shrugged. "Then we die."

"We?"

Mac turned to him. "Maybe I can't beat thirty men, but I know I can get you before they get me. But even if I don't," Mac pointed to *Phoebe* with his head, "see that number two carronade? She's loaded with grape, and she's pointed right at you, mate." Mac smiled wickedly. "I fall, they fire, and there ain't enough left of you for your mother to bury."

The man stepped back.

Brumby jerked open the door to the captain's cabin without any preamble and strode in. The doctor turned and saw Brumby standing there.

"Get out!" he snapped.

"Mind your manners, Doc," the mutineer said. "I've brought you a visitor."

Greene stepped past him into the cabin.

"Five minutes, Lieutenant," Brumby said, then left and closed the door.

Greene looked around and saw that the cabin was little changed since Brewer's occupancy. He was about to introduce himself to the doctor when a voice called out, "Mr. Greene!" And a young man entered the cabin from the day room.

"Mr. Short!" Greene clasped the young midshipman's shoulders and looked him over.

"Doctor," Short said by way of introduction, "this is Lieutenant Greene from the *Phoebe*. Sir, this is Doctor Ellington."

The two men shook hands.

"I haven't much time, Doctor," Greene said. "How is your captain?"

"Not good," Ellington said. "But come, see for yourself."

He led Greene into the day cabin. Captain Gerard was lying on the settee beneath the open stern windows. His head rolled toward the newcomers, and Greene could see his eyes were open and trying to focus. His face was covered by sweat, and his shirt was plastered to his skin. Greene knelt beside him.

"Gerard," he said, "can you hear me?"

The effort to focus and concentrate was too much for him, and the captain fell asleep. Greene turned to the doctor.

"Whatever he's got," The doctor said, "it's determined to kill him. I can't get it out of his system."

"What's wrong with him?" Greene asked.

The doctor leaned in and spoke quietly. "I believe he was poisoned."

"Poisoned?!?"

The doctor nodded emphatically and stole a quick look at the door. "It's the only explanation that makes sense. A lesser man would have died long ago, but he is holding on for dear life."

"Is there anything we can do for him?" Greene asked as he stared at the captain's unconscious form.

"Nothing more than we are," came the answer. "Mr. Short's been a tremendous help. We need to get the captain to a hospital."

"We're working on a plan to rescue you," Greene said, but he had no chance to say anything more, for the door opened and Brumby reappeared.

"Time's up," he said. "Let's go, Lieutenant."

Greene looked at Gerard. "Take care of him, Doctor." He left the cabin. Brumby followed him out and closed the door behind him.

Greene stepped out onto the deck and headed straight toward Mac. When he reached the rail, he turned to Brumby and his men.

"The only chance you have is to surrender now!"

"Ha!" Brumby cried. "What chance is that? Leave while you still can."

Greene descended to the launch, and Mac followed. They shoved off and pulled for *Phoebe*. Greene resisted the urge to turn around. Instead, he concentrated on what Ellington had told him.

Once aboard, Greene and Mac reported to the captain's cabin. The sentry admitted them. Neither man was surprised to find the captain playing chess with Doctor Spinelli.

"Good," Brewer said, as he stood and greeted them, "you're back. Come to the day cabin, if you please, gentlemen."

The four men moved aft and found their seats. Alfred arrived with four glasses on his silver tray. Brewer turned to his premier. "Mr. Greene, your report."

Greene sighed. "First, let me talk about the situation in general, then I will get to Captain Gerard." Hearing no objections, he continued. "Brumby is in control. I only saw the men who were on deck. I saw no one else on my way to Gerard's cabin or on the way out again. The ship looks undamaged for the most part. Anything to add, Mac?"

"No, sir. They made no advance on me while you were below. Kept their distance, in fact. I did see some old *Revenge* hands, Captain, but they didn't seem like they wanted to talk none."

"So," Brewer said, "we still have no idea if we can turn the crew against Brumby. Let's set that aside for now. What about Gerard?"

"Not good. He was conscious for a few moments when I first arrived, but then he fainted. The doctor over there is convinced he's been poisoned. He also said it would have killed a lesser man days ago, but it looked to me like Gerard is too weak to last much longer. Sir, if we are going to save him, we don't have much time."

"And Mr. Short?"

"He seemed in good health," Greene said, "and handling himself very well, all things considered."

Brewer rose and began to pace. "So, what do we have? We don't have a good count of their numbers, other than the thirty or so who appeared on the deck. Can we sweep the deck with grape and board her?"

"I don't know if we could get to the hostages before they were executed in reprisal," Greene said.

Brewer looked at his officers. "I'm open to suggestions, gentlemen."

"The way I see it," the doctor said, "we only have two choices where the hostages are concerned: either we take them or we trade for them."

The captain stopped in his tracks and stared at the doctor. "Trade for them, you say? Pray tell, what would you suggest we trade for them?"

Spinelli leaned forward. "What do these mutineers want most at this moment?"

The others looked at each other and then back to the doctor.

Spinelli shrugged. "Their freedom."

"You expect," Greene said in disbelief, "us—the captain, rather—to barter with mutineers? What, they give us the hostages, and we just let them go free? Are you *mad,* Doctor?"

"Do you have a better idea, Lieutenant?" Spinelli sat back and crossed his arms.

Greene glared at him through eyes narrowed to angry slits. Finally, he turned his eyes to the captain and shot him a question with his eyebrows.

Brewer thought furiously. He looked to the doctor. "Adam?"

Spinelli's silence was not what he wanted. He sighed.

"Gentlemen, please give us the room."

Greene opened his mouth to protest, but closed it again without speaking. Instead, he rose and led Mac out of the cabin.

After the door was shut, Brewer sat down opposite his friend. "You know I can't do that, Adam. The Lords of the Admiralty would never approve negotiating with mutineers."

Spinelli shifted in his seat. "William, you have a choice to make. You can either take out the mutineers, or you can save the hostages. We have been unable to come up with a plan that accomplish do both."

Brewer slapped his knees in frustration and rose again to pace. The doctor moved to the settee in order that his captain could walk the entire breadth of the room unimpeded. He watched as Brewer did just that, five steps across and five back, over and over again, his chin tucked down to his chest, mouth pressed into a thin line.

The doctor had seen this from his friend many times during their voyages together. He was glad of it, because it meant that the captain's mind was working, turning over every option he could think of rather than simply saying "No" and hiding behind the Admiralty. So he sat back and waited as patiently as he could for Brewer to make up his mind.

When the captain made his next turn, his chin came up and he said, "I cannot conceive of a plan that would allow us to capture or sink *Revenge* and yet save the lives of Captain Gerard, Mr. Short, and the doctor. If, as you say, I must choose between two options—either take the mutineers or rescue the hostages—what choice do I have? Pass the word for Mr. Greene and Mac, if you please."

The doctor rose and went to the cabin door to have the sentry pass the word. When he returned, he found Brewer sitting on the settee, elbows on his knees and his forehead resting in his hands. Spinelli resumed his seat silently. He did not envy his friend his decision; if Brewer did what he expected him to do, the captain might well have some explaining to do, either in Port Royal or in London.

A knock at the door preceded the sentry admitting Greene and McCleary. Brewer sat up when he heard the knock.

"You sent for us, sir?" Greene asked. The doctor's brow rose slightly; he could still hear the disagreement in the first lieutenant's voice.

"Yes," Brewer replied calmly. "Sit, please, both of you. I have made my decision. I cannot in good conscience condemn the hostages to die, which is what would almost surely happen if we fire on the mutineers or try to board. Lieutenant Greene, I am sending you and Mac back as envoys. You will present Brumby with the following offer: If he surrenders his hostages immediately, I promise not to pursue him until after we have delivered them to the naval hospital at Port Royal. If he declines, return to *Phoebe*."

Behind him, Mac stared into empty space and clamped his jaw firmly shut.

"I know this is not to your liking, Benjamin," Brewer said, "but how else can we ensure the lives of the hostages?"

"So you will let Brumby and his murderous mutineers go free?" Greene demanded.

Brewer responded to the tone of his first lieutenant's voice. "Lieutenant, will you have a problem carrying out my orders?"

Greene snapped to attention. "None, Captain."

"Very good," Brewer said. "Off with you both, then."

The two men came to attention and left the cabin without a word. After they were gone, Brewer stood absolutely still. Suddenly, he felt very tired.

"Do you think he'll be all right?" Spinelli asked without taking his eyes from the door.

"Yes," Brewer replied. He laid his head back and closed his eyes. "Benjamin will do his duty, Doctor; have no fear. No, the question is, what will Brumby do?"

Mac glanced sideways at the first lieutenant. They were in the stern sheets of the launch, on their way to the mutineers' ship. Mr. Greene had not said a word since they left the captain's cabin. Even now, his jaw was set, his face a mask of rage. The coxswain's eyes turned forward again.

"Pull together now!" he chided his men. "Those mutinous scum are watching, you may be sure of that! Show 'em how a British crew behaves! Together now!"

His crew responded, and the launch picked up speed. Mac smiled and turned to Lieutenant Greene, but the look on the premier's face was unchanged. The smile vanished from the coxswain's face.

When they reached their destination, Greene didn't wait for Mac to ascend to the deck first, as he had on their first trip over. Instead, the first lieutenant vaulted up to the entry port, leaving Mac to scramble after him. By the time Mac set foot on deck, Greene was face to face with the mutineers' leader again.

"I bring a... proposal from my captain," Greene said.

"Really?" Brumby crossed his arms over his chest, a gesture of defiance and contempt. "And why should I listen?"

Greene stepped aside and pointed toward HMS *Phoebe's* guns. "Because if you don't, my captain will blow this ship out of the water."

Brumby scowled, his eyes darting from his visitor to the British frigate and back again with undisguised hate. Then his eyes slip sideways to take in the expressions on the faces of his men.

Mac and Greene both saw this movement. Mac slowly scanned the faces of the men. "In the interest of saving the lives of your hostages, Captain Brewer makes the following proposal: If you will surrender your hostages immediately, alive and well, he promises not to pursue you until after he has delivered them to the naval hospital at Port Royal."

"That's it?" Brumby said, incredulous. "And what if I refuse?"

Greene showed his teeth in something that was not a smile. "In that case, he will blow you out of the water. Hostages or no hostages."

The mutineer's eyes narrowed. He stepped around the officer for another look at the menacing frigate in the distance. The eighteen-pounders pointed at him were intimidating, enough to strike fear into the coldest heart. Worse, from his point of view, were the glints of telescopes on the deck observing everything on his ship.

Once again Brumby took stock of his crew. In their eyes he saw a warning.

"Well?" he said. "You heard the man."

The men looked at each other. Finally, Jenkins stepped forward.

"Give them what they want, and let's get out of here."

Brumby saw heads moving up and down in agreement. He looked each man in the eye to be sure.

"Tell your captain he has a deal."

"Good choice." Greene turned and nodded to Mac. The coxswain leaned over the rail and whistled. On this signal, the eight marines in the long boat climbed up and over the side to stand on the deck. "We will be taking the hostages back to the ship. Sergeant, take two men with you below and fetch them. You'll find them in the captain's old cabin.

Back on-board HMS *Phoebe*, Captain Brewer watched the events unfolding aboard *Revenge* through his glass. His heart leapt when he saw Mac lean over the railing and whistle. He watched as two British officers appear on deck—

presumably Mr. Short and the doctor—followed by two of his marines maneuvering a stretcher bearing Captain Gerard,. A lift was raised, and Gerard was slung over the side and lowered to the boat, where he was secured for the trip back to *Phoebe*. He saw Short and the doctor climb down the side of the ship and take their places next to Gerard. Brewer was careful to count the marines as they disembarked, followed by Greene and Mac last of all.

He kept watch on the deck of *Revenge* all the while the boat was in transit. There was a large part of him that longed to give the order to fire, to simply blow the mutinous scum to Davy Jones' locker now that the hostages were safe, but his loyalties to his oath and his word prevented him from giving the order. He watched in frustration as the mutineers raised sail and got under way. Their course was to the southeast, but Brewer was fairly sure that would change the moment they were safely below the horizon. He lowered his glass and frowned. There would be a reckoning. He would make sure of it.

Brewer turned to the officer of the watch. "Mr. Rivkins, make ready to receive our boat. Have a sling readied to bring Captain Gerard aboard and men standing by to take him to sickbay."

"Aye, Captain."

Under Rivkins' direction, the bosun and his men rigged the sling and brought Captain Gerard aboard. Brewer saw that his friend was unconscious, so he stood back and let the men take him below.

"Sir," Greene said, approaching, "May I introduce Dr. Ellington? And you remember Mr. Short."

"Doctor," Brewer said, as he shook the man's hand. His grip had no energy behind it. "I am happy to make your acquaintance. I presume you wish to go below and see

Captain Gerard settled into our sickbay; Mr. Greene, will you please lead the way? Introduce Dr. Ellington to Dr. Spinelli."

"Aye, sir. Doctor, if you'll follow me?"

After they had gone below, Brewer said, "Mr. Short, it's good to see you again." Brewer was actually shocked, seeing the boy up close. He was a full half-head taller than Brewer remembered, but he looked leaner; it was almost as if he were starving.

The boy smiled. "Thank you for the rescue, Captain."

"I'm glad we were able pull it off. After you've rested, please dine with Mr. Greene and myself. I want to hear your observations of what happened on *Revenge*."

"Aye, sir." Short swayed wearily. "May I go to sickbay and check up on Captain Gerard?"

"Of course, lad," the captain said. "We'll talk later."

Short knuckled his forehead and made his way awkwardly to the sickbay. It was clear that fatigue was hitting him hard.

"Mr. Sweeney," Brewer said, "please set your course for Port Royal."

"Aye, sir."

* * * * *

Adam Spinelli checked on his patient before leaving sickbay. Gerard slept soundly, and Spinelli smiled at the sight of the faithful midshipman, Mr. Short, seated beside his captain, his chin on his breast and his eyes also closed in exhausted slumber. Dr. Ellington was likewise asleep, in a hammock slung near to Gerard. Spinelli pulled his watch from his coat pocket as he reached for his patient's wrist, counting silently as he felt Gerard's pulse beneath his fingertips. Spinelli nodded and returned the wrist to its owner's side.

In the two days Commander Gerard had been aboard, his pulse had strengthened, and his breathing seemed less labored. Gerard had slept most of his time since coming aboard *Phoebe*; in fact, Spinelli had not really begun to treat the man as of yet. Ellington and Short were no help; they were so exhausted by their ordeal that they slept almost as much as Gerard.

Dr. Spinelli made his way aft to the captain's cabin, to find his friend sitting in the day cabin, staring at a cup of coffee.

"William? What are you doing?"

Brewer stirred, but just barely. "Something that both Lord Hornblower and Captain Bush warned me never to do, second-guessing myself." He took a drink and set the cup down. "I'm wondering if I did the right thing."

Alfred appeared in the doorway, and the doctor nodded to him. The captain's servant withdrew and returned with coffee for the doctor. Spinelli took his cup and went to his usual seat at the captain's left. He sipped his coffee and set the cup down.

"Talk to me, William."

Brewer shrugged. "What is there to say?"

"Think out loud, then."

Brewer drew in a long, slow breath and sighed loudly. "Thinking hurts right now." He rose and began to pace across the cabin. "Did I do the right thing? Was there *really* no other way for us to return with the hostages alive? I couldn't just let them go—we both know that—so it was either bargain with them or board the ship and hope we could get to the hostages before Brumby could have them killed. Not bloody likely, I must say. I... didn't know what else I could do."

Spinelli took a long, slow drink of his coffee as he watched his captain through the steam. Brewer paced back and forth, five paces and turn, five paces and turn, eyes never leaving the deck before him. The doctor had seen this before in his captain. He thought to himself, *As long as he keeps talking it out, all should be well.* It was the times he'd gone silent that concerned the doctor.

"It ended well, William," he said. "Gerard and the others are safe, and I have no doubt we will track down the mutineers."

The captain kept pacing, as though he had not heard a word. Spinelli was not concerned—yet. He decided to try something different.

"I do have a report, Captain," he said. Brewer nodded, but did not cease his pacing. Spinelli sighed and continued. "Commander Gerard seems to be improving."

"That's good," Brewer said. "You've done well, Adam."

"That's just the thing," Spinelli said, "I haven't done anything yet. The commander's been asleep most of the time since he's been with us. His temperature is coming down and his breathing has been closing to normal, so I've let him rest. I tell you, William, I'm beginning to wonder just what went on over on that ship. Was Brumby drugging Gerard's food to keep him sick and helpless? And why did neither of the other two ever show any symptoms?"

"That's a question you should ask their doctor," Brewer said absently. He continued to pace. "Did I do the right thing, Adam? Will Admiral Cartwright—will the *Admiralty*—think I did the right thing?"

"I can't say, William," Spinelli said. "What I can say is this: *I* think you did the right thing. Because of your resolve, three men are alive and well in my sick bay."

Brewer ceased his pacing and sighed. He sat back down with a tired plop. "Alfred! More coffee, if you please! Thank you, Adam; your words are a comfort." Alfred arrived and refilled both their cups. "Thank you, Alfred. Pass the word for Mr. Greene and Mac, would you please? Now, Adam, has anyone questioned the doctor or Mr. Short since they've been aboard?"

"I don't think so. Doctor Ellington has either been watching over Commander Gerard or been asleep. Same goes for Mr. Short."

"It's time to change that." Brewer took a drink of his coffee and smiled. Alfred made the best coffee in the world, no doubt about it. "Here's what we'll do. Adam, I want you to return to sick bay and send Mr. Short to me. Hopefully, with Mr. Greene here, and especially Mac, he'll feel comfortable enough to open up and talk to us. After he's gone, I want you to question the doctor. He told Benjamin while there were on *Revenge* that he thought Gerard had been poisoned. Would the commander's apparent improvement since he's been here seemed to bear that out?"

"Yes, I'd say so."

"Talk to the doctor, Adam, take his measure. And keep your eye on Gerard. Please inform me when he is up to having visitors."

"Aye, sir." The doctor drained his cup and left the room just as the sentry admitted Greene and the coxswain.

"You wanted to see us, sir?" Greene asked.

"Yes. The doctor is going to send Mr. Short to us. Let's see if he can tell us anything that might give us a hint as to where Brumby might go. Please, be seated."

Greene sat off to the captain's right while Mac took up his usual post inside the day cabin doorway. There was a knock at the door, and the sentry admitted Mr. Short.

His step seemed steady enough, but Brewer thought he swayed a little more than the motion of the ship necessitated. His eyes held the strange look of a boy who had been traumatized almost beyond his limits mixed with the joy of = rescue. Brewer rose and stepped up to shake his hand.

"Mr. Short, it's good to see you again," he said as he guided the lad to the settee. "I do wish it was under better circumstances. How are you? Are you hungry?"

Short's eyes lit up at the captain's last word. "Well, sir, maybe a little?"

Brewer smiled and summoned Alfred.

"Our guest needs something to eat. Do we have any of that ham left from last night?"

"Yes, sir," Alfred replied. "There are also a few slices of fresh-baked bread I could bring. Perhaps with marmalade?"

Brewer looked to Short, who nodded happily.

"Oh, yes," he said. "Thank you!"

"In that case," Brewer said as he rose, "gentlemen, let us adjourn to the table."

They made their way to the dining room and sat, Mr. Greene at the captain's right and Mr. Short on his left. Mac took up his post near the door.

"Mac," Brewer said, "I'd like you to join us today." He inclined his head slightly towards Short, who only had eyes for the plate of cold meat and bread that Alfred set before him.

"Of course, Captain," Mac said, and took the seat next to Short.

"Dig in, Mr. Short," Brewer urged him. "We can talk while you eat."

"Oh, aye, sir!" The youth took a big bite of ham and chewed hungrily.

After Short downed a couple good-sized pieces of ham and a slice of bread, Brewer addressed him again.

"Mr. Short, I need to ask you some questions about what happened aboard *Revenge*. When did you begin to notice trouble aboard?"

"About two weeks into the cruise, sir," Short replied between mouthfuls. Alfred brought him a cup of water. Short nodded his thanks and drank half of it in a single draught. "The first and second lieutenants, they came over to *Revenge* from *Phoebe*, and they began harassing some of the old *Phoebe* hands. Little things that you or Mr. Greene would warn about and correct on the spot, men were getting flogged for! Us *Revenge* hands couldn't believe it, sir! Eventually, one of 'em protested—it might have been Kelly, but I'm not sure—and that's when they turned on us as well." The lad shivered.

Brewer and Greene shared a knowing look. Mac patted Short on the shoulder.

"It's all right, Will," he said. "You're here now."

"Thanks, Mac," Short said as he took a bite.

"Is that when Brumby and the others began talking mutiny?" Greene asked.

"Aye, sir." Short's head bobbed up and down as he chewed.

"Was Captain Gerard sick by this time?" Brewer asked.

"No, sir," Short replied and took another bite. "Not yet. He saw what was happening, sir, at least I think he did, because he intervened a couple times on behalf of the men."

"And when did Captain Gerard begin to get sick?" Brewer asked.

"Not long after that, I think. He complained of stomach cramps and went to his cabin. We rarely saw him after that. The doctor tended to him, and after a few days, the first lieutenant assumed command of the ship." Short looked down at his empty plate. "That's when the trouble really started."

Mac rubbed the boy's back reassuringly and urged him to take another drink of his water.

"Mr. Short," Brewer said. "I have one final question for now, and I want you to think carefully. Do you remember Captain Gerard's steward? Good. Did he remain aboard *Revenge* with the mutineers, or did he get in the boat with Kelly and the others?"

"Oh, he stayed, Captain! He said he wanted to look after the Cap'n, but I could tell he was with them all the way."

Brewer rose, and the rest followed suit. "Thank you, Mr. Short. Mac, why don't you give our young friend a tour of the ship?

"Aye, sir," Mac said cheerfully. "Come along, Mr. Short. Wait till you see the guns we got on *Phoebe*! 18-pounders look huge when you're used to the twelves!"

The two departed, and Brewer led Greene back to the day cabin.

"So," Greene said, "it was his servant."

"Had to be. He was the one is a position to make sure only Gerard got it and not the other two. Stetson, the first lieutenant, probably had him put something in Gerard's food. Brumby figured it out and had the man keep it up after the mutiny."

Greene sighed. "I can't imagine what a hell *Revenge* became with those two in charge." He shook his head. "You know, if Brumby hadn't killed them both, he might have had a chance at his trial."

"Feeling sorry for him, Benjamin?"

"No, sir," Greene replied. "Mutiny is a choice."

Brewer leaned back and caressed the bridge of his nose between his thumb and forefinger. "So is survival." Greene chewed his lip and said nothing.

Brewer rose. "If you will excuse me, Benjamin, I need to write a report. Please keep Mr. Short and Mac on the deck and out of the sickbay until the doctors are done talking."

"Aye, sir." Greene came to attention and left the cabin.

When Dr. Spinelli got back to the sickbay, he saw that both Mr. Short and the doctor was awake and keeping silent watch over the sleeping Gerard.

"Doing better, Dr. Ellison?"

The doctor rose and took his hand. "Yes, thank you. A little better every day."

"And how's the commander today?" Spinelli asked.

Ellison looked to his sleeping captain. "Making remarkable progress. His temperature is nearly back to normal, and his breathing is not nearly so labored as before."

"That bears out your diagnosis, doesn't it?" When Ellison looked confused, Spinelli elaborated, "You told Lieutenant Greene you thought your captain had been poisoned."

"Ah, yes," Ellison said. "It seems so."

"Were you the doctor on *Phoebe* before you were assigned to *Revenge?*"

"Yes," Ellison said sadly, "but I'd hoped to leave all that rottenness behind when I got to *Revenge*. Too bad Stetson and Kirby didn't."

Spinelli didn't know what to say, so he reached down and felt Gerard's forehead. It was almost cool to the touch now.

"So, what do we do now?" Ellison asked.

"Our course is for Port Royal," Spinelli explained. "The captain has to deliver the three of you to the naval hospital there, and then we are going back out after the *Revenge*."

Ellison looked down at his sleeping captain and sighed.

"And what happens to *him*?"

Spinelli shook his head. "I do not know. Let's get him well first, shall we? I'll relieve you for a few hours. You can lie down on that cot by the bulkhead and sleep." Ellison looked unsure, torn between his duty and his desire to close his eyes. Spinelli touched his arm. "I'll wake you if he regains consciousness, I promise."

Ellison nodded and made his way to the cot against the wall. In minutes Spinelli heard gentle snores coming from that direction, and he smiled.

HMS *Phoebe* continued on her course to Jamaica. They were still thirty-six hours out when there was a knock on the captain's door and the sentry announced Mr. Short. The midshipman came to attention.

"Yes, Mr. Short?" Brewer said as he set down his pen. "What can I do for you?"

"Dr. Spinelli sends his respects, sir. He says to tell you that Captain Gerard is awake now, sir."

"Thank you, Mr. Short. Please tell the doctor I shall be down to see the commander in a little while."

"Aye, sir!"

Short left the cabin, and Brewer walked to his desk and got out his writing materials. Soon his ship would deliver their passengers to Port Royal, and he wasn't going to miss the chance to add another letter to the stack he had waiting for the next mail bag.

My dearest Elizabeth,

I pray this letter finds you and our darling Anne safe and happy. It is hard for me to write you; I already have five letters waiting for the next mail bag, and I don't want to ask you the same things in every one!

There is still no news in the hunt for Black Rose. We are cruising as many likely shipping lanes as we can, but so far we have come up empty. I fear that if we do not end this pirate's activities in the Caribbean very soon, merchant captains may begin to refuse to take their ships to sea without direct Royal Navy escort to guarantee their safety. We do not have enough ships to guard every merchantman on the waters, so we would have to convoy ships from port to port. This would slow the movement of goods so much that the various economies of the islands would be jeopardized. Fear is a powerful weapon, Elizabeth.

I have run into our old friend Gerard. You will remember him as Lord Hornblower's aide. He attended our wedding with His Lordship and Lady Barbara. He sends you his greetings.

Know that I am well, and that I miss you both very much. I look forward to hearing your plans for our move to England—what sort of house you want to look for, in what part of the country, by the sea or not.... What should our lives together look like? You ask my opinion? I can sum it up for you easily: you, me, and Anne living together in comfort and safety. All else is merely icing on the cake.

As ever, I am
Your Loving Husband,
William

Brewer entered the sickbay to find Gerard sitting up in bed, surrounded by his doctors and Mr. Short.

"Hello, Gerard," he said as he stepped up. "Good to see you awake and alert."

"It is good to see you, Captain," Gerard said. "I understand I have you to thank for my life."

"On the contrary," Brewer said as he sat beside the commander's bed, "you have the doctor and Mr. Short to thank for that. If not for them, you'd have been dead long before I came along." He addressed the others. "Gentlemen, may I have a few moments alone with the commander?"

They moved to the far side of the sickbay, and Brewer turned to his friend. "It's good to see you awake, Gerard," he said softly.

"Your doctor tells me you traded our lives for the mutineers' freedom," Gerard said. "I wish you hadn't done that."

"I did no such thing, sir," Brewer chided gently. "I merely promised them I would not pursue them until after I deposited you in the naval hospital at Port Royal. I fully intend to hunt them down and either return them for trial a or deal with them summarily."

Gerard grimaced. "Glad to hear it. Hate to think you let them go for me." Brewer gave him a concerned look, but Gerard waved him off. "Spasms in the stomach wall. Dr. Ellison tells me it's normal for my recovery. Believe me, these are nothing compared to the ones on *Revenge*."

Brewer looked concered "What else have the doctors told you, Gerard?"

The commander's chin went down to his breast. "That I was poisoned; that's why I was so sick and lost command to that... maniac." Brewer could hear a ragged gasp. "What he did to my crew... my ship!" Gerard's shoulders shook. "I should have seen it coming. I should have prevented it."

"You were gotten out of the way, Gerard," Brewer said. "You were the only one poisoned; the doctor and Mr. Short were unharmed. But the poison wasn't enough to *kill* you, only to incapacitate you, resulting in your first lieutenant assuming command and the volatile situation exploding. The only course that halfway makes sense to me is that Stetson subverted your servant and got him to poison you, allowing him to take command. After the mutiny, Brumby discovered what had happened and ordered the servant to continue with the poison. That way, you stay incapacitated." Brewer shrugged. "Of course, we' may never know the truth. Maybe we'll get lucky and take him alive."

"If you do," Gerard said, "I'll kill him myself."

"Yes, well," Brewer said as he rose, "I shall do my best to give you the opportunity. Get some rest; we'll talk more at a later time."

Gerard closed his eyes, and Brewer stepped over to the doctors and said, "Call me at once if he remembers anything that might give us a clue where Brumby may have gone."

The next day, HMS *Phoebe* was approaching the Port Royal harbor entrance. Brewer and Greene were on the quarterdeck when Skimpy ran up to them and saluted.

"Begging your pardon, Captain," he said, "but the doctor sends his respects and asks that you come to the sickbay at once, sir."

"Right behind you, Skimp," Brewer said. "You have the deck, Mr. Greene."

"Aye, sir."

Brewer followed Skimpy down and forward until they reached the door to the sickbay. He saw Gerard, dressed and sitting on his cot, looking better than he had the day before. Spinelli was at his desk, writing.

"Adam," he said, "what is it? Gerard looks healthy."

"Oh, it's not Gerard," Spinelli said. He rose and led the captain to a darker corner. Brewer saw one of his midshipmen, James Drake, lying in the bed, his shirt plastered to his chest by sweat.

"He was brought in this morning with a high fever," Spinelli said. "I want to transfer him ashore along with Commander Gerard."

Brewer frowned. "That would leave us short a midshipman."

"Not necessarily," Spinelli said. He pointed over his shoulder with his thumb at Mr. Short. "There's one sitting right over there. Perfectly healthy, at least physically."

"Do you think he's up to it, after what he's been through?"

Spinelli shrugged. "Who knows? Might be the best thing for him."

Brewer met his friend's eyes. "Back on the horse, and all that, eh?" He took a deep breath and quickly considered his options. In the end, he went with his doctor's advice. "Mr. Short, may I speak with you?"

The midshipman stepped over. "Yes, Captain?"

"Mr. Short," Brewer said softly, as he pointed to the young boy in the bed, "this is James Drake, one of my midshipmen. The doctor here says he should be sent ashore with Mr. Gerard when we get to Port Royal. I agree with him, but that will leave me short a midshipman. So I ask you, do you want to sign on to take Drake's place?"

Short's eyes got big.

"Please understand, William," Brewer said, "I am not ordering you to do this. It is entirely your decision. If you think you need to spend some time ashore, I fully understand. William, look at me. You proved yourself to be a good midshipman when we sailed together on *Revenge*. No matter what you decide, my estimation of you will not change. You would be welcome on my quarterdeck any time. What do you say?"

Short smiled broadly. "I'd love to sail with you, sir!"

"Very well!" Brewer said. "Then you'd better go say goodbye to Commander Gerard and Dr. Ellison."

Short slipped away, and Brewer turned to Spinelli. "One problem solved. Now, if only the admiral doesn't relieve me of command, we may be all right."

He climbed back to the quarterdeck and informed Mr. Greene of the change in midshipmen. He was just about to go below and gather his reports when a familiar call came from above.

"Deck there! Merchantman approaching on the starboard beam!"

"Mr. Greene!" Brewer cried. "Hoist 'Heave to'. Mr. Sweeney, stop us within speaking distance."

"Aye, sir." Sweeney worked a miracle, and *Phoebe* ended up a mere thirty yards from the merchantman's quarterdeck. Brewer made a mental note to congratulate him later. He picked up a speaking trumpet and moved to the rail.

"Ahoy, Captain!" he shouted. "Are you heading into Port Royal?"

"Aye, that we are!" came the reply.

"Might I beg a favor of you? I have two officers who need to go to the naval hospital, as well as reports and mail to be turned in, and I need to head out after Black Rose. Can you take them in for me?"

"Only if you promise me that pirate's head on a pike!"

Brewer laughed. "Done! I shall send over a boat!"

The merchant captain waved his acknowledgement, and Brewer turned to make preparations.

"Mr. Greene, order all ready mail collected. I shall bring up my reports for the admiral. Have Commander Gerard, Dr. Ellison, and Mr. Drake brought up from sickbay. Ready the launch to take our guests to their chariot! Bosun's mate, ready the sling to lift Commander Gerard and Mr. Drake over the side."

The two men were brought up on deck on stretchers. Brewer stepped over to his ailing midshipman.

"I'm sorry, sir," Drake croaked.

"Nonsense," the captain chided him. "It's not like you chased this illness until you ran him to ground and forced him to infect you, is it?"

Drake smiled in spite of himself. "No, sir."

"Get well, Mr. Drake. I expect to have you return to the ship the next time we make port."

The midshipman closed his eyes and swallowed hard.

"Aye, sir."

Brewer patted him on the arm. "There's a good lad."

The bosun's mate gave the order, and Drake was lifted over the side. Brewer held his gaze until he disappeared over the railing. Then he turned to Gerard and took his friend's hands. "I hope you make a speedy recovery. We need you back out here."

"Small chance of that," Gerard said. "I lost my ship to a mutiny. There will certainly be an inquiry, either here or in

London, and possibly a court-martial. I shall be lucky to end up on the beach at half-pay."

"I'm not so sure. You're overlooking some considerations that should operate in your favor. What about the fact that the doctor here can now swear that you were incapacitated by poison, most likely administered in small doses by your own servant to incapacitate rather than kill you? I interviewed two of your crew, Kelly and Jones, who served under me on *Revenge*, and they gave a pretty convincing account of what went on below decks. Unfortunately, Admiral Simpson is dead, so we cannot have him held accountable for the hands he authorized to be transferred from *Phoebe* and placed under a newly-frocked commander, but I'm sure we can make that point plain to any court." Brewer patted his friend on the arm. "Never fear, Gerard; I know what kind of man you are, and so do many other people. You will always be welcome to sail with me."

Gerard closed his eyes for a moment and tried to smile.

"Thank you for your kind words, Captain. I shall remember your offer."

Brewer looked up to the bosun's mate. "All right, gentlemen, easy now with the commander."

Brewer stepped back. Gerard turned his head to look at the captain, and Brewer saw the hopelessness in his eyes. He did the only thing he knew to do—he came smartly to attention and saluted. Mr. Greene beside him quickly followed his captain's lead. Gerard raised his hand in farewell as he disappeared over the railing.

Dr. Ellison stepped forward.

"Thank you for rescuing us, Captain," he said. "I never thought I would see England again."

"You're welcome, Doctor. Watch out for the commander, won't you? It's a hard thing to lose a ship, and we must keep his spirits up."

"I shall do my best. Goodbye, Captain, and thank you again. Mr. Greene, thank you." He shook hands with both men and made his way over the rail.

Soon, Brewer was leaning against the larboard rail watching the launch make its stately way to the merchantman. He might have some explaining to do with Admiral Cartwright the next time he put in to port, but he hoped to have Brumby and his mutineers in irons, and possibly Black Rose alongside them, by then.

"Mr. Greene," he said, "when we recover the launch, set your course South-Southwest. We've got mutineers to catch. Will you and Mr. Murdy join me in my cabin afterward? We need to inform him of his new midshipman."

Greene's face lit up. "Aye, sir."

CHAPTER EIGHT

Brumby stood on the quarterdeck of a *Revenge*—no longer HMS *Revenge*—barely discernible in the dense fog bank that surrounded them. He'd sailed away from HMS *Phoebe* heading southeast, only to change course at midnight, first to the east, putting in at an uninhabited island for water and what fruits they could scavenge. He'd then taken a chance and made his course northeast through the Mona Passage, avoiding any English traffic going between Jamaica and St. Kitts. Once through the passage, he'd steered them northwest, just out of sight of the coast of Hispaniola. His intention had been to see if the rumors he'd heard of the resurgence of Tortuga were true, but when he saw this lovely fog bank off their starboard bow, he'd headed for it with abandon. They'd only been hidden for a day, but he was already beginning to hear some grumblings from his "crew."

"How long we going to stay in this God-forsaken pea soup, that's what I want to know."

Brumby turned to peer at Emery, standing beside him. The topman was known for being light on his feet; rumor had it he could appear or disappear at will. Emery was one of the transfers from the old *Phoebe*.

"Till I say otherwise," Brumby answered in a low, menacing growl. "You want to risk running across Brewer and his eighteen-pounders again?"

"I think mebbe we ought to raid a fat merchantman for supplies before heading south. Mebbe make for the South Pacific islands like them *Bounty* boys done. I wouldn't mind settling down in some nice hut with a couple of them island beauties for company."

Brumby grunted.

"I been talking to some of the lads," Emery continued, "and they agree with me. I didn't mutiny against the Royal Navy to hide in some fog bank until they hunt me down. Let's load up and disappear south! Mate, what're we waiting for?"

"We leave when I say so, that's when," Brumby said fiercely. He stared the other down until Emery finally backed and turned away. Brumby watched him slink off.

His hold over the crew was based on their fear and his bravado, but that could change if enough of them turned against him. He considered Emery's request to head south, and he could see the appeal of such a plan. The South Atlantic was a big ocean and easy to get lost in; the Pacific even more so. So far as he'd heard, none of them Bounty boys was ever caught, so it might be possible to disappear and settle down comfortably. The more he thought about it, the more the idea appealed to him.

He scowled as the reality of his situation closed in on him again. They all would be hunted men for the rest of their lives. While they breathed, there would never be a day when they were not looking over their shoulders. Damn Stetson and Kirby anyway! When *Phoebe* had put in to Port Royal and Captain Judah and the others went ashore, he'd hoped things might get a little better. His prospects had actually been bright when he was transferred to HMS *Revenge*, but then Stetson and Kirby joined the ship, and he knew from the way Stetson smiled at him that nothing had changed but the ship. Captain Gerard had seemed like a good man, but he was new to command and seemed to be taken in by Stetson's suave manners. Then he got so sick —all very sudden and mysterious, that —and Stetson had what he always wanted: command. Brumby and the others were at his mercy, and he proceeded to make Captain Judah look like a saint by comparison.

Brumby shivered at the memories of how he and the others were driven beyond human endurance until they finally acted to save their lives and reason. He took a deep breath and shook his head decisively. *It is what it is.*

His thoughts turned back to Emery and his plan. Perhaps he ought to call a council and see what the men thought of the idea. He had no problem with the plan to raid a merchant ship for supplies; the penalty for that would not be any more severe than for mutiny. He was about to act on this new resolve when he was preempted by a shout from the fo'c'sle.

"Ship coming out of the fog off the larboard bow!"

Brumby ran to the larboard rail and saw a brig emerging from the mist. The ship bore no flag, and he could not see her deck clearly. Then the stranger suddenly swung across their bow and fired.

Grape shot swept down the deck. Brumby felt something hit him in the shoulder; he was spun by the force of the blow and went down on the deck. His head throbbed with pain and shock. He tried to rise, but he collapsed back on the deck. He heard a faint cry from the other ship for them to stay where they were, and he knew they were about to be boarded.

He felt a hand on his arm, and he opened his eyes to see Junior looking him over. Junior was a landsman, known for being a little slow in the head, but having a big heart. He'd just gone along with the mob when the mutiny happened. Junior got Brumby to his feet and leaned him against the rail for stability.

Men were bounding over the rails and on to the deck, each one armed with saber, daggers, or pistols, screaming at the top of their lungs and waving their weapons menacingly. His men were for the most part unarmed, and many of the deck hands had also been wounded by grapeshot.

The pirates secured the deck, and then waited. A second group stepped onto deck. Their leader was a small man, slim, with a mask covering his face and as large hat pulled low on his head. He spoke to one of the hands who was held at sword-point. He must have asked who was in charge, because the man pointed to Brumby. The leader and his entourage made their way over. Brumby struggled in the arms of his captors.

"You are the captain?" the leader demanded.

"No captain here," he answered in a surly voice, "but I speak for the men."

Brumby saw the other's eyes narrow. "What ship is this?"

"*Revenge*," Brumby gasped. The pain in his shoulder was getting worse.

The effect upon the pirate leader startled Brumby.

"*Revenge?!?!*" he cried. "This is HMS *Revenge*? Your captain, he has a cook, a little man named Alfred?"

Brumby was mystified by the leader's questions and he looked to the crew for help. One of the old *Revenge* hands stepped forward.

"The little man, he were Cap'n Brewer's servant," the man said. "He transferred to HMS *Phoebe* along with Captain Brewer."

The pirate captain howled in rage. He pulled a pistol from his belt and shot the hand who'd given him the unwelcome news.

"I have been cheated!" he screamed, as he threw down his pistol and pulled his saber from its scabbard. "I find his ship, only to find the murderer gone!   I will not be denied my vengeance!"

He turned on his heel and stalked back toward the entry port. Brumby was about to say something, anything, that might save their lives, when the pirate suddenly stopped and spoke to his lieutenant.

"Kill them," he said. "Kill them all."

"And the ship?" the lieutenant asked.

"Burn it."

Diego stiffened at the order, even though he'd expected it. He looked around at the ship; it was the best prize they had ever taken. He leaned in and spoke in a low voice.

"May I speak to you privately?"

Rose's eyes flashed angrily at him, but she nodded curtly. They moved to the rail for privacy.

"I think we should consider keeping this ship," Diego said.

"Why?"

"I have heard of this ship. The English took it from Jean Lafitte and put it in their navy. If we keep it, it will be the most powerful pirate raider the Caribbean has ever seen! We keep a few of the prisoners to give her the appearance of an English crew on deck, and we have the perfect disguise! We can even rename it—although the name *Revenge* would suit our purposes. We can call her the *Cofresi*. Think of it, Rose! Everyone would know of your revenge and fear you!"

Her eyes snapped to his at the mention of the name. She nearly lashed out at him, but something in his words stayed her hand. What he said had merit; perhaps Cofresi would even approve of the scheme.

"Very well," she said. "I am returning to the island. Choose your prisoners and kill the rest of the crew. Keep a prize crew to work the ship." She looked around, sighed, and held out her hand. "Do you have it?"

"Of course." He handed her the flower.

"Load the dead into the ship's largest boat," she said. "Put this in the captain's hand and set the boat adrift."

Diego smiled. They were now in possession of a sloop-of-war, complete with naval grade armament. "It shall be done," he said.

"Good." She looked up at him with a grim smile. "It seems our hunt is not yet over, eh, Diego?"

* * * * *

Captain Brewer sat at the desk in his cabin, the quill in his hand hovering above the paper as a result of his hesitation. He was trying to compose a letter to Elizabeth in which he would lay out his vision for their lives together. The trouble was, he was coming up with absolutely nothing. His mind was a blank. He had no idea what sort of house she would like, or where she would like to live. Near to Plymouth would suit him just fine; it was very convenient for times when his ship was fortunate enough to return to England. But what if Plymouth wasn't to her liking? And now it was looking more and more as though she was going to have to return to England and set up house without him.

He was saved by a sharp knock at the door. The sentry opened it and announced Mr. Short. HMS *Phoebe's* newest midshipman came to attention.

"Yes, Mr. Short?" Brewer asked.

"Sir!" Short answered smartly, "Mr. Greene sends his respects. He wishes to report a ship on the horizon. Lookout says she's hove to, sir. Mr. Greene says he has altered course to intercept."

"Thank you, Mr. Short. My compliments to Mr. Greene. Please inform him I shall come up on deck."

"Aye, sir!" Short came to attention and departed.

Brewer set his quill on the desk and capped his inkwell. He threw one last regretful glance at the unfinished letter before grabbing his hat and heading out the door. He stepped out on deck and was joined by Lieutenant Greene, who handed him a glass and pointed toward the horizon off the starboard bow.

"There, sir," he said. "A single merchantman, apparently hove to. She's just hull up."

Brewer found her easily. The ship did not look damaged from this distance. She looked too small for an Indiaman, but she was large enough to hide a smaller ship behind her. Brewer lowered his glass.

"Beat to quarters, if you please."

"Aye, sir." Greene reached for a speaking trumpet and began bellowing the orders that sent the ship's complement to battle stations. Nine minutes and thirty seconds later, he reported, "Ship rigged for action, Captain. Shall I run out the guns?"

"Not yet," Brewer replied. He raised the glass to his eye again and studied the ship they were approaching. He was now within range to see the ship plainly, and there seemed to be a group of hands gathered at the far rail, looking over the side. Brewer lowered the glass. "What do you think, Benjamin?"

"I don't know, sir," Greene said as he studied the ship. "Strange."

"Yes." Brewer turned and stepped over to the wheel. "Mr. Sweeney, heave to when we get close. Put us in speaking distance."

"Aye, sir."

"Mr. Henry," Brewer called the midshipman of the watch. "Raise the colors!"

"Aye, sir!"

Sweeney slid the ship to within speaking distance of the merchantman, turning broadside to her at the last minute. That was show Phoebe's colors, and also her armament. Lookouts on the merchantman had alerted her master. The man picked up a speaking trumpet and came to the rail.

"Ahoy!" he called. "What ship are you?"

Brewer picked up a trumpet and answered, "We are His Majesty's Frigate *Phoebe*. Do you need assistance?"

"Thank God!" the master answered. "Can you please come over? We have something you should see on the other side!"

"Very good. We shall lower a boat."

The other waved his acknowledgement.

Brewer handed the trumpet to a hand and joined Sweeney and Greene by the wheel. "I'm going aboard. Mr. Greene, you have the deck."

"Are you sure that's wise, sir?" Greene asked. "What if it's Black Rose again?"

Brewer shook his head. "It doesn't feel like that, but just in case, have Mr. Rivkins take a boat with six marines in it around the bow and down the other side. Have them loaded and ready to shoot before they round the bow."

Greene looked relieved. "Aye, sir. I'll alert Mac to have your gig ready. Will you take Alfred?"

Brewer got irritated and turned on his first lieutenant, but the feeling disappeared when he saw only concern in the other's eyes. "Very well," he said.

The crossing to the merchantman was quickly done, and Brewer made his way up the side of the other ship. Mac followed close behind. They were met by the man who had spoken to them.

"Greetings, gentlemen," he said. "I am Tiberius Hawk, master of the *Liverpool*."

"Captain Brewer of HMS *Phoebe*." Brewer offered his hand, and Hawk shook it. "What did you want me to see?"

Hawk indicated the far rail. "We found a boat adrift on the sea. All the occupants appear to be dead. They all seem to have been killed in a violent action, and quite recently. It looks very much like pirates' work. We're bringing it aboard now."

The boat was hauled over the side and settled on the deck. Brewer and Mac followed Hawk to the side and scrutinized the corpses. Most of them had obviously been killed by swords.

"Captain," Mac said, "this one's Brumby!"

"What? Mac, are you sure?"

"Aye, sir! This be he!"

"Do you recognize anyone else?"

Mac walked around the boat, trying to look at as many faces as possible. "Aye, I do. Many were on *Revenge* when I went aboard with Mr. Greene."

"Captain?" Hawk said.

"That man was a mutineer we've been hunting," Brewer explained. "Apparently, someone else found him first."

Mac looked into the boat again and suddenly grabbed Brumby's arm and lifted it in the air. The dead man's hand clutched a crushed—but still very recognizable—black flower.

Hawk went white at the sight. "Is that what I think it is?"

I'm afraid it is," Brewer said. "Black Rose." He turned suddenly. "Mr. Hawk, have your men lower the boat back into the water. We shall take it to HMS *Phoebe*." He left the master and went to the rail. Looking over, he said, "Mr. Rivkins! All is well! They are going to lower a boat to the water! Tow it back to the ship!"

"Aye, sir!"

"Brewer turned to the master. "Mr. Hawk, where are you bound?"

"Martinique, Captain."

"Then that is now *Phoebe's* next port of call as well. If you will remain under my lee, we shall escort you there." Hawk looked very relieved. "Thank you, Captain. Recent as those corpses are, the pirates cannot be far from here."

Back on board *Phoebe*, Brewer met with Greene and Sweeney on the quarterdeck.

"They found a drifting boat, crewed by the dead, one of which Mac has identified as Brumby."

Greene's eyebrows nearly flew off his head. "Really? Someone found them before we did. I wonder who?"

"Oh, there's no mystery about that," Brewer replied. He reached inside his coat and pulled out the crushed black rose.

"Well!" Sweeney exclaimed. "Isn't that what you might call poetic justice!"

"Mr. Greene," the captain said, "ask the doctor to examine the men in the boat. I imagine they were all murdered, but I want his confirmation."

"Aye, sir," Greene said. "Disposition of the remains?" Brewer's face grew hard. "Put them back in the boat. Light it on fire and set it adrift. The sharks can have what's left. After that, set our course for Martinique. We shall be providing escort."

The two officers watched him disappear below decks without looking back. When he was gone, Sweeney let out a low whistle.

"Mr. Greene," he said softly, "our captain has a cold-blooded streak in him. I for one would not like to be on the receiving end if it were ever let loose." Greene could only agree.

Mr. Short found a place by the starboard long nine to sit on the rail and watch as the lifeboat was lit on fire and set adrift. His felt numb as he watched the bodies of his tormentors burn. *Revenge* had very nearly driven him mad. He barely noticed the single tear that escaped his eye.

Suddenly he realized he was not alone. He wiped his eye with the back of his hand and his nose with his sleeve. He turned to see Lieutenant Reed standing beside the number two carronade.

"Hello, William," he said. "It's good to see you sailing with us again."

"Hello, Mr. Reed."

Reed stepped up. "Are you all right?"

Short shrugged. "I suppose so."

"Many men would not to be," the lieutenant said. "Not be all right, I mean. You've been through an ordeal that would kill most men."

Short shrugged. "I did what I had to do. Captain Gerard and the doctor depended on me."

"And you stood by them," Reed said. "I heard the doctor telling Captain Brewer what a tremendous help you were in keeping Captain Gerard alive." He placed a hand on the lad's shoulder to reassure him, but he withdrew it immediately when he felt Short recoil at the touch. Reed stepped back and studied the young midshipman. Mr. Short looked tense as he watched the boat—now engulfed in flames—drift away. Even the lad's jaws were clenched.

Reed guessed the boy's age at eleven or twelve, and he was small for his age, but Short's eyes were filled with rage and hate, yet tears slid down his cheeks. Reed stepped up and put his arm around the boy's shoulder. Short flinched at the contact, but Reed held him tight.

"I'm sorry, William," Reed said softly. "I'm sorry I could not be there to save you this time. I would give anything to be able to change things so that you came to *Phoebe* with us or I stayed on *Revenge* with you. All I can promise you is that it will never happen again." He felt the boy begin to tremble as he lost the battle to control his emotions. "And William?" Reed went on, "it's all right to cry when you need to. I do too. It doesn't make you any less of a man."

All at once, Short turned and buried his face in the lieutenant's chest and wept openly. Reed wrapped his arms around him and let him cry. Finally, the sobs subsided.

"Better now?" Reed asked. He felt a nod, so he released the boy and stepped back. Short sniffed; he pulled a handkerchief from his pocket to wipe his eyes and blow his nose. He stuffed the kerchief back into the pocket before looking up at his friend.

"Thanks," he said quietly. "I think I needed that. Do you really cry?"

Reed nodded. "Every time I need to."

Short looked again at the burning boat that was drifting toward the horizon.

"They're gone now, William," Reed said, "and they're never coming back. Leave them in the past and never think about them again. I find that's the easiest way." Short nodded again without taking his eyes from the boat. "William," Reed said firmly. Short turned to him. "That's better," Reed said. "Now, Mr. Drake was the midshipman in my division. Since you have taken his place in the crew, that job now falls to you. Are you up for it?"

"Me? Work for you, Mr. Reed! Why... yes!"

"Well then, straighten up, Mr. Short!" Reed said, his eyes smiling. Short happily sprang to attention. "Straighten that shirt, and blow your nose!" Short merrily complied. "Now," the lieutenant said, "are you ready to get to work?"

"Aye aye, sir!"

"Good," Reed said. "We have the next watch. I'll see you on the quarterdeck at eight bells."

Two days later, Brewer paced back and forth across the quarterdeck in the early morning sun, talking out loud to nobody in particular.

"There ought to be a way for us to narrow the search area a little," he said. "There's too much ocean to search willy-nilly like this, too many islands for Black Rose to hide behind." He paused at the turn to look out over the featureless sea. "Too bad we can't see past the horizon, to see if Black Rose was hiding, there beneath the horizon, waiting for us to sail past so he—or she—could emerge to plunder safely in our wake." He turned his back to the sea, lowered his head to his chest, and resumed his pacing.

Ten feet away, Lieutenant Greene shared a concerned look with the sailing master, Mr. Sweeney. They had seen their captain in this state of mind only once before, when he wanted to go out after the pirate El Diabolito. It had not been good then, and they feared this boded ill again.

They were rescued by the lookout in the mizzen tops.

"Deck there! Sail on the horizon! Starboard quarter!"

The two men were met at the railing by the captain. All could see the speck of white bobbing on the horizon.

"Alter course, Mr. Sweeney," Brewer said. "Let's see what she's about. Signal *Liverpool* to proceed to Martinique on her own."

"Aye, sir." Sweeney went to issue the orders. HMS *Phoebe* came about on her new heading with the ship settled into the larboard tack. Brewer lowered his glass.

"Let's go forward, Benjamin."

"Right behind you, sir."

They moved smartly up the starboard rail and settled in just forward of the forward carronade. With the telescope again to his eye, it seemed to Brewer that the sail split into two for a moment before coming together again.

"Lookout! Let's hear you!"

"Looks like two ships, sir! Hard to tell yet! They should be hull-up in a few minutes!"

Brewer swallowed hard to force himself to wait. Beside him, Greene's telescope come down and he stared at the horizon.

"Benjamin?"

"Did you hear it, sir? On that last gust of wind? I'd swear I heard gunfire."

"Gunfire?" Brewer looked to the growing patch of white. The next gust of wind brought a hint of sound to his ears as well. "Good enough for me. Mr. Greene, I'm going aft to call for all sail. I want you to stay here. Call for Skimpy to be your runner. Let me know when we're in range for the long-nines."

Greene's hand went automatically to his hat. "Aye, sir."

Brewer headed aft. Mr. Sweeney met him before the wheel.

"Call the hands to make sail, Mr. Sweeney. We heard gunfire. Midshipman of the watch, I want a runner sent up to the foretop lookout. Tell him to report anything he sees."

"Aye, sir!"

"Aye, Captain!"

Brewer walked to the rail. He was sure now that they were approaching two ships, and from the way they were acting, he'd bet one of them was a pirate. He was about to raise the glass to his eye when he saw a tar approaching. The man slid to a halt two feet from his captain and knuckled his forehead.

"Sir! The lookout sent me to report that we are approaching two ships. One has has been fired upon! She's trying to run, but the lookout thinks the second ship will board her very soon."

"Thank you. Return to the lookout."

"Aye, sir." The man knuckled his head again and was gone.

So a pirate was attacking and looking to board a merchant ship. A quick glance skyward showed Brewer that *Phoebe* was carrying every stitch she could get away with. He clenched his fist in frustration as the gap closed, far too slowly.

Thirty minutes later, the runner was back.

"Captain!" he skidded to a halt. "Lookout says to tell you both ships have heaved to!"

Brewer crossed over to where his first lieutenant was standing with the crews of the two long-nines. Greene turned and touched his hat as the captain approached.

"Report, Mr. Greene."

"Still out of range, sir," the premier said.

"Lookout reported both ship hove to," Brewer said. "I expect the pirates to raise sail the moment they see us, but they are on the far side. If they have only sent a boat or two over to the merchantman, we may be able to do the same. My goal is to save as many of the crew and passengers as possible."

"Aye, sir."

Brewer thought for a moment. "Benjamin, take two boats and make ready to board the merchantman. You may well have to fight if they have already put a prize crew aboard. Take Mac and Alfred. When we get close, I'll back the mains'l long enough to put your boats in the water. We'll come back for you after we've dealt with the pirate ship. Go now! They will spot us any minute now, if they haven't already."

"Aye, sir!"

Greene went aft, calling for the bosun as he went, and Brewer turned his glass upon the pirates again. Could this finally be Black Rose?

Josiah Pendleton had thought he'd achieved all his dreams. Just three months ago, he had been appointed master of the *Sea Breeze,* an old sloop purchased from the Royal Navy at Port Royal and converted to carry cargo around the Caribbean. This was all he ever wanted from life, but now it was all turning to ashes before his eyes.

The stranger had come up on them suddenly, emerging from the pre-dawn mist and putting a shot across their bows. Pendleton had ordered all sail, but the stranger had overtaken them within two hours and fired again.

Pendleton hove to in an effort to spare the lives of his crew. The stranger came to a halt less than a hundred yards away, and Pendleton could now see plainly the row of 8-pounder cannons protruding from gun ports down the side of the ship. A boat was lowered to the water and began to make its way across the divide.

Pendleton had never seen a pirate, but that was the word that exploded across his mind when he saw the first stranger set foot upon his deck.

"Who is the master?" the man demanded. Pendleton silently stepped forward. The man had a wicked grin on his face as he approached. "I have a present for you, *Señor*," he said. Two more pirates were already on the deck behind their leader, and more were coming aboard.

The color drained out of Pendleton's face as the first pirate handed him a single black rose.

The killing began almost at once. Three of the pirates used their swords on members of his crew. Pendleton pleaded with them to take anything they wanted and go, but the pirate leader laughed at him and raised his sword to strike the poor master down. He was interrupted by a call from the rail.

"Pedro! Pedro! Come see!"

The man shoved Pendleton to the deck and ran to the rail, yelling, "What is it, José?"

José gesticulated wildly at their ship. "They are leaving us!"

"What!?!"

Pedro leaned over the rail and stared. It was true. Diego was making sail!

"Diego!" he shouted, knowing he would not be heard. "Diego! Wait!" He turned to José. "Why is he doing this?"

José pointed again. Pedro saw that he was not pointed at their ship, but rather past it. He eyes went wide as he saw a frigate fast approaching.

José sank to the deck in despair. "We are dead men."

"Not yet," Pedro said. "Get up! Gather this ship's crew and take them below. Take our men with you. Leave the master up here with me. If you hear a shot, kill the crew."

"*Si!*" José scrambled to his feet and began shouting orders. The merchantman's remaining crew were hustled below.

Pedro turned to see his ship sailing away as fast as she could fill the sails. He could see Diego standing on the quarterdeck. Neither man waved.

Brewer paced the quarterdeck waiting for any fresh information from his lookouts. He was about to go to the rail for another look when the runner appeared.

"Sir!" he gasped as he saluted. "The pirate ship has cleared the merchantman and is on a course directly away from us."

"Thank you," the captain replied. "Return to the lookout. Mr. Sweeney! Have to just long enough to drop Mr. Greene and two boats, then I want every inch of sail she'll carry! If that is Black Rose out there, I do not want them to get away!"

"Aye, sir!" Sweeney picked up a speaking trumpet and began bellowing orders. The effect on the ship was as though a giant hand lay hold of her and brought her to a stop.

Brewer turned to the waist, where Lieutenant Greene was waiting, and nodded.

"Good luck to you!" the captain called.

Greene saluted, then gave the orders that sent the boats over the side. Sweeney watched, and as soon as the boats were in the water and free of the ship, he bellowed the orders that set *Phoebe* off in pursuit of their quarry.

Greene sat in the stern sheets of the launch, Mac at his side. The gig behind them had Lieutenant Cromwell and Alfred in the stern. The ship they were approaching looked like a sloop, or maybe a sloop-of-war; he could see the outlines of the gun ports running down her side. There was no sign of activity on the deck or in the yards above. His eyes narrowed as they darted back and forth.

"Mac," he said quietly, "I don't like this. When we hook on, take the marines and secure the entry port. I'll follow with the rest. Cromwell's men will be right behind us."

"Aye, sir."

When the boat reached the ladder, Mac and the marines scrambled up, followed closely by Greene and his men. When Greene stepped onto the deck, he found it deserted except for two men standing by the wheel. Judging by their dress, Greene took one to be a pirate and the other a member of the merchant crew, possibly the master. The pirate had his sword raised with the tip at the other man's throat. Greene stepped forward.

"I am Lieutenant Greene of His Majesty's Frigate *Phoebe*," he said loudly. "Who are you?"

The pirate nudged his prisoner.

"Josiah Pendleton," he said, "master of the *Sea Breeze*. This murderer is a pirate. Aaah!" Blood seeped down the master's neck where the pirate dug in the tip of his blade.

"That was not very nice, *señor*," the pirate said.

"Your name, sir?" Greene demanded.

The pirate smiled. "You may call me Black Rose."

"Really?" Greene replied. "You are not what I expected. Where is the crew?"

"My men have them below," the pirate said. "If you do not leave immediately, they will all be killed."

"And if I leave?"

"I will set them free." The man shrugged. "Tomorrow, maybe the day after."

"I don't believe you. The Black Rose leaves no one alive. This is probably the only hostage you have, and you are bluffing. Your own crew has deserted you, leaving you behind."

By now, Cromwell and his men had ascended to the deck and spread out. The pirate's smile faded as he watched developments warily.

The pirate looked around, careful to keep the tip of his cutlass on the master's throat, counting the men and taking stock of their weapons. There were twelve of them. That meant he had numbers on his side, as well as hostages. He did not think this officer had the stomach to watch men slaughtered before his eyes. "José!" he called out. "Bring the hostages up on deck!"

Slowly, seventeen pirates came up on deck, a hostage in front of each of them like a human shield.

"Do you still think I am bluffing, *señor*? Depart now, or these men die, slowly and painfully."

"Do you think we will not kill you all if you shed another drop of blood?" Greene countered.

The marines raised their rifled muskets and took aim.

"Pedro?" One of the pirates spoke in a voice that shook. "What do we do?"

Greene suppressed a smile. Now he had the man's name.

The tension was thick on the deck, and Greene expected open warfare to erupt at any moment. Suddenly, Alfred stepped forward and faced Pedro.

"You, sir, are a coward," he announced, loudly, for all to hear.

Pedro reacted as if Alfred's words were a slap in the face. He shoved his prisoner aside and charged the little man with a growl of rage and his cutlass high. Alfred dodged the blow to his left and brought his own sword down hard on his assailant's thigh. The man screamed and fell to the deck. Alfred hit him in the side of the head with the hilt of his sword and then stood in front of the master, one foot placed atop Pedro's silent form.

Greene yelled out to the rest of the pirates, "Surrender! Now!"

The pirates looked at each other. The man who had spoken before stepped out from behind his hostage and dropped his sword on the deck. One by one, the others followed suit.

"Sergeant," Greene called, "have your men take these below deck and secure them. Mac, see what you can do for this one's thigh. I need him alive and talking. Mr. Cromwell, free the hostages and tend to them."

"Aye, sir."

His men went to work. Greene walked over to speak to the master of the *Sea Breeze*. That was when he noticed the single black rose in the man's hand.

CHAPTER NINE

Brewer paced back and forth between the bow and the quarterdeck. They were closing the gap, but he was fast coming to the conclusion that the pirate would escape into the darkness before he got into gun range. The ship was a large brig, which matched reports he'd received from witnesses in St. Kitts. That meant it *might* be Black Rose out there, and if it was, he had to find a way to slow him or her down.

He joined Lieutenant Rivkins at the long-nines.

"Can we reach them?" he asked.

"No, sir," Rivkins replied as he touched his hat. "If we had an 18-pounder...."

Brewer's lips pressed together. He bounced the telescope in his hand as he glared at the fleeing ship. He hated feeling helpless.

Lieutenant Greene sat in the master's cabin of the sloop *Sea Breeze*. Across from him sat the pirate named José, flanked by two marines.

"So, José, is it?" Greene asked. "I take it this... Pedro... he was in charge of your boarding party?"

"Sí," the pirate confirmed. "How is he?"

"He's alive. How long he stays that way is another matter." Greene leaned forward. "The same goes for you."

"Eh?"

"You will be charged with piracy on the high seas," the Lieutenant said matter-of-factly. "The penalty for piracy is death by hanging."

"I will get a trial, no?"

"Yes."

José sighed and looked at the floor.

"Pedro was in charge?" Greene repeated.

"Sí."

"And who is the captain of the pirate ship?" Brewer asked.

A look of utter terror came over the prisoner's face. "Señor, I cannot say! It would mean my life!"

Greene reached around behind him and held up the single black rose that had been given to Pendleton.

"This rose has already condemned you," Greene said, softly and coldly. "I cannot help you if you withhold information."

José looked at the floor miserably and shook his head.

"Very well," Greene said as he rose. "Sergeant, take this prisoner back to the holding area. We shall turn him over to the Admiral in Port Royal for trial with the others."

The marine grabbed José under the arm and lifted him from the chair. "Come on, you!"

"Wait!" the pirate cried as he struggled. "Please, Señor Greene!"

Greene nodded at the Sergeant, and José was allowed to settle into his chair again.

"I'm listening," Greene said ominously.

The pirate drew a ragged breath and looked toward the deck above. "I am a dead man!" he whispered.

"Talk to me now, José, or the Sergeant shall remove you," Greene prompted.

"The pirate chief is called Black Rose," José said quietly, "but Diego commanded the ship."

"Describe Black Rose," Greene commanded.

"Small," came the reply. "Maybe only to here?" He put a hand just below his neck. "Thin. Dark eyes." He met the lieutenant's eyes. "Let me tell you, Señor, the devil is in those eyes of hers. She also has long, black hair."

"She?" Greene asked. "You mean Black Rose is a woman?"

The pirate threw back his head and laughed. "Sí, Señor! You did not know? Make no mistake," José warned. "Black Rose may be a woman, but a deadlier pirate never sailed the Caribbean. She will have her revenge."

"Revenge?" Greene was surprised at the revelation. "Revenge for what?"

José took a deep breath and told him.

* * * * *

It was three bells in the forenoon watch the next day before HMS *Phoebe* rejoined the merchantman, having lost sight of the pirate ship after darkness fell. Greene and Cromwell returned to the ship, along with Mr. Pendleton. The master of the *Sea Breeze* gave his report to Captain Brewer and thanked him for coming to their aid. The prisoners were transferred to *Phoebe* for the journey to Port Royal, and the merchantman was allowed to proceed to her destination.

After the ships parted, Brewer ordered a course for Jamaica and retreated to his cabin. Mr. Greene joined him for supper, along with the doctor. After the meal was finished, the three men removed to the day cabin for coffee.

Brewer held up his cup appreciatively. "Gentlemen, do you know what I like best about serving in the Caribbean? The ready abundance of coffee!"

"Here! Here!" the doctor chimed.

The three men made themselves comfortable. Brewer set his cup on the table, and the meeting was called to order.

"Benjamin," he said, looking at the black rose that had been given to him by Greene, "I know you are still writing your report, but I want you to tell us about your time on the merchantman."

Greene told his companions all about the boarding of the *Sea Breeze*, Alfred's defeat of the pirate leader Pedro, and the surrender of the remaining pirates.

"After we had the pirates secured, sir, I interrogated one of them," Greene said. "The man's name was José. He provided us with two very important pieces of information."

Greene leaned forward, elbows on his knees as he counted off the points on his fingers.

"First, sir, José confirmed for us that Black Rose is indeed a woman."

The doctor's look of disbelief nearly made Brewer laugh. "I thought as much," he said. "The descriptions pointed to that conclusion."

"Second," Greene said as he raised a second finger, "José told us who Black Rose is after."

That news brought the captain to the edge of his seat.

"*Who?*" he said. "Do you mean Black Rose is doing all this in order to get revenge on someone in particular?"

"Aye, sir," Greene sat back and refolded his hands. "Rose is plundering every ship she can in search of the man who killed her fiancé. They were to be married, but the wedding was postponed when the groom-to-be was persuaded to take part in one last voyage. He told her their share would be enough to allow them to run away to South America and live like royalty for the rest of their lives. She wanted to accompany him, but he talked her into staying behind and waiting for him to return. So he sailed... with El Diabolito."

A stunned silence settled briefly over the room. Spinelli's eyes darted briefly to his captain, who killed El Diabolito.

Brewer found his voice first. "You said, *with* El Diabolito. Then El Diabolito was not the fiancé, correct?"

"No," Greene said, "he was not."

"Then who?" Spinelli asked.

Greene looked from one to the other before answering.

"Roberto Cofresi."

The three sat in stunned silence. The name on all their minds was whispered by the doctor.

"Alfred."

* * * * *

Diego set course for home. He felt badly about having to abandon Pedro and his boarding party, but there had been no time to spare. He stood at the fantail, looking out over their wake.

He'd hoped to get some fine wine and provisions from the merchantman. The arrival of the frigate had foiled that plan, of course. They had been fortunate to keep their distance until the darkness shrouded them and allowed them to escape the warship.

173

He stared into their wake and thought of Rose. A dark cloud had descended upon her ever since she discovered the identity of Cofresi's killer. She retreated inside herself, eating very little and saying even less; he feared this mood more than any other. He knew she would not stop until she faced this Alfred and repaid him for the pain he had caused her. But how could they get to him, when he was safe aboard a Royal Navy ship?

Her original information had been that this Alfred was the captain's servant on the sloop HMS *Revenge*. They'd found that ship, only to find it in the hands of mutineers, and Alfred long since transferred to a frigate, HMS *Phoebe*. He hoped taking her quarry's old ship and using it to their ends might mollify her somewhat, but that remained to be seen. Knowing her as he did, he did not think she would not settle for less than her enemy's head on a pike.

So, the problem remained. The answer seemed obvious to Diego: if they could not get to him while he was on the ship, they would have to seize this Alfred when he was ashore. But how? They dared not make the attempt at Port Royal, so what did that leave? Any British port would be too risky, so that left only the French or Spanish ports. Many of the Spanish governors in the Caribbean had arrangements with pirates in the area, so it was unlikely that a British warship would enter one of their ports for shore leave. That left the French. Which French port was a British ship likely to visit for a short rest? Diego smiled. There was only one answer to that question.

Martinique.

Yes, he thought, *it could be done there, but how do we get his ship to visit the city? We cannot just camp out and wait for them!* It looked as though they would have to depend upon luck or an act of Providence to catch this man.

He scowled; he did not trust luck and did not believe in Providence. No, there had to be a better way....

Alfred stepped into the day room and cleared his throat.

Captain Brewer looked up.

"More coffee, sir?"

"Ah, no, Alfred, thank you," Brewer said. "Alfred, please, join us. Something has been brought to our attention that concerns you."

Alfred took a seat facing his captain, his hands resting on his thighs. "What is it, sir?"

"Alfred, ..." the captain began, stopped, and took a breath. "We have discovered that Black Rose was responsible for the attack on the merchant ship yesterday. Lieutenant Greene interrogated one of the captured pirates. First of all, he confirmed for us that Black Rose is indeed a woman."

Alfred waited. There was clearly more.

Brewer forged on. "He also uncovered a particular piece of information. There is a reason that Black Rose has been terrorizing the Caribbean. She has been seeking revenge against the man who killed her fiancé."

"Really?" Alfred said. "And who was her fiancé?"

Brewer looked at Greene and the doctor before meeting Alfred's eye.

"Roberto Cofresi."

Alfred's eyes grew wide for just a moment before his iron control reasserted itself.

"I see," he said evenly. "Black Rose is looking for me, because I killed Cofresi."

"That is our information," Greene said.

Alfred dropped his gaze to the deck and said nothing.

After a few moments, the doctor leaned forward.

"Are you all right, Alfred?"

Alfred blinked his eyes back into focus. "Yes, of course, Doctor." To the captain, "Will that be all, sir?"

"Yes, Alfred. Thank you."

The captain's rose and retreated to his pantry.

No sooner was he out of sight than he had to sit down and take several deep breaths to calm himself. He knew about blood feuds, and once in his youth had nearly become involved in one, but this was different. Black Rose wanted him dead as revenge for Cofresi, but she was turning her fury on everyone she met, killing them indiscriminately. Alfred shivered in his chair. Something had to be done to stop the killing.

* * * * *

Diego made his way up the path from the harbor. He had been informed that Rose wanted to see him right away.

The summons both pleased and concerned him. He was annoyed to be called away from the refitting of the *Cofresi*, making changes that would render the vessel the premiere pirate raider in the history of the Caribbean. But Rose had secluded herself for the week since their return, and he was glad she was emerging from her isolation, even if he had no idea what her mood would be. On board *Revenge* he had been alarmed by her reaction; he had never seen that level of mindless rage from her before. He quietly resolved to keep a closer watch on her.

He knocked once at the door as a courtesy before entering. Rose sitting at the table, wearing an oversized shirt that had been Cofresi's and playing idly with a dagger. She did not look up as he entered, and he saw that her eyes were staring into space just beyond the blade. He went to the cupboard and got a plate, on which he placed a few pieces of fruit and cheese —taken from their last prize—and set it on the table before her. Then he retrieved her glass and filled it with wine. After setting it beside the plate, he sat opposite to her. Still, she did not acknowledge his presence.

"Rose," he said firmly.

She blinked, finally focusing her gaze on him. She glanced down, saw the food and drink before her and nodded her thanks. She sat up and picked up a piece of cheese.

"Are you all right?" he asked.

Rose nodded as she took a bite of cheese. He watched her as she chewed, looking for signs that she was not being entirely honest and finding none. He relaxed a little as she drank from her goblet.

"I was remembering Cofresi," she said as she examined the fruit and chose a piece of melon. "I am glad you stopped me from destroying the sloop, Diego. I think Cofresi would be pleased that we have his murderer's ship and will use it to our own ends." She stopped and picked up the dagger again, standing it with the point on the tabletop and balancing it with her forefinger. "He would also expect me to avenge him." She let the blade fall to the table and looked at him. "How do we do that, Diego?"

His eyes went swiftly from her to the blade and back again. He rose and poured himself a goblet of wine. He sat again and downed the dark liquid in a single draught, then set the goblet hard on the table. When she did not react, he shrugged.

"I do not know," he said softly. He found her stares unnerving, so he rose and began to pace. "He is protected on his Royal Navy frigate with his Royal Navy captain. Even with the new sloop, that is a battle we dare not fight; it would be suicide."

She resumed playing with the blade. He glanced at her, wondering what she was thinking as he continued his pacing. *Is there a way?* he wondered. *Other than a happenstance meeting in some random port, what else was there?* He turned around at the wall, chin still down on his breast. "The only thing I can think of is to force him to come to us somehow."

Diego glanced her direction when there was no reply and found her still playing with the dagger. He thought she had ignored him when the blade suddenly fell to the table. He resumed his seat at the table and waited. She was leaning forward now, elbows on the table and her forefingers steepled and tapping the end of her nose. The only indication of how fast her mind was racing was her eyes darting randomly from place to place.

"Yes," she muttered. "But how do we make him come to us? We have no leverage to compel him to come, even if we could get word to him. He has no family we can threaten..."

He looked up when she stopped speaking. Her head was raised, and her eyes and mouth were open, as though an idea had struck her.

"Rose?" he said.

A smile crept over her face, one dripping with evil and revenge. She picked up the dagger and sat back in her chair, tapping the side of her forehead with the flat of the blade as the smile grew.

"The little cook," she said slowly. "*He* has no family, but his *captain* does! Did we not hear in Martinique that his captain...? What was his name?"

"Brewer."

"Yes, Captain Brewer, he was married recently, was he not? To the daughter of... St. Kitts, wasn't it? Yes! To the daughter of the governor of St. Kitts!" She looked him in the eye and nodded. "Now *that's* what I call leverage! How many soldiers are we likely to find in the garrison?"

Diego shrugged. "Not much more than a hundred or so. They have really cut back since the wars ended, and there are very few slaves on the island."

"Good," she said. "Very good. Then it is possible."

Diego said nothing as he followed her train of thought. He walked over and leaned on the table with both hands. "Kidnap the captain's wife?" he said. "Force him to bring your cook to us, at a place of our choosing? Is *that* your idea?" He slapped the table with both hands and resumed his pacing. "What makes you think he won't bring his frigate along as well?!?!" He marched back to his seat and sat down hard. "Do you wish to avenge Cofresi or join him? Please explain to me how this does not lead to our deaths?"

He sat there, breathing hard, his mind slowly regaining control from his outrage and frustration. Never had he spoken to her in this way, and he now feared her reprisals. To his surprise, Rose stared wide-eyed at him until his tirade ended, then she blinked and began to play with the dagger again. He rose and refilled both their goblets, then sat back down to see what would happen.

Rose alternated balancing the dagger tip-down on the table with holding it in front of her face, her dark eyes never leaving the gleaming blade. He knew she was deadly with the blade; how often had he seen her flip just such a blade in her hand and send it flying into an enemy's chest faster than he could blink? He half-expected to find the blade embedded to the hilt in his chest at any moment and was pleasantly relieved when it did not occur. He let out the breath he had been holding as quietly as possible when she dropped the dagger and reached for the goblet.

"Obviously, we will tell him to come alone," she said quietly, "and he must believe we are serious." She took a drink and stared off into space again before saying, "What if we went in at night, quietly. Perhaps send a small boat in ahead, to capture the harbor master and prevent him from sounding the alarm. You will take ten men and rush to the governor's mansion. Your goal is to kidnap Captain Brewer's wife and return with her. As soon as you are back aboard, we head out to sea."

He considered for a moment. "We will have to fight our way back to the ship."

Rose shrugged. "Possibly."

She picked up the dagger again and resumed playing with it. He watched her with growing frustration, hoping for her to recant, but no sign came. He tapped the table with his forefinger, but she ignored him completely. He took a deep breath and expelled it loudly before snatching his goblet and drinking deeply to give himself time to go over her plan.

Diego rose and resumed his pacing. Her plan did have some merit—going in at night and using a small advance force to silence the harbor master gave them a good chance of success, providing they could do it before anyone was able to raise the alarm. But once they had the woman and were heading back to their boats, the garrison would surely be out and they would have to fight for their lives. He could not imagine the alarm not being raised by that time. How could they make it off the island with the woman still alive? He sat back down and rested his forearms on the table.

"Rose, your plan is daring, and it may possibly succeed, but the odds of our making it off the island with the captain's wife alive are small. Are you sure there is no other way? Perhaps we could wait at Martinique for them? They stopped there before, if we were waiting for them the next time they came into port..."

"Then we should have the British *and* the French after us," she said coldly, her eyes never leaving the twirling blade. "*Leverage*, Diego, leverage is what we need! We must be able to force the good captain to turn over his cook to us—and the only way he will do that is to retrieve his wife safe and well." She let the knife drop and lifted her eyes to meet his. "I can see no other way. However, I will give you one week to come up with a better plan. Leave me now; tell the others that I am not be disturbed."

He left the hut without a word. After leaving notice not to disturb Rose, he went to his own quarters and gathered his bedroll and several days' provisions. He put his lieutenant, Tomas, in charge of the work on *Cofresi* and left the camp. He hiked to the north side of the island, to the top of Rackham Hill, the highest point on the island. He needed to be alone in order to think. He had to come up with a better plan, one that would allow them to come out of this with their lives. He set up camp before walking out to his throne— that was the name he gave a large rock near the cliff that allowed him a magnificent view of the northern horizon. He felt like Neptune when he sat on it, the god of the sea surveying his domain.

Diego sighed and shook his head, banishing such fantasies from his mind. He stared out over the empty ocean and thought about Rose's plan. He agreed that they needed leverage to pry the cook from the safety of his frigate; the question was, did they have to kidnap the captain's wife to get to the cook? Not that he minded kidnapping; he was trying to think of a way to do it that would minimize their losses.

The setting of the sun roused him from his thoughts. He returned to camp and made a small fire. After cooking and eating his evening meal, he sat silently by the fire, but staring into the flames brought no new ideas to mind. He doused the fire and went to sleep, hoping tomorrow would bring a better plan.

The mid-afternoon on the fourth day, he made his way slowly down the trail that led to the pirate camp. He went to his own quarters and dropped off his kit before heading to her bungalow. He was not looking forward to this meeting.

He knocked on the door frame, and she bade him enter. The curtains drawn back, making the room relatively well-lit. Rose had bathed—her face and hair made it obvious—and she wore one of her best tunics. It was almost as if she were celebrating, and he wondered whether he should be worried. To top it off, on the table before her was a bottle of Cognac and two glasses.

"Diego! Welcome! Come in, we have much to talk about." She opened the Cognac and poured them each a generous portion.

Diego picked up his glass but did not drink. "Rose? Are we celebrating something?"

She seemed to be enjoying herself; he thought the devil himself was in her mischievous smile, and there was a twinkle in her eye that he had not seen for a long time.

"Your plan, Diego!" she cooed. "I want to hear all about your marvelous plan that will bring me revenge for my Cofresi."

He sighed and gulped down a large portion of his drink. "I regret to say that I have not come up with a better plan," he said dourly, "only a few recommendations."

"Really?" Her surprised expression mocked him, but he knew better than to challenge her over it. Better to let her get past her gloating so they could finalize their plans. Rose downed her Cognac in a single draught before hurling the glass into the empty fireplace.

"Don't ever question me again, Diego," she said, her voice hard and menacing. "My heart knows how to gain my revenge for my Cofresi, and I shall have it. Never doubt that."

She paced back and forth across the room. He could hear her breath slowing as she calmed down; soon she would sit again, and then the planning could begin. When she did sit, she buried her face in her hands and took long, slow breaths. He rose without a word and got her another glass. He set it on the table in front of her and filled it with three fingers of Cognac before resuming his seat. Finally, he heard a loud breath expelled from behind her hands. Rose lowered her hands and smiled at the Cognac; she nodded her thanks and picked it up and savored a long, slow drink.

"Tell me what you did come up with," she ordered.

"I want to suggest a few ... modifications, for you to consider, Rose. For one, I think the advance party should be larger, perhaps twenty-five or thirty men. As you said, we must take the harbor master's office before the alarm can be sounded, but we also have to get to the governor's house before the captain's wife can flee into the hills. Then we may have to fight our way out of town and back to the ship. Our losses could be considerable, including the captain's wife."

Rose nodded her agreement as she considered his advice.

"Also," Diego continued, "I think *Cofresi* should appear at the harbor entrance and fire into the harbor and the town to cover our escape and distract the garrison."

"Sounds reasonable," she said. He relaxed and leaned forward, one elbow on the table.

"Once we have the woman," he concluded, "it is only a matter of time before word gets to the captain, and he brings the cook to us."

Rose refilled her glass and smiled. "Actually, I have been thinking while you were gone. Tell me what you think of this."

They talked and drank long into the night, and the moon was high in the sky when Diego left the bungalow with a smile on his face.

* * * * *

With the ship back on course for Martinique, Captain Brewer invited his officers to dinner. He included Mr. Sweeney, Dr. Spinelli, and Captain Enfield. They were seated around the table, nursing glasses of Cognac after dinner, when Lieutenant Greene spoke up.

"It's amazing that Black Rose found the mutineers and dispatched them for us. How's that for irony?"

"I agree," Mr. Sweeney said, "but you're missing the more important question."

Greene stared at him over his glass. "And what would that be, sir?"

Sweeney put his glass down. "What happened to the ship?"

Mr. Rivkins' eyes snapped up from his drink. "What do you mean?"

"Just what I said," Sweeney continued. "What happened to *Revenge*?"

"The pirates probably burned her," Greene said.

Sweeney wouldn't let it go. *"What if they didn't?"* He looked around the table and got no answer. "What if they took the ship? Now Black Rose has a Royal Navy sloop-of-war armed with 12-pounder guns to go with her original ship mounting 8-pounders. If this keeps up, we'll be back to the days of Henry Morgan, when pirates had fleets that ruled the Caribbean."

"You raise a good point," said Brewer, "One that adds urgency to our mission. We are on our way to Martinique to see if we can pick up any fresh information that might lead us to Black Rose."

"And I know just where to start," Spinelli chimed in. "That little pub off the waterfront. Remember, Captain? I went there on our last visit while you went to see the governor." He paused for a drink. "I had an interesting conversation with a pretty little barmaid on that visit."

Enfield looked up. "Barmaid?"

"Yes," the doctor said, reliving the memory. "She had long black hair and dark eyes that would steal a man's soul. She was very interested to hear about how we went after El Diabolito."

"Was she?" Brewer said. "Tell me, Doctor, did she ask about Roberto Cofresi as well?"

Spinelli pursed his lips as he tried to remember. "Let me see," he said, as his eyes narrowed. "Yes, I believe that name did come up."

Brewer shot a glance to his first lieutenant. "And what did you say about Cofresi?"

"Hum ... when I told her you had killed El Diabolito, she asked if anyone else of note had died. I told her Cofresi was also among the dead. She asked if you had killed him also, and I said no, that Alfred had done the deed."

"And what did you say she looked like?" Greene asked.

Spinelli didn't have to strain his memory to answer this question. "Short, slender, pretty, long black hair and dark eyes."

"What was her voice like, Adam?" Brewer asked. "Was it deep?"

"Oh, no; it was rather high, soprano, I'd say, not contralto. Why?"

Brewer raised his eyebrows at Greene in a silent question, and Greene nodded. Brewer sighed loudly.

"Would someone tell me what's going on here?" Spinelli demanded.

"Doctor," Brewer said, "it's possible the barmaid you were speaking to was Black Rose herself. Your description matches the one we got from a pirate we captured." He leaned forward. "If so, it was you who gave her Alfred's name and described him. She knows where to find him now."

"I...I," Spinelli stammered. "I'm sorry, Captain, I had no idea who she was. I didn't mean—"

"Of course you didn't, Doctor," Brewer stopped him. "It sounds like you didn't say anything anyone else at this table wouldn't have said, were he in your place."

"Dear God," Spinelli whispered. "Have I put Alfred in danger?"

"At most you changed *when* she found out, not *if*, Doctor," Mr. Greene said. "Black Rose was already looking for Cofresi's killer. Her intelligence gathering network is supposed to be a very good one, so she would have come upon the information sooner or later. The battle was too well known for her not to find out eventually."

Spinelli shook his head uncertainly. "Still, if I hadn't..."

Brewer cut him off. "Adam, stop. You had no way of knowing who you were talking to—if that's even who it was.

In any case, Alfred is here, safe with us. No pirate can get to him without going through every man in this room. Don't blame yourself. I shouldn't have told you."

Agreements arose from all around the table, but the doctor stared gloomily at his drink.

The captain stood. "Gentlemen, let me summarize everything we know so far regarding our mission. Based on the boat full of dead bodies, complete with the crushed flower, found by the *Liverpool*, we are reasonably sure that Black Rose found the *Revenge* and doled out the justice those mutineers merited, possibly surer and swifter than His Majesty's government would have. As Mr. Sweeney said, we do not know if they kept the ship or burned it. In any case, we can close the book on Brumby and his mutinous filth."

Brewer caught himself; he was not at all happy with his words. He looked at the table for a moment to gather himself. "Sorry, I got carried away there for a moment. But our original problem still remains: finding Black Rose. I don't know about you, but I for one am sick and tired of sailing around hoping we bump into her. There has to be a better way. Any ideas?"

It was Lieutenant Greene who answered. "We lay a trap."

Brewer looked at him. "How?"

"We use what we know about her," he nodded towards the doctor, "and we use what she knows about us."

"Aye!" Mr. Sweeney said. "After all, we have the perfect bait."

Mr. Crawford was confused. "Bait? What bait?"

Captain Enfield leaned over and spoke softly. *"Alfred."*

Crawford's eyes widened and he nodded sheepishly.

"I hate to sound crass," Lieutenant Rivkins said, "but what we're talking about is hanging Alfred out in the wind to see if Black Rose snaps at the chance to take her revenge."

"Absolutely not," Brewer said firmly. "We must come up with a plan that will ensure Alfred's safety as much as possible. We make sure that Mr. Crawford and Mac are close at hand." He interlaced his fingers before his face, forefingers steepled. "So, *if* we decide to do something like this, how do we make it work? I mean, obviously it can't *look* like a trap."

"Easily said," Sweeney growled, "not so easily done."

Brewer rose and said, "Which is why I am giving all of you twenty-four hours to think it over. Do not talk about this in front of or around the crew. We meet again here at the turn of the second dog-watch. Dismissed."

In the pantry, Alfred absently-mindedly wiped a drying cloth over a plate. He was thinking about what he had just overheard of the conversation around the table. He did not mean to eavesdrop, but it's hard *not* to overhear what is said around the table if one is in the pantry. *So*, he thought, *they want to use me as bait to lure Black Rose out of hiding. Makes sense, I suppose, since I'm the one she wants.* He traded the dry plate for a wet one. He trusted the captain; Brewer was certainly kinder and more considerate than many of the gentlemen he had worked for. *Still, I wonder what they will come up with?* He sighed as he made a decision. *Captain Brewer has never given me cause to doubt him,* he reasoned, *and I won't start now. I have to hear them out, at the very least.* He reached for another plate only to discover there was nothing left to dry. He put the plates away and looked around to make sure the pantry was ship-shape. Satisfied, he hung the drying towel on the bulkhead and left the cabin, hoping the cool sea air would clear his head and calm his mind.

CHAPTER TEN

The men stayed low in the crowded boat. The lack of moonlight would leave them nearly invisible as they crept toward the shore through the sleeping harbor. Diego couched in the bow and used hand signals to communicate with the man at the tiller. He chose a secluded beach on the western end of the harbor; from there the short trek through the jungle to the governor's mansion would allow them to approach unseen. But the way in was not what worried Diego. It was the way out that concerned him. If the guard boats patrolling the harbor were alerted to their escape, they could make things very hot for him and his men. To that end, Diego had brought two blue rockets they found in *Cofresi's* hold while making their modifications to the ship. Should the guard boats chase them, he would fire these into the night sky. The signal would bring Rose and *Cofresi* to the harbor's mouth to provide cover fire to chase the guard boats away.

The dark of the moon meant they had very little warning of the approaching shore. Diego was caught off guard when the boat grounded, and his cheek was cut when it hit the railing. He cursed silently as he jumped over the rail and into the surf. The boat was dragged up on to the beach and camouflaged. Three men of his party had been born on the island; Diego sent them off as the advance guard to lead the way through the woods. Two men were left at the edge of the beach to guard the boat; the rest followed the three scouts.

Progress was slow but steady; just over two hours' march brought them to the mansion. A search to the right and left found no guards patrolling the grounds. A barn for the animals and a building for the servants' quarters were on the far side of the house from their position. A boy was left with a lantern at the spot where they emerged from the forest.

Diego led the others as they ran to the lone door at the back of the house. He tried the handle and put his shoulder to the door, but it was barred on the inside. He nodded to a burly hand beside him, who drew his dagger and used its handle to break the narrow pane of glass in the window beside the door. He reached in and groped until he had the blade under the bar and levered upward with all his might. He grimaced as his shoulder was cut by the jagged glass that remained in the frame, but his reward was of the sound of the bar, falling to the ground. The door opened easily now.

"We move swiftly and quietly," Diego reminded them. "Quanto, take three men and make sure no servants interfere. Felipe, take five men and secure the bottom floor of the house. Do not let anyone out! Move!"

Quanto sprinted from the group, tapping three men on the shoulder as he passed them as the signal to follow him to the outlying building where servants where quartered who did not live in the household. The building was little more than a large cabin, probably one large room with bunks for eight or ten men.

The four of them moved as swiftly as silence would allow —there must be no noises from any startled chickens or horses to alert the hands. Quanto halted about twenty paces from the door and hunkered down. His men followed his lead.

"We take no prisoners. Everyone inside must be dealt with swiftly and silently. No shooting! Understand?" He looked each man in the eye and saw resolve that mirrored his own. He nodded to Gabriel, and the big Dominican crept to the cabin and tested the door. It opened, and he slipped inside. Quanto and his men followed Gabriel.

Inside were bunks for twelve men, their occupants asleep and defenseless. The four men fanned out and attacked, starting with the men closest to the door. Quanto heard a ragged gasp from a man as a dagger slit his throat. He turned to his left in time to see another draw a pistol from beneath his pillow. He moved swiftly to plunge his cutlass into the man's chest. A commotion arose at the back corner of the cabin, where one of the hands had succeeding in surprising one of his men, killing him with a dagger. He then picked up the fallen pirate's cutlass and moved to attack another, but was felled by a knife thrown by Gabriel. Sounds of scuffles and one muffled yell ended as the pirates' blades did their fell work. A silence descended upon the room, broken when Gabriel spoke.

"Plunder?" he asked.

Quanto laughed. "Here? These are servants, Gabriel. What would you find, eh? A few coins?" He shrugged. "Search if you wish, and take the pistol and any other weapons. Then we go. We must make sure there is no one in the barn."

As Felipe led his men away to search the ground level of the house, Diego turned to his remaining men, holding up a finger to draw their attention. "We move upstairs. *Everyone we encounter must be taken alive! I will kill the man who harms anyone upstairs!"* We are seeking the wife of the British captain Brewer. We gag and bind everyone we find. Now follow me." They set off into the darkness of the house.

Elizabeth Brewer sat exhausted on the edge of her bed and watched as Sally, the upstairs maid, took a turn pacing back and forth, humming in an effort to lull little Anne to sleep. Elizabeth looked at the clock on the wall and groaned. Nearly two o'clock! She herself had walked the selfsame path with her stubborn daughter for the last two hours before Sally had gently knocked at the door and offered her assistance.

Watching her now, Elizabeth envied the older woman her patience with the child.

"Shhh," she cooed to the babe. "Hush now, my precious."

"Sally," Elizabeth said wearily, "you are a Godsend. Here, let me... What was that?"

The maid looked up. "What was what?"

"It sounded like something fell against a wall."

"I didn't hear anything."

Elizabeth's next words were interrupted by breaking glass. She went to her bedroom window, which was on the front of the house, and looked out warily. She saw nothing. Still, she felt uneasy.

"Sally, I think—" A heavy thud was heard from below, and Elizabeth's eyes grew wide in alarm. "Wait here. I shall go wake my father."

She ran past the maid and down the hall three doors to her father's bedroom. She burst in without knocking and shook the governor into wakefulness.

"Elizabeth?" her father said, once his eyes were able to focus. "What is the meaning of this? What's..." A scream was heard from below, followed by the sound of plates smashing on the floor. The governor sat up. "What's happening?"

"It appears we have thieves below, Father." She went to his window and looked out. Her father's room was at the back corner of the house, and she hoped to signal the servants' cabin for help. Instead, she saw what she took in the darkness to be a man bearing a cutlass come out of the cabin. "No, not thieves," she said. "Pirates."

"Pirates?"

"Yes, and it looks like they've killed everyone in the servant's cabin. I must get back to Anne. Excuse me, Father."

She dashed from the room, leaving her bewildered father to his own devices. Her heart nearly froze in fear as she heard footsteps coming up the stairs. She entered her bedroom, closed and latched the door, and turned to find Sally sitting on the side of her bed, holding little Anne.

"Mistress, what is happening?" Sally whispered.

"Pirates, Sally," Elizabeth said. She looked around the room and cursed herself for not having a pistol hidden somewhere. Her eyes went back to her daughter in Sally's arms and a horrifying thought occurred to her. What if they'd heard of Anne's birth? What if the pirates were here to kidnap the governor's grandchild and hold her for ransom? She ran to the bed and knelt before the terrified maid.

"Sally," she said quickly in a hushed tone, "you must listen to me. I cannot explain now; the pirates are almost here. Listen to me! Anne is *your child!* Do you understand? Tell the pirates that Anne is your child! Do you hear me? Good! Tell them the father is Jason, one of the hands in the barn. No, don't worry about their asking him; I fear he's dead now."

Sally gasped.

"Sally! The only thing that matters now is Anne! *We cannot let these beasts know she is the governor's granddaughter!* Do you see now? That is why you must tell them Anne is your daughter."

Sally blinked and swallowed hard. "Yes, I understand."

At that moment, the door burst open, and four pirates brandishing cutlasses charged in. Elizabeth saw blood on one of the blades. One man stepped forward and surveyed the room before speaking to his companions.

"Take them to the parlor below," he ordered, directing two of his companions forward. He left the room with the fourth man. One buccaneer stepped to the side and motioned toward the door with his blade.

"Ladies," he said with a sneer, "if you please."

The governor sat up in his bed and watched his daughter dash from the room; he was barely awake enough to comprehend what she had said. When the full force of her words hit him, he jumped from the bed and went quickly to the window. Sure enough, he could make out three men standing outside the cabin, all with weapons in their hands.

He stepped back from the window. Pirates? Here? Now? What could they want? It was well known that St. Kitts was not a particularly prosperous colony. The spoils available to them for such a raid would not be large; so why? His eyes opened wide as a thought burst in upon his terrified mind. The pirates were not looting the town—they were here, *at his house!* He cursed himself for disbanding the guards who had formerly protected his residence day and night. He went to the chair and hurriedly put on the pants his valet had laid out before he retired. He took a pistol from the drawer of his nightstand and tucked it in his waistband. He opened his wardrobe, and barely managing to draw his sword from its scabbard when his door burst open and four men entered.

The governor stepped out from behind the wardrobe door. He shot the first pirate and threw the pistol at the second as a distraction. He charged as the man raised his arms to deflect the flying pistol and thrust his sword into the man's chest and through his heart.

He stepped back to ready himself for the next attack. The remaining two men stepped apart and charged him simultaneously. He parried a blow from the one to his left, only to feel his companion's blade bite deep into his forearm. The governor cried out and dropped his sword, falling to his knees as he cradled his wounded arm. The pirate raised his cutlass to bring the death blow down on the governor's neck when a voice interrupted him.

"Julio!"

The pirate's blade halted in mid-air. The governor looked up at the pirate standing in the doorway; this was obviously the leader of the raid.

"I said, *no killing* upstairs," he said. "Pick him up and bring him downstairs."

Julio growled as he grabbed the governor under his wounded arm and hauled him to his feet. The governor exclaimed in pain. Julio struck him on the temple with the hilt of his cutlass. Only the pirate's strong grip stopped him from crashing to the floor again. Julio then dragged him out the door and down the hall toward the stairs.

The doors to the parlor were open, and Diego led this final group of captives in. Julio threw the wounded governor to the floor.

"Father!" Elizabeth cried, and rushed to his side. "You're hurt! Jane, get towels from the washstand. Good. Here, wrap one around the wound and hold it tight." She stood and turned to Diego. "What did you do to him?"

"Not half what he deserved," the pirate said, "so hold your tongue." He turned to confer with his comrades.

Elizabeth took a second wet compress from Jane and applied it gently to the wound on her father's head. "Father, hear me," she whispered in his ear. "Anne is Sally's daughter tonight."

His eyes flashed to hers, lit with comprehension.

Diego turned back to her. "You are the governor's daughter?"

Elizabeth rose and tried her best to put on a brave face. "Yes."

"You are the wife of the English captain Brewer?"

Her eyes went wide at his name. "Yes. What have you done with him?"

Diego grinned ferociously. "Nothing… yet. You will come with us, Señora."

"Where," her father gasped, "are you taking her?"

"That is none of your business, Governor." Diego took a letter from inside his shirt and tossed it to the ground before the governor. It landed in a pool of his blood. "You may open that after we are gone, Governor. If anyone pursues us, your daughter dies."

"You swine!" the governor spat.

"Count yourself lucky, Governor, that I let you live," Diego said coldly, "for I could allow Julio to avenge his comrades upstairs. You and you," he pointed at two of his men, "escort Señora Brewer back to the boat. Guard her carefully, or I shall be angry."

"Sí, Diego." One of them put his hand on her arm, but she shrugged him off and made to strike him.

"Elizabeth!" her father said firmly. "It will do you no good if they kill you before William has a chance to rescue you."

Diego laughed. "Listen to your father, child; he speaks truth. I am ordered to bring you back alive, but I will kill you if you resist again. Your husband will not know the difference until it is too late."

Elizabeth looked to her father, his eyes imploring her to cooperate, at least for now. Her eyes flew to Anne, and without thinking she went over to kiss the child on the forehead. Sally gasped, and Elizabeth realized her mistake. She quickly embraced and kissed Sally on the forehead as well, then stepped away from them.

"The child means something to you?" Diego demanded, his eyes narrowing. He gestured, and Julio stepped forward to hold the point of his cutlass next to her father's neck.

"She was born to my lady's maid," Elizabeth said. "Sally was kind enough to name her after my mother."

"And her name?"

"Anne."

The pirate stepped around her to get a closer look at the child cradled in her mother's arms. He reached out, but Sally drew the baby away. Diego warned her with a look, and then reached out and softly brushed the child's cheek with the back of his finger. He straightened up and untied a bag from his belt, opening it and taking a gold coin out. He dropped it in Sally's lap.

"Anne was my mother's name," he said. "Take good care of her; she is precious." He turned to the governor, who was now sitting upright with his back against a chest, Jane still holding the makeshift bandage tight on his forearm. "Governor, you have your instructions. Remember my warning."

He led his remaining men from the room. Elizabeth held his eyes as they dragged her out, begging him to look after Anne. He nodded just before she disappeared out the door.

"Jane," he said quietly, "as soon as they have gone—wait until they are out of sight—go out the front door and fetch the doctor and the garrison commander."

Two hours' time found the governor seated in a chair in the parlor, with Dr. Underhill to tend his wounds. The governor's head ached and he felt dazed; the area was bruised and swollen but not actually bleeding. The doctor sat on a stool to the governor's side with his assistant behind him. He spent little time looking at his temple before moving on to the arm. Underhill carefully removed the bandage to expose the wound, handing the dressing to his assistant. He probing drew a sharp hiss from the governor.

"Have you any whiskey about, Governor?" Underhill asked.

"Yes. Jane can get some for you."

"Not for me," the doctor looked up. "Jane? Get the governor a stiff drink, and bring the bottle."

She returned a moment later with a glass of whiskey and the bottle on a tray. The doctor nodded to the governor. "Drink up, sir. It will steel you for what I have to do."

The governor picked up the glass in a shaky hand and downed it in one swallow.

"Good," Underhill said. "Jane, lean hard on his shoulder and arm. Don't let him move."

Jane did so. The governor began to protest, but the doctor was quicker. His assistant clamped down on his patient's other arm and shoulder as the doctor picked up the bottle and poured a generous portion onto the open wound.

The governor screamed in pain and tried his best to jump out of the chair. The doctor's assistant—whose name turned out to be Brutus—and Jane held him in place. Jane actually had to lean on him with all her weight, practically sitting on his arm to keep him in the chair. Next the doctor dabbed away the alcohol and once again began gently probing the wound. Several minutes later, he set his probe down.

"My apologies, Governor," he said as he wiped his hands on a towel, "but experience has taught me it is better to beg forgiveness that ask permission in cases like this. I needed to verify how badly the blade damaged the bone. Thankfully, the blade bit into but did not break the bone completely in half. It should heal in time, so long as we can prevent infection. I will sew up the arm, but first I need to find something to act as a splint."

The doctor stood up and went in search of a splint. As he was exiting the room, Captain Erikson, the garrison commander, entered.

"Governor," he said in greeting, "I'm glad you survived."

That brought a wince to the governor's face. "How bad is it?"

"Ten dead in the cabin, one of them a pirate," Erikson reported. "Four more in the barn, all ours. Three dead in the room off the kitchen, looks like two women and a teenage boy. Two pirates dead upstairs, in your room, I think. Your work?"

The governor nodded dully as he took in the captain's report. All those people, members of his household, some of them for years, dead in his service. He had failed to protect them. They were like his *family*... Oh, God! *Elizabeth!*

Elizabeth Brewer at that moment was seated in the middle of the boat being rowed out of the harbor. The pirate leader, Diego, warned her that any attempt to signal the guard boat or overturn the boat would result in her immediate death; with her father's warning ringing in her ears, she chose to believe him.

Once they were clear of the harbor, the mood on the craft lightened considerably. Not long after, she could see a boat approaching them. Her hopes for an early rescue were dashed when the pirates rowed directly for it. When they were alongside, Diego was the first up the entryway ladder, and she was ordered to follow. When she stepped up on deck, it finally dawned on her that she was still dressed in her nightgown, and she tried her best to conceal herself. Diego snapped his fingers, and one of the pirates produced an overcoat, long enough to cover her. She thanked him as she put it on over her shoulders and held the front closed. Diego touched her arm.

"Come with me," he said. "This way."

She felt something vaguely familiar about this ship, as he led her down the stairway and aft to the main cabin. He opened the door, and she entered to find a woman sitting at a table. Before her was a bottle of rum and three glasses. She rose as Diego closed the door.

"Welcome, Mrs. Brewer," she said. "Please be seated."

Elizabeth stayed where she was and watched as the woman poured three glasses half-full of rum. She had mesmerizing dark eyes and raven hair that glided down her back well past her shoulders. She was small—Elizabeth was literally head and shoulders taller—and petite to the point of being thin. The only flaw—if it could be called such—was a nose just prominent enough to spoil the natural beauty of the hair and eyes.

Diego nudged her toward a chair, and Elizabeth reluctantly sat. The woman pushed one of the glasses to her and another to Diego, who took the third seat at the table. The woman sat, raised her glass in salute, and drained it in a single swallow. Elizabeth watched silently. The woman set her glass down and smiled.

"You may call me Rose," she said.

"Why am I here?" Elizabeth asked.

Rose smiled. "Direct," she observed, "and no fear. I like that. You are here, my dear, because your husband has something I want. The letter I left with your father proposes a trade."

Elizabeth's head tilted to the side and her eyes narrowed. "Some *thing*?"

Rose shrugged. "Very well. Some *one*."

"And you expect him to trade that person for me." Elizabeth snorted. "My husband does not respond well to blackmail."

Rose met her eyes and held them. "And how do you think he will respond to murder?"

Elizabeth did not flinch. "With vengeance."

A frightening curl appeared at the corner of Rose's lips. "Then we will be even."

Elizabeth lifted her glass and took a slow sip and she looked around the cabin. Again she felt a familiarity, as though she had been here before.

"You have a question, Mrs. Brewer?" Rose asked.

"No, not exactly," came the reply. "It's just that, for some reason, all this feels familiar to me."

Rose stood. Diego followed suit, and Elizabeth finally did so as well. Rose led the way to the day cabin aft and sat on the settee beneath the stern windows. Elizabeth looked around the room and turned to her host.

"This... was my husband's ship," she said. "HMS *Revenge.*"

"Why do you think that?" her host asked.

"That chair," Elizabeth pointed to a chair up against the bulkhead, upholstered with a gaudy bright red fabric and accented by yellow tassels. "I remember that chair from when my husband gave me a tour before we were married. I told him that was the ugliest chair I had ever seen, and I asked him why it was here. He said it was part of the original decoration left behind by the previous owner—the pirate Jean Lafitte, I believe. A friend of yours?" Rose shook her head. "Never met him."

Elizabeth shrugged. "It's still ugly. Why do you keep it?"

"It was left behind by the previous owner," Rose said, "and I have grown partial to it. And yes, Mrs. Brewer, this was once your husband's ship. When I came upon it, it had been liberated from the Royal Navy by some mutineers, and I liberated it from them. I renamed it *Cofresi.*"

"Cofresi," Elizabeth said quietly. Where had she heard that name before? Some time ago; before her marriage? Yes! That was the pirate.... She stared wide eyed at her captor.

"I see you have made the connection, Mrs. Brewer," Rose said, her voice suddenly low and menacing. "Cofresi and I were to be married, but he put it off to go on one more voyage with El Diabolito; he said his share would set us up for the rest of our lives. He never came back."

"My husband did not kill your fiancé," Elizabeth said.

"No, he killed El Diabolito. But the man who did is on his ship," Rose retorted. "I want *him.* His name is Alfred. He is your husband's servant."

Diego stepped around her and handed something to Rose.

"What makes you think my husband would turn over any member of his crew to you?" Elizabeth asked desperately. "I can tell you he would not. Not even for me."

"I hope you are wrong, Mrs. Brewer, for your sake." Diego now stepped back, so Elizabeth could see the flower Rose was holding between her thumb and forefinger. Her eyes grew wide and an icy fear gripped her heart.

"My God!" she whispered. *"Black Rose!"*

Rose smiled as she twirled the rose beneath her nose. "A pleasure to make your acquaintance, Mrs. Brewer."

* * * * *

The sun was high in the sky when HMS *Phoebe* slid into the harbor at Martinique. The pilot guided the frigate to her berth, and Mr. Greene thanked him and escorted him from the deck. He came over to join the captain, Mr. Sweeney, and Mr. Rivkins by the fantail.

"We'll do shore leave by divisions," the captain said. "Mr. Rivkins, your division and Mr. Cromwell's can go ashore with the forenoon watch tomorrow. The other two divisions can go the next day. Remember, keep your ears open for any news of Black Rose. Mr. Greene and I shall go ashore and pay our respects to the governor."

"Sir?" Mr. Rivkins said, "shall we increase security around your quarters?"

Mr. Greene raised an eyebrow. "And your reason for that would be?" he asked.

"Well, sir, Governor Roussin has tried every other conceivable way to convince Alfred to defect to the French, so I was sure that when he heard we were in the harbor, he would send his garrison aboard to kidnap the poor man." The others stared at him.

"Of course," Rivkins deadpanned, "the governor would send a politely worded note saying that Alfred had finally agreed to take him up on his offer."

Captain Brewer turned to his first lieutenant.

"Double the guard," he said, "and tell Mac to carry his pistols inside the cabin."

Greene smiled and winked at Rivkins. "Aye, sir."

An hour later the captain and his first lieutenant were walking up the lane to the governor's house. They were politely received by a servant at the door and shown into a waiting area off the foyer. The door closed behind them, and the two men looked around the room. It was Greene's first time here, and he admired the portrait of Louis XVIII by Jean-Baptiste Jacques Augustin which hung above the hearth. Brewer smiled when his premier only gave a passing glance at the bookshelves filled with works on philosophy and French influence on Caribbean history—they were in French, and Greene did not speak the language. A display case in the corner of room held a handwritten document; this, too, only received a cursory glance. Brewer knew it to be a copy of the report written by Admiral Francois-Joséph-Paul de Grasse-Rouville, Comte de Grasse, detailing his victory over the British fleet at the Battle of the Capes, forcing the surrender of General Cornwallis' army at the Battle of Yorktown during the American Revolution. Brewer knew that Roussin kept it on display to impress the Americans who came to visit.

The door opened without preamble, and the two officers turned to find, not the expected servant, but the governor himself.

"Captain Brewer!" he exclaimed. "Lieutenant Greene! So good to see you again!" He shook hands with each of them. "To what do I owe this unlooked for pleasure?"

"Merely a courtesy call, Governor," Brewer assured him.

"I was hoping you would have fresh information on Black Rose. I would, of course, be willing to reward such information with one of Alfred's feasts."

Roussin hung his head and placed his hand over his heart in mocking regret. "Alas! I am afraid I can add nothing to what we have already discussed. No ships have arrived with any information as to her whereabouts or activities." He looked up. "Does this mean the dinner is off?"

Captain Brewer grasped the governor's shoulder and gave a friendly squeeze. "I don't think Alfred would forgive me if I were so inhospitable, Governor! But first, we have some news regarding our favorite lady pirate."

The governor's eyes widened in anticipation, and he led the way to his office. A servant brought in Cognac for three and left the tray on the table before he bowed to the governor and retreated from the room. Roussin handed out the glasses and held his up in a toast.

"To Black Rose," he said. "May she live just long enough for us to hang her."

The toast was drunk, and the three men took their seats. Roussin set his glass on the table. "Now, Captain, what is it you have to tell me?"

Brewer set his glass down. "A short time ago, we came upon a pirate ship attempting to board a British merchantman. The ship ran at our approach, abandoning the prize crew. I stopped just long enough to send Mr. Greene over with a boarding party before I pursued. We lost them, but when we returned to the merchantman, Mr. Greene gave a very strange and informative report."

Greene picked up the tale. "One of the pirates talked, you see, and gave us several bits of information. First, he confirmed that Black Rose is a woman."

"Ah!" Roussin said softly. "As we surmised."

"Yes," Greene continued. "He also let us know her purpose in the increase of piratical activity. Did you know Black Rose was engaged to be married? Her fiancé was a pirate who persuaded her to postpone their nuptials just long enough for him to go on one more voyage. He promised his share would be enough to set them both up for life. But he was killed when his ship was boarded by our ship, HMS *Revenge*."

Roussin's eyebrows rose. "El Diabolito?"

"No," Brewer said. "Roberto Cofresi."

"I see. And was it you...?"

Brewer shook his head. "Alfred."

The governor's eyes went wide at the news, then he shook his head ruefully. *"Mon Dieu!"*

The captain nodded for Greene to continue. "It appears she is out for revenge. The prisoner who talked said it is common knowledge in their camp that she will pay a fortune to anyone who discovers Alfred's location."

The governor steepled his fingers under his chin. "And how will you use this information?"

"We're are working out a plan," Brewer said, "to make Alfred's whereabouts known and lure Black Rose into the open, where we can engage the pirates and defeat them, or seize them by stealth."

Roussin pursed his lips as he considered. "That will be tricky. How can it be done without the pirates seeing it as a trap? They must be convinced that they are the ones taking you by surprise. Perhaps you might leave him here and let it be known that he is awaiting Black Rose to settle accounts with her once and for all?" He sounded almost hopeful. Not doubt the prospect of having Alfred as part of his household was the inspiration for this idea.

Brewer shook his head. "She would simply put a bounty out on him, a fortune to anyone who brought her Alfred's head. He wouldn't be safe, and we wouldn't apprehend Black Rose."

"What if he turned pirate himself?" Roussin wondered aloud.

Brewer was interested. "What do you mean?"

"Perhaps," the governor tapped his forefingers thoughtfully, "he could run off into the hills outside of town. Alfred simply would not return from shore leave, for example. This island has many places where someone could hide from a search party. After your crew comes ashore, it will be known all over the city that you seek Black Rose; this would easily explain why you cannot stay long to seek him. You might also spread the rumor that a note was found, left for you in your cabin by Alfred before he left, saying he could not bear responsibility of putting you and your crew at risk, so he was leaving to employ his considerable skills to turning a profit for himself. What do you think?"

Brewer leaned his head back slightly and looked at the governor through hooded eyes. He turned the idea over in his mind before looking to Mr. Greene, who was staring at the floor as he weighed the pros and cons of the plan. The captain turned his gaze back to their host, who was sitting back in his chair and observing his guests over his glass.

"An intriguing idea, sir," he said. "I have some reservations, however."

"Such as?" Roussin asked from behind his drink.

Brewer sat forward. "For starters, how would we stay close enough to intervene when the crisis came? In order for your plan to succeed, Alfred would have to feign ignorance of

Black Rose's intended revenge and seek her out before her hired assassins found him. So we would need the location of her hideout, or at least knowledge of her immediate plans, and if we had those, we would not need the plan."

"Perhaps we could send several of our men along with him," Greene posited. "Mac and Mr. Cromwell, for instance."

"Cromwell?" Roussin lowered his glass. "Who is this?"

"A new lieutenant we picked up at the start of this voyage," Brewer explained. "He also happens to be the only man among us to ever score a point against Alfred in swordplay."

"Indeed?" The governor raised his eyebrows. "In that case, the solution presents itself, *mon capitan!* Alfred deserts. You search but cannot recover him before you are forced to leave to resume your search for Black Rose. Leave this Mr. Cromwell behind as well. After a week or so, I will discreetly let it be known that Alfred has been captured by Cromwell, who is willing to turn him over to Black Rose for double the current bounty. We could even have a small force secreted nearby, ready to help at a moment's notice."

He watched for any reaction from the Englishmen. *Capitan* Brewer's eye were hooded again, but his head was bobbing up and down slowly with his eyebrows raised; his expression indicated a generally good impression of the plan. Lieutenant Greene sat silently, watching his master. Like any good premier, he waited to see what his captain thought of an idea before voicing his own position.

"Well, *mon capitan?*" Roussin asked.

"An interesting plan, Governor, and one I will bring to my officers for their consideration. Alfred will, of course, be there as well. We shall see." He turned to Greene. "Benjamin, please give me some time alone with Governor Roussin. Perhaps you could check on our shore leave parties, make sure they are behaving themselves? I'll see you back on the ship."

"Of course, sir." Greene rose and came to attention before his captain, before bowing to the governor. He marched from the room, closing the door softly behind him.

Roussin watched the door even after it was shut. "That is an excellent officer, Captain."

"I know," Brewer said.

Roussin refilled their drinks. Brewer nodded his thanks.

"Now, Captain," Roussin asked, "what did you wish to discuss?"

Brewer took another drink and stared into the glass for a while before answering. "There is something you need to know, Governor. I have reason to believe that Black Rose has been here, in Martinique, as recently as our last visit here."

Roussin shrugged. "I would not be surprised if this were true, Captain, but why do you think so?"

Brewer relayed Dr. Spinelli's tale of the interview with the barmaid. "I believe that barmaid was Black Rose and that she discovered Alfred's identity from the doctor."

Roussin waved his free hand in a *there-you-have-it* sort of gesture. "Entirely probable, Captain. Do not be so surprised! Martinique has been known for decades as a place where pirates are known to visit, discretely and incognito, for the purpose of gathering information. They usually do not cause trouble while they are here."

He saw the Englishman set down his glass before looking down to his hands and begin to twist what Roussin took to be a wedding ring around the third finger of his left hand. Such things were not unheard of—although usually the bride was the one to wear the ring. Roussin had known a few sailors in the French navy to wear such rings, to remind themselves of the love awaiting them at home. Apparently, Brewer was one such as well.

"Tell me, Captain," he asked, "how is your dear wife?"

Brewer looked up, surprised by the question. "She is well, Governor," he said, "or at least she was when I last heard from her."

"She is in the Caribbean, is she not?"

"Yes. She and our daughter are staying with her father, the governor of St. Kitts."

"Daughter! *Mon Dieu!* Captain, you have been keeping secrets from me! *Georges!*"

The steward appeared in the doorway.

"Find the box of cigars I received from Havana yesterday, if you please. Captain, we must celebrate the birth of your daughter!"

The steward returned and held the box for both Roussin and Brewer to select a cigar, then he struck a match and lit both cigars.

"Fine tobacco," Brewer said after puffing his cigar to life. "It's good to see you are still in communication with the Spanish."

The governor blew a cloud of smoke toward the ceiling and smiled.

"Tell me, what did you name the little cherub?"

"Anne," Brewer said, "after Elizabeth's mother."

"I can see you miss them," Roussin said. "I miss my own Isabella. You should meet her, Captain! A true Spanish beauty if ever there was one!" He shook his head. "Unfortunately, she cannot be spared to join me; she must care for her sick mother in Cadiz."

"I'm sorry," Brewer said. "How long has it been?"

"Two years now. I kissed her goodbye when I sailed to join the South Atlantic squadron." He reached inside his waistcoat and brought out a locket. He opened it and gazed at the contents longingly before handing it over. "This is my Isabella."

Brewer accepted the locket and looked inside to see a miniature of a woman with dark hair piled high on her head, dark eyes, high cheek bones, and a long, graceful neck. He handed the locket back. "She is beautiful, Governor. You are a lucky man."

"Yes, I know." Roussin looked again at his wife's face before closing the locket and returning it to his pocket. He looked up in time to see Brewer pull a locket of his own from inside his uniform coat. The captain opened it and handed it to his host.

"This is my Elizabeth."

Roussin took the locket and admired the beautiful miniature inside. He handed it back with a smile. "Your bride is stunning, Captain. I pray the child gets her looks from her mother."

Brewer actually blushed, much to the amusement of his host. "Let's hope so," he said. "Right now, Governor, I need some provisions from my ship before we go out after Black Rose."

Roussin rose, and Brewer followed suit. "Of course, Captain." He turned toward his desk and stopped. When he turned again, Brewer thought he saw a devilish glint in the governor's eye.

"I am sorry, Captain," he said, "but we have recently had a number of ships come through requesting supplies, including several of His Majesty's warships. I'm afraid our resources are somewhat limited at the moment."

Brewer eyed the governor suspiciously. "I see. Well, Governor, what can you do for us?"

Roussin held out his hand, and Brewer shook it. The governor held his grip and said, "I am afraid, Captain, that I can only give you enough supplies to get as far as St. Kitts. Perhaps you can get what you need there."

Brewer smiled. "Governor, I am grateful for what you can do."

Lieutenants Greene and Cromwell walked down the waterfront lane toward the tavern where the doctor had his encounter on their last visit. Greene had met Cromwell and his division as they landed on the wharf, and had taken the opportunity to address those going on shore leave.

"Listen to me, you men!" he'd said in a loud voice. "Remember that we are guests in this port and conduct yourselves as such. Don't do anything that would embarrass the king or the captain! The last boat leaves for the ship at sundown; anyone who causes a delaywill have to answer to the captain! Dismissed!" He turned to the petty officer in charge of the boats. "Mr. Petrie, your men are scheduled for shore leave tomorrow, correct?"

"Aye, sir."

"Good. Then keep them here; don't let any of them wander. When you get enough returning men to fill a boat, go ahead and send them back. Be sure to have at least one boat here until sundown. You'll have to keep a good count of the men."

"Aye, sir."

Now the two lieutenants approached the inn, and Greene turned to Cromwell. "Let me know what you find out, if anyone even remembers her being here."

"Perhaps she makes a habit of it," Cromwell postulated, "coming here to gather information. According to the doctor, nobody took any particular notice of her. Maybe the staff was used to seeing her around."

Greene shrugged. "See what you can find out while you are inside. I shall be down the lane a piece." He pointed with his chin further on. "I remember Captain de Robespierre telling me about a little café where the food is exquisite."

Cromwell grinned. "Enjoy yourself, sir." Greene sauntered down the lane. Cromwell turned to see that only two of his division remained: Mr. Short, his divisional midshipman, and old Christian, the foretop lookout. Christian was notable because his uncle had been one of the ringleaders in the HMS *Bounty* mutiny of 1789. That Christian had been his mother's older brother and his namesake. He didn't like it to be known—he'd had some trouble with young lieutenants early in his career over it, so now he kept quiet. The man had taken a shine to Cromwell, probably because they both had "dark" ancestors in their past.

"You two are staying with me?" Cromwell asked them.

"Someone has to keep you out of trouble, sir," Christian said simply.

"What else do we have to do, Mr. Cromwell?" Short added.

The lieutenant chuckled and waved for them to follow him. He entered the inn and looked around before heading toward the table on the far wall, where the doctor had told him he'd sat when he met the barmaid. They took their seats, and Cromwell ordered three ales from the barmaid.

"Mr. Short, you go easy on the ale," Cromwell warned. "Christian, you better help him, so it looks like he's drinking it all."

Christian brightened up immediately. "Oh, aye, sir!"

Cromwell looked around. Their barmaid obviously was not who they were after; she was nearly as tall as he was, plus she was plain and blonde. He looked around and saw another moving between tables on the far side of the room. She was short and had dark hair, but Cromwell discounted her as well—there was simply no way anyone could call her pretty. The only other barmaid in the place was an Amazon who stayed behind the bar with the barkeep; she was certainly not the girl who had spoken with the doctor.

The barmaid returned with their drinks, and Cromwell dropped a couple coins on the tray. She turned to go, but he put his hand on her arm. She turned to see him holding three shillings in his hand.

"I have a question," he said.

She set the tray on the table and put her hands on her hips, her right hand close by the hilt of a dagger concealed in the waistline of her skirt.

Short noticed the weapon. "Lieutenant?"

"I see it, Mr. Short," he said quietly. "There's no need for that, Madam, I assure you. I am seeking a woman who worked here at one time. Some months back, my ship was here, and a shipmate came in here. He said the barmaid who spoke to him was the most beautiful woman he had ever seen, and I am here to see if he spoke the truth. What is your name?"

The barmaid eyed him suspiciously. "Darla."

"Well, Darla," Cromwell placed one of the shillings on the tray, "my shipmate said this woman was a barmaid. She was short, but she had long dark hair and a fair complexion. He also said she had dark eyes that could swallow a man's soul. Sound familiar?"

The corners of Darla's mouth curled ever so slightly upward, and she crossed her arms over her ample chest. Cromwell placed a second shilling on the tray and raised his eyebrows.

Darla looked around before leaning over and placing both hands on the table so she could speak quietly. "I think you mean Annie."

"Annie?" Short echoed.

Darla shot him a look before turning back to Cromwell. "Anne Bonney," she said in a near-whisper. "At least, that's what she said her name was. She shows up every few months and works for a few weeks, then she's gone again."

"Any idea when she might be back?" Cromwell asked.

Darla shook her head. "None. She comes and goes as she pleases." She pointed with her head at the barkeep. "Drake there is sweet on her, so he lets her work whenever she comes around."

"Does she come often?"

Darla shook her head. "I've seen her maybe five or six times, and I've worked her more than three years."

Cromwell set the third shilling on the tray. "Thank you, Darla."

The barmaid smiled. She picked up the tray and was gone.

"So," came a voice from the next table, "is that how Englishmen get the attention of a wench in these parts?"

Cromwell turned to see a man about his own age standing beside the next table over. He was thickly built through the chest and shoulders, and wavy brown hair hung down just past his shoulders. The scar that decorated his left cheek gave him a menacing look. A saber hung on his right hip. He eyed the tray as the barmaid passed by.

"Three shillings?" he sneered. "It seems you got one of the cheap ones."

"Why don't you enjoy your drink elsewhere and leave us alone," Cromwell said.

The man's face clouded over with anger, and the scar turned a deep red. He took a step in their direction when a voice bellowed from the bar.

"*Andre!*"

They turned to see the barkeep and the Amazon each holding two pistols. It was the barkeep who spoke.

"Sit down and enjoy your drink, or leave," he said. "Choose now."

Andre directed a menacing glance toward the bar before resuming his seat. Drake the barkeep set his pistols under the bar, but the Amazon held on to hers.

"That's better," Drake said. He began pouring drinks. "Darla, refills all around."

The barmaid picked up the tray from the bar and delivered drinks to Andre and his friends before coming to the Englishmen.

"Take care," she said quietly as she set the drinks on the table and collected the empty glasses. "He is a bully, that one."

"Who is he?" Short asked.

"Andre Suchet," she said, "youngest son of the Viscomte de Rochambeau. His father owns a large plantation outside of town, and Andre thinks that gives him privileges. He's the reason Drake has pistols under the bar." She picked up the tray and walked away.

"Finish your drinks," Cromwell said to his companions, "then we can explore the town."

"Good idea," Andre said. "The further you are away from here, the better."

Cromwell had enough at that point and started to rise, but old Christian gripped his forearm and held him down.

"Mr. Cromwell," he said, "I think we'd better go. We got what we came for."

Andre's head snapped around. "Cromwell? Did you say *Cromwell*? Would you by any chance be related to Oliver?"

Oh, no, Cromwell thought, *here we go again.* "Yes, I am," he said.

Andre rose. "Good! Now this is what you English would call a fortuitous development. You see, I am a direct descendant of your Charles the First through his son during his time in France, before he was called back to the throne of England as Charles the Second." He drew his saber, a slow, deadly sound. "Now I shall have revenge for my family."

Cromwell stood up. Behind him, Christian leaned over and quickly whispered in Short's ear. The midshipman nodded and slid out of his seat and made his way out of the inn.

The barkeep and the Amazon had their guns out again. "Andre, not in here."

"Stay out of this, Drake! This is none of your affair!"

"Anything in my place is my affair, Andre," Drake said. He cocked his pistols. "Remember what the governor said after the last time. I *will* shoot you where you stand; I don't care who your pater is."

The sound of the hammers being pulled back got Andre's attention. His eyes shifted quickly to the bar, and he saw two barrels pointed squarely at his chest. He turned to his quarry.

"Let's step outside, murderer," he said.

"I haven't murdered anyone," Cromwell said.

"Your ancestor murdered mine," the Frenchman insisted. "That's enough for me."

"I hold to no such reckoning."

Andre raised his saber until the tip was no more than an inch from the lieutenant's chest. The Amazon now cocked her pistols. Andre's friends looked nervously to the bar.

"I don't calculate," Andre said, "that Drake can shoot me before I can run you through. Not from this distance. It's your choice; in here, or outside."

"Mr. Cromwell," Christian said from behind him, "outside would perhaps be best. There are civilians in here, and I don't think he cares."

"Yes, of course," Cromwell said. He looked at Andre. "After you."

The Frenchman grinned wildly and rammed his saber home in its scabbard. He pointed to Darla. "If you try to scurry out the back door, Englishman, I will come back for her."

"No need for threats. I'm right behind you."

Andre turned and marched out the door and into the street.

Cromwell turned to his companion.

"As soon as I'm outside, go out the back door and make for the wharf. I'm the one he wants, not you. You need to get back with the information."

"I'm not leaving you, sir," the old tar said. "Besides, there's no need."

"What? Why?" He caught himself and looked around. "Where's Mr. Short?" Christian just stared at him, and Cromwell smiled. "Very well, Mr. Christian, let us step outside."

On the way out, he said to the barkeep, "Sorry for the fuss."

Drake shrugged. "Something of the sort usually happens with that one. He looks for any excuse to start a fight."

The lieutenant nodded to Darla and stepped out into the sunshine.

Andre was standing on the far side of the lane, stripped to his shirtsleeves. His saber was in his hand. Cromwell noticed that Andre's friends were posted at either end of the lane, whether to prevent his escape or attack from behind was anyone's guess.

Andre stepped forward into the street. "So, now the son of the murderer of kings is called out, eh?"

Cromwell removed his coat and handed it to Christian, along with his hat. "I will give you one chance to walk away," he said as he drew his blade.

The Frenchman raised his saber. Cromwell sighed and did the same.

Andre moved to the left and attacked immediately. Cromwell easily turned the heavy blade away and sidestepped to let his enemy pass. Andre turned quickly and moved in behind a flurry of vicious slashes up high. Cromwell gave ground grudgingly as he searched for a weakness in his adversary's attacks. One near-miss cut a neat rent in his shirt, a move which distracted him just long enough for Andre to close in and deal a blow to the jaw which sent the lieutenant flying backward and to the ground. The Frenchman followed up quickly with a savage kick to the ribs. Cromwell was able to roll just enough to get his hands up and block the next kick; he even managed to twist the foot and bring the Frenchman hard to the ground. Cromwell rose quickly and retrieved his sword, although he found that pain in his ribs now restricted his movements. Ten yards away, his opponent rose as well.

"Traitors beget traitors!" Andre taunted him. "All your kind should have gone with Robespierre to the guillotine! That is the only just price for regicide!"

"You know," Cromwell said, "neither Charles nor Louis would have died had their friends known how to fight, rather than merely talk!" He raised his sword again.

Andre roared like a raging bull and charged with his saber high, ready to slice down from on high and split the Englishman's skull. He never got the chance. Cromwell ducked inside the strike and drove the hilt of his sword into the Frenchman's gut, causing him to almost double over in pain. With all his might, Cromwell drove his fist into his enemy's cheekbone, the hilt around the fist acting like brass knuckles. The Frenchman flew up and back, nearly senseless from the blow, and even further dazed when the back of his head struck the road. His vision clouded, and when it cleared he saw the point of his opponent's sword one inch from his throat.

Old Christian saw the Frenchman's friends begin to close in. "Mr. Cromwell!"

"Your friends best stay where they are," the lieutenant said to his enemy. "There is certainly no way they could get to me before I could spit your throat. Even should they shoot me, I will fall on my sword and drive it through you with my dying breath." The sword tip pressed the Frenchman's skin. "Tell them!"

"Stay where you are!"

"Mr. Christian?"

"They have stopped, Lieutenant."

"Good." He twisted the sword point into the neck a little, and the Frenchman hissed in pain. "Now, my friend..."

"Mr. Cromwell!"

He looked up to see Lieutenant Greene pushing his way through the crowd with Mr. Short right behind him. The two men said nothing, but volumes were spoken by the eyes of both men. Finally, Cromwell nodded, and the sword point lifted, allowing a trickle of blood to drip down Andre's neck. Cromwell put his foot on the other's chest and leaned in close.

"My ship will be here another day or two," he said. "I suggest you remain at home until after we have left the island. If I see you again, sir, believe me when I say, *history will repeat itself.* Do you understand?"

"Oui."

"Bloody good." Cromwell cleaned the tip of his blade, directed his sword into its sheath, and turned away from his opponent. He marched up the lane with old Christian beside him and Lieutenant Greene and Mr. Short right behind. They were nearly to the wharf when they met the captain, returning from his meeting with Governor Roussin. The men came to attention and saluted.

"Gentlemen," Brewer greeted them. "Mr. Cromwell, you look like you've had a bit of exercise. Anything I'd be interested in hearing?"

Cromwell hesitated and turned to look at Lieutenant Greene behind him. The premier said nothing, so Cromwell faced his captain. "I don't think so, sir. But Mr. Short, Mr. Christian, and I were able to pick up some significant intelligence on the barmaid Doctor Spinelli spoke to on our last visit."

"Really? Then let us return to the ship, and I will hear your report, Lieutenant."

Brewer and Greene headed for the wharf, and Cromwell turned to his companions.

"Thank you both for how you conducted yourselves back there," he said. "You are free to stay ashore until sundown, if you wish."

The two looked at each other and shook their heads. "Thank you, sir," Short said, answering for them both, "but we've had about all the shore leave we can handle. We'll go back now."

Aboard the *Phoebe*, Brewer led the way below, followed by Greene and Cromwell. The sentry closed the door behind them. Alfred appeared in the pantry door.

"Alfred, refreshments, please," Brewer asked.

"Aye, sir."

The three officers went to sit in the more comfortable day cabin. After Alfred delivered their wine, Lieutenant Cromwell related everything told to them by the barmaid Darla. When he was done, Captain Brewer looked satisfied. "Well," he said, "that cinches it, doesn't it?"

"I don't understand, sir," Greene said.

"Don't you? Benjamin, Anne Bonney was a famous pirate a hundred years ago," Brewer explained. "She was arrested for piracy along with Calico Jack Rackham in the 1720s. He was hung, but she pleaded pregnancy and so escaped the noose. The plan was to execute her after she gave birth, but somehow she disappeared. Nobody knows what happened to her."

Cromwell grunted and took a drink.

"Mr. Cromwell?" Greene prompted.

"Nothing, sir." He could see nobody believed him, so he spoke up. "Well, what with the doctor quite probably speaking to Black Rose herself and not knowing it, wouldn't it be strange indeed if this Black Rose turned out to be a descendant of Anne Bonney?"

Greene laughed. "That would certainly add to our tally of descendants of the famous and infamous." He turned to Brewer. "So, sir, what about provisions?"

Brewer smiled. "That, too, is a tale, Benjamin. When the good governor heard about the birth of my daughter, his supply situation changed radically. It seems that he can only spare us enough supplies to allow us to make it to St. Kitts. So, gentlemen, I propose a toast to the conscientious Governor Roussin."

The other two officers raised their glasses and drank to the governor's health.

Brewer continued. "Tomorrow, Lieutenant Rivkins' division has shore leave. We shall use the time to provision for the voyage to St. Kitts and sail with the morning tide the next day. Any questions? Benjamin?"

"None, sir," Greene said. "And I look forward to meeting your daughter myself.

* * * * *

HMS *Phoebe* sailed gracefully into the harbor at St. Kitts. Captain Brewer stood in his usual spot, aft of the wheel on the starboard rail, where he watched as Mr. Cromwell conned the ship to the point where they would heave to and receive the pilot. Mr. Greene stood beside him and scanned the harbor with a glass.

"Sir?" Greene said. "Seems like the garrison is on alert. The guns are all manned and run out, and lookouts are at every posting."

"Really?" Brewer reached for a glass and confirmed the sighting for himself. "You're right, Mr. Greene. I wonder what it means? I shall ask the governor when I pay my respects."

The pilot came aboard, but rather than go to the wheel, the man made a beeline for the captain. He stopped and knuckled his forehead. His hand trembled as he held out a letter.

"Beggin' yer pardon, Captain," he said, "but the governor said you was to get this as soon as you entered the harbor." He saluted again and headed for the wheel.

Brewer swallowed his puzzlement at this strange turn of events and examined the letter. He noted the governor's seal on the wax as he broke it and unfolded the single page within. Mr. Greene stopped what he was doing and watched his captain's expression change to one of concern.

"Midshipman of the watch!" Brewer suddenly bellowed. "Call away the gig! Alert Mr. McCleary I am going ashore! Mr. Greene, with me!" He called that last over his shoulder as he was headed for the companionway stair.

Greene caught up with his captain as they reached the cabin door. Once inside, he asked, "Captain? What is it?"

Brewer handed him the letter as he called to Alfred for his best uniform to see the governor. Greene read slowly.

Captain Brewer,

The governor requests that you come to his house immediately upon receiving this letter. He will explain when you arrive.

Your Obedient Servant,
Captain Nathaniel Erikson
Garrison Commander

"I'm going ashore, Benjamin," Brewer said. "No shore leave until you hear from me. You may send Mr. Rivkins to make arrangements for provisioning. Be ready to leave on the morning tide if necessary."

"Sir, are you sure this is necessary?" Greene asked.

Brewer grabbed the letter from Greene's hand and held it up between them. *"He did not write this himself, Benjamin! Something is very wrong. I must go at once."*

Brewer made the journey ashore in complete silence. It took all his control to stop his mind from racing and to remain seated, there in the stern sheets of the gig, beside his coxswain. McCleary stole an occasional glance sideways at his captain; to say he was concerned would be an understatement. In all his years as coxswain, he had never seen Brewer like this. But he knew his captain well enough to know that he should remain quiet for now; the captain would talk when he was ready. When they reached the wharf, Brewer was up and gone leaving only a curt order to wait for him.

At the end of the wharf, Brewer found a carriage waiting for him. He was further alarmed to find that Drury, the governor's normal driver, was not at the reins. Brewer resisted the impulse to question the footmen and boarded the carriage. The driver whipped up the horses, and they sped through the streets toward the governor's house.

Brewer was met at the door by a uniformed officer. "Captain Brewer? I am Captain Erikson, commanding the garrison of St. Kitts. Will you follow me, please?"

The officer turned without waiting for a reply and led Brewer to the governor's study. He knocked once before opening the door and entering. Brewer followed him inside and found his father-in-law seated before the window with dressings around his head and forearm.

"Henry?" he exclaimed as he rushed to his side. "What happened? Where's Elizabeth?"

"Sit down, William," Governor Danforth replied, nodding toward the seat opposite him. Brewer sat, elbows on his knees. "Something strong for the captain! Steel yourself, my son. Elizabeth is gone. There was a pirate attack three days ago, and she was kidnapped."

The blood drained from Brewer's face. He closed his eyes and gripped the arms of the chair to help regain control of himself. He drew in a long, slow breath and expelled it before opening his eyes again and leaning forward. "Anne?"

"She is here, safe and sound," Danforth reassured him. "Elizabeth instructed the girl, Sally, to claim the child as her own."

Brewer's mind whirled possibilities about like a hurricane. He looked up and asked, "What did the pirates say?"

The governor shut his eyes in pain at the memory. "They brought us into this room after killing many of the servants. Their leader asked which one was the wife of the English Captain Brewer. Elizabeth stepped forward, and they took her."

Brewer shuddered. He fell back against the chair, breathing heavily. His father-in-law eyed him with concern. At last, the captain opened his spoke, his voice husky. "May I see Anne, please?"

His father-in-law's face softened. "Of course." He looked to Captain Erikson, who stood next to the door. "Please send for Sally and my granddaughter."

A servant appeared at Brewer's elbow and held out a try with a glass containing an amber liquid. Brewer nodded his thanks and took a long, slow drink, allowing the liquor to calm his nerves. He set the glass on the table just as the door opened and a maid entered, carrying his daughter. Brewer bounded from the chair and took the babe in his arms. He gazed at her face and saw her smile as she recognized her long-absent father. He held her cheek to his own, feeling a tear escape his eye and touch them both. He kissed her gently on the forehead and looked to the maid. "What is your name?"

"Sally, sir." She curtsied.

"Ah," the captain said. "Then it is you I have to thank for my daughter's life."

"Oh, no, sir. That was all Miss Elizabeth. She instructed me what to do."

"I see." He returned the baby to her. "Still, I am in your debt."

The maid curtsied again and departed with the child.

"William."

Something in the tone of his father-in-law's voice struck fear in the captain's soul. He turned slowly and saw the older man was now holding a letter stained with blood. Brewer resumed his seat, and the governor handed him the letter. Brewer took it and stared at the blood before looking again to his father-in-law.

Danforth shook his head. "The blood upon it is mine. You will find the seal broken; I judged it necessary to read it as soon as they left."

"Yes, of course." Brewer took a deep breath to steel himself again, then he opened the letter.

Captain Brewer,

You have someone I want. His name is Alfred, and I understand he is your servant. He killed the love of my life, Roberto Cofresi, and now I shall have my revenge.

You will bring him to me at Porto Bello in Panama. From the bay, you will see a fortress upon a hill to the southeast. It is called La Venganza del Pirata. Ask one of the locals, if you must. I'm sure they can point out the path to you.

I strongly advise you to come at once upon receipt of this note. Should you delay, or if my patience should run out, you will never see your wife again.

At the bottom of the letter, he found not a name, but a drawing of a black flower.

"Black Rose," he whispered without looking up. "Black Rose has my wife." He dropped the letter into his lap and buried his head in his hands.

"I am sorry, William," his father-in-law said softly. "Is this Alfred still aboard your ship?"

Brewer lifted his head and sighed. "Yes," he said. He picked up his drink and drained it in a single draught. Danforth noticed a change in his son-in-law's countenance: anger, combined with a fierce resolve. When he spoke, his voice carried a promise of vengeance. "Black Rose just made the last mistake of her career."

He rose and scanned the letter again. " *La Venganza del Pirata.* That means 'The Pirate's Revenge', doesn't it?"

He tossed the letter on the governor's desk and began to pace the room. After a few crossings, he addressed his father-in-law. "Henry," he said, "I must leave at once. My ship must be provisioned for sea immediately."

"I shall send a note to the docks to give HMS *Phoebe* unconditional priority."

"Thank you. May I use your desk? I must write a report. I need you to send it to the admiral at Port Royal as soon as possible."

"A packet was to leave today with my own report. When we saw you enter the harbor, I ordered a delay. It can leave as soon as your report is delivered."

Brewer rose and placed his hand upon the governor's good shoulder and squeezed by way of thanks. He went to the desk and sat.

"Writing paper is in the top drawer on the right," Danforth said over his shoulder.

Brewer opened the drawer and pulled out several sheets. He picked up the quill and reached for the inkwell, only to pause and look at his father-in-law. "Henry, I promise to do my best to bring Elizabeth back to you."

Danforth met his son-in-law's eye. "I know you will, William."

Brewer began writing his report for Admiral Cartwright. He hardly noticed the servants come in and take the governor upstairs to his bed. When he finished the report, he read it over again and, satisfied with the contents, folded and sealed it. He looked up to see Captain Erikson still standing at the door.

"Captain," he said, holding out the report, "please see that this makes it to the packet that is to carry the governor's report to Jamaica."

"Yes, sir," Erikson said.

Brewer rose and came around the desk. He stopped at the captain's side. "How badly was the town damaged in the attack?"

"The town wasn't damaged at all," Erikson said. "The pirates took a round-about path through the woods so they could arrive here without being seen by anyone."

"I see. So, kidnapping Elizabeth was the entire purpose of the raid."

"So it seems."

Brewer sighed. "What was the butcher's bill?"

"Ten dead in the cabin out back, one of them a pirate," Erikson reported. "Four more in the barn, all ours. Three dead in the room off the kitchen, two women and a boy. Two pirates dead upstairs, apparently killed by the governor when they entered his bedroom."

"Good for him," Brewer said under his breath. He looked to Erikson. "I am going upstairs to say farewell, then I shall return to my ship. We sail as soon as provisioning is complete."

Erikson shook his hand. "Good luck, Captain."

Brewer went upstairs but found his father-in-law asleep. He stood in the doorway and tried to imagine the combat that allowed Danforth to take down two pirates and still walk away with his life. He shook his head in wonder and breathed a silent thanks to God for preserving the old man.

On his way out, he found Sally and Anne in the baby's room. Sally was seated in the same rocking chair where Brewer had watched Elizabeth nurse their child. Anne was asleep in her crib. The maid was startled by his sudden entrance and made to rise, but Brewer waved her back into the chair and went to his daughter's crib. He gazed at her: sleeping peacefully, completely unaware of what had happened to her mother. He envied her that peace. He reached down and tenderly brushed her cheek with the back of his finger, careful not to wake her. "Farewell, little one," he whispered to her. "I must go now and bring your mother back to you. That is my promise to you." He looked up to see Sally now standing before the rocker.

"Thank you again for all you did to keep Anne safe," he said. "You have my gratitude."

"I haven't been here very long, sir, but your wife has been kind to me, and it is a joy to do whatever I can to help her."

Brewer took her hands in his. "I will bring her back. Pray for us."

"I shall. God be with you."

He stepped back and bowed to her. He blew a kiss to his sleeping girl and left the room.

CHAPTER ELEVEN

The journey back to the ship passed quickly. Once aboard, Brewer called for the first lieutenant, sailing master, and Dr. Spinelli to meet him in his cabin. When they were assembled, Brewer took the unusual step of closing the door to the day cabin and stationing Mac outside it as a guard.

"Gentlemen," he said after he resumed his seat beneath the stern windows, "I have called you here as a de facto council of war. Black Rose raided the island three days ago and kidnapped my wife." He paused for a moment, taking in the expressions of outrage on the men's faces. Mr. Sweeney actually lunged forward, as if he could somehow apprehend the kidnappers by sheer force of will. Brewer described the event as the governor had told him, then pulled the letter out of his pocket and showed it to them. "We are commanded to deliver Alfred to them at Porto Bello in Panama." He handed the letter to Mr. Greene. "Mr. Sweeney, work me up a course. Mr. Greene, how goes the provisioning?"

"Nearly complete, sir. Alfred and Winfield are ashore now, along with Mr. Franks, the purser. The lighter is scheduled to come alongside at first light to top off the water tank. After that, we shall be ready to go."

"Good," Brewer said.

"Well, so much for our springing a trap," Dr. Spinelli remarked. "What will we do when we get to Panama?"

Brewer looked at him sternly. "We take my wife back."

"How?" Spinelli said. "We can't just give them Alfred in trade."

Brewer blinked and lowered his eyes. "No, of course not. I have no answer for you, Doctor, at least not yet. That is part of the reason I have called you all together. Mr. Sweeney, do you know that coast?"

"I was there once, Captain, several years ago. Porto Bello's got a lovely harbor, nice and deep, well sheltered against anything less than a hurricane. At one time, it was Spain's main port on the Atlantic. Captain Morgan sacked it in 1668 and demanded nearly a half-million pesos ransom from the Spanish governor-general or he would burn the town. The governor-general refused, so he burned it."

"Well, we won't be doing any of that," Brewer said. "The letter said the fortress is to the southeast and visible from the harbor. That means they'll be able to see us as we approach."

Greene handed the letter to the doctor. "Perhaps there's a way to get to the fortress without being seen? Could we find an inlet where we could land and send a force through the woods? Surprise them as they did the governor's house?"

Brewer looked to his sailing master. "Mr. Sweeney?"

Sweeney thought for a minute, but finally he shook his head. "I don't know of any, sir."

Brewer pursed his lips as he thought. "I'll have Mac check the crew, see if we have anyone who is familiar with that coast. Who knows? We might get lucky." He rose and began to pace. "For now, this information must remain in this room. The crew will be told after we sail. In the meantime, I want you all to be thinking about what we might be able to do when we get there. Dismissed."

He heard them file out of the room behind him and was irritated when he turned and found the doctor still in his seat. "What part of 'Dismissed' do you not understand?"

"So that's how it will be, is it?" the doctor replied. "I'm worried about her, too, William."

Brewer stopped pacing and swallowed the frustration that was brewing up inside him. He looked at the deck. "I'm sorry, Adam. I know you are. I feel so helpless. I want to scream and rip Black Rose's head from her shoulders, and I can't." The doctor looked at him with concern, and Brewer sighed. "I also know I can't take it out on the crew. I'll be careful."

Spinelli rose. "I'll stop in later to check on you. See if you're up for a beating in chess." He headed for the door, then stopped and turned back. "William? You need to decide now what you're going to say to Alfred when he gets back. At the latest, he'll know everything after we leave harbor in the morning."

Brewer nodded. "Thanks, Adam."

After the doctor departed, Brewer looked around the cabin again, as though reassuring himself that he was truly alone. He went and sat on the settee, buried his face in his hands, and wondered what he was going to do. *How can I ask Alfred to surrender himself for Elizabeth? Would I ask him if it weren't my wife in question?* He shook his head in agony and pushed his face harder into his hands. Suddenly, he heard a young voice clearing his throat and looked up to see Pudge standing sheepishly in the doorway.

"Yes, Pudge?" the captain said as he sat upright.

The boy shifted, fidgeting from one foot to the other. "Well, sir, begging yer pardon 'n all," he said, "but Alfred taught me that when you come in, if he's not here I'm supposed to ask you if there's anything I can get for you."

Brewer found himself touched by the lad's simple devotion to his duty. "Has Alfred taught you how to make coffee yet?"

Pudge's face lit up. "Yes, sir! I mean, he's been helping me, but I think I can do it myself! Shall I?"

"Yes, please." Pudge's head bobbed up and down in excitement and he turned to run back to the pantry. He was a step into the run, and Brewer was about to correct him on it, when suddenly the lad caught himself and came to a screeching halt that was almost comical in its intensity. He took a deep breath and forced himself to walk (albeit swiftly) to the pantry to complete his mission. Brewer had to put his hand over his mouth to stop himself from laughing out loud.

The captain sat back and leaned his head on the back of the settee, grateful for the interruption. He rose and walked to the cabin door to ask the sentry to pass the word for the doctor. He turned to find Pudge sticking his head out of the pantry, probably to see if he had left.

"Pudge," he said, "I've just sent for the doctor. Could you please make that coffee for two?"

The young head bobbed excitedly again. "Oh, aye, sir!"

Brewer went to his desk and opened it, taking out the box that held his *Légion d'honneur*, presented to him on St. Helena by the Emperor Napoleon himself. He returned to his seat and opened it, staring at the white enamel cross with a gold medallion in the center surmounted by a gold crown, resting on a cloth of velvet. He touched it lightly, and memories of the Emperor flooded his mind. "What would you do?" he whispered to the medallion.

A knock at the door signaled the arrival of Dr. Spinelli. The sentry admitted him and closed the door, leaving the doctor to find his own way aft. Spinelli stopped at the door of the after cabin and watched in silence as his captain gazed at the box in his hand.

"Is that what I think it is?" he asked.

Brewer sighed and sat back in the settee. "Probably," he said, and he held the box out for the doctor's examination. Spinelli stepped into the room and took the box, admiring the medallion before handing it back.

"Asking for advice?"

The captain shrugged. He closed the box and rose, stepping past his friend to return the box to his desk. He pulled out his chess set and motioned toward the table. The doctor sat dwn across from him, silently accepting the challenge. The two men set up the board as Pudge emerged from the pantry carrying Alfred's silver platter with two steaming cups of dark, aromatic coffee upon it. He set one in front of each man and stepped back.

"What's this?" the doctor asked.

"Pudge's first solo attempt at coffee," the captain said. He raised his cup to his opponent. "Shall we?"

The two men brought their cups to their lips and sipped cautiously. To their surprise, the brew was good. Not up to Alfred's standards, but definitely on a par with Mac's coffee.

"Well done, Pudge," Brewer said as he raised his cup in salute.

"Yes," the doctor agreed. "Very good, Pudge."

The lad's face beamed, but he managed to control himself and bowed at the compliments. "Thank you, gentlemen." He turned and left the room.

Spinelli set his cup down. "Captain, what is this you have created?"

Brewer shook his head and looked toward the pantry. "I'm not sure, but I think it will be interesting to find out." He took another drink and set his cup down. "You go first."

The doctor turned the board so he was playing white and moved his king's pawn. Brewer replied with his queen's knight and was rewarded when the doctor raised an eyebrow. He was determined to concentrate on his game, and so relieve the anxiety that was preying upon his mind, and the best way he could think of to do that was to try new strategies. All went well for the first fifteen moves or so, but then the doctor found a gap in his defenses and swiftly moved his queen and a bishop into threatening positions. Brewer frowned as he studied the board.

The doctor sat back in his chair. "Still thinking about Alfred?"

Brewer nodded. He reached out to move a rook but thought better of it and rubbed his face with both hands. "What am I supposed to do? I can't imagine asking Alfred to give himself up; I have no right do make that kind of command decision. Besides, I've pretty much come to the conclusion that the question would never come up if it weren't *my wife* we were talking about. So Alfred stays. We have to find another way to rescue Elizabeth."

"William," Spinelli paused to move a knight, "you may want to watch Alfred when we arrive in Panama. I wouldn't put it past him to dash off on his own to try to trade himself for Elizabeth."

Brewer castled to his queen's side. "Yes, I'd thought of that. I will have to have that talk with him, but I can't do it just now."

Spinelli moved a pawn, which opened up an attack by a bishop and consequently sealed his captain's doom. "Checkmate."

Brewer leaned back and smiled. "Well, that didn't work out very well, did it?" He stared at the board. "Tell me, Adam: how do we announce this to the crew—or how do we let them find out about it—without it seeming like a personal vendetta on my part? I'd rather tell them about it than to have rumors running rampant about the ship! But how do I? What can I say?"

The doctor crossed his arms over his chest in a gesture of mild rebuke. "You tell them, Captain; that's all. I think you will find that the fact that Elizabeth is your wife will pull the crew to you rather than the other way around. It boils down to this, sir: we have orders to track down Black Rose and eliminate her as a threat. Black Rose has kidnapped a British citizen, and we know where she is being held. So, we go rescue her, just as we would any other British citizen. The crew will follow you."

Brewer's eyes flashed to his friend before returning to the board. "I hope you're right," he said, as he began to set the board up for another game.

* * * * *

The lighter finished its work and pulled away from the ship, and HMS *Phoebe* was, in all respects, ready for sea. Captain Brewer ordered the ship warped out of the harbor, and boats were swiftly dispatched over the side for the work. The ship's anchor was lowered into one of the boats, which then rowed off toward the harbor mouth. When the anchor chain was paid out, the boat dropped the anchor. Hands were put to the capstan to take in the chain, which action actually pulled the ship toward the anchor. This sequence was repeated three times before the ship was clear of the harbor and able to catch a wind.

"Mr. Greene," Brewer said from the quarterdeck, "please give the boats' crews and the men at the capstan a 'Well Done!' from me. Mr. Sweeney, as soon as the boats are back aboard, set a course southwest for Colombia."

"Aye, Captain," replied the sailing master.

As soon as the boats were aboard and secured, Brewer turned to his premier.

"Mr. Greene, I wish to address the crew. Please have them assemble aft."

"Aye, sir," Greene touched his hat and picked up a speaking trumpet. "All hands lay aft! All hands! Lay aft!"

The men assembled, and their captain stepped forward to address them with a loud voice. "Men of *Phoebe*! I shall bring you up to date on our mission. As you know, we have been pursuing Black Rose, prepared to devote the entirety of our cruise on seeking her out. Well, now she has saved us the trouble! She sent some of her men onto the island of St. Kitts and kidnapped a British citizen, my wife Elizabeth. This took place three days before we arrived. Her father, the governor, valiantly killed two of the pirates, but he was wounded in the struggle and those whom the pirates did not kill were compelled to surrender at sword's point. The pirates left a letter for me: their prisoner will be held at a fortress outside of Porto Bello in Panama. That is where we are heading. One way or the other, Black Rose's reign of terror will end. I'm telling you this, because I want no rumors or idle gossip flying around the ship. Do your jobs, and all will end well."

"Sir!" a voice came from the crowd. "What about your daughter? Is she safe?"

"Yes, thank God!" Brewer said. "Elizabeth kept her wits about her, and did not let the pirates discover the potential for a second hostage."

"We're with you, Captain!" The cry brought a cheer that rose from the crew. Brewer was touched by this demonstration and lifted his hat to the crew. He turned to Greene. "Dismiss the men, if you please."

"Aye, sir." Greene raised the speaking trumpet again and gave the order. The men dispersed, and Dr. Spinelli stepped up.

"You see, Captain, they are with you," he said softly.

"Yes," was all he could say aroubd the lump in his throat.

Brewer made his way below to his cabin. As he entered, he found Alfred awaiting him, standing in the pantry doorway. Brewer motioned to the table.

"Won't you sit down, Alfred?"

The captain took his seat, and Alfred tookthe chair on Brewer's left. "How much do you know?"

"Pretty much everything, sir," he said. "Black Rose has your wife?"

"Yes."

"And she has offered to trade her for me."

"Yes."

Alfred gazed upward for a long moment before saying, "I will do it, sir."

Brewer nearly teared up at that. He'd always thought well of Alfred, and he was pretty sure the feelings were mutual, but this was the first time Alfred had said anything to indicate a depth of regard. Brewer looked at the table and closed his eyes for a moment before looking up again. He shook his head.

"Thank you, Alfred, but that will not be necessary. I have no intention of trading you for Elizabeth; neither do I plan on abandoning her to Black Rose. We are working on a way to rescue Elizabeth. According to the note left for me, Black Rose has taken her to a fortress outside of Porto Bello in Panama. It is on a hill southeast of the harbor. I am to deliver you there in exchange for Elizabeth." Brewer grinned, but his servant thought there was not much confidence in it. Brewer went on, "But we will have a few surprises worked up by the time we get there. Tell me, Alfred, do your talents extend to planning operations?"

The servant's head raised a bit. "Why, yes, sir. I have some experience in this."

"Good. In that case, I want you to sit in on our next council and help us plan the rescue."

"It will be my pleasure, sir," Alfred said as he rose. "If there's nothing else, I believe I need some time on deck."

"Of course," Brewer said. He watched his servant bow and leave the cabin, and he wondered what was going on inside his head.

Alfred found, to his consternation, that his walk on the deck did nothing to help him. He came to the conclusion that there was only one thing to be done, so he headed below deck. He stuck his head in the gun room and found the one he was looking for. Lieutenant Cromwell was sitting at the table, reading a newspaper and sipping a glass of wine. He looked up when Alfred knocked on the door frame.

"Alfred? Is there something I can do for you?"

"Yes, sir," the diminutive man said as he stepped inside the doorway and held out a pair of wooden practice swords.

"If you have a few minutes." Cromwell closed his book and rose. "At your service, sir."

The lieutenant followed the older man out of the gun room, and the two men made their way up a deck and went forward. Alfred was hoping for a modicum of privacy (the noise of their workout was bound to draw the attention of off-duty onlookers eventually), but he found Pudge there, practicing his knife-throwing. The two men stopped and watched the boy throw his knife four times at a white circle painted on the wall from about ten paces; three of the four stuck, and two of those were in the circle.

"You're getting better, my young friend," Alfred said as they approached.

"Thanks to your instruction," he said. "Hello, Lieutenant."

"Hello, Pudge," Cromwell replied. "I see your training is proceeding. How is your schoolwork coming along?"

Pudge scowled. "Writing letters is dull, Mr. Cromwell. And doing sums seems pointless. When am I ever going to need that stuff?"

The two adults shared a smile. "Well, Pudge," Cromwell said as he took the lad's knife and backed up another ten paces before throwing the knife, sticking it in the very center of the circle.

Pudge stared at him.

Cromwell went on, now sure he had the lad's attention. "Letters will be very important when you wish to write a letter to a pretty girl." Pudge gave him a look that said what he thought of that possibility. Cromwell ignored the look and went on. "As for sums, Mr. Rivkins told me not long after I came on board that our captain had, as he put it, 'a nose for prize money.' Is that true?" Pudge looked to Alfred, who nodded. "Well, then," Cromwell said, "how are you going to know if you are getting your fair share if you can't divide?

And how will you know how much money you have if you cannot add? Sums are very important to a gentleman."

The boy sighed. "I guess that' so." He noticed the swords. "Are you going to fight? May I watch? I'll keep score for you!"

Cromwell looked to Alfred, who shook his head.

"Not this time, Pudge," Alfred said. He paused as the ship's bell rang four times. "Besides, don't you have an appointment in sickbay with the doctor?"

The boy hung his head. "Yes, sir." He sheathed his knife and made his way below.

Cromwell watched him go and smiled. "I hope I'm around to watch him grow up."

"You will be." Alfred tossed him a wooden sword. He held the other up in the *en garde* position. "Shall we?"

The lieutenant saluted with his sword and extended it to touch his opponent's. They began. Alfred made a couple probing attacks, easily parried by Cromwell, before moving swiftly to his right and making a thrust at the taller man's ribs. Cromwell deflected the blow and moved to his right as well. "Shall we dance?" he asked.

"Let's," Alfred replied.

And the two men went to battle. Cromwell struck with a high slash and jumped quickly back to avoid Alfred's counterstroke. The lieutenant made a series of thrusts designed to put Alfred squarely on his heels and on the defensive, but he was only partly successful. Alfred sidestepped the final thrust and brought his sword down sharply on Cromwell's forearm.

The lieutenant rubbed his arm as they reset to begin again. "I should have seen that coming."

Alfred smiled and attacked low. Cromwell blocked, forcing Alfred to the side while the lieutenant got in beside him and landed a blow to the side of his head. The next advance was a slash by Alfred; Cromwell parried and rushed in behind it. This allowed him to get close enough to grab his opponent by the front of the shirt and hurl him backward and to the deck. Alfred sat up from the deck and looked astonished.

"Your mind is elsewhere today," Cromwell said. "Not that I blame you. What say you work out your frustrations, eh? Come on!"

Alfred jumped to his feet and ran at Cromwell. The lieutenant dropped to the deck, allowing his opponent to sail over him, but he was not prepared for what came next. Alfred landed, turned, and dove at Cromwell's legs, his sword stabbing the man in the thigh. The lieutenant was staggered by the blow and went backward a couple steps. This gave Alfred time to attack from the left, fend off a weak parry on Cromwell's part, and slash at his kidneys.

The two stepped back a few paces, each one breathing heavily.

"So, that's how it's going to be," Cromwell said. "Very well; the kid gloves are off, sir!"

And so the battle became a war. Attack was met by parry and counterstroke, a thrust to the chest by a slash landing on the side or leg. Cromwell fought in close whenever he could and one time succeeded in grabbing Alfred and throwing him across the deck again; twice Alfred was able to sweep Cromwell's legs out from under him and send him to the deck. Alfred struck with all the pent-up frustration and fury that he had held within, while Cromwell did his best to fend off the attacks and strike back when he could.

Of course, the sheer rage of their attacks and the noise of wood striking wood with such force was bound to attract attention on a ship as small as a frigate. Soon nearly every man who was off duty was in attendance, cheering for one or the other whenever a blow was landed. The ruckus even brought the doctor and Pudge up from the sickbay. At one point, the crowd parted to allow the captain and first officer passage to the front.

Brewer winced at the force of the blows being landed by both men. He'd half-expected Alfred to need some sort of release like this, but he'd thought the victim would be Mac. As it was, both men would be severely bruised and lucky to have nothing broken nbefore this match concluded.

"Sir," said Lieutenant Greene beside him, "do you think we should break this up before one or the other takes a serious injury?"

"Probably, but truth be told, Alfred needs an outlet just now, and Mr. Cromwell is probably the only one who could stand up to his fury. Even Mac would mainly be a punching bag for Alfred. He couldn't fight back as effectively as Cromwell."

Just at that point, Cromwell worked in close, grabbed Alfred by the arm, and swung him around, sliding him down the deck.

"Now, Benjamin," Brewer said.

Greene stepped forward, calling for the fight to stop, but Alfred was already past him, his sword raised for another blow. Greene grabbed his wrist. "Enough, I said!" he bellowed.

Alfred reflexively grabbed the first lieutenant's hand and pulled his wrist, twisting and taking Greene down to the deck in front of him, his sword arm raised to deliver a blow .

"Alfred!" Brewer called out.

The cook stopped in mid swing. He blinked and recognized the first lieutenant at his feet.

"Mr. Greene!" he cried. "I am sorry, sir! I didn't realize it was you!" He quickly assisted the premier to his feet.

"It's no matter," Greene announced, clearly enough to dispel any concerns that the incident might result in disciplinary action. "I see you and Mr. Cromwell were having some fun here! Isn't that right, Captain?"

The two combatants turned and came to attention as the captain stepped up. "Quite right, Mr. Greene. Really, Alfred, you should sell tickets when you have one of these training sessions of yours. You could buy an Indiaman by the time you retire!"

Doctor Spinelli stepped up. "Let's get you, er, *gentlemen* down to my sickbay, and I'll have a look."

"Thank you, Doctor," Cromwell said, "but we're fine, aren't we, Alfred?"

Spinelli looked to the captain, who nodded.

"Very well," he said, "but if you need me, come to sickbay."

"Understood, Doctor," Cromwell replied. He picked up the swords and turned to his opponent. "Alfred, shall we?"

"Aye, sir." The two men left. Brewer and Greene stood beside the doctor and watched them go.

"Sir," Greene asked, "have we just seen the greatest swordfight in British naval history?"

"I can't say," Brewer said, "but it's certainly the greatest I have ever beheld."

The gun room was empty when the two men entered. Alfred stood inside the doorway and watched as Cromwell set the swords on the table and gingerly sat down. The lieutenant looked at Alfred and pointed at him.

"No smiles out of you, sir!" he said. "I wager you're feeling it about now as well." He winced as he probed his rib cage. "Please, sit. Would you have something to drink?"

"No, thank you, sir." Alfred lowered himself gently onto a seat. He winced at the effort, and Cromwell smiled.

"That's more like it." The lieutenant slowly removed his shirt and began examining the bruises that were rapidly covering his upper body. "You know," he said, "my brother and I used to get in donnybrooks like this, usually when I said or did something to show him up. So, let me ask you, dear sir: *What have I done to you to earn a beating like this?*"

"Nothing, sir," Alfred looked down at his hands, curled tightly in his lap. "It's nothing you've done. I'm sorry if I went too far."

Cromwell put his elbow on the table despite the pain. "Alfred, what's going on?"

His guest drew a long, slow breath and exhaled it even more slowly. He studied the deck beams above for a moment before looking the lieutenant in the eye. "I must beg your forgiveness, Mr. Cromwell. The captain's wife is in danger because of me. She was kidnapped because I killed Roberto Cofresi." He scowled in frustration. "I have been fighting all my life, but I've never been in a position where my actions resulted in the endangerment of someone entirely innocent." He sighed. "It's a new feeling, a new *realization* for me, that someone like Black Rose wants to fight me bad enough that she would resort to kidnapping a woman."

Cromwell hissed as he checked out a bruise on his side.

"Oh, I seriously doubt she wants to fight you."

"Excuse me?" Alfred said.

"Alfred, you bested Roberto Cofresi in a fight. Black Rose does not want to fight you, *she wants you dead!* You beat

Cofresi, therefore she knows *she* cannot win in a fight against you, and if she knew of any of her men who could, she would have sent them out to kill you and rewarded them handsomely for it. No, she knows her only chance for her revenge is to hamstring you in some way. Hence, Mrs. Brewer is kidnapped to distract both you and the captain. She knows he's not going to trade you; no British captain would trade a member of his crew for any hostage. She wants to lure both you and the captain into a situation where you face overwhelming odds and kill you both. Afterwards, she may send a ransom demand to the lady's father at St. Kitts."

Alfred said nothing; he merely nodded pensively. Cromwell tapped the table with his fingertip, and Alfred looked up at him.

"Don't you believe for a second that the captain will allow that to happen," he said, quietly but firmly. "We'll think of something. We will stop Black Rose, once and for all."

"I hope so."

CHAPTER TWELVE

Brewer stood in his day cabin, looking out the stern window and watching their wake flow behind them until it was swallowed by the sea. What little he had seen of Alfred's "practice" with Mr. Cromwell was becoming more disturbing the more he thought about it. The realization that Alfred had that much power and had nearly lost all control while on his ship was something to be concerned about. If Greene had not successfully made light of the situation, he as captain would have been compelled to treat the incident as an attack on an officer. This situation with Elizabeth obviously had upset Alfred much more than he let on.

The captain looked around the dining cabin and pantry to assure himself that he was alone, then he returned to the day cabin and began to pace. His chin was on his breast, and his eyes saw only the deck one step in front of him. He pursed his lips and allowed his mind to roam.

The first image that came to him was Elizabeth. She was holding Anne and waving goodbye to him. She was in their room at her father's house on St. Kitts. *What is she going through?* he wondered. *I pray Black Rose is not hurting her.*

The woman has no interest in her other than using her to compell me to bring Alfred. Perhaps Elizabeth will sit quietly and await rescue. Brewer grunted bitterly. *Doubtful. When has she ever sat quietly and waited upon others do do what needed doing?* He stopped pacing and took out the locket. He opened it and gazed at her face before looking at the strand of Anne's hair tucked inside the lid. *I will bring your mother back to you, little one.*

He put the locket away and resumed his pacing. A dark image filled his mind now, with a black hat and a black scarf pulled up to conceal the face. Black Rose. Brewer's anger rose as the image in his mind seemed to laugh at him, at his impotence, lauding her own ability to snatch his wife from her bed chamber. Brewer felt his jaw tighten, and the muscles in the back of his neck began to ache. He stopped pacing and stretched, allowing his muscles to relax a bit. He looked out the stern window and saw that dusk was setting in; he vowed that Black Rose had not many sunsets left.

Brewer turned, and his eyes fell on his desk. He went to it and took out his *Légion d'honneur*. He took the decoration and sat in the day room. As he stared at the cross, in his mind's eye he saw Bonaparte as he had been the last time they spoke, in his office on St. Helena. The image frowned at him.

'M. Brewer, I have an idea as to what you are feeling— anger at this outrage, fear for her safety. You must push all these aside, mon ami; bury them as deeply as you can, and focus on your mission. That is your only hope. The vision vanished.

Brewer closed the box and held it tightly to his chest. He squeezed his eyes shut and screamed inside his head. He panted hard for several seconds before he closed his mouth and took several long, slow, deep breaths through his nose.

Slowly he could feel the calm returning to his body, and his head began to clear. He pulled the box from his chest and viewed the cross again, and he knew the Bonaparte-image was right. He closed his eyes and hugged the box tightly.

I have to focus, he told himself. *I must succeed. Black Rose must be stopped.*

He rose, replaced the box, and turned. Rage was in his eyes, and his face was like a flint. *No matter what the cost.*

Over the next couple days, Brewer rarely left his cabin. Lieutenant Greene and the doctor were concerned, and Greene quietly spoke with Alfred and Mac to make sure one or the other was always in the pantry to keep watch.

Doctor Spinelli entered the gun room during the middle watch to find Mr. Greene sitting at the table, staring at a cup of cold coffee.

"Benjamin?" he said. "Trouble sleeping?"

Greene shook his head, then shrugged. "I don't know. I suppose I'm worried about the captain."

"So am I. Who has the watch tonight?"

Greene rose and picked up his cup. He motioned with the cup to the doctor, who nodded. Greene moved off and returned with two steaming cups.

"Mac," he said. "I gave him instructions that if the captain went up on deck to pace, he was to send word to me, but otherwise to leave him be and watch."

"Good," Spinelli replied. "So what has you so worried?"

Greene looked up at him and grunted. "The captain has not been himself these past few days," he said. "Not that I blame him, you understand. If I got the news he got, I'd be fit for an asylum by now." He took a drink and considered. "Still, I'm concerned about what effect that will have when we reach Panama." He stopped and shook his head. "What does that make me, Adam? The captain's wife has been kidnapped, and I'm worried about operations when we get to Panama."

Spinelli smiled. "It makes you a good first lieutenant." He drank his coffee and set the cup down. Then he tapped the table with his forefinger. "Right now, I don't think we have anything to worry about where the captain is concerned. Yes, he's got what I can only call 'family issues' to work out in his own mind. Remember, his own father disowned him when he joined the Royal Navy, and he has not returned to his home from that day to this. The Navy was his only family until Elizabeth, and now he is in danger of losing her as well." The doctor sighed. "I've been playing chess with the captain long enough to know his mind fairly well. I believe he will do his duty."

Greene considered for a moment before raising his eyes to meet the doctor's. "And if something happens to Elizabeth?"

Spinelli's face grew stern. "Then God save Black Rose," he said quietly, "because no one else will be able to."

Mac sat at the table in the captain's cabin, trying to work his way through *Robinson Crusoe,* which he'd borrowed from the captain's book shelf. He set the book down and stared at the flame of the single candle on the table. A noise from the sleeping cabin drew his attention, and he sighed. Soon the captain would begin pacing back and forth across the day cabin. This would be the third night in a row the captain had not slept. Oh, he'd managed to doze for an hour or so here or there, but anyone looking at his face could tell that fatigue was catching up with him.

He picked up the book again and resumed his reading. He had to admit, he liked the story. When the captain had offered him the chance to borrow a book to read, Mac had politely refused, outwardly. Inwardly, he'd scoffed at the notion or wasting time reading, but over time, it began to seem like a good idea after all. He'd gone back to Captain Brewer and asked if the offer was still open, and the captain had said yes immediately. Mac had scanned the bookshelf and narrowed his choices to two: *Ivanhoe* and *Crusoe*. He'd chosen the latter for two reasons. One, it dealt with the sea; and two, the captain had said it was based on a true story. Mac turned the page, then became aware that he was not alone.

He looked up to see the captain standing there. Mac jumped to his feet.

Brewer held up his hand. "So," he said, "you've got the duty tonight, eh?"

The coxswain nearly denied the reason for his presence, but decided against it. "Aye, Captain," he said.

Brewer nodded. "I thought I'd step on deck for some fresh air, maybe take a turn or two around. What were your instructions if I did?"

Mac sighed in surrender. "Mr. Greene said I should send word to him."

Brewer picked up his hat. "Come along, Mac." As he passed the sentry, he remarked, "Pass the word to Mr. Greene that I've gone up on deck."

"Aye, sir," the sentry replied. He gave Mac a questioning glance, but the Cornishman only shrugged and followed his captain.

The two men arrived on deck and turned forward up the starboard side. Mac hung back a respectful distance, but Brewer motioned him forward.

"Stay with me, Mac," he said. The coxswain quickly caught up.

"Nice little world we have here, wouldn't you say, Mac?" Brewer said as he gestured at their surroundings. "No trouble to speak of, everyone does their job and we all live in peace and safety." They reached the bow, and Brewer stopped beside one of the long nines. He patted the gun. "And if we find anyone who wishes ill upon us, or simply wants to fight, then we have the weapons we need to enforce the peace." He patted the breach again, and the two men began their walk down the larboard side. "But then," the captain continued, "there are times, Mac, when something happens that shows us just how powerless we really are." The captain lowered his chin to his chest, his eyes on the deck, and said nothing more.

Mac decided his best option was to say nothing. He wished he had an idea that would rescue the captain's wife and put Black Rose in her grave in the bargain, but he didn't. His mood improved marginally when he saw Mr. Greene and the doctor on the quarterdeck.

"Sir?" he said. Brewer looked to him, and Mac pointed forward with his chin. Brewer glanced that way and saw his welcoming committee.

"So," the captain said, "checking up on me at night now, are you?"

"I beg your pardon, sir," Greene replied.

Spinelli stepped up. "We're concerned, Captain."

"Really?" Brewer said dryly.

The doctor stepped in close and put his lips near to the captain's ear and whispered, "We don't want to do this here, in front of the crew, do we?"

Brewer glared at his friend, with only a brief glance offered to his premier. He turned to his coxswain. "Mac, you're dismissed. Thank you for the walk, now get some sleep. Report to me at the turn of the forenoon watch."

Mac knuckled his forehead. "Aye, sir."

"As for you," Brewer said to the remaining two, "would you please join me in my cabin for a drink?"

"With pleasure, Captain," Spinelli said.

Brewer led them to his day cabin. He tossed his hat on the settee and indicated the bottle and glasses to the side.

"Benjamin, if you please?"

The first lieutenant silently obeyed and returned with three glasses of wine. The three men sat and drank. Nobody seemed to want to be the first to speak. Nobody looked up; all eyes were on the deck or their glass.

It was the captain who finally broke the silence. He set his glass down and leaned forward, elbows on his knees and hands clasped in front of him. His eyes were on his hands.

"All right," he said. "Tell me what's on your minds. You may speak freely."

His guests shared a look before Lieutenant Greene spoke up. "As the doctor said on deck, Captain, we're concerned for you. You haven't slept in days, and soon it will catch up to you. Worst of all, sir, Panama is less than a week away now, and we still don't have a plan to rescue your wife and deal with Black Rose when we get there."

"William," Spinelli said, "I pray you do not take this amiss, but this ship needs her captain. Right now, you cannot afford to be Elizabeth's husband, you must be Captain of HMS *Phoebe*." He paused to swallow hard before continuing. "I'm sure you know this, but if 'Elizabeth's husband' goes to Panama to rescue her, then she is dead already, along with you and many of us, and Black Rose wins. In addition, she will most likely escape in the confusion and resume her pillaging of the Caribbean. We need the Captain, and that at the top of his game, to lead us in the rescue of a hostage. You must focus on the mission, Captain, and put off any revenge until it's over."

Brewer said nothing for several minutes before looking to his first lieutenant.

"You agree?"

Greene's expression was one of total concern and sympathy. "Aye, Captain."

The captain pursed his lips and nodded slowly. He rubbed his hands together and rose.

"Thank you, gentlemen," he said. "You are, of course, completely correct, and I am grateful that you cared enough to tell me. Benjamin, I want a council of war assembled here tomorrow, say, two bells of the forenoon watch. Make it yourself, Mr. Sweeney, Mr. Rivkins, Mr. Cromwell, and Captain Enfield. Alfred will be there as well. You may attend, Doctor, if you have a mind. Have the bosun and gunner nearby in case we need them for a question. Tell Mr. Reed he has the deck during the council. He won't like that, but tell him you will brief him personally when it's over. Have we found a crewman who is familiar with that coast yet?"

"No, sir," Greene replied.

"Hmm." Brewer paced two steps out and two back. "Very well. Time to stop being discreet about it. Make an announcement to the crew that we are looking for any men who have been to the coast around Porto Bello. Have them report to their divisional officers immediately."

"Aye, sir."

"Anything else for the moment?" the captain asked. When neither man replied, he said, "In that case, I must ask you to excuse me. I want to turn in and get some sleep before Alfred brings breakfast. Oh, and Benjamin, you can tell Mac and Alfred their services will no longer be needed overnight."

Greene smiled. "Aye, sir."

"Then goodnight, gentlemen."

The ship's bell had just finished ringing two bells when the sentry's knock was heard at the cabin door.

"Enter!" Brewer called.

The door opened and HMS *Phoebe's* council of war entered. The captain took his place at the head of the table with Mr. Greene on his right and the good doctor on his left. Next to Greene sat Rivkins, Cromwell, and Captain Enfield, while next to the doctor were Mr. Sweeney and Alfred. Mac and Pudge served coffee to everyone before Pudge retired to the pantry and Mac took his place by the door. The captain rose and addressed the company.

"Thank you all for coming. We are here to take the first steps toward a plan of action for when we reach Panama. We should be there in six or seven days, Mr. Sweeney?"

The sailing master nodded. "About that, sir, if the wind blows fair."

"Good. Please understand, I do not expect to leave this room today with a plan in place and ready to go. I view our gathering today as more of a round-table discussion to get ideas out in the open. You may all speak freely on the matter. Let me all remind you what the pirate's note said. The fortress would be visible from the harbor to the southeast. They will know when we arrive, even if they don't have watchers on the coast."

"Agreed," Greene said. "That means they will also be able to see who disembarks, or at least in what numbers." He nodded at Alfred. "I expect they'll be looking for Alfred to go ashore. His size makes him distinctive."

"Yes," Brewer said meditatively. "I have an idea. Mac, I want you to search the crew and see if there is anyone about the same size as Alfred. I'm looking for someone who may be mistaken for Alfred from a distance."

"Aye, sir."

"You're planning a distraction," Spinelli said.

"Just throwing out ideas, Doctor," the captain replied. "Captain Enfield, do you or any of your men have experience fighting in jungles such as those we're likely to find in Panama?" "I do not, Captain," Enfield replied. "I will ask my men."

"Thank you. Any tips we may gather from experience will only help. There is one thing that bothers me, and that is manpower. I don't believe Black Rose has enough men to effectively defend a fortress. I also do not believe that it is her base of operations."

"Agreed, Captain," Cromwell said. "It makes no sense for the pirates to lure a British warship to a location they plan to use in the future. This has to be a trap designed to lure Alfred to his death, and probably yourself as well, sir." He paused and looked toward the captain to see if he'd gone too far.

"Please, continue, Mr. Cromwell," Brewer said. "You may speak freely. I am interested in any ideas I can get."

"Well, sir," Cromwell continued, "I think it's safe for us to assume that Black Rose does not put a high priority on keeping her word. Therefore, I... I believe she will try to kill your wife no matter what we do. She has to know that you will not allow the kidnapping to go unavenged, so she must be planning on killing you as well."

"Perfectly sound," Brewer said. "Go on."

"Captain, I wonder if Black Rose is even in Panama. She wants Alfred dead; she doesn't care how or who does it. I can only imagine the bounty that would be paid to the man who brings her his head while she lurks elsewhere, or continues her raids." He paused as a thought struck him. "Say, can't we do that?"

"Do what?" Sweeney asked.

"Bring Black Rose Alfred's head!" Everyone at the table looked at Cromwell as though he'd lost his mind, but he went on. "Look, as far as we know, none of the pirates have ever seen Alfred. They only have a vague description gleaned from Rose's conversation with the doctor and whatever they may have learned from *Revenge's* crew before they were killed. What if we put word out that we had Alfred and would deliver his head to Black Rose for a price?"

Brewer watched as those around the table debated the idea. The only man who did not participate was Alfred; he sat silently at the end of the table, his chair turned so he faced the captain and his left arm resting on the table top. His face was an unreadable mask.

Lieutenant Greene raised his hand to get everyone's attention. "I have a problem with that idea," he said. "Maybe not so much a problem as a flaw. If I were Black Rose, I would not pay a single piece of eight for a head, especially the head of someone I did not know by sight. I would instruct my emissaries to question the man while he is alive, and if they were satisfied as to his identity, pay the captors, behead the man, and then bring me the head. Or, better yet, bring me Alfred alive and allow me to run him through myself."

Brewer smiled behind his cup as he watched Cromwell frown at the holes the first lieutenant punched in his scheme. Personally, he agreed with everything Mr. Greene said, but he thought the plan good enough to keep around as a last ditch emergency option.

"Good points, Mr. Greene," he said, "but let's not discard Mr. Cromwell's idea entirely. Anything else?" Nobody said anything, so Brewer dismissed the meeting, saying they would meet again tomorrow at the same time. Mr. Greene and the doctor remained.

"You know," Greene said, "Mr. Cromwell's idea might be a way to get Alfred in front of Black Rose herself to where he could kill her. We would have to be close enough to come to his rescue at once, though. Tough, but it could be done."

"You're not serious?" Spinelli said. He looked incredulous as the first lieutenant shrugged.

"No, Adam," Brewer said, "I have no intention of doing anything of the sort. Yes, desperate times call for desperate measures, but we're not there yet, not by a long shot. Alfred, you were quiet during the meeting."

The other two turned to see the diminutive servant standing in the doorway.

"I had nothing to offer, sir," he said. "I thought it best to listen."

"Hear anything that interested you?" Spinelli asked.

The little man's head tilted to the side as he considered. "I rather liked Mr. Cromwell's idea, but I saw the same flaw in the plan that Mr. Greene did. I was just about to say something when he spoke up. However," Alfred paused for a moment and drew a deep breath, steeling himself for what was coming. "I heard what Mr. Greene said just now, Captain, and I am willing to do it, if it can be done in such a way that ensures the safety of your wife."

Silence descended over the cabin. Brewer's chin edged up, almost of its own accord, so that he nearly appeared to be looking down his nose at Alfred. The captain glanced at the other two men in the room; the doctor was shocked and the first lieutenant embarrassed. His eyes went back to Alfred, who was standing very still and erect in the doorway. Brewer forced his chin down and pursed his lips to cover his turbulent emotions. He exhaled forcibly.

"Alfred," he said, "you cannot know how deeply I am moved by your offer. However, I cannot accept. I have no intention of knowingly trading the life of anyone on this ship for a hostage—*any* hostage—to a pirate, even my wife." He grinned. "For one thing, Elizabeth would never forgive me. She has visions of you cooking for us the rest of our lives."

Greene and Spinelli chuckled, and even Alfred had to look down to hide his grin.

"Very well, sir," he said, "but please know that the offer is genuine, and I am ready to take the risk if it becomes the only way to save her." He met his captain's eye. "As you said, sir, desperate times."

"Thank you, Alfred. Let us hope it never comes to that. I will certainly work to see that it does not."

Alfred bowed and retreated into the pantry.

Lieutenant Greene shook his head. "Egad."

The next day, Mac turned up aces for his captain. Just prior to the council of war, the sentry knocked on the door and announced the coxswain. Mac entered the day cabin with a hand beside him.

"Yes, Mac?" Brewer asked.

"Captain, this here's old Stoney," Mac said. "He's been on ships man and boy since he was seven, in so many ships and on so many oceans that nobody remembers his real name. Anyway, he says he's been to Porto Bello, sir."

"Really?" Brewer turned to the tar. "Is that so, Stoney? When were you there? How long ago, I mean?"

The old man pulled his cap off his head and wrung it nervously in his hands. "Aye, Captain. I've been off that coast four or five times. The last time was, let me see, maybe 1816 or 17, sir."

Brewer pulled out the pirate's ransom note. "Can you read, Stoney? No? Then listen to this." He read the letter through twice, more slowly the second time to give Stoney time to take it all in. When he finished, Brewer watched the old tar stare off into space for a while before looking at him again.

"Yes, sir," he said. "I know the coast. The fortress in the letter is perhaps an hour or so's march through the jungle from the bay."

"How good a view would they have from the fortress?" Brewer asked. "What I mean is, do you think they would be able to identify people, say, on the quarterdeck or in a boat going to shore?"

Stoney thought it over. "Maybe with a good glass they could tell numbers, but I don't think from there they'd be able to see who was who, unless someone was wearing an officer's uniform or the like. Of course, there are any number of places to hide spotters along the tree line around the bay who could notify the fortress by runner."

"Thank you, Stoney," Brewer said. "If you think of anything that might help us, please let Mac know. Dismissed."

"Aye, sir," Stoney said. He knuckled his head and left the cabin.

"Anything else, Mac?" Brewer asked.

"As a matter of fact, yes, sir." The coxswain turned and whistled. A hand stepped into the day cabin who, except for his blonde hair, might actually be mistaken for Alfred from a distance. Brewer stared in amazement.

"Captain," Mac said by way of introduction, "meet Joshua."

Brewer nodded as the tar knuckled his forehead. "Mac, get Alfred." The Cornishman stepped out and returned with the captain's servant. Alfred stood next to Joshua, and their outlines were similar, the biggest difference being Alfred's mane of black hair.

Mac grinned. "Good enough from a distance, eh, Captain?"

Brewer nodded slowly, then addressed the newcomer. "Joshua, has Mac told you why you're here?"

"Nay, sir," he said. "Only that I was to report to you."

"I see. You are aware that Black Rose has demanded we turn over Alfred in exchange for the release of her hostage?"

"Aye, sir. For yer wife, sir."

"That's right. We are looking for someone who could pass for Alfred from a distance, in case we need to deceive the pirates about his whereabouts."

Joshua was confused. "Deceive?"

Mac leaned over and murmured, "Fool them" in the tar's ear. Joshua face cleared and he said, "Ah!" then, "Aye, sir, anything I can do to help get yer wife back, I'm yer man, sir."

"Thank you, Joshua," Brewer said. "That means more to me than I can say. Tell me, what's your last name?"

Joshua blushed. "I don't rightly know, sir. I grew up a slave of the Barbary pirates, and they only ever called me Joshua. They sold me to work on a slaver, and when the Royal Navy took her, I joined up right willingly. But I never learned my last name, so I just go by Joshua."

Brewer stood. "Good enough for me. I thank again, Joshua. Dismissed."

The tar saluted and left the cabin.

"You've earned your pay this month, Mac." Brewer patted his coxswain on the shoulder. "I hope Stoney will be able to help us plan some strategy for when we arrive in Panama. Come, it's time for the council to begin."

The sentry knocked on the door and admitted the council. By prior arrangement, Mr. Cromwell had the deck today so Mr. Reed could attend the meeting.

The captain opened the meeting without preamble. "Thank you all for coming. For those who do not know, Mac has again worked a miracle. He has found us a hand who has been to the Porto Bello coast. We will be talking to him over the next day or so to see if he can be of any help to us. He also brought me a hand who should be able to pass for Alfred convincingly enough from a distance, although we may need to dye his hair black."

"Bravo!" cried Captain Enfield. "Now we can get to work."

The discussion lasted over an hour, the consensus being that a way should be sought to send a raiding party discreetly to the fortress while the captain and fake-Alfred appeared to row to shore from the ship and proceed up to the fortress. Brewer asked Alfred his opinion of the plan, and the steward agreed in principle. The captain sent Mac to bring Stoney back for consultations. Mr. Sweeney produced the only chart they carried of the region. Brewer hoped the old tar would remember a few points to make it better. Brewer dismissed the assembly and ordered them to meet again tomorrow.

Brewer and Lieutenant Greene awaited Mac's return with Stoney. "Benjamin," Brewer said, "I am actually beginning to think we may have a chance to come through this with the best possible outcome."

"And that is?"

"Elizabeth and Alfred alive and unharmed, and Black Rose dead."

"Amen to that, sir."

A knock at the door foretold the return of Mac and Stoney. Brewer motioned the tar over to the table, and Mac took up his usual position at the door.

"Look at this, Stoney," Brewer said, indicating the chart on the table. "This is the only chart we have of the Porto Bello coast. I cannot tell you how old or how accurate it is. Study it for a moment, and tell me what you think. This may help." He handed the old man a magnifying glass.

He stood back beside his premiere to give the man access. Stoney bent over the chart, holding the glass barely a half inch above the paper and moving in very slow, incremental shifts up and down the coast. Fully fifteen minutes later, he straightened up and stretched his back.

"Well?" Greene asked.

"Not too bad as charts go, Captain," the old man said. "I've seen much worse. There's nothing much I can add, other than a shoal or two that I don't see indicated."

"We are thinking of running a deception," Greene explained, "with the captain and a crewman standing in for Alfred leaving the ship in the harbor while a force makes its way secretly to the fortress to surprise the pirates. Do you know of a place where such a force could land, say at night?"

Stoney turned and studied the map again, his arms crossed over his chest and his chin resting between a thumb and forefinger. He picked up the glass again and scrutinized an area of coastline for a while before standing erect again. He set the glass down.

"Here," he said, laying his finger on the coast slightly south of Porto Bello. "There's a small bay with a good beach. If I remember right—I'm sorry, but I'm working from a memory that's over twenty years old—there was a small animal trail away from the coastline, which some of our crew investigated. We might be able to use it to get to the fortress. But I must tell you, it will be an all-night trek. The force will have to be landed immediately after dark at the latest, and I cannot guess at what perils will await you in the jungle."

"Do you think they will have it guarded?" Brewer asked.

The old man considered. "I shouldn't think so, Captain. This bay is separated from the fortress by several miles of forest. There are several landing places closer to the fortress that would demand guarding first."

"But you're sure we can get to the fortress from this bay?" Greene demanded.

Stoney turned and faced the premiere. "Sure? No, sir. I have no way to be sure about this. I merely said this is the best place to be able to land a sizable force unobserved. As I said, there are places nearer to the fortress where such a force could also be put ashore, but the closer you are, the greater the chance that you will be observed by someone in the pay of the pirates."

"Mark the bay on the chart, Stoney, if you please," Brewer said. "Thank you. Do you have any experience with the jungles of Panama?"

The old tar shook his head. "Sorry, Captain, but I never went ashore there myself."

"Very well," Brewer said. "If you remember anything else, please come and inform me immediately. Dismissed, and thank you."

Stoney knuckled his head. "You're welcome, sir. I wish I could do more."

When they were alone, Brewer led his premiere to the day cabin and plopped down on the settee, suddenly conscious of how tired he was. "Alfred!" he called. That good man appeared. "Wine for three, if you please."

Alfred's left eyebrow rose slightly, as he saw there were only the two officers in the cabin. "Aye, sir." He returned with the order, and after handing out the two glasses, stood holding the tray with the third.

The captain smiled. "Sit down, Alfred, please. The wine is for you. Join us."

"Thank you, sir."

Brewer drank and addressed his first lieutenant. "Mr. Greene? What do you think?"

Greene frowned. "I'm not sure the information Stoney provided helps us, sir. We run a great risk of losing a large portion of the ship's company in the forest."

The captain turned to Alfred. "You heard what Stoney said?" Alfred nodded once. "What do you think?"

"What would the plan be, exactly, sir?" Alfred asked.

"Well," Brewer said, "at the moment, the proposition is that we drop a large force at this bay—what's it called, Benjamin? Bastimentos—that's right—just after sundown. That puts them about seven or eight miles from the fortress. That force would consist of Mr. Greene, Mr. Crawford, Mac, yourself, and as many hands with combat skills and marines as we can spare. At dawn the next morning, I take the ship into the harbor at Porto Bello, where Joshua and I will take a boat to the shore and make our way slowly to the fortress. I'm banking on our men reaching their destination before we have to enter. With their help we take the fortress, rescue Elizabeth, and kill or capture Black Rose. Now, what do you think?"

Alfred didn't answer at once. Instead, he looked at his wine and then took a stiff drink. Finally, he sighed and raised his head. "I'm afraid I agree with Mr. Greene, sir. I believe there's too great a risk that the landing force will be lost or at least significantly delayed in the forest. That would leave yourself and young Joshua in grave danger."

Brewer pursed his lips as he studied the clouds in his wine and thought. "Do either of you have a better idea?"

"Sir," Alfred said, "I think that the force should be landed much earlier, perhaps even at dawn the day prior to your arrival at Porto Bello. We can't expect them to make good time through an unfamiliar jungle traveling at night. But they may be able to make their way by daylight. True, that greatly increases the risk of their being discovered, but Stoney did say that the bay at Bastimentos was unlikely to be watched by the pirates. It is a calculated risk, sir, but I believe it is worth taking. We can even dress the landing force as pirates. That way, even if they were discovered, Black Rose may not immediately think they were here to rescue Mrs. Brewer."

Brewer nodded. "Benjamin?"

The first lieutenant considered Alfred's proposals. "I like it, sir. I think landing the force early to give them more time to get to the fortress is a good idea. In fact, I would go one further—land them *before* dawn. Give them the chance to disappear into the jungle before the sun comes up and they become vulnerable to detection. I like the idea of the disguises, too. At least it may make Black Rose hesitate if she thinks another band of pirates is coming for her treasure. She may even send men to attack them in the forest. That may give you and Joshua a chance to rescue Miss Elizabeth yourselves."

"Well, then," Brewer said, "we'll propose the plan to the council tomorrow. Now, if you'll excuse me, gentlemen?"

Mac lingered behind. "Yes, Mac?" Brewer asked.

"Well, sir, it's about the plan. Or at least my part in it."

"What about your part?"

"Forgive me for saying so, Captain, but my place is with you."

"I'll be fine, Mac. I want as much power in that landing force as possible."

"Sir, you can't get much more power than Alfred and Mr. Crawford. My place is with you, Captain. You can court-martial me when we get back to Port Royal, but I'm going with you."

Brewer's irritation at his coxswain's stubbornness disappeared the moment he turned and saw the other's face. It was a mask of concern and duty, a devotion to the officer who had given him a chance to prove himself. Brewer sighed.

"Very well, Mac. You're with me, but—"

He was interrupted by a sharp wrap at the door. The sentry opened it and announced Mr. Murdy. The senior midshipman marched into the room and came to attention. "Mr. Rivkins' respects, sir. He requests you come up on deck. The lookout reports a strange sail to the south."

"I shall be up directly," Brewer said. Murdy came to attention and left.

CHAPTER THIRTEEN

Captain Brewer emerged onto the quarterdeck and was met by Lieutenant Rivkins.

"Sir," he said, "in accordance with your instructions, I have altered course to investigate."

"Very good," Brewer said. He raised his voice. "I have the deck! Mr. Rivkins, send Skimpy to be runner for the foretop lookout. Send Pudge to the maintop to run for the lookout there."

"Aye, sir!"

"Mr. Sweeney, make all sail!"

"Aye, sir!"

"Mr. Rivkins, you may clear for action!"

"Aye, sir! Clear for action! All hands! Clear for action!"

The hands crowded all the canvas the ship could carry on her yards and HMS *Phoebe* sprang forward. Captain Brewer stood off to the side of the quarterdeck, saying nothing, but his eyes missed nothing as his men carried out their tasks. The first lieutenant joined him; he saluted and took his place next to his captain. The captain turned to Rivkins.

"I'm going forward," he said. "You have the deck."

"Aye, sir."

Brewer started forward. "Mr. Greene, you're with me."

The captain marched forward to the long nines. With a nod he accepted a spyglass from a hand and raised it to his eye. He sighed inside; they were not yet close enough for him to distinguish anything. He looked up.

"Lookout! Let's hear you!"

"Looks like two ships, sir!" the lookout called.

"Two ships?" Lt. Greene lowered his glass. "Do you think we've caught up with Black Rose?"

Brewer shook his head. "I don't see how. They had a four or five day head start. Besides, even if they have *Revenge*, they wouldn't want to tangle with us at sea." He looked at one of the guns beside him as he turned possibilities and strategies over in his mind.

"I have them, sir," Greene said. "Definitely two ships. One of them much smaller than the larger one."

Brewer frowned as he stared at the growing white speck on the horizon. "Beat to quarters, Mr. Greene."

Greene saluted and headed aft. "Beat to quarters! All hands! We shall beat to quarters!"

Brewer heard the marine drummer boys begin their rhythm that would send the hands to their stations and made the ship ready for battle. He heard a throat clear behind him, and he turned to find Mr. Short standing at ease. *God bless Benjamin!* he thought. *He sent me a runner.*

"Mr. Short," he said, "glad to see you. Kindly run up to the foretop lookout and get a report."

"Aye, sir!" Short sprang to the shrouds and climbed swiftly, disappearing from view. A few minutes later, he descended. "Lookout says it's definitely two ships, Captain.

He says it looks like one is circling the other, and he says it looks like a pirate attack, sir!"

Brewer lowered his glass. "Thank you, Mr. Short. I'm going aft. I want you to return to the foretop. Skimpy was up there as well, correct? Good. I want one of you to report to me with updates."

"Aye, sir."

"Good. Go."

"Aye, sir!"

The captain went aft to the quarterdeck. "I have the deck!" he called. "Mr. Greene, we may have caught pirates in the act. Grape for the carronades, ball for the rest, if you please."

"Aye, sir."

Skimpy came running up. He skidded to a stop and saluted. "Lookout says it looks like a brig and a merchantman, maybe the size of a small Indiaman."

"Thank you, Skimp," Brewer said. "You may return to the lookout."

Brewer watched the dance growing more and more visible before him as the two ships maneuvered and counter-maneuvered. He lowered his glass. "Mr. Rivkins!"

The second lieutenant appeared and saluted. "Sir?"

"Man the long nines," Brewer said hurriedly. "Let me know when you think we're in range. I want you to fire on the brig as soon as we're able."

"Aye, sir!" Rivkins touched his hat and headed forward.

Brewer walked over to the waist. "Mr. Greene!" he called. "Stand by! Remind your gun captains to be sure of their target! We don't want to hit the merchantman."

"Aye, sir!"

He moved back to the rail and again raised the glass to his eye. He could make out the action ahead much better now. The brig wanted to take the merchantman intact, Brewer judged, as she passed on opportunities to rake the vessel's stern. *Whoever is conning that brig is good,* he thought as he watched the smaller ship turn sharply in response to the merchantman's attempts to escape. *The merchantman's luck can't last forever; soon the pirate's patience will wear thin and he'll fire into the merchantman and make her heave-to.* Moments later his fears were confirmed when he saw the splash of a shot off the merchantman's beam. It was possible, he realized, that a lookout on the brig had spotted the approaching Phoebe and the captain had decided to make certain of his prize. As he watched through his glass, the big ship hove to.

Brewer's mood brightened considerably when Mr. Short appeared and informed him that Mr. Rivkins thought the brig was in range now. The captain sent him back with permission to fire at will. Three minutes later the larboard long nine erupted, and Brewer was able to spot the splash off the pirate's larboard quarter. It had the desired effect; the brig veered off and turned toward the *Phoebe*.

"Mr. Dye!" Brewer called over his shoulder, "run up the colors!"

"Aye, sir!"

The sailing master stepped over to the captain's side. "He's cutting it close, sir; half-pistol shot, I'd say, maybe less."

"I see it, Mr. Sweeney," the captain replied without lowering his glass. "Let's see if—Wait! What's he doing?" The brig ran up the flag of the United States.

Brewer was surprised by the flag and crossed the deck to the larboard rail to get a better look at the approaching vessel. He could see one or two officers in uniform on the deck as the ships were about to pass each other, but several of the hands were not in uniform at all. He'd heard rumors of the loose codes in the American Navy, but he'd never thought....

"Captain!" came a shout from behind him. "Look out! It's a trick! *Captain!*"

Brewer turned in time to catch a glimpse of a blurry form flying at him. He didn't even have time to brace himself before the form collided with him and took him to the deck. The captain lay there, the breath knocked out of him and his assailant on top of him, when he heard the unmistakable sound of a broadside being fired very close to his ship. Ball crashed into woodwork and caused damage to the sails and rigging, while grape mowed down any flesh that happened to be in its path. Even through the stunned sensation caused by his head hitting the deck, Brewer heard the cries of the wounded that were cut down.

A moment later, his assailant rose and pulled him to his feet. Brewer leaned against a quarterdeck carronade and shook his head clear. His eyes cleared to find Mr. Knight, the bosun, holding him up by his lapels.

"Are you all right, Captain?" Knight asked.

"What? Mr. Knight? Yes! Yes, I'm fine, or I soon will be. You saved my life, sir! How did you know it was a trap?"

"Me mum lives in Pennsylvania now, sir," the bosun explained. "That's in the United States, sir. Anyway, I got a letter from her in the last mail call that said the American flag now had twenty-four stars."

Brewer looked confused.

"Sir," Knight explained, "that flag only had *twenty-two*."

Brewer's eyes grew wide at the news, and he spun to his right to see for himself. It was the wrong thing to do; his head whirled and he nearly went down. Only his leaning on the carronade and Knight's steadying hand kept him on his feet. By the time his vision cleared the telltale flag was down. He saw the pirate ship coming around to starboard.

"Mr. Sweeney!" he croaked as he stood erect, "hard-a-starboard! Course due west!"

"Aye, sir! Due west!"

"Midshipman of the watch! Pass the word for Mr. Greene and Mr. Rivkins! Lookout, let's hear you!"

"Brig's coming around, sir! Looks like she's heading for the merchantman again!"

"Mr. Sweeney! Bring us around to larboard! Smartly, now! I want to get in between that ship and the merchantman!"

"Aye, sir!"

Greene and Rivkins arrived and saluted.

"Damage report, Mr. Greene?" Brewer asked.

"Eight men hurt, sir. Hull intact. No guns out of action."

"Good. Mr. Greene, you're here with me. Mr. Rivkins, I want you to go below and take over the gun deck. I will send your orders presently."

"Aye, sir."

Greene looked the captain over and asked, "Sir, are you all right? Should I send for the doctor?"

Brewer took a deep breath and pushed off the carronade. He accepted his hat from Mr. Dye with a nod of thanks and put it on. "That won't be necessary, Mr. Greene, but thank you."

Greene looked past his captain at the approaching brig. "Their captain must be a maniac! Why doesn't he head north and try to escape? He must know he has no chance against a frigate."

Sweeney stepped up. "Don't get cocky, sir. Remember the *Speedy*."

"*Speedy*?" Greene asked.

"HMS *Speedy* was Cochrane's brig during the Napoleonic wars. In 1806, I think it was, he took the 32-gun Spanish frigate *El Gamo*."

Greene looked incredulous. "Should we turn and run, then Captain?" he asked.

"Now, Mr. Greene," Brewer answered wryly, "do I look like a Spaniard?"

Greene grinned broadly. "Not in the least, sir."

Brewer turned to his sailing master. "Mr. Sweeney, where are those two ships?"

"The merchantman is heading south as fast as she can, but she has no chance of escaping the brig, which is following her."

Brewer looked up and eyeballed the distances of the closing triangle made up of the three ships. He didn't like what he saw.

"We're not going to make it, are we?"

Sweeney shook his head. "It doesn't look like it, sir."

"Mr. Greene, what do you think? Parallel course for a broadside?"

Greene nodded. "Might slow them down a bit, sir, but a hit at this distance would be sheet luck."

"Let's hope not *sheer* luck, Mr. Greene," Brewer deadpanned. "Please tell Mr. Rivkins to stand by. I want the carronades to hold their fire."

"Aye, sir."

"Stand by to turn to starboard, Mr. Sweeney," Brewer called.

"Aye, sir."

He watched the pirate's progress with only an occasional glance to the merchantman. Finally, he turned to Mr. Sweeney. "Now."

The sailing master picked up the speaking trumpet and issued the orders. HMS *Phoebe* can around to her new heading smartly. When her captain was sure of their new course, he stepped over to the waist. "Mr. Rivkins! Fire!"

"Captain!"

Brewer made his way back to the rail as the broadside went off. Before the smoke obscured his view, he saw the brig begin evasive maneuvers, and he knew his broadside was wasted.

"Deck, there!" It was the mizzen lookout. "The brig's approaching, sir!"

"Where away?"

"Dunno, sir! I lost her in the smoke!"

"Captain!"

Brewer had wandered forward. He now turned back and saw the brig coming out of the smoke on *Phoebe's* larboard side at the beam. She turned aft and loosed a broadside before moving away.

"Fire!" Brewer shouted. "Carronades! Fire!"

The larboard carronades fired, but they could not depress their muzzles enough to hit the brig. All they did was put a few holes in its sails. Brewer pounded the railing in frustration as he watch the pirate turn away.

"Mr. Sweeney!" he called. "Two points to larboard!" He rushed to the waist. "Mr. Rivkins! Fire with any guns that will bear!"

"Aye sir!"

He stood there on the quarterdeck and almost willed the bow over until he heard two or three of the great 18-pounders go off. His adversary avoided the broadside.

"Steady as you go, Mr. Sweeney," the captain said. "Try to keep us between the pirate and the merchantman."

Brewer moved to the rail and raised his glass to study his enemy. He could see movement on their deck as well as repairs being made to their rigging. *Well,* he thought, *at least we did some damage.* He took advantage of his first chance to study his enemy up close as they ended their run away from the British frigate and turned to follow the merchantman again. The brig looked well-built, and she was certainly fast—no, not fast, *quick.* That ship could not compete in a race against *Phoebe,* but she could turn much quicker and sharper than any frigate, and this made her a very difficult target to hit. Of course, with that size ship, just one solid hit from a 18-pounder could be enough to reduce it to a wreck. The trouble was hitting it.

The captain chided himself for the distraction and resumed his study. From what he could see, the ship had a mixed armament—not unusual for a pirate. He thought he caught sight of one carronade on each side surrounded by maybe five or six long guns. Eight-pounders, he guessed. Not heavy, but enough to do some damage to his ship if he got away with a few more passes like that last one.

Brewer lowered his glass and stared at his enemy. *There has to be a way,* he thought desperately. *We have to be able to catch him by surprise, to appear out of nowhere, as he did to us... But not quite like he did to us!* The captain smiled wickedly as an idea formed in his head. He turned and found Mr. Sweeney and the first lieutenant near the wheel.

"Gentlemen," he said hurriedly, "I believe I have it. If I read this rascal right, he'll try that same trick again—coming in through the smoke of our broadside to take us by surprise. Only this time, we won't be here to surprise. Mr. Sweeney, upon my command, we will again turn to starboard to fire a broadside at our friend out there. Mr. Greene, have Mr. Reed fire as well this time, we shall need the extra smoke. As soon as we fire, I shall give the order to bring the ship about. That should give us the time and distance to pound him with a full broadside from the starboard battery! One hit, two at the most, should do it for him. Mr. Sweeney, after we fire, we shall head directly for him, but bring him down our larboard side, in case Mr. Rivkins or Mr. Reed need to finish him off. Mr. Greene, kindly go below and explain our plans to Mr. Rivkins. The larboard battery must reload in double-quick time if we are to pull this off. If we can damage him with the starboard guns, the sight of the larboard battery ready to blow him out of the water may be enough to make him surrender."

"Aye, sir," Greene said and departed on his errand.

"Captain," Sweeney said with a wolfish grin, "I know you read the Bible, but I'd swear there are times you have the very devil in you."

"Thank you, Mr. Sweeney," Brewer said, bouncing on his toes with his hands clasped behind his back. "Stand by."

He stepped over to the rail and watched the range close. He wondered what the pirate thought was on that merchantman? It must be something valuable, considering the way he was willing to cross swords with a Royal Navy frigate rather than abandon the chase. Brewer grinned. *I shall have to remember to ask him. If he survives, that is.* He gauged the distance once more, and then turned to his sailing master.

"Now, Mr. Sweeney," he said calmly. "Hard to starboard." He moved swiftly to the waist. "Fire as your guns bear!"

"Aye, sir!"

The ship steadied up on her new course, and the broadside erupted, shrouding the ship in smoke.

"Now, Mr. Sweeney!" Brewer cried. "Hard to starboard! Make it a wide loop! I want room so the starboard battery can do some damage!"

"Aye, sir!"

Brewer moved to the waist. "Stand by, Mr. Rivkins! As soon as he appears from the smoke, fire every gun that will bear!"

"Aye, sir!"

The captain stepped away, aiming for the starboard rail. He stopped involuntarily when he saw the brig emerge from the smoke. *He did it!* Brewer thought with vast relief. *He fell for the ruse!*

The eruptions of the first guns jolted him back to the moment. He rushed toward the rail, but smoke obscured his vision. As soon as the gunfire ceased, he turned to the sailing master.

"Hard to starboard! Remember to bring them down the larboard side!"

"Aye, Captain!"

HMS *Phoebe* swung around obediently, and within seconds they were clear of the smoke. A cheer rang up on deck at the sight that greeted them: the brig had lost its foremast about ten feet above the deck. The ship had also taken several hits between the carronades and the long guns and was now adrift. Brewer saw no activity at all in her upper works and few men moving on the deck.

"Mr. Sweeney," he called, "heave to at half-pistol shot. I want the larboard battery plainly visible to everyone on that deck."

"Aye, sir." The sailing master went to confer with the quartermaster before reaching for a speaking trumpet.

The first lieutenant appeared at the captain's side.

"Well done, Benjamin," Brewer said.

"Not me, sir," Greene corrected him.

Brewer looked up in surprise. "Rivkins?"

Greene nodded. "Sited every gun himself."

"I see," the captain commented. "We're coming up on the pirate. I'm hoping that he's either too damaged to resist or that he pulls down his colors when he sees we're ready to fire. I want you to take a boarding party over. Take Mac with you, but leave Alfred here. Bring the captain back if he's still alive. If you think she's still seaworthy, we'll put a prize crew aboard her and send her back to Port Royal."

"Aye, sir."

"Don't take any longer than necessary, Benjamin," the captain warned. "I want to get back under way as soon as possible."

"Aye, sir." Greene saluted and left on his mission.

HMS *Phoebe* hove to, her larboard battery loaded and run out, ready to blow the pirate out of the water if he so much as twitched. There were no colors showing, which was not really a surprise, but neither was there any movement on the deck at all. Brewer called out to them with a speaking trumpet, but there was no response. He turned to the wheel.

"Once around, Mr. Sweeney," he called. "Let's see if they've abandoned ship. All the way around, then heave-to on her stern."

"Aye, Captain."

Sweeney gave the orders, and the ship began to move. They rounded the pirate's stern and came up his starboard side. There were no boats in the water, and still no movement aboard.

Sweeney joined his captain. "There's no way they could have rowed away so quickly," he said to no one in particular, "and there's only about a dozen or so bodies on the deck. Not enough for a crew. You don't think that's all there were of them, do you?"

Brewer lowered his glass and shook his head, his lips pursed as he considered his options.

"Captain! Captain!"

Brewer's eyes flew to the mizzen shrouds where he found Mr. Short gesturing frantically toward the pirate.

"I saw him, sir! I saw him! A man looked through a gun port at us!"

"Well done, Mr. Short!" Brewer grabbed a speaking trumpet and went to the rail. "Attention, pirate ship! Attention! This is Captain Brewer of His Majesty's frigate *Phoebe*. All crew still able to move must come on deck with your hands up! All crew still able to move must come up on deck with your hands up! Surrender now, or we shall fire! Move, now!"

After a moment, the hand Mr. Short had seen stood up where he was hidden between two guns and raised his hands. Within ninety seconds, roughly a dozen more came up from below decks and surrendered.

"Where are the rest?" Brewer called.

"This is all there is left," came the reply.

The captain called for the midshipman of the watch. "Pass the word for Mr. Greene to go." The boy saluted and left, and he raised the speaking trumpet again. "We are sending a boat to board you. Any movement on your part, and I shall open fire! Remain where you are!"

"We understand!"

The passage of Mr. Greene, Mac, and the marines took place without incident, and soon they were on the deck of the pirate vessel. Greene estimated there were twenty to twenty-five dead, and he counted fifteen living.

"Who is your captain?" he asked.

One of them stepped forward. "I speak for the men now, The captain was killed in your broadside."

"Your name?"

"Flint."

"Sergeant of marines, take Flint here and clap him in irons. Put him in the boat under guard for transport back to *Phoebe*." Some of the pirates made like they would resist, but Mac and the other marines took aim, and they stopped. Greene ordered the marines to hold those on deck at the fantail. He also dispatched Feathers, carpenter's mate, and a team to check the ship for damage as well as sending Mr. Murdy and Mac to search the captain's cabin. Thirty minutes later, the mate reported.

"In my opinion, sir, the ship's not worth saving. She's rotting below the water line, and at least one of our hits is letting in a good bit of water, filling up the hold. Even with repairs, I'd not like to wager on her even making Jamaica."

"Thank you, Feathers," Greene said. "We'll get everyone off and burn her. Get it ready, if you please."

"Aye, Mr. Greene." The mate knuckled his forehead and motioned for two men to follow him below.

"Mr. Murdy!" Greene called. "I am returning to the ship with the pirate captain. You shall be in command here. Keep Mac with you. Make sure you bring all papers found in the captain's cabin back with you. I know, I know," he acknowledged the midshipman's incredulous look, "pirates aren't big on papers, but you never know what you might find. We shall send boats back to take our crew and the pirates off the ship. Feathers is setting her up to burn."

"Aye, aye, Lieutenant."

Greene descended into the boat, and they pushed off for *Phoebe*. Greene studied his prisoner. Flint was of medium height and wiry build. His hair was brown and his beard was grizzled; neither looked like they'd seen any grooming in weeks. The pirate's eyes were close set, sunk deep in his head, and shifty. Mostly he stared at the bottom of the launch, but Greene caught him casting quick glances around him. Upon reaching the ship, he was taken below and held under guard while Greene reported to the captain. The sentry admitted him, and he found the captain working on his report to the admiral.

"Well, Benjamin?" he said as he set the quill down. "What did you find?"

"Feathers says she's not worth saving, sir. She was already rotting below the water line before the damage we inflicted. I left Mr. Murdy and Mac to search for any papers. We'll need to send two or three boats to take off our men and the prisoners, then I ordered her burned in accordance with your standing orders. I brought the pirate leader with me. Says his name's Flint; he sort of took command when the captain was killed in our broadside."

"We'll speak to him after Mr. Murdy makes his report. Alfred!" Brewer called, and the faithful steward appeared. "Madeira for two, if you please. Thank you. Now, Benjamin, about the plan we were discussing to land the force in Panama. The more I think about it, the better I like it. My only concern is that it will leave the ship practically indefensible. Mr. Sweeney will barely have the hands to handle her, let alone defend her."

Greene shrugged. "Part of the calculated risk, sir. I don't see how Black Rose can have sufficient forces to defend the fortress and launch a boarding action in the harbor. In fact, you might say it would benefit us immensely if she tried. That means less men to guard your wife."

Brewer looked at his wine. "Do you think she'll be there? Black Rose, I mean."

The first lieutenant took a deep swallow of his wine before answering. "Yes, I do."

"Why?"

"Two reasons. First, she may not trust anyone else with custody of Elizabeth. Rose will want to be there to make sure nothing goes wrong. Second, I think she will want to be there when, according to her plan, Alfred is killed."

The sentry knocked at the door and announced Mr. Murdy. The young gentleman marched into the room with a book under his arm and came to attention.

"As you were, Mr. Murdy," Brewer said. "Alfred, another glass of wine for the senior midshipman. Thank you. Come, Mr. Murdy. What do you have for us?"

Murdy placed the book down on the table. "These pirates didn't have any papers other than this book. It looks to be some sort of ledger. I found entries about each man's share of a treasure buried somewhere—the name's in code."

"Any references to Black Rose?" Greene asked.

"Not that I noticed sir," Murdy replied. "But I only had a glance at it."

Brewer flipped through a few pages before closing the book. "Well done, Mr. Murdy. And the prisoners?"

"Under marine guard below, sir."

"Very well," Brewer said. "Mr. Murdy, on your way out, please pass word for this Flint to be brought here."

The senior midshipman came to attention. "Aye, aye, Captain!"

When Flint entered the cabin, he joined an exclusive club:those whom Brewer instinctively and intensely disliked upon first meeting, and it had nothing whatsoever to do with his being a pirate. In Flint's case, it was his eyes. Brewer saw something there; the man had a secret, a piece of knowledge he was sure was going to get him out of trouble. Brewer was resolved that it wouldn't.

The captain and first lieutenant received him in the day cabin, standing beneath the stern windows. The sergeant-at-arms brought the prisoner forward and stood him just inside the room. Mac followed and took his station at the door.

"I am Captain Brewer, of His Majesty's frigate *Phoebe*, and this is Lieutenant Greene. Your name is?"

The pirate didn't answer right away. Brewer was about to repeat his question when the sergeant-at-arms took two steps to the side, allowing Mac to take position immediately behind the pirate's left shoulder. He leaned in and whispered in the man's ear. Brewer could only imagine what was said, but the pirate's eyes went wide. The captain saw him swallow. "Flint."

"Sir." Mac prompted.

The pirate glanced over his shoulder, but Mac stared straight ahead. Flint swallowed again. "Sir."

"Why were you attacking the merchantman?"

When no answer was forthcoming, Mac leaned in and whispered in Flint's ear. The pirate's eyes went to the left and he scowled. "Weren't attacking nobody."

"Sir!" Mac prompted.

"Sir."

"Then what do you call it?" Greene asked.

When Flint again refused to answer, Mac took a step forward and grasped the pirate's upper arm. The man winced.

"Captain," the coxswain said, "request permission to step outside for a moment."

The captain kept his face expressionless. "Of course, Mac."

"Come on, you," the coxswain growled and jerked the pirate around toward the door.

"Just a mo', guv!" he protested. "You can't do that!"

Mac jerked him savagely, and the two ended up nose-to-nose. "My captain just said I *could*, you pirate scum. Unless you want to be more respectful."

"All right, mate," Flint said. "You win."

Mac let go, and Flint resumed his place in front of the two officers. "Ask your questions," he said. Brewer noticed the glint in his eye had returned, like he had a secret.

"Why did you attack the merchantman?" Greene asked.

Flint shrugged. "Looking for supplies. Food, fresh water, gold. You name it. We could either use it or sell it."

"How much treasure did you have in the hold?" Brewer asked. "A king's ransom?"

"No. Sir," he added with a nervous glance in Mac's direction. Then he grinned and added, "Well, maybe a prince's."

The captain smiled. "That's too bad."

"Why's that?" Flint asked.

Brewer was about to answer when an explosion was heard. "Because that was your ship exploding. It was too damaged to salvage, so I ordered it burned. I presume that was the fire reaching the magazine."

The pirate grimaced and shook his head in regret. "Too bad, all right. It took us near six months to gather all that. Ah, the lads will be crying, that's for sure."

"They'll be crying for more than that," Brewer said. "The penalty for piracy is death by hanging."

Flint smiled and bobbed up and down on his toes.

Here it comes, Brewer thought.

"Now, Captain," Flint oozed, "you're not going to hang me, or anyone in my crew."

"Really? Why not."

"Because I know something you don't."

Brewer shrugged. "I doubt it, but I suppose it's possible."

"Oh, I do, believe you me."

"And what would that be?"

Flint scoffed. "Oh, come now, Captain. You can't really expect me to show my hand this early. What about me and my men?"

Brewer shrugged. "Your information would have to worth more than the gold that just sunk with your ship for me to agree to a deal."

"It is."

"All right, Mr. Flint," Brewer said as he sat down on the settee and relaxed. "What is your information?"

Flint hesitated. "My men?"

Brewer shrugged. "I told you, it depends on the information."

Flint smiled and leaned forward.

"I know where Black Rose is hiding."

Brewer and Greene looked dumbfounded, their eyes wide. Greene made a dramatic shake to clear his head.

"Let me get this straight," he said. "You know where Black Rose is hiding?"

"Yes, Lieutenant."

Greene took a step forward. "*You know* where Black Rose's hideout is? You know which island? And you're willing to trade that information for your freedom and that of your men?"

"That's right, Lieutenant."

Greene looked to his captain. "Sir?"

Flint turned to the captain and was surprised to find him smiling.

"What?" the pirate asked.

Brewer leaned forward. "Oh, Mr. Flint, I thought for a moment you were serious. You see, *we already know where she is!* In fact we're on our way to meet her now." He sat back and enjoyed the look of disbelief on the pirate's face. "Sergeant-at-arms, take him below and hold him with his men. We'll drop them off for trial after we've dealt with Black Rose."

The sergeant had to lead the prisoner away; he was so devastated that he didn't move of his own accord. When they were gone, Greene turned to see a very serious look on his captain's face.

"She will be there," he said barely above a whisper. "She *will* be there. She's got to be."

The next morning, the council met again. Panama was now only three days away, and everyone present could feel the tension rising. Brewer rose from his seat at the head of the table.

"I have decided to go with the plan for a landing force to make its way through the jungle to the fortress. The force will be landed at Bastimentos before dawn. They will have about thirty hours to cover the eight or nine miles to the fortress. In addition, the landing force will be dressed like pirates. We hope that, if they are sighted, Black Rose will think it is a rival pirate captain trying to catch her by surprise. The landing force will be commanded by Lieutenant Greene and Captain Enfield. It will consist of Lieutenants Reed and Cromwell, as well as Alfred and approximately 150 of the marines and crew." Heads turned at the large number assigned. Brewer held up his hand for quiet. "I know, but we need the numbers to hit the fortress hard and fast. The next day, I shall take the ship into the harbor at Porto Bello. The pirates should be able to see us from the fortress. Even if they have someone on the beach, Joshua should should sufficiently resemble Alfred after we dye Joshua's hair black. Joshua and I will go ashore and make our way slowly to the fortress. I plan to arrive at the door right at eight bells of the forenoon watch."

The captain saw heads bobbing up and down as he paused for any comments or criticisms, but there were none of either, so he continued. "The force shall be landed on the third morning hence. Mr. Greene, please begin assembling and outfitting your men. I want Captain Enfield and yourself to report to me at the turn of the first watch with an update.

Any questions? No? Dismissed."

CHAPTER FOURTEEN

The second dog watch ended with eight bells, and as soon as the eighth sounded there came a rap on the cabin door. The sentry admitted Lieutenant Greene and Captain Enfield. Brewer received them in the day cabin.

"Sit down, gentlemen, please," he said as they entered. "Alfred! Wine for three, if you please! Now, gentlemen, what have you to report?"

"I think we're in good shape, sir," Greene said. "The overwhelming issue is, of course, arriving at the fortress on time. Captain Enfield has a proposition that may help in that regard."

"I have three or four men who have jungle experience," Enfield elaborated. "Not in Panama, but it should still help. I want to send them out ahead of the main force to scout the best route, along with some men armed with machetes and axes to clear the path for the main force. Everyone will have a sword, or axe, and we will try to avoid use of pistol or musket before we arrive at the fortress."

"Good. Ah, thank you, Alfred," Brewer said as the wine was delivered. "What about the disguises?"

"No problem there, sir," Greene answered with a grin.

"Some of the men's Sunday best would qualify, I'm afraid." Brewer chuckled, remembering the somewhat... *colorful* garb they had picked up on shore leave. "What about the final number?"

"We're still coordinating that, sir," Enfield said.

"We want to make sure we leave enough of the right people on board to handle the ship, sir," Greene added. "We hope to have that number for you by tomorrow morning."

"Fine. Then if you'll excuse me, gentlemen?"

"Of course, sir." Greene answered. The two men rose and came to attention before leaving the room. Brewer stared at the door for several minutes after they'd gone. So intense was his distraction that he did not notice Alfred had returned until that worthy cleared his throat rather loudly.

"Alfred?" he said.

"I came to see if you wanted anything, sir."

"No, nothing," Brewer sighed. "Thank you, Alfred."

"In that case, sir, I think I'll take a turn around the deck."

Brewer nodded and retreated to his desk. He did not see his servant's eyes narrow.

When Alfred left the cabin, he made a detour to the sickbay before he went up on deck. When he got there, he stepped inside and realized he was interrupting school. Pudge was seated in front of the doctor, who was in the midst of leading a spelling lesson.

"Try it again, Pudge," the doctor said.

The boy sighed. "K-A..."

"*C*-A-T, Pudge!"

"Aw, who cares how you spell it?" the boy whined. "I know one when I see it!"

The doctor began counting off on his fingers. "The captain, Mr. Greene, Mr. Sweeney, Mac, me, and Alfred, that's who! Now try it again."

Alfred stepped forward. "Excuse me, Doctor, but may I have a minute?"

"Thank God," Alfred heard the boy whisper.

The doctor stepped over. "What may I do for you, Alfred?"

"It's the captain, Doctor," Alfred confided in a low voice. "I'm afraid he's becoming despondent. Perhaps you might look in on him when school is out? Please do not mention our conversation."

"Of course," Spinelli agreed. "I think I can talk him into a game of chess."

"Thank you," Alfred said. He nodded toward Pudge. "Is the boy giving you trouble?"

The doctor shrugged. "Let's just say the allure of learning to become a gentleman has definitely worn off."

"I see. Let me see if I can't help a bit." Alfred looked to the doctor for permission.

"By all means," Spinelli said.

Alfred stepped forward. "Pudge!" he called, and the lad turned. "From this day forth, I will be checking with the doctor and Mr. Sweeney every day regarding your lessons. If they tell me you did not do your best, there will be no training in weapons that day. Instead you will spend that time making up for your lack of effort. Do you understand?"

The boy was absolutely crestfallen. "Yes, sir."

Alfred turned to the doctor and made a *there-you-have-it* gesture. "I shall speak to you later, Doctor," he said.

Brewer sat alone in his cabin, the space lit by a single candle on his desk before him. He had his miniature of Elizabeth set out on the desk. He could feel remorse and doubt growing within him as they got closer to Panama. He disliked the idea of using his ship and crew to rescue Elizabeth. He would do it without hesitation to save any British citizen kidnapped by pirates, but Elizabeth was not just any British citizen. She was his wife, and nobody laid hands on his wife. Every fiber of his being told him that he should be out there on his own, rescuing her. Suddenly, he chuckled. *Well, maybe not alone,* he realized. *I imagine I'd have a hard time leaving Mac behind.* He picked up the miniature and caressed it with his thumb. *I will see you soon. We shall be together again, my love. I swear it.*

A knock at the door interrupted his thoughts. "Enter!"

The sentry stepped in. "Sir? Do you have a moment for Doctor Spinelli?"

Brewer sighed. "Send him in." He set the portrait down and turned to see his friend march in.

"What can I do for you, Doctor?"

Spinelli's eyebrows rose a pitch. "Just coming to check on you, Captain. We haven't played chess in a few days."

Brewer put the portrait away. "I'm afraid I've been busy."

"No doubt," Spinelli agreed. "But now that the plan's been decided and Greene and Enfield are getting ready, I thought you might have time for a game or two."

Brewer looked at him. "And if I say no?"

Spinelli smiled. "You can even have white."

The captain surrendered. He opened the desk and handed the chess set to the doctor. The two men went to the table and the doctor set up the pieces.

"Alfred!" Brewer called. He looked a little confused when Mac and Pudge appeared.

"Alfred's up on deck, sir," Mac explained.

"Ah, yes, that's right. Well, wine for myself and the doctor."

"Aye, sir."

Brewer sat down behind the white pieces, and the two men went to war. Spinelli could tell right away that his opponent's mind was not on the game. After two moves, the doctor sat back. "Where's your mind, William?"

Brewer almost protested—indeed, he debated for a moment throwing the doctor out of his cabin—but in the end he thought better of it. "In a fortress at Porto Bello."

Spinelli moved his rook. "I thought as much." He took the captain's bishop. "Check."

The captain moved his king, then, two moves later, sprang a trap himself. "Check." He sat back. "I know what I'm supposed to be—captain of the ship, leader of the crew. Impersonal, like it's not my wife that's being held or I'm not being asked to trade her life for a member of my crew." He shook his head. "I don't know if I can do it."

"You don't have to." Spinelli took his opponent's pawn. "Not anymore. No, I should say not much longer. After that, you can do what you need to."

"What do you mean?" Brewer asked.

"The planning is over," Spinelli explained. "The operation is set, and Mr. Greene and Captain Enfield are putting it into motion. That was the dangerous part, William, and you held yourself together and got through it in good order. Now, all you have to do is to hold yourself together another few days. You don't want to give it away before Greene and Enfield can reach the fortress. After that, all need for pretense is gone.

Checkmate."

Brewer frowned at the board, but his mind wasn't on the game.

"Look, William," Spinelli said, "I know that Black Rose hit you in a sensitive area. Elizabeth and Anne are the first family you've known since you left your father's house to join the navy and he disinherited you. You don't want to lose another one." The doctor shrugged. "You're allowed to be human."

Brewer inhaled a deep breath, long and slow, then let it out just as slow, letting the air take as much of the tension as he could let go of. He shook his head from side to side, as though he was getting rid of the proverbial cobwebs that dulled his thinking. He looked to his friend.

"Thank you, Adam."

"Not at all," Spinelli replied. "I owe you for saving my life in Martinique."

Brewer opened his mouth to protest but closed it again. He remembered the incident.

Two nights later, Captain Brewer came up on deck at four bells of the middle watch. He made his way over to the quartermaster. "What's our position?"

"Good morning, Captain." The quartermaster touched his hat and reached for the chart. He held it up so the captain could see it more easily in the moonlight—Brewer had ordered darken ship when they began their run toward the coast three hours earlier. "By my reckoning, we should be about here, sir." He pointed to the position. "I make it about six or seven miles now, Captain; about two more hours at our present speed."

"Good, Mr. Gentry," Brewer replied. "Slow and quiet."
"Aye, sir."

Brewer went forward to find Captain Enfield going over the final instructions with his scouts. The idea had come up in the council meeting yesterday and had been quickly approved. A small boat with five of the scouts would be sent ashore, ahead of the main force, and while *Phoebe* was still a good way out at sea. If the beach was clear, they would alert the ship with a white light. If the beach was not clear, a red light would be used and the scouts would return, hopefully unseen. The operation did not have to go off on any particular night, so long as it took place in the next week at the outside. That was about the limit of time that they could justify by claiming a slow passage from St. Kitts. Brewer stopped short so he didn't interrupt the meeting.

"Remember," Enfield was saying, "the most important thing is stealth. We can always try again, so long as nobody knows we're here. Go in *quietly*. If you can secure the beach, use the white light. Thirty seconds on, then cover it for thirty, then show it for another thirty. Do that a maximum of three or four times. If nobody comes in and it gets near dawn, get back in your boat and get out of there. We'll try it again tomorrow. Any questions?"

"What if someone wanders on to the beach or approaches after we've sent the white light?" a scout asked.

"After the white light is sent, anyone who comes upon you must be killed if they are hostile or taken prisoner. That is the only way to ensure secrecy once the main force is on its way to the beach."

"And who makes that decision?" the same scout asked.

Enfield nodded toward one of the scouts. "Sgt. Clark is in command of the mission. Any decisions will be his, as will any responsibility. Anyone who doesn't think they could follow his orders, I need to know now."

No one said a word, and Enfield nodded his approval.

"Good. Now get this stuff loaded in the boat. Harrison, make sure the white and red lights stay dry."

"Yes, Captain."

Enfield turned to leave his men to their tasks and saw Brewer standing three paces away. He touched his hat. "Sorry, Captain. I didn't know you were there. Did you want to address the lads before they go?"

"No, thank you, Captain. I think you did just fine."

"These are my best men, Captain," Enfield confided. "They'll do right by ye. If you'll excuse me, sir, I need to see Lieutenant Greene."

"Of course, Captain."

Enfield touched his hat again and headed aft, leaving Brewer to watch the scouts at work. He was careful to step back so his presence didn't disturb them. They worked silently and efficiently, and he longed to go with them. He turned and made his way aft, knowing he had his own part to play in the drama. When he reached the quarterdeck, he found Mr. Gentry and Mr. Sweeney looking over the chart. The two men saluted as he approached.

"Another two miles or so, Captain," Sweeney said. "Thirty minutes, then we'll heave-to and put the scout party over the side."

"Very good," Brewer clasped his hands behind his back to hide his nervousness. "I'd feel better if we had some reliable maps showing the way to the fortress."

Sweeney shrugged. "We know the general direction. They should be able to take a sighting from a hilltop or treetop by mid-afternoon. Hopefully, they'll see the fortress and head for it."

"Yes." The captain studied the deck for a moment before wandering aft. *This is no good,* he thought. *All I'm doing is distracting them.* He turned on his heel and headed for the companionway. "Mr. Sweeney," he called over his shoulder, "see that I am called when we reach the disembarkation point."

"Aye, sir."

When Brewer got to his cabin, he flopped down on the settee in the day cabin, exhausted by frustration and inactivity. He closed his eyes and breathed in deeply. *I'm not cut out for this sort of thing,* he mused. *Give me a straight up gun battle any day.*

He jumped as he heard a familiar voice say, "Can I get you anything, Captain?"

"Mac? What are you doing here?"

"Sorry I startled you, sir," Mac said, "but I knew Alfred would be getting ready to go ashore, so I thought I'd best be around in case you needed anything."

Brewer grinned. How like his coxswain. "Yes, a glass of wine, if you please."

"Aye, sir." The big Cornishman returned in a moment with the wine. Brewer held it up in salute. "Hopefully, the day after tomorrow will be our turn, Mac."

"Aye, sir." He made to go, but then he stopped and turned back. "We'll get her back for you, Captain, don't you doubt it. And Black Rose will pay for this."

Brewer held up his glass again in silent salute and agreement. Mac nodded and left his captain to his thoughts. As it was, Brewer had barely finished his wine when a knock at the door admitted Mr. O'Reilly, midshipman of the watch.

"Mr. Sweeney's respects, Captain," the boy said as he came to attention. "He says we've reached our destination and requests that you come up on deck."

"My compliments to Mr. Sweeney, and I shall be up directly." The boy came to attention and left the room. "Mac," Brewer said, "my coat and hanger."

He stepped up on deck to find Greene, Enfield, Sweeney, and Gentry all crowding around the chart. Brewer could see the flickering light of a single candle lighting their faces. Greene was the first to notice him, and someone immediately snuffed out the light. Captain Enfield turned and saluted.

"Scouting party ready to go, sir," he reported. "Request permission for them to proceed."

"Granted," Brewer returned the salute. "Tell them I wish them good luck."

"Thank you, sir." Enfield went forward.

Brewer walked to the larboard rail with Mr. Greene to watch the scouts row toward the shore and disappear into the darkness. "Well, Benjamin, we are committed now." He turned and leaned against the rail and crossed his arms over his chest. "I want this to be over, with Elizabeth safely home with Anne, and Black Rose with several holes in her." He shrugged. "I'm afraid I'm not very good at waiting."

"Nor am I, sir," Greene confessed. He hesitated, and then continued in a low voice. "William, every man on my team knows what's at stake, and every man has the same priority— Elizabeth's safe return." He saw his friend open his mouth to protest and cut him off. "With all respect, sir, it will do no good for you to protest. Please do not put us in the position of disobeying an order to put Black Rose's capture or death above Elizabeth's safety, for it would not be obeyed."

The captain's eyes jumped from the first lieutenant to the deck and back again. "You know, Lieutenant, I had thought to issue you an order regarding the disposition of said pirate, but I suddenly find myself forgetful of what I was about to say." He grinned.

Greene looked out over the railing. "Thank you, sir. If you'll excuse me, I need to check on my men." He saluted and disappeared into the darkness forward.

Sweeney and Gentry joined their captain. "Mr. Greene estimated thirty minutes to reach the shore," Sweeney said. "Sounds about right. Give them thirty minutes to determine if the beach is secure. Allow for surprises like tides, etc., and that means we can start looking for a light in about seventy minutes. If we don't see anything within ninety minutes, we head in to close the distance."

"Agreed," Brewer said. "I want extra lookouts in the larboard shrouds and extra runners along the rail."

"Aye, sir," Gentry said.

The captain paced the deck as the minutes ticked slowly by. He had no idea what time it was when he became aware of activity on the deck. He turned and saw Skimpy running aft toward Mr. Greene on the quarterdeck. Greene patted him on the head and escorted him toward the captain. Brewer stopped pacing as they approached. The boy knuckled his forehead.

"Old Christian sent me to report, sir," he said. "White light!"

"Is he sure?" Brewer asked.

"Aye, sir!"

Brewer noticed Mr. Short approach and speak to Greene. The first lieutenant smiled. "Confirmed, sir! White light from the beach, and in good time, too."

"Mr. Greene, get your men into the water," Brewer ordered. "As soon as the last boat is recovered, *Phoebe* shall retreat out to sea. I shall enter the harbor at Porto Bello tomorrow morning as planned. Good luck."

"Thank you, Captain." The two saluted, and Greene was gone.

"Mr. Sweeney, prepare to get under way," Brewer said.

"Aye, sir."

Brewer stood by the rail and watched as the boats containing the strike force dissolved into the gloom. It was nearly an hour before they appeared again. The petty officer who conned the first boat back came aft to report.

"Strike force landed successfully, sir," he said after his salute. "Mr. Greene sends his respects and said to tell you they would be away into the jungle before dawn. He will see you in the fortress tomorrow afternoon."

"Thank you. Return to your boat and get it stowed. When the last boat is secure, report to Mr. Sweeney."

"Aye, aye, Captain!" The man saluted again and was gone.

"Mr. Sweeney," Brewer said, "after you are notified that the last boat is secure, head due north away from the beach. I want it noted in the order book: any sightings are to be logged, and then turn the ship away from the contact. We must hide until we pull into the bay at Porto Bello tomorrow morning. Also, notify me with every sighting. I shall be in my cabin."

"Aye, sir," Sweeney replied.

It took thirty minutes to get the boats aboard and secured, after which HMS *Phoebe* turned her back on the Panamanian shore and disappeared over the northern horizon just as the sky lightened.

* * * * *

Lieutenant Greene made his way halfway up the beach before turning to look out over the water. The last of the boats were unloading their men and supplies, and he could already see several that were on their way back to the ship. Mr. Murdy was by his side. Greene pointed to him and three others.

"You four!" he said. "Follow me!" He led them to a tree at the edge of the beach. "I need you to find Captain Enfield, Lieutenant Cromwell, and Alfred and bring them here to me. Swiftly now!"

The four spread out up and down the beach. The council had decided some days ago that the four of them would all come to the beach in separate boats; that way no single accident could claim more than one of them. The three were brought to the tree in short order.

"Any problems?" Greene asked. The others shook their heads. "Good. Captain, what's our bearing."

Enfield took out his compass and allowed it to steady itself on true north. He indicated a direction northwest into the jungle. "Our orders are to take the best path leading between north and northwest, staying closer to northwest. At noon, or somewhere close to it, we are to try to get a sighting by climbing a tree or hill. Remember to shade your telescopes so the lens does not reflect in the sun and give us away."

"Right," Greene said. "There you have it. Captain, have the scouts set out first with your group right behind. We shall follow you, one group at a time."

A commotion was stirred off to their left, and a group brought up a native they had taken prisoner. "Report!" Greene demanded.

"Caught this one coming out of the woods, Lieutenant," a scout said. "He was surprised to see us and surrendered right away."

"Do you speak English?" Greene demanded, and the man nodded. "What is your name, and what are you doing here?"

The native looked around, obviously fearful. "My name is Roberto. I often come to this beach at dawn to fish. What are you doing here? You are English pirates?"

Greene glanced at Enfield, who nodded. "Never you mind that. I am going to give you a choice, Roberto. You can help us, or you can die."

The fisherman's eyes grew wide. "H-help you with what?"

"We need a guide to help us through the jungle," Enfield said. "We are going to the fortress that is just southeast of the harbor at Porto Bello."

The man tried to run, but the scouts had him securely by the arms. "No, *Señor*, please! I beg you! I have a family! I cannot go there! I do not want to die!"

Alfred drew his sword and set the point against Roberto's chest. The effect was immediate; the man ceased struggling.

"Why do you not want to go there?"

"Because," he answered, his voice choking in fear, "Pirates are there, *Señor,* very bad men, and five days ago, their leader returned. We cannot go there! It is too dangerous. We will all die."

"Black Rose?" Greene asked. Roberto's eyes grew wide again, and Alfred nudged him with his sword's point. "Black Rose is there? Now? Did you see him?"

"No, *Señor,* I hear it from others."

Greene considered for a moment before looking at the scouts. "Hold him here." He signaled the other three to step away with him.

"What do you think?" Greene asked after they stepped ten feet off to the side.

"He's telling the truth," Alfred said without hesitation. "Or at least what he believes to be the truth."

"Did you notice something?" Cromwell spoke up. "He knew *exactly* which fortress we were talking about. That means he could probably lead us to it."

Greene looked to Enfield, and the captain nodded.

"Agreed."

"Very well." Greene led them back to their captive. "Roberto, you still have the same choice I gave you earlier. You can help us, or we will kill you where you stand. Take us to the fortress, or die."

The fisherman opened his mouth to scream for help and thrashed about desperately to break free, but a scout clamped his hand over Roberto's mouth, and Alfred rested the point of his blade at the unfortunate man's throat. Resistance ceased, but his eyes were still wild with terror.

"Listen to me, Roberto," Greene said, but the man paid him no attention until he pulled a gold coin from his pocket and held it up before him. "I have twenty-five coins exactly like this one. We looted them from a Spanish ship two weeks ago. They are yours, along with your freedom, unharmed, if you take us to the fortress."

The fisherman was tempted by the coin and the promise of more. "H-how do I know you will keep your w-word?"

Greene smiled viciously. "You do not. But know that I will have my men kill you if you refuse us."

Roberto looked at the coin again. "B-but, the coins—all of them—*and* my freedom? Do you swear this?"

"I do."

Roberto nodded. "I will take you there."

"Good," Greene pointed to Enfield. "You will go in front with the captain and his men."

"Sí, *Señor*," Roberto accompanied Enfield and the scouts into the jungle.

About an hour into the jungle, Enfield and Roberto were walking right behind the scouts, who were clearing a pathway with their machetes. Suddenly from behind them came intense cries of pain.

"Stay here!" Enfield told the scouts. "Be on the lookout for an attack! Roberto, come with me."

They made their way back down the path as quickly as they could until they came on a group of men on the ground, one of whom was writhing in pain while the others were holding body parts as though they had been burned.

"What happened here?" Enfield asked.

"Not sure, sir!" one of the sailors standing off to the side said. "I saw this one—he pointed to the one writhing on the ground—eat one of these little apples off a tree, but I think all the rest of them did was lean against the trees for a rest."

"Oh, no! *Señor*!" Roberto cried and grasped Enfield's arm. "It is the manchineel tree! Poisonous! Very poisonous! The sap! It will burn the skin! Look at this man's hand, and that one's arm! See the burns? That is where the flesh touched the tree, or got some of the sap on it!"

"What about him?" Enfield indicated the writhing man.

Roberto looked about him. "Did anyone see if he ate the fruit, or just put it in his mouth?"

"I think he ate one," a bystander said.

Roberto shook his head. "I do not know if he will live or not. Some die from eating the fruit, but others do not. It is called *manzanillas de la muerte*, or 'little apples of death'. One thing I do know, he will be in great pain for many days.

These who leaned upon the trees should recover. At least they can walk with us." He pointed at the leaves. "The sap is in all parts of the tree. Anywhere is touches the skin, it will burn. If it gets in your eyes, you will be blind for several days, but you will recover, if the pain does not drive you mad. My uncle's mule got some in his eye, and they had to shoot him because he went *loco,* kicking everything and everyone."

"Everyone stay away from the bloody trees!" Enfield sighed. "I need one man to go report to Lieutenant Greene and bring him here."

"I'll do it!" said a hand.

It took twenty minutes for the lieutenant to arrive, and another two for Enfield to brief him on the situation. The man who ate the fruit—he turned out to be a cooper's mate named Dimwiddle—had briefly passed out from the pain but was now groaning again.

Greene studied the trees and shook his head. "Well," he mused aloud, "we obviously can't take him back to the ship. Roberto, is there anything that can be done about the pain so that he could march?"

"No, *Señor,* there is nothing. Most people are in severe pain for days, and many die from it."

Greene studied the trees again and thought quickly. "Captain, I confess to being a little out of my depth. What would you do in the army?"

Enfield looked down at his man with a frown borne of a dislike of a duty that must be followed. "We are behind enemy lines," he said in a voice low and devoid of compassion. "If he is found, we shall be betrayed, and our mission will fail." He went down on one knee and leaned in close. "Dimwiddle, I need you to concentrate on my voice. You must understand what I am about to tell you. Are you listening?"

"Yes, Captain." The man bit his lip against the pain and forced his eyes toward his captain.

"I need to know if you can travel silently. If you betray us with a cry of pain or even a moan, I will have to kill you. Can you do this?"

Dimwiddle squeezed his eyes shut, clamped his jaw closed, and nodded.

"Good man." Enfield stood and turned to Greene. "Sir, I recommend he be put on a makeshift stretcher and brought along with us."

Greene opened his mouth to question the recommendation, but closed it again. "Very well, Captain. Please see to it. We need to get moving again."

"Aye, sir."

Thirty minutes later, the party was moving again. Captain Enfield and Roberto again were at the front with the scouts. Greene took his place with the vanguard. When Dimwiddle was carried past him, he noticed that someone had gagged the unfortunate man to keep him from making any noise.

Shortly after midday, Greene saw a messenger from the vanguard approaching. The man began to salute and caught himself before his arm rose. Greene nodded to himself—the men had been warned against behavior that would identify them as Royal Navy.

"You're needed forward, sir," the messenger said.

"Right behind you," Greene said. The man led him to where Enfield and Sergeant Clark were standing at the base of a large tree. Greene was thankful to see it was not a manchineel tree.

"Yes, Enfield?" he asked.

The marine nodded up the tree. "I've got Crosby up this tree with a glass, sir, looking for the fortress. Roberto estimates we've come about three miles, give or take, so I thought we'd take a chance."

Movement from above caused them to look up and then step away to give Crosby room to descend. The man leaned against the tree trunk and massaged his shoulder. "Nothing, sir," he said to Enfield. "Hills and low clouds make it difficult to see."

"All right, Ethan," Enfield clapped his man on the shoulder. "We try again in an hour or so." He turned to Greene and shrugged. "Sorry. I thought we'd have better news for you."

Greene shrugged. "We'll get there."

The group had a quick meal before setting out again. The heat and humidity became brutal as the day wore on, and Greene was quietly thankful not to be wearing his uniform. Progress was slow through the dense jungle. They didn't have a great deal of time to waste, so the best the scouts could do was to clear a narrow pathway, which limited their speed. Greene guessed it was two or three hours before he saw the messenger coming his way again—only this time, the man was running.

"We've got it, sir!" the man said a little too loudly. "Crosby says he's sighted the fortress. Captain Enfield wants you to come, sir." The two men hurried forward. "Roberto went up the tree," the messenger continued. "He confirmed that it's the fortress we're looking for. Crosby estimates we're about two miles north of it. Here we are, sir." Greene found Enfield and Clark at the bottom of another tree, only this time they were looking up for any sign or signal from Crosby. "Report," he said.

"Crosby!" Enfield called. "Come down! Just a moment, sir; Crosby will report."

The topman scrambled down the tree in a hurry, landing in a shower of leaves and insects.

"The fortress is about two miles to the south, give or take," he said. "There's a ridge in between where we may be seen if we're not careful."

"Good work, Crosby," Greene said. "Captain?" He indicated a private conference, and Enfield stepped aside with him.

"Well?" Greene asked.

"Sir," Enfield said, "I recommend that we send Sergeant Clark with half the scouts and twenty or twenty-five men to occupy the ridge immediately. From there, we should be in a position to move against the fortress in the morning."

Greene looked around, wishing for the horizon but seeing nothing but trees. He nodded. "Do it."

Ten minutes later, Sergeant Clark was leading his men forward. One hour later, Greene, Enfield, and the rest of their force joined them on the far side of the ridge from the fortress. The sun was beginning to set as the two British officers crawled up to the crest of the ridge to observe the fortress, taking care not to be visible. Lights illuminated several windows, and sentries could be made out, walking the battlements.

Greene lowered his glass. "They certainly aren't trying to hide, are they?"

"No reason to," Enfield replied. "They expect their package to be delivered to them any day now." He lowered his glass. "How right they are! But it won't happen as they expect." The two men retreated slowly down the slope. Sergeant Clark met them at the base of the ridge.

"No fires tonight!" Enfield ordered.

"Right, sir," the sergeant replied. "I suggest we split the group into four teams and spread them out for the night. That way, if one group is discovered, the others might still be able to complete the mission."

"Good idea," Enfield said. "Implement it at once. Organize the watch schedule. I want to be over the ridge and on the way to the fortress before dawn."

Clark saluted and jogged off on his errand. Enfield sat down and opened his pack. Greene stood apart, thinking,. *Tomorrow is going to be an interesting day.*

CHAPTER FIFTEEN

Dawn found Captain William Brewer on the quarterdeck of HMS *Phoebe*. The ship's course, since dropping off Greene and Enfield, had been northeast on a direct line away from the beach, but Brewer stood at the fantail wishing he could see over the horizon. He was uneasy about the whole operation. The truth was that he felt uneasy about entrusting Elizabeth's safety to anyone but himself. He sighed in frustration as he stared at the horizon. There were two things he wanted more than anything at that moment: Elizabeth, safe and by his side; and Black Rose, dead. Preferably by his own hand.

The sound of footsteps alerted him that he was no longer alone. He turned to see Lieutenant Rivkins standing two steps behind him.

"Something I can do for you, Lieutenant?" he asked.

Rivkins touched his hat. "No, sir. I was thinking about asking you the same question." Brewer shook his head and turned back to the horizon.

Rivkins stepped to the rail, careful to keep a respectful distance. "Not like the Med, is it?"

The captain turned his head. "Excuse me?"

Rivkins nodded to the horizon. "All this. Not like the Med at all. That was much more straightforward, don't you think? Perhaps I'm using the wrong word. That fight wasn't so *personal*."

Brewer turned back to the horizon, his face an emotionless mask. "No."

Rivkins moved to his captain's side and lowered his voice so no one else would hear. "But this one is personal. Sir, I—we, actually; the entire crew—want you to know that it's personal to us as well." Brewer looked at him with one eyebrow raised a touch. Rivkins continued, "Nobody goes after our captain that we don't feel it, too. Forgive me if I've crossed the line, Captain, but you need to know that you are not alone."

Brewer held the eyes of his second, and he saw there the same concern and loyalty he had seen in Mac's eyes earlier.

He nodded once—more of a bow of the head.

"Thank you, Mr. Rivkins."

The lieutenant touched his hat as his captain returned to his study of the horizon. Rivkins left him to his solitary vigil and returned to the wheel.

Mr. Sweeney made way for Rivkins and nodded toward the captain. "How's he doing?"

Rivkins crossed his arms over his chest as he stared at his captain's back. "He's fine."

Sweeney stepped around until he was in front of the lieutenant. "What is it you're not telling me?"

The lieutenant blinked at that; the question caught him off guard. "How's that?"

The sailing master chuckled. "I have made a life out of standing back beside my wheel and studying the officers as they go about their business on the quarterdeck." He motioned toward the captain at the fantail. "I've been studying *him* for more than three years now. It doesn't take a spiritualist to see how worried he is, let alone how hard he's trying to control it. *You,* on the other hand, my dear lieutenant, are not so open a book. So, I will ask again. *What is it you're not telling me?"*

Rivkins' eyes went from the sailing master to the captain slowly. "When I was in the Med with the captain—he was a lieutenant then, my divisional officer—I got the feeling while we were fighting the pirates that there was something more to him, a rage that he managed somehow to keep buried. The trouble with that is, something is bound to come along that will reveal that rage to the world. He will lose control of it, and then God only knows what the consequences will be. And he will have to bear them all alone." He turned back to the sailing master. "I'm afraid that the kidnapping of his wife will be the thing that causes the volcano to erupt, so to speak. If that is the case, I wouldn't want to be Black Rose when that happens."

"Lieutenant," Sweeney said quietly, "you're not far wrong."

Sweeney moved away to check the chart again. Rivkins returned to his study of the captain until he heard the sound of someone emerging from below. He greeted the doctor as he stepped free of the companionway.

Spinelli motioned toward the captain. "Did he leave orders to be left alone?"

Rivkins shook his head. "Not to my knowledge."

"Excellent," the doctor said. "Excuse me."

He stepped past the lieutenant and made his way to the captain's side.

"I was wondering when you'd show up," Brewer commented.

"Well," Spinelli said with a smile, "good morning to you, too, my dear captain. Enjoying the view? Or wishing you were with them rather than here?"

Brewer turned just enough to see the doctor with the corner of his eye. "How many times have I asked you to confine your medicine to my body and leave my feelings alone?"

"Oh, hundreds, I'm sure," Spinelli deadpanned. "Still, how can I learn if I don't try?" He clasped his hands behind his back and stared at the ship's wake. "How are you holding up?"

"How do you think?"

Spinelli's eyebrows rose and he pursed his lips. "That answers that question. Captain, shall we adjourn to your cabin for a drink and a game? Or perhaps you'd rather try Pudge's coffee again."

Brewer turned and opened his mouth, but he closed it again without speaking. He met the doctor's eye, and knew that his friend was right.

"Follow me, Doctor, if you please."

The two men went below. When they entered the captain's cabin, Pudge appeared in the pantry doorway.

"Anything I can get for you, Captain?" the boy asked. Brewer ignored him and went to the day cabin.

"Don't mind him," the doctor said. "Can you bring us two cups of coffee?"

"Right away, Doctor!"

Spinelli stepped into the day room to find his captain seated on the settee, elbows on his knees, his head in his hands. The doctor silently took a seat beside him. Pudge appeared in the doorway, carefully holding a tray with two steaming cups on it. Spinelli gently nudged his captain.

"What?" He said, then he saw Pudge holding his tray. "Oh, thank you, Pudge. Come in." Each man took a cup. "Thank you, Pudge. That's all."

"Aye, sir."

They sipped tentatively and were pleasantly surprised.

"The boy's getting better," Spinelli said. He set his cup down. "Can you hold on until tomorrow?"

Brewer buried his head in his hands again. "I don't have much choice, do I?"

"No," the doctor agreed, "but that doesn't make it any easier."

Brewer only grunted.

"Trust them, William," Spinelli said. "Greene is very good at his job. Not only that, he has Alfred and Mr. Cromwell with him. They will be there, and on time. The only real question for you is whether there will be any pirates left when you arrive tomorrow at noon."

Brewer raised his head and took a drink of his coffee. He nodded his agreement at the lad's improvement, then set his cup down and leaned back to rest his head on the top of the settee.

"I know you're right, Adam," he said, sounding very tired, "but I've never been very good at this waiting business. Captain Bush used to tell us stories, and it seems that every time they were in a spot like this, Captain Hornblower—he was a captain then—could always be found in the same place, the lee of the quarterdeck, pacing back and forth. Sometimes he even took his meals there, pacing the whole time. I guess he wanted the crew to see him, to know that he wasn't worried, so he paced back and forth to keep himself busy. I'm just not built that way."

Spinelli shrugged. "Nobody expects you to be. William, nobody *wants* you to be that way." Brewer just stared into space, so the doctor went on. "You are not Hornblower. You are not Bush. You are Captain William Brewer of His Majesty's frigate *Phoebe*. You are the best we have in this part of the world, my friend, and you got that way by learning from everyone you could and then putting your own stamp on it."

The captain's eyes turned to him. "But what if she dies?"

"She's not going to die."

"But what if she does?"

"Elizabeth is not going to die."

"But what if she does!" Brewer shouted, but he quickly regained control and returned to staring into space. "What do I do then? What do I tell Anne?"

Spinelli's heart broke as he remembered feeling something very similar after he received the letter telling him that Mary had died. He had walked the valley the captain had feared he would enter, but he knew the way out.

"You go on, William," he said frankly. "And you tell Anne the truth."

The captain was silent, but his face betrayed his fear.

"William," the doctor said, "I believe the phrase is, *'Don't borrow trouble.'* You have a plan, and you have good men ready to deliver a hammer blow shortly. You must let the plan unfold now. You keep them busy at the front door, so to speak, and trust Greene and Enfield to rescue Elizabeth."

It took a minute, but Brewer squeezed his eyes shut. He took a deep breath and exhaled it loud and slow. He opened his eyes and then rubbed his face with both hands.

"Thank you, Adam," he said. "I needed that." He picked up his cup but frowned when he noticed the dregs had grown cold. "I need another. One for you, Doctor? Good. Pudge!" The lad appeared.

"More coffee, if you please."

"Oh, aye, sir!"

The boy came back with a steaming pot, from which he carefully refilled both cups before bowing and retreating from the room.

"You know," the doctor said, "I wonder if he's not after Alfred's job as well as Mac's."

Brewer chuckled. "I'll have no objection, providing his coffee continues to improve."

The night was moonless, but the sky was clear as Alfred sat against a rock and looked up at the stars through a gap in the forest cover. He tried to focus on the points of light to keep his mind off what the morning might bring. He remembered reading somewhere that each star was a sun like their own, only a very long distance away. If that were so, was it possible that one of those suns had planets orbiting it? And might it also be possible that one of those planets would have people on it? So, there might be someone out there looking back at him. *Fascinating thought,* he mused. *I wonder if we shall ever develop technology that will allow us to sail to other planets through space the way we travel to other lands across the oceans?*

Footsteps approached, and he turned to see Mr. Cromwell standing there.

"May I sit?" he asked. Alfred shrugged and motioned to the ground. "Thank you. How's Dimwiddle doing?"

"Better, now that he's not being jostled around," Alfred replied, and pointed to where the man was sleeping. "I'm going to ask Mr. Greene if he can remain here with his stretcher bearers when we move out. They can take him down to the harbor and hopefully get him to the ship while we're busy in the fortress. It'll get him to the doctor quicker."

"Good idea," Cromwell said.

Alfred shrugged. "I just hope it's over tomorrow, one way or the other."

"I've never been in a fight like this before," Cromwell said. "So much riding on it, with the captain's wife and all. Not the same as boarding a pirate ship. Then you only care about securing the deck or what have you. Now we have to get into the fortress and find Mrs. Brewer before Black Rose and her men realize they are under attack and kill her out of spite."

Alfred nodded. "That about sums it up. I ask one favor."

"What's that?"

"Black Rose is mine."

Cromwell looked to his friend, but Alfred's eyes were on the heavens. Cromwell considered, then rose to his feet. "I'll try to remember that." He left to go check on his men.

A short distance away, Lieutenant Greene and Captain Enfield were going over their plans.

"So," Greene said, "we are agreed that, as much as possible, stealth should be the order of the day?"

Enfield nodded as he took a drink of water. "The more time we have to search for Mrs. Brewer before we're discovered, the better her chances of coming through this alive."

"Agreed. Send the scouts out at the very break of dawn to look for doorways or a good spot to use the grappling hooks to climb a wall."

"I'll speak to Sergeant Clark. I suggest we approach to within two hundred yards of the fortress, be there at dawn."

"We still need to wait for the captain to approach at noon. That will distract them, especially Black Rose."

"I know. I just want to be ready, in case we get an unexpected opportunity."

Greene thought it over. "Sounds reasonable."

* * * * *

Ever since returning from his interview with the captain, Flint had sat near the entrance to the cable tier, watching and planning. The events of the past twenty-four hours had drawn his attention, and now he was looking for an opportunity.

"Well?" It was Spot who sat down uninvited. He was called 'Spot' because of a large mole on his upper right arm. He had been a gun captain on the old ship; he had also been a pirate nearly as long as Flint had walked the earth. That kind of longevity earned respect.

"Well what?" Flint growled.

"Have you figured out what's going on yet?" Spot whispered loudly. "Near as I can tell, the captain has not changed course for Jamaica, and early this morning a large part of the crew was put ashore. Any idea what's going on?"

Flint shrugged. "One or two. I've been talking with the boy who brings us our food, and he tells me they're going to attack a fortress."

"Fortress? What fortress?"

"I have no idea. But the captain did tell me that they knew where Black Rose was hiding and that they were on their way for a meeting. I wonder if that force they put ashore was going to sneak up on the pirate's fortress from the rear?" Flint scratched his chin for a moment. "I wonder how many that leaves aboard ship?"

Spot grinned savagely. "Not many, I reckon. That was a large force they put ashore."

Flint leaned back against the bulkhead and closed his eyes. A moment later, they sprang open, and he looked at Spot. He moved in close and lowered his voice.

"Suppose that's exactly what's happening. Suppose they are going to meet Black Rose, only they mean to use that force in a surprise attack on that fortress the boy mentioned.

You know what that means for us, Spot?"

The pirate shook his head.

Flint leaned back and closed his eyes again. "Opportunity, Spot ol' son. Stay ready."

There was a marine assigned to guard them, and he was armed, but he was only one man....

Captain Brewer heard the sound of four bells of the middle watch from the ship's bell as he stepped on deck. The night sea air was cool and refreshing, a definite blessing on a night that offered precious few. The officer of the watch was the senior midshipman, Mr. Murdy; he touched his hat to his captain but was careful to maintain a discreet distance. HMS *Phoebe* was traveling north under reduced sail, awaiting her master's order to turn southwest for her approach to the harbor. His eyes drifted from the deck to the sails to the stars to the sea, and he made his way to the fantail.

He couldn't sleep, and he was beginning to feel it in his eyes. Each time he'd tried to sleep, the same nightmare came to him: Elizabeth, beautiful and alive, running to him from the cabin where they spent their honeymoon, only to be intercepted by a laughing Black Rose who drags her into a forest, Elizabeth screaming his name all the while. Before he can make a move, he wakes up, pouring sweat. After the third time, he'd decided that a turn around the deck might do him some good.

He began to pace across the stern, back and forth, back and forth, as though the sheer monotony would clear his mind. After fifteen minutes of getting no help at all in this regard, he ceased his pacing and headed for the wheel.

"Good morning, sir," Mr. Murdy said.

"Good morning, Mr. Murdy. How long until we make the turn?"

"Six hours, Captain."

"Very good, Mr. Murdy. I shall be in my cabin."

"Aye, Captain."

Captain Brewer breakfasted early and was up on the deck by six bells of the morning watch, just in time to see the sun begin its ascent into the eastern sky. The breakfast was good —better, in fact, than he thought Mac was capable of producing in Alfred's absence. For a moment he wondered if Alfred had prepared it for him before he left, but he decided not to ask. He didn't want to hurt his coxswain's feelings on the off chance that the concoction was really his own.

The ship was on course for Porto Bello. Brewer did his best to control his impatience and stand on the quarterdeck to inspire his crew. He stepped over to the wheel. He was greeted by Lieutenant Rivkins.

"Captain," he said as he touched his hat.

"Good morning, Lieutenant. How long?"

"Mr. Sweeney estimates another four hours or so, sir."

Brewer frowned. "We may need to slow that down, Mr. Rivkins. We don't want to show up too early. I want to go ashore just before midday. Notify me the instant we sight land; if we are too early, we may need to reverse course quickly before we are seen."

"Aye, Captain."

Doctor Spinelli came up on deck and made his way aft. "Good morning, sir."

"Good morning, Doctor."

Spinelli bounced on his toes nervously. "Today's the day."

Brewer turned to his friend, his face a tightly-controlled mask. "Today's the day."

The doctor swallowed hard at the look in his captain's eyes.

The sun was well on its way through the morning sky when HMS *Phoebe* slid into the bay at Porto Bello. Lieutenant Rivkins conned the ship to a spot in the middle of the harbor. The fortress was plainly visible in the hills to the southeast; Rivkins estimated a two-mile trek would get the captain and his party to the door. He took the time to study the beaches and the tree line, looking either for a greeting party or a sentry posted to alert Black Rose of their arrival. He lowered his glass and squinted, dissatisfied at finding nothing along the beach other than a few small, worn-out fishing boats. He judged the harbor a superior one, with good natural protection from the weather. There was a fishing village a short distance to the north, but all the boats must have been out working on the day's catch.

"Mr. Short," he called, "I'm going below to report to the captain. You have the deck. Let no one approach from the shore."

"Aye, aye, sir."

Rivkins went below and was admitted to the captain's cabin by the sentry. His first sight was of young Joshua, seated at the table with his hair dyed black to match Alfred's. The glass of wine in his hand was doing little to calm his nerves.

"Where's the captain?" he asked.

Joshua motioned with his glass toward the day cabin, then he slowly drained the whole thing. Rivkins raised his eyebrows but did not comment. He found the captain getting dressed with Mac's help. The lieutenant came to attention and cleared his throat. Brewer looked up.

"Yes, Lieutenant?"

"We are currently hove-to in the middle of the bay, Captain," Rivkins said. "The fortress is plainly visible atop a hill to the southeast. I estimate two miles to the door."

"Very good. The time?"

Rivkins pulled a watch from his coat. "I make it just coming up on six bells, sir."

"Excellent!" Brewer said. "My compliments, Mr. Rivkins. Please pass them along to Mr. Sweeney and the Quartermaster. You timed it perfectly." He paused while Mac hooked on his sword and a brace of pistols was hidden in his waist under his coat. "Now, you know what to do next?"

Rivkins clasped his hands behind his back. "Aye, sir. As soon as you and Joshua are safely ashore, I am to put a boat over the side and turn the ship around so the bow is pointed at the harbor mouth, ready for a quick escape. I shall also have a boat ready to warp us out of the harbor, should the necessity arise."

"Good."

Mac stood back to admire his handiwork and nodded in satisfaction. His captain had a sword on his left hip and a pistol visible on his right. He also had the two pistols hidden in the small of his back, ready for use. The two had spent two hours yesterday practicing drawing them from beneath the coat. "I think you're ready, sir," the coxswain said.

"I hope so," Brewer said. "Mr. Rivkins, return to the deck. Mac, get the gig over the side and ready to go. Send word when it's ready."

"Aye, sir," Rivkins acknowledged. "Good luck, sir." He came to attention, and he and Mac left the room. Brewer walked out to the table and sat down across from Joshua.

"Ready?"

The lad swallowed hard. "I think so, sir."

"How old are you, Joshua?" Brewer asked.

"Just turned nineteen, sir."

"How long have you been in the navy?"

"Going on three years now, sir," Joshua replied. "I joined up just before the ship headed to South America."

"Able seamen yet?"

"No, sir. I believe Mr. Cromwell has me scheduled for the examination in two months."

"Good bump in pay, is it not? Moving from ordinary seaman to able, I mean."

"Aye, sir, it is."

"Well, Joshua, after we get through this, I will look into shaving those two months off your time and getting you to able seaman as soon as possible."

"Thank you, sir!"

Brewer was about to reply when a knock came at the door. The sentry admitted Mr. Short.

"Beg your pardon, Captain," he said. "Mr. Rivkins says they're ready for you."

"Thank you, Mr. Short." The midshipman came to attention and departed.

Brewer turned to his seaman. "Remember, Joshua: you are to make them think you are Alfred. Hang your head down, and let me or Mac do the talking. Got it?"

"Aye, sir."

The two men left the cabin and made their way on deck, where Brewer led them directly to the entry port. Joshua descended first and found his place in the gig, followed by the captain, who took his place in the stern sheets beside Mac. The boat shoved off and made an easy pace toward shore.

"Keep your eyes peeled, Mac," Brewer said softly.

"Aye, sir."

"Who will mind the boat while we are away?"

"Mr. Murdy, sir."

"Very well."

They made it to the beach without incident, seeming to draw no attention at all, save for a few birds who disliked having the serenity of their beach disturbed. The three men disembarked, and Brewer turned to Mr. Murdy.

"Guard her well, Mr. Murdy," he said. "If you are attacked, return to the ship immediately."

"Aye, sir. Good luck."

The two men exchanged salutes, and the captain's party walked up the beach to the edge of the forest, where they met a path they hoped would take them to the fortress.

"Mac," Brewer said, "you take the point. We're right behind you."

* * * * *

Dawn was about to break as Lieutenant Greene and Captain Enfield crouched in the undergrowth about 150 yards from the fortress and waited for Sergeant Clark to return with his report. A closer look, even from their current vantage point, showed the fortress to be older and in much poorer state than they had thought, which raised hopes that Clark would find one or more openings they could exploit. The sergeant reappeared just as the sun cleared the horizon.

"Report?" Enfield asked.

"Well, sir," Clarke said, "I scouted around the fortress. As you can see," he indicated the walls visible from their perch, "the outer walls are in very bad repair. The opposite side is worse." Enfield handed him a canteen, and he took a healthy drink before handing it back. "Thank you." He drew a hasty map in the dirt. "We are here, looking at the north side, here. The path the captain will take from the beach leads to a door on the east side, here. I found two places where the perimeter walls are broken down somewhat. The first is here, about a third of the way down the west wall. There's a breach where some men could climb up and gain entry without much trouble. The second is here, where the west wall meets the south wall. The wall there is also broken down, and entry is possible. I did see sentries patrolling the walls and also around the fortress itself. I saw them when I passed the openings in the walls."

"Thank you, Sergeant," Enfield said. He handed him the canteen again.

"Thank you, sir."

Enfield and Greene studied the crude map. Greene pulled out his watch to check the time.

"Six o'clock," he muttered. "Six hours before we need to be ready for the captain." He sat back on his heels and rested his chin in his hand. "Stealth. We must remember stealth."

"Agreed," Enfield said as he squatted. "I wish we had some long bows."

"Long bows?"

"A quiet way to kill your enemy from a distance."

"Ah."

Enfield cleared his throat. "I thought of something that never came up during a council."

Greene looked up. "What's that?"

"What do we do if we get an opportunity *before* the captain gets there?"

Greene stared at him. What indeed? "I'm not sure," he admitted. "It would have to be a *damned good* opportunity. We'd be risking the captain's wife, remember."

"I still think we should keep our eyes open," Enfield urged.

Greene thought for a moment before nodding. "Agreed."

* * * * *

Flint and his men were ready; they had been ever since the ship was turned around, and the time had come to strike. When the boy brought their meals, the entire company rushed the door. The boy was knocked back against the marine sentry, who was quickly mobbed by several pirates and killed with his own bayonet. Another pirate grabbed the boy by the hair.

"No!" whispered Flint. "I'll not be known as a killer of children. Bind and gag him, then leave him behind."

The pirates made their way forward through the ship until they came to the armory. The marines guarding it raised a cry, and one of them got off a shot with his pistol, killing one of the pirates before several others overpowered him.

"Quick!" Flint said. "Arm yourselves! McClarity! Stanton! You two start loading pistols and passing them out. We've got to move fast!"

"What's the plan, Flint?"

"We take the deck, see? We get control of some of those carronades I saw up there, and we can hold off anyone trying to board the ship long enough for us to put to sea." He looked around. "How many pistols do we have loaded?"

"Four!"

"That'll do for now," Flint growled. "We got to move. Stanton! Follow us when you get another armful loaded! All right, you blokes! Let's move!"

Up on the deck, Lieutenant Rivkins head jerked up at the sound from below. He turned to the quartermaster's mate at the wheel.

"Did you hear that?"

"Didn't hear nothing, sir."

A shot broke the silence, and the mate's eyes grew big as saucers. "I heard that one, sir!"

"Beat to quarters!" Rivkins screamed. "The pirates must be trying to make a break for it! The buggers couldn't have chosen a better time! Mr. Dye, find the marine sergeant and tell him to take his men below. Go!"

Mr. Sweeney appeared. "What's happening, Mr. Rivkins?"

"The pirates have broken their confinement and are trying to take the ship. I have sent the marines below, but our problem is to keep control of the deck!"

"Agreed!" Sweeney hurriedly turned and took inventory. Twenty hands were on the deck. "Should we send a few men below to make a quick sweep for any weapons?"

"Granted. Mr. Henry! Take two hands and make a sweep below deck for any weapons; bring all you can carry up on deck and place them on the quarterdeck. And bring up any hands you find below. Under no circumstances are you to fight, should you encounter any pirates. Bring everyone you meet up on deck. We shall make our stand here."

"Aye, aye, sir!" Henry headed toward the aft companionway. "You! Weezil! And you, Johnson! Follow me!"

Rivkins looked to the shore and saw the single boat that had taken the captain and his party ashore. There were ten men or so in that boat.

"Mr. Sweeney!" he called. "Who is in charge of the captain's gig?"

"Mr. Murdy, I believe, sir."

"Signal him to return to the ship at once! We need all the numbers we can get, and his men may make the difference."

Sweeney turned to the quartermaster's mate. "Fire the signal gun! Recall Mr. Murdy and the captain's gig at once!"

"Aye, sir!"

Flint and his men made their way to the berthing deck and found it nearly empty. Some of his men wanted to go aft, but he called them back.

"No, you lubbers!" he hissed. "We need to take the deck! Carronades and sails, that's what we need to get out of here alive! Stay together now! Up!"

On the gun deck, they ran into about five hands who looked to be gathering pikes and swords. They ran for the aft companionway when they saw the pirates. Some of Flint's men took off in pursuit, but again he called them back and urged them upward.

Rivkins turned when Henry and his men burst from the companionway, arms full of pikes, swords, and a couple of pistols.

"Mr. Rivkins!" Henry cried. "They're coming up the forward companionway!"

"Right!" Rivkins answered. "You and the mate stay here and get Mr. Murdy aboard as soon as possible. I'm heading forward. Mr. Henry, follow me!" He ran for the fo'c'sle, calling as he went. "Men! Grab a pike and defend the companionway! The pirates are coming up!"

Four hands grabbed pikes in time to discourage the pirates from using the companionway. Rivkins heard four shots; one of the defenders fell with a bullet hole in his temple, and the other three fell back out of caution, allowing the pirates to emerge on the deck.

Rivkins drew his sword and dove into the fray. Two vicious slashes to the shoulder and chest felled the closest pirate, and he recovered just in time to parry a strike from his left. *Thank God for Alfred's training,* he thought as he pulled a pistol from his belt and shot the man in the chest. He used the pistol as a club on a man attacking from his right before whirling and burying his sword into the man's ribs. Rivkins looked around quickly before putting his foot on the corpse and pulling his blade free. The job was not done yet.

On the beach, Mr. Murdy turned with a start at the sound of the signal gun. "What's going on?"

"Dunno, sir," a petty officer replied. He handed Murdy a glass.

"A couple people are gesticulating wildly," Murdy said. "Wait! Men are rushing forward with pikes! Come on! We've got to get back!"

"What about the captain?" the petty officer asked.

"We'll come back for him after the ship's secure," Murdy said. "Now, shove off!"

CHAPTER SIXTEEN

Lieutenant Greene pulled his watch from its pocket. 10:30 in the morning. The captain would soon be coming ashore, if he wasn't already. The idea was for him to make a slow, steady march up the path to the door of the fortress, keeping as much attention on himself and 'Alfred' as possible. He replaced the watch and joined Captain Enfield, hunkered over the makeshift "map" in the dirt.

"I suggest we send Alfred and his team to the opening in the west wall," Greene said, pointing with his finger to the site of the breach. "At the same time, we can send Mr. Crawford and Mr. Reed and their teams to the breach at the corner, here. Once they're in, they can go two different directions in the search. The last team will stay with us, and we'll try the front door after the captain and his party are inside. Hopefully, the din from within once our men are discovered will provide enough cover for us to force an entry."

"So much for stealth, eh?" Enfield teased. He looked at the map again and nodded. "Sounds good to me. I'll give the order to move out."

Greene frowned. "How will they know when to move in? How can we get word to them?"

"Oh, believe me," Enfield said as he rose, "they'll know."

* * * * *

Mac paused where the pathway veered away from the forest line and ended in a large clearing that held the fortress. There were two men standing atop the perimeter wall keeping watch. A large wooden door stood in the center of the wall facing them. He turned his head when he heard the captain and Joshua approach.

"So, that's it, eh?" Brewer said.

One of the two guards disappeared.

"They know we're here, Captain."

Brewer studied the woods on both sides of the fortress, praying his men were there but seeing nothing. Suddenly a familiar sound drifted to their ears. Brewer turned and looked back down the path. "Mac?"

The coxswain shook his head. "Sounded like a signal gun, sir."

"Well," the captain said as he turned back to the fortress, "we don't have time to investigate just now. 'Alfred', keep your head down, like this is all your fault and you're sorry. Let's go, Mac. Look sternly."

They made their way slowly toward the door. The second guard reappeared and took station on the opposite side from his fellow. Mac walked up to the door and pounded on it with his fist. The door opened to reveal a small man dressed in ostentatious pirate finery, complete with gold earrings and necklace.

"Captain Brewer?" he asked.

Mac looked hard at their host before shaking his head and stepping to the side. Brewer took one step forward. "I am Captain Brewer."

The man nodded and looked at Joshua. "And this is Alfred?"

"Yes," Brewer answered.

The pirate looked to Brewer in mild surprise. "He does not speak?"

"I have ordered him to remain silent. He has brought enough trouble upon my house."

Their host's eyes darted from the captain to Joshua and back again, and he smiled, showing teeth. He waved them into the fortress. When Mac went to follow, the pirate stopped him.

"Not you," he said.

Mac nodded to the captain. "I go where he goes."

The pirate considered for a moment and then shrugged. "Very well," he said. "You shall both remain outside."

Mac reached out swiftly and grabbed the man by the front of his tunic.

The pirate remained calm. "I return with those I am to bring. If I bring more, or if I do not return, she dies."

Mac snarled and pulled the man up onto his tiptoes. The pirate merely smiled.

"Mac," Brewer said in a tone that would not be questioned. "Let him go." To their host: "I am allowed to escort Alfred?"

"Oh yes, you are expected," he said. Brewer turned to his coxswain.

"Sir," Mac said desperately, but the captain shook his head. Brewer took Mac by the arm and turned him away. He looked over his shoulder to the pirate. "Excuse me for a moment, would you please? Alfred, come here."

Joshua move away before the pirate could stop him and joined Mac and the captain a short distance away from the wall.

"Sir, you can't be serious," Mac pleaded.

Brewer held up a finger. "One, Mac, I would ask you to remember I am always serious. Two, my wife is in there. You will remain here while I go inside and make sure they don't slaughter 'Alfred' as soon as the door closes. *Keep your eyes open.*" He didn't dare say anything aloud of their plans, but he signaled with his eyes to remind Mac that Lieutenant Greene, Captain Enfield, and their men were nearby. Then he inclined his head in a barely perceptible tilt in the direction of the sentries on the wall.

"Aye, sir," Mac said, with the smallest of acknowledging nods. "But I don't like it."

"Neither do I."

Mac scowled, moved off, and Brewer and Joshua returned to the entrance. They followed the pirate inside, and the door closed loudly behind them.

Alfred left his team and, bent low, made his way to the edge of the tree line. The wall was about ten yards away, and the break in the wall formed a roughly arch-shaped opening . One guard walked back and forth along a parapet. Alfred slunk back into the forest.

"I need one man," he said quietly when he got back to his men, "to disable the wall perimeter guard quietly, and look around to see if it is safe for us to enter. Remember, we must get in *unseen* and *unheard*." He looked around. "Any volunteers?"

"I'll go." One of the hands from Lieutenant Rivkins' division, named Davy, spoke up.

"You understand what is riding on this? You must be unnoticed, like a shadow of leaves on a wall."

Davy nodded once, and Alfred motioned for him to follow him to the tree line. When they arrived, they knelt behind a tree, and Alfred whispered in his ear. "Watch the guard as he makes his round. Choose the best moment, then sprint out and leap through the opening. You must be silent when you take the guard out. Signal as soon as it is safe for us to follow."

Davy nodded his understanding, and Alfred backed away from him. The boy—Alfred judged him to be eighteen at most—studied the guard as he went back and forth on his watch. Suddenly, he put his hand on the hilt of the dagger at his hip and sprinted for the opening while the guard was at the far end of his patrol. He leapt through the opening and disappeared just as the guard made his turn. Alfred watched as the guard came back, ready to run forward and hurl a knife at him to prevent his sounding an alarm, but it wasn't necessary. When the guard made his turn and headed away again, he did not notice Davy step up on the parapet only a step or two behind him. The tar closed the gap silently and quickly. He caught the guard from behind, clamping his hand over the man's mouth so he couldn't cry out as he plunged his dagger into the man's throat. Davy let the dead man fall to earth outside of the wall, and he disappeared again. A few minutes later, he appeared in the opening and waved for Alfred and the others to come.

Mr. Cromwell's way into the fortress wasn't quite so easy, as he had to deal with two guards patrolling the walls, not to mention the fact that his men had seen three men relaxing in a small yard on the other side of the wall. The lieutenant retreated several yards into the forest to brief his men.

"It would be best if we could wait for the men on the ground to leave on their own," he said quietly. "Then we would only have the two guards to deal with. The problem is, who knows when they will leave?"

They were interrupted by a hand who came running up. "Lieutenant! Lieutenant! You won't believe this!"

"Pipe down!" Cromwell hissed as he grabbed the man by the shirt and pulled him down. "What's going on?"

"Sorry, sir," he said hurriedly, "but they're all gone!"

"What do you mean, gone?"

"A pirate ran up to the men in the yard and said something, then all the men in the yard ran for the front of the fortress! The guards on the wall went, too!"

Cromwell was stunned. "You mean there's nobody guarding the breach in the wall?"

"No, sir!"

The lieutenant turned back toward the wall. "But why..."

"The captain," the petty officer beside him said. "The captain and Joshua have entered the fortress."

"That has to be it!" another added.

"Lieutenant," the petty officer said, "we need to move!"

"Agreed!" Cromwell said. He pointed at ten men to his right. "You men follow me. We're heading into that breach. You!" He pointed at the petty officer. "Get the rest of the men and follow us. Quietly now! Let's go!"

Mac stood in front of the closed door, fuming at being left behind. He thought he felt something whizz past his ear, and he swatted away the imaginary insect. A minute or two later, a clump of dirt burst when it hit the wall two feet to his left.

He looked up and saw the lone remaining guard on the wall, down by the corner; the second guard had disappeared after the captain went inside. He turned quickly and saw Lieutenant Greene's face for just a moment in the trees. He walked toward the spot.

"Hey!" the guard said, "where are you going?"

"If I have to wait out here," Mac replied over his shoulder, "I want to do it in the shade, if you don't mind!"

The guard laughed but paid him no more attention after Mac sat at the base of a tree.

"What are you doing out here, Mac?" Greene's voice came from behind the tree.

"The pirate who met us at the door wouldn't let me in. He had orders only to take the captain and 'Alfred'."

Greene peered at the front of the fortress from behind the coxswain's shoulder. *Now what do we do?* he wondered. *There's too much open ground—we'd be seen before we could get close enough to try to silence the one on the wall, and shooting him would only announce our presence to everyone inside.* He sighed in frustration. "Any ideas how we get in, Mac?"

Mac's eyes never left the guard. "Not a one, sir."

Brewer and Joshua stood to the side, under the drawn and aimed pistols of three pirates, while their host closed the door, bolted it, and laid a thick drawbar into the braces on the wall to secure it. Satisfied, he turned to his guests.

"Welcome, Captain," he said with a bow. "My name is Lucifer. Will you please follow me? You are expected within."

"Lucifer?" Brewer said. "Your mother actually named you Lucifer?"

The small man smiled. "No, of course not. But I believe that names should inspire. Don't you?"

The two men's eyes met, and Brewer's face grew cold and hard. He nodded.

Lucifer led them down a wide corridor that had several open doors on each side. Brewer glimpsed the occupants as they walked past, and several pirates came to the doorways to gawk or jeer at the two prisoners as they made their way toward the large door at the end. By the time they got there, Brewer estimated they had passed twenty pirates. *Good,* he thought. *The more that are watching us, the fewer there are to catch Greene and Enfield.*

Lucifer knocked three times in quick succession before opening the door. He stepped inside and announced their arrived.

"Captain Brewer, and the murderer Alfred!"

Brewer and Joshua entered the room. It was dominated by a single long table with an unlit candelabra in the center and tall-backed chairs down each side an

342

d at each end. At the far end of the table, a man sat and drank from a glass of wine. He had black hair and bright, almost grey eyes, and there was a noticeable scar down his left cheek. He set the glass down and beckoned with his arm.

"Captain Brewer! Join me!"

The two men made to step toward the table, but Lucifer stopped them. "Only you, Captain."

Brewer shook his head and nodded to his companion. "He goes with me."

"I don't think so," Lucifer said, and the three pirates with him leveled their pistols at his head.

"'Tis all right, sir," 'Alfred' said softly. "I'll wait here." When Brewer turned to go, Lucifer called out to him.

"Captain!" he said. Brewer paused and turned. "Your weapons."

Brewer drew his sword and set it on the table, then did the same with the pistol at his side.

"Now may I go?" he asked.

Lucifer smiled and gestured for Brewer to proceed. Brewer walked up the side of the table; his guest did not rise to greet him.

"Sit, Captain," he said. "Have some wine." He filled two glasses and pushed one to Brewer.

"Where is my wife?" Brewer asked.

"All in good time, Captain," his host said. "Sit." Brewer did so, but he ignored the wine in front of him.

"What about my friend?"

"I do not drink with murderers."

Brewer laughed out loud. "That's ridiculous! Pirates murder innocent people all the time. Alfred murdered no one; he simply won a fight against a man who was trying to kill him, that's all." He leaned forward and put his forearm on the table. "Now, where's my wife?"

"She is not here."

Brewer's face went stone cold. "That wasn't the deal."

The pirate shrugged. "Deals change."

"Not ones you want to walk away from."

Now it was the pirate's turn to laugh. "I like a man with guts!" he said. "Oh, Captain, I shall be sorry to kill you!"

"Where is my wife?"

The pirate sat back, and he face grew stern. "My friend, you should know better than to use that tone of voice with me."

Brewer got control of himself and sat back as well. "All right, let's try something else: Where is Black Rose?"

The pirate smiled again. "With your wife."

"Good," Brewer said. "Now we're getting somewhere. And what is your name? Not that I care, mind you; I just don't want to keep saying, *'Hey, you'*."

The pirate chuckled. "That is a good one, Captain. My name is Diego."

"Thank you," Brewer said. "Now, Diego, I also have a change to make in our deal."

"And that is?"

Brewer leaned forward again. "Tell me where Black Rose is holding my wife, and you may live to leave this room."

All the pirates laughed at that, but their laughter was cut short.

Suddenly there were sounds of gunshots going off somewhere in the fortress. Brewer took advantage of the distraction and threw his heavy goblet at his host, hitting his face above his right eye and drawing blood. Diego tried to jump out of his chair, but he only succeeded in toppling it over and himself with it. Brewer leapt from his chair and drew the pistols secreted in the small of his back. He put a bullet squarely in the middle of Lucifer's forehead and shot a second pirate in the chest. Joshua grabbed the captain's pistol off the table and shot the third pirate in the face. He immediately flung the empty pistol at the remaining pirate, a move which bought him enough time to pick up a pistol off the floor and shoot the man dead.

"Alfred!" Brewer called, holding out his hand. Joshua tossed his sword to him, hilt first. Brewer caught it just in time to bring the point to Diego's throat before he could rise.

"It will do you no good, Captain," he said. "My men will be here soon."

"Stand up," Brewer said. Diego did so, and Brewer nudged him with the sword's point in the chest. "Against the wall." Diego backed up slowly, never taking his eyes from his adversary. They stood there, listening to the sound of battle coming closer and closer. Finally, there was a crash against the door. It held, but just barely.

"Goodbye, Captain," Diego said. "You are about to die."

A moment later, the door turned to kindling, as Mac broke through with a powerful shoulder. Lieutenant Greene and Captain Enfield were right behind him. Brewer almost laughed at the look of disbelief on Diego's face.

"Welcome, gentlemen," Brewer said. "Mac, come here and keep my friend company." The coxswain stepped over and pointed a pistol at Diego. Brewer stepped away to speak with his officers.

"Have you searched the fortress?" Brewer asked. "Diego here says Elizabeth and Black Rose are not here."

"We have teams doing that now, sir," Enfield said.

Brewer nodded and walked over to where Joshua was sitting. He patted him on the shoulder. "Well done, Joshua. You played your part well."

"Joshua?" Diego cried. "This is not Alfred?"

"No," Brewer said. "This is Alfred." Brewer indicated the little man standing in the doorway. Diego closed his eyes and buried his face in his hands.

Lieutenants Cromwell and Reed arrived. "Sir," Reed reported, "we searched the entire fortress. Neither your wife nor Black Rose is here."

Brewer's heart sank. "You're absolutely sure?"

"Aye, Captain," Reed said. "I'm sorry, sir."

Brewer looked over at Diego, who was smiling. It was absolutely the wrong thing to do.

"Mac," Brewer called. The coxswain rose and backed over to his captain. "Hand me your pistol." Mac looked questioningly at him, but he complied. "Give me the room, please," Brewer called. "Wait for me out front."

His men looked at him, but none questioned his orders.

Soon, Brewer was alone with the pirate leader.

"May I sit?" Diego asked.

"You may not. I will give you one chance, and one only, to walk out of this room alive. Where are my wife and Black Rose?"

The pirate shook his head. "You will not shoot me. That is not something English captains do."

"At this moment, I am not an English captain. I am your judge, jury, and executioner. You have been charged with piracy and kidnapping. You have been found guilty and are sentenced to death. My only regret is that I cannot make it slower and more painful." He raised the pistol.

Outside, Greene and the others were startled to hear the single gunshot ring out. Greene turned to the assembly and said, "If any one of you ever mentions this day to anyone, anyone at all, I will hunt you down." A few minutes later, the captain came out alone. Nobody asked about Diego.

"Sir," Cromwell asked, "did you find out where they are?"

"No," the captain replied, "but we have one more chance."

"Aye, sir."

"Let's get back to the ship," Brewer said.

* * * * *

Rivkins and his men had been pushed back to the quarterdeck. He had the edge in numbers, he thought, but the pirates had raided the arsenal and were making full use of the weapons they had liberated. At that moment, the pirates were trying to force the starboard gangway, and the battle was hard fought. The narrow gangway hurt the attackers, giving the British a chance to hold on until relief arrived. Rivkins had just defeated a thrust on the larboard gangway and was crossing the quarterdeck to aid those defending the starboard when he saw Pudge emerge from the companionway. He had his dirk, a pistol, and his sling with him. Rivkins was about to send him below when Pudge reached into his bag, pulled out a ball, and put it into his sling. He began to twirl it over his head as he searched for a target. Rivkins watched transfixed as the lad looked to the mizzen shrouds and let fly. The lieutenant spun in time to see a pirate let go of the shrouds to grab his head before he fell backwards into the sea. He turned back to the quarterdeck, but Pudge wasn't wasting any time; he was already reloaded and searching for a new target. Rivkins kept count as he hung back to protect the lad: Pudge had five musket balls for 'live' ammunition, and he took down four pirates with them.

347

"All right, Pudge," he said sternly, after the last missile missed, "get below."

"Can't, sir. Got to help defend the ship!"

"But you're out of ammunition!"

"Only for now, sir," the boy replied. "I can scavenge any that are rolling around the deck."

"No—" But then Rivkins was distracted by the battle for the starboard gangway. When he turned around again, Pudge was nowhere to be seen. "I hope he stays out of the way," he said to himself as he headed starboard.

Flint saw that the battle for the ship was at a tipping point. One more good shove and they would break through to the quarterdeck and force the British to haul down the flag.

"Flint!"

He turned to see one of his men running toward him and pointing toward the shore. The gig was returning! Making its way to the larboard entry port. They had to load and aim one of the carronades before the boat got too close. One shot would blow it out of the water! He looked around, but he could only find three men who were not already in the fight.

"You three!" he pointed at them. "Get over here and help me with this gun! We got to take out that boat!"

They got to work on it, but it was slow going, and it soon became apparent to Flint that they were not going to be ready in time.

"Never ye mind that now!" he cried. "Everyone grab a pike and head to the entry port! We got to stop them from coming on board!"

They arrived at the entry port just as the boat was hooking on. The four of them poked down the ladderway with their pikes and stopped the men from making their way up. Then suddenly a volley of musket fire rang out, and two of his men cried out and fell overboard. Three more shots drove the last man away and wounded Flint in the arm. Murdy and his men clambered up the ladder and over the rail.

"You three head aft!" he ordered. "Report to Lieutenant Rivkins or whoever is on the quarterdeck! The rest of you, head forward and circle around behind them on the starboard gangway! We'll have them trapped!" His men took off, and he looked down at Flint, bleeding from his wound. He grabbed the pirate by the lapels and lifted him up. "I think the captain is going to want to speak to you, sir."

Murdy's men turned the tide. The pirates surrendered, several of them tossing their swords or pikes into the waist and raising their hands.

Lieutenant Rivkins leaned against the carriage of a carronade and took a deep breath. He looked up and saw the captain and his party beginning to arrive on the beach.

"Mr. Short!" he called. "Get a crew into the gig and run ashore to bring the captain back. Mr. Murdy! See that these scum are returned to the cable tier. Shackles on all of them, if you please! Mr. O'Reilly!"

"Mr. O'Reilly's dead, sir!" the hand pointed to the young midshipman's body lying beside a long nine forward.

"Mr. McClelland!" Rivkins called a petty officer he saw. "Gather those who are not injured, and get the wounded below to the doctor. Report back to me when that's done."

"Aye, aye, sir!"

He was at the entry port when the captain came aboard.

"Report, Mr. Rivkins!" Brewer said.

"Sir, the pirates managed to break out of their confinement, after you left the ship. They were able to raid the armory and made their way up on deck by means of the forward companionway. I gathered everyone I could on deck. We signaled for Mr. Murdy to return to the ship, and we made our stand on the quarterdeck. The surviving pirates surrendered approximately twenty minutes ago, and I sent Mr. Short to the beach in the gig to fetch you."

"I see," Brewer said as he looked around. "Casualties?"

"I don't know yet, sir; we're just getting the last of the wounded down to the sickbay."

Brewer nodded. "As soon as you can, get the boats in the water so the crew can get back aboard." He looked around again. "Did Flint survive?"

"I believe so, sir," Rivkins responded. "The doctor's mate is probably working on him in the cable tier as we speak. He was wounded, sir. Took a musket ball in the arm."

CHAPTER SEVENTEEN

It took nearly three hours to get the crew back aboard, the deck restored to some sort of order, and the ship clear of the harbor.

That night, Captain Brewer held another council of war in his cabin. Present were Lieutenants Greene, Rivkins, and Reed (Mr. Cromwell had the deck), Captain Enfield, Doctor Spinelli, Mac, and Alfred. Pudge was entrusted with serving the wine.

The captain stood at the head of the table. "I want to thank you all for the valiant effort you made in Panama. Unfortunately, our original problem remains—finding Black Rose and her prisoner. Now, however, we need to do it before she learns of what happened in Panama." He took a drink and paused for a moment before he was able to continue. "First, Mr. Greene, report on taking the fortress."

"Sir," Greene said formally, "scouting by Sergeant Clark of the marines revealed two openings in the wall of the fortress, one on the west side and the other at the southwest corner. Captain Enfield and I decided to divide our force, taking a quarter of the men to the front. Alfred took a quarter of the men to the opening on the west wall, and Lieutenants Reed and Cromwell took the remainder to the one at the southwest corner. Mr. Reed?"

"We had an easy way in, Captain," Reed said. "I guess when you entered the fortress, every pirate in the place—at least in our section of it—decided to leave their post and go watch you come in." Brewer nodded as he remembered the pirates lining the corridor. Reed continued, "Knowing that Alfred was working on the west wall entrance, I took my men around and up the east wall of the fortress. We were spotted about halfway up the side, and we attacked the pirates. It was a running fight until we met the others, inside the front door."

"I see," Brewer said. "Thank you, Mr. Reed. Alfred?"

"We gained entrance through the opening in the west wall, sir. We turned north and were able to subdue what sentries we came across without any alarm being raised. We found ourselves at the front door, so we simply removed the drawbar and let Mac, Mr. Greene, Captain Enfield, and their men in. We came upon the pirates retreating in front of Mr. Reed's men and attacked. That battle ended when Mac broke in the door and we found you."

"Very good. I need a written report from each of you." He took a deep breath and let it out. "As I said earlier, neither Black Rose nor my wife were present in the fortress, so we're still at square one, as far as that goes."

Doctor Spinelli tapped the tabletop. "Neither one? Where does that leave us then? Did the pirate leader you spoke with say anything?"

"No, Doctor, he didn't. About the only thing he did say was that Elizabeth was a dead woman, and Black Rose would never stop trying to get her revenge on Alfred."

Spinelli looked hard at his captain, obviously unhappy with the answer. He opened his mouth to say something, but thought better of it and closed it again. Brewer knew there would be more questions later, when they were in private.

Rivkins leaned forward. "Where does that leave us, sir?"

Brewer leaned back in his chair and stared at his hands folded in his lap. "I have one more card to play, Mr. Rivkins, after which I shall be able to answer that question. Gentlemen, please give me the room. Lieutenant Greene, please remain."

Brewer saw a few surprised glances exchanged as his guests obeyed the captain's unexpected request to depart. The look on the doctor's face was a strange mixture of confusion and compassion; he was wondering what the captain was hiding. Nevertheless, he, too, departed as he was bid. When they were alone, Brewer turned to his first lieutenant.

"Bring in Flint."

Greene went to the door and passed the word for the pirate leader to be brought to the cabin. Minutes later, he was there, escorted by the sergeant-at-arms and still in irons. Brewer indicated a chair, and the pirate sat. Mac emerged from the pantry and took his place before the door; Brewer was amused to note that he wore a dagger and a pistol on his belt.

"So, Captain," Flint said, "here we are again. I take it your information on Black Rose turned out to be wrong?"

"Not entirely," Brewer replied, content to let the pirate talk for the moment. "We found several of her men there, along with her second-in-command, a man named Diego. However, Black Rose and her prisoner were not there."

"Aye," Flint said, shaking his head in mock sadness, "yer wife. Yes, I heard about that. A shame, that is."

Brewer noticed Mac tense, and he stopped him with a gesture. "Then you know why you're here."

"Aye." He leaned forward and said, "But the price has gone up."

Brewer nodded to Greene, who turned to the sergeant. "You're dismissed, Sergeant. Wait outside."

"Aye, sir." After he was gone, Brewer leaned forward to get Flint's attention.

"You have no idea how right you are, Mr. Flint," he said. "The price is now your life." He sat back, smiling at the look of uncertainty on the pirate's face. "You see, the last thing Diego said to me before he died was that my wife was a dead woman. Our infant daughter was killed in that raid when my wife was kidnapped, Mr. Flint. If Diego's prophecy comes true, my reason for living will be gone. As you can see, I have nothing to lose." He stood and walked around the table, sitting on the edge of it in front of the pirate. "Bear all this in mind as you answer my next question. And that is, *Where is Black Rose?*"

Flint stared wide-eyed at his captor, his mouth hanging open in a fear-fueled gape. He quickly squeezed his eyes shut and turned his head toward the deck below. His breaths were ragged.

"I need an answer, Flint."

"It's not that easy," the pirate replied. "They'll kill me if they discover I said anything."

Brewer crossed him arms over his chest. "Mr. Flint, you tried to take over my ship. I can have you executed right now."

Flint's eyes narrowed as he stared at his captors, going back and forth between them very rapidly as his mind desperately searched for a way out of this mess. He had no loyalty to Black Rose, only the fear for his life, should the captain's plan fail and she survive. All he wanted now was to get out of this without getting his neck stretched, with his crew if possible, but if not, then so be it. After all, he would expect nothing less from them, were the positions reversed.

"Captain," he said cautiously, "let's speak frankly, shall we? I have information you need, and at this moment my life is in your hands. If you kill me, I take that information to the grave with me, and your wife dies." The captain stiffened at that, but Flint pressed on. "Can we not come to some sort of arrangement where you get your information and I keep my head?"

"You are hardly in a position to bargain," Brewer said coldly. "Remember, I have already been told my wife is dead. If I decide to torture you in order to get information on Black Rose, what do you think the Admiralty would do? The worst they would do is to court martial me and dismiss me from the service, at which point I would retire to an English country house with my prize money. With all this in mind, I shall ask you one last time: *Where is Black Rose?*"

The pirate writhed in agony of desperation, his breaths now coming fast and ragged for all to hear. Brewer shrugged and turned to his coxswain.

"Mac, pass the word for the bosun, if you please."

"Aye, sir." Mac opened the door and spoke to the sentry.

Brewer stood. "As for you, sir," he said formally, "you are charged with piracy and insurrection against a ship of the Royal Navy. You are found guilty, and you are sentenced to death by hanging. Your sentence will be carried out at once."

Flint gaped at the captain in shock and disbelief. A knock at the door was followed by the entrance of the bosun.

"You sent for me, sir?" he asked.

"Yes, Mr. Knight," Brewer said. His eyes never left the pirate. "Prepare for a execution on the deck if you please."

The bosun looked hard at the prisoner. "Aye, sir," he answered. He came to attention and left the room.

The look on Flint's face was now one of stark terror. "Captain!" he cried. "What are you doing?"

Brewer glared at him for a moment before sighing heavily. "Give me the room, please."

Lieutenant Greene's head snapped around at that. His eyes met his captain's, and that worthy nodded. Reluctantly, Greene stood and headed for the door. "Come, Mac," he said, and he stepped outside.

Mac looked at Brewer and nodded. "We'll be right outside, sir."

The door closed softly. When Brewer was sure they were alone, he pulled a chair over so he could sit face-to-face with his prisoner.

"We are alone now," he said softly, "so I can say what I need to. You hold the one piece of information that may allow me to save my wife. She may already be dead, but your withholding of Black Rose's location ensures it. There is no way under God's heaven that I am not going to make sure you die by my hand."

Flint looked away, trying furiously to come up with some sort of offer that would be tempting to the captain, and failing miserably. Finally, he turned back to his captor.

"And if I tell you?"

Brewer sat back in his chair and studied his nails in his lap while he considered. "I would delay your execution long enough to verify your information. If you lied, or even if you were simply wrong, your death would be immediate."

"And afterwards? If I'm right?"

The captain shrugged. "Can't say right now."

Flint scowled and looked away again. *A bloody cornered rat, that's what I am,* he thought miserably. *What do I do? If I don't tell him, this bloody Brit'll haul me up on the deck and hang me from the yardarm! But if I do tell him and I'm wrong, for any reason whatsoever, he'll hang me. Still, what was it ol' Roberts was supposed to have said? 'As long as yer breathing, you got a chance.' It's worked so far, so why change?*

Flint turned back and sighed. "All right, Captain, you win. I'll tell you what I know."

Several minutes later, Brewer opened the door and called for the sergeant-at-arms.

"You may take him below, Sergeant," he said. "Keep him in irons, and keep him away from his men."

"Aye, Captain." The sergeant stepped in and hauled the unfortunate pirate to his feet. "Come on, you!" he growled as he practically dragged his charge from the room.

After they were gone, Brewer addressed Greene and Mac. "You may come back in."

He led them into the day cabin and motioned for them to sit down while he stepped over to the table in the corner to pour each of them a drink. Greene smiled; he recognized what his captain was doing. It was a ritual he did whenever he was pleased with himself—by serving others, he humbled himself before God. Greene remembered the day on HMS *Revenge* when he came upon his captain reading his Bible in his cabin. Brewer had shown him a verse that said something about God resisting the proud but giving grace to the humble. The captain had closed his Bible and set it aside before telling his first lieutenant that he meant to live by that verse. So far, to Greene's knowledge, he had.

Brewer passed out the drinks and sat down on the settee in his usual place. He raised his glass. "A toast," he said. "To the end of Black Rose."

Mac raised his glass and took a sip, but his eyes never left his captain. It did not escape his notice that the captain had not toasted the safe return of his wife.

Greene motioned to the captain with his glass. "Good news, sir?"

"As good as could be expected, Benjamin," came the reply. "Flint gave me the location of Black Rose's camp. It's on an island northeast of Puerto Rico."

"Was Flint able to tell you anything about the island," Greene asked, "or what their camp is like?"

The captain shook his head. "Claims he's never been there. He said he got the information from a hand he shipped with once. They've used the place for years; El Diabolito and Roberto Cofresi worked from there for much of their careers." He picked up his glass and drained its contents in a single draught. "If he means where I think he means, it's a wonder to me why they haven't been caught by now."

"Maybe they found someplace like Brest," Mac said. "Someplace where the bay is hidden from the sea, and you have to go through a channel to get there."

"When were you at Brest?" Greene asked.

"When I was a ship's boy like Pudge," Mac explained, "on HMS *Victory* during the Hundred Days. We were attached to the Channel Squadron. More than once I saw our frigates head up the channel to get a look into the harbor." He shook his head at the memory. "Always wished I was with them."

His captain smiled. "You may just get your chance."

* * * * *

Elizabeth Brewer awoke with a start in the darkened room, hoping her nightmare was over. As her eyes adjusted to the darkness, she could see it was not so. She was still imprisoned in the same tiny, windowless hut with a single wooden door, guarded, as she knew from experience, by two burly pirates. It was opened during daylight hours to allow sunlight into the prison, a small thing for which she had learned to be grateful. A girl brought her food and water twice a day, but evidently she had been warned against speaking with the prisoner; all she did was deposit the tray and leave.

She had lost count of how many days she had been a prisoner here. She had thought, from what she had overheard, she would be taken to Panama to await her husband's arrival, but on her third day at sea, they had rendezvoused with a brig. Diego and several men had transferred to the brig, and the ship she was on had changed course and come here—wherever "here" was. She had been taken off the ship and had met Black Rose on the pier. "Mrs. Brewer," the pirate had said, "welcome. Come with me."

Without another word, she had turned her back on Elizabeth and marched off. A guard had nudged her in the back, so she'd had little alternative but to follow. The pirate leader had lead the way to a camp, then entered a hut near the middle of the encampment, and Elizabeth had followed. The guards had remained outside.

Elizabeth stood inside the door while Black Rose busied herself pouring them drinks. She brought them to the table and motioned for her guest to take a seat. Elizabeth did not move, and the pirate sighed and leaned on the table.

"Mrs. Brewer," she said, "if it will make things easier for you, I can have you killed now rather than later. Personally, I would consider that a great loss."

"And why is that?"

Rose waved to the chair again. "Because you have what I always wanted, Mrs. Brewer—a home, a husband, someday a family. That was taken from me, and I want my revenge."

Elizabeth sat and pulled her drink to her. "Cofresi should have chosen a less dangerous profession."

Rose shrugged. "Perhaps. He knew the danger; we both did. Still, it does not deaden the shock or the pain when the news comes that your worst fears have been realized." She drained her drink, then spent a moment looking in the empty glass before setting it down. "Believe it or not, I harbor no ill will towards you or your husband. You are a necessary means to an end in getting my revenge. I want Alfred. I wish to see him dead for what he did to my Cofresi and for how he shattered my life. Franco!" One of the guards came in. "This man will take you to your quarters. Do not leave them unattended, Mrs. Brewer. If you are found outside alone, you will be punished. That is all."

Without preamble, Franco dragged her from her chair and out of the hut. She'd barely managed to get her feet under her when they arrived at the small hut she now occupied. Franco opened the door, threw her inside, and slammed it behind her. She had neither seen nor spoken to Black Rose since.

Now, the door opened, and the girl stepped inside to bring her morning tray of fruit. This morning's assortment included a surprise—a small wedge of cheese. Elizabeth picked it up and smelled it, surprised at the quality. "Thank you," she said to the girl, more out of habit than anything else, but it had a result. The girl paused at the door and smiled at her before leaving.

Elizabeth sat at the small table in the middle of the room and ate her meal. Her constant fear now was that William would never find her, that she would never see her husband or daughter again. Every time she felt overwhelmed by this prospect, she forced herself to remember that William was the finest captain in the Caribbean, and he would find her. She wrapped her arms around herself as tight as she could.

* * * * *

Unknown to the pirates, HMS *Phoebe* was just over the horizon, sailing away from the island after a night of reconnaissance. The captain convened a council of war to see what they had learned. Present were himself, Lieutenants Greene, Rivkins, Reed, and Crawford, Captain Enfield, Sergeant Clark, Alfred, Mac, Mr. Sweeney, and the doctor. The captain sat at the head of the table.

"Report, Mr. Greene," he said.

"Captain," the first lieutenant responded, "I believe we have a good idea of what is happening on that island. I will let the individual leaders report. Mr. Rivkins?"

"Captain," Rivkins said, "Mr. Reed and I took a boat to explore the channel to the bay. The channel itself is about two hundred yards long. There's a small cove on the coast line, and the channel leads from there to the bay. We saw a ship in the bay that might have been the old *Revenge*, sir, but she was dark and we didn't want to get too close."

"Is there any way to get *Phoebe* down the channel?" Sweeney asked.

Rivkins shared a rueful look with Reed before answering. "I don't think so. It was dark, no moon either, so we didn't have as good a look as we would have liked. Frankly, the channel is rather narrow. Trees come right up to the water's edge for most of the run."

"Any defenses?" Brewer asked.

"None that we noticed, Captain," Reed said. "To our knowledge, we raised no alarms from any outposts along the channel."

"Then we should be able to send several boats up the channel just before dawn and surprise them with a landing?" the captain asked.

"Yes, sir," Rivkins replied. "I believe so."

Brewer nodded and looked to Greene.

"Captain Enfield?" Greene said.

"Captain," the marine said, "I led a small force consisting of myself, Sergeant Clark, and four of the scouts from Panama. We landed on the far side of the island from the cove and explored inland. We found the pirate encampment about a hundred yards away from the bay. It's a collection of huts, sir, like a village. Surprisingly, there were no sentries posted, except two men outside a small hut, one of whom was sleeping. That may be where your wife is being held, but I have no certain evidence of that. I did see a well in the center of the village. As far as we know, we made it away without being seen."

"From the size of the encampment," Brewer asked, "can you estimate how many pirates may be housed there?"

The two marines shared a questioning look before Sergeant Clark answered. "Perhaps as many as two hundred, Captain, if every hut is filled to capacity."

"I'm inclined to believe there are fewer than that, Captain," Enfield added. "Remember, Diego had seventy-five or a hundred with him in Panama. I think many of those huts are empty."

"Captain Enfield," Brewer said, "assume for a moment that the guarded hut is where my wife is being held. Could she be rescued without rousing the village? Do you think we could get a team in there before dawn to free her and get her out of the village before the real fighting starts?"

"Yes, sir," Enfield replied.

"Good. Make that part of the plan. Pudge!"

The boy appeared in the pantry door. "Sir?"

"Wine for everyone, if you please."

"Aye, sir!" The boy re-appeared bearing Alfred's silver tray with eleven glasses on it. He went around the table handing them out.

"Captain," Mr. Rivkins said, "have you read my report on the fighting aboard ship at Panama?"

"I glanced at it, Mr. Rivkins, but I haven't had the chance to study it in detail."

"Then, sir, may I point out to you that Pudge here took an active part in the fighting to defend the ship? He took out several pirates with his sling. You'd have been proud of him, Alfred."

"I already am," Alfred said.

"Good man, Pudge," Mac added.

"Pudge, come here," the captain said. The boy came and stood before him. "Is this true?"

"Aye, Captain."

"So, all that practice paid off?"

"Aye, sir," Pudge said, "but I need to practice more."

"Why is that?"

Pudge looked embarrassed and ashamed as he said, "I missed one."

Brewer laughed and clapped the boy on the shoulder. "For a first battle, four out of five counts as well done, Pudge. Thank you."

The lad bowed, as he'd seen Alfred do on so many occasions, and left the room.

The captain watched him go and nodded once to himself, before turning back to the council. "Right, then," he said, "let me outline the basic plan as it now stands. We shall have three parts. First, we leave enough men on board to move the ship, but no more. Mr. Sweeney will remain here along with..., ah, Mr. Greene, who drew the long straw?"

"Mr. Reed, sir."

"Right." Brewer turned to the poor lieutenant. "Mr. Reed will be in command. Second, we shall send three boats up the channel. Their primary job will be to secure the sloop, after which the men will move ashore and approach the pirate camp. This group will be under the command of Lieutenant Greene. You shall have Lieutenant Crawford and fifty men."

"Aye, sir," Greene replied.

Brewer took a drink and continued. "That leaves the ground force, which will land just after midnight on the far side of the island and make its way across in order to be at the edge of village, arriving approximately one hour before it starts getting light. That force will be under the command of Captain Enfield. Along with this force shall be the team that will attempt the rescue of my wife. I shall command that team personally."

"Captain?" It was Mr. Greene who spoke up. He was about to say that he thought this was a bad idea, but when he saw the captain's eyes, he closed his mouth and looked at the tabletop in shame. "Aye, sir."

"As I was saying," Brewer continued, "I will lead this team, and I shall have Mac, Alfred, Sergeant Clark, and the doctor. When we get to the village, we will take out the two sentries on that hut and hopefully extract my wife without raising the alarm. Only after she is free of the area will we attack. Any questions?"

"I'm sorry to play devil's advocate, Captain," Alfred said, "but what do we do if an alarm is raised, either by one of the sentries or a pirate who happens to be up and taking an early stroll?"

"We attack immediately," Enfield said, "if only to cover the withdrawal of Mrs. Brewer."

"Agreed," Brewer said. "Attack, and the louder the better. I don't want their first thought to be that their prisoner is escaping."

"Do we go in as pirates again?" Rivkins asked. "As we did in Panama?"

Brewer considered for a moment before shaking his head. "I see no need for subterfuge on this occasion, Mr. Rivkins. Besides, I want them to know that the Royal Navy has come to put an end to their reign of terror."

Rivkins grinned and slapped the table with his palm. "Aye, sir!"

"Once we get into the village," Brewer continued, "our number one job is to find Black Rose. We know she is small and has black hair and dark eyes. Be wary! If we take them by surprise, Black Rose may try to pass herself off as a captive herself, in order to gain an advantage or even escape into the jungle. Take her alive, if possible, but under no circumstances is anyone to allow her to do any more harm. If she will not lay down her sword and surrender, do not hesitate to kill her." He looked around the table to make sure his order was understood. "Remember, we are to end Black Rose's career in the morning, one way or the other. I do not intend to fail."

"Captain," Mac spoke up in a hesitating voice, "please don't take this the wrong way, but if we do find Black Rose alive, should we regard her as yours?"

Silence descended on the cabin, for all knew that Mac was offering the captain the opportunity for revenge on the pirate queen for the kidnapping of his wife. The captain opened his mouth and was about to speak, but another beat him to it.

"No." It was Alfred who spoke. He had a look on his face that was both sad and determined, as though he had to right a wrong. "Forgive me, Captain, if I overstep myself here, but no. Black Rose is mine."

To the surprise of everyone at the table, the captain did not argue with him. "Any other questions?" he asked. "No? Then you are dismissed. Coordinate your team rosters with the first lieutenant. We move tonight."

Brewer turned and stepped into the day cabin. Behind him, he heard the sounds of the council making their way out. He was not surprised when he turned and found the doctor standing in the doorway.

"Well?" the captain asked.

Spinelli shrugged. "Just wanted to see how you were doing. Care for a game to pass the time?"

"No, thank you," Brewer replied. "Pudge!" The lad appeared.

"Is Alfred still here? Or Mac?"

"No, sir, they went out with Mr. Greene."

"Coffee, if you please." Brewer looked to the doctor, who nodded. "Make that two, please."

"Aye, sir."

The doctor took his usual seat. "So, tomorrow it ends."

"That is my intention."

Pudge arrived with the coffee on a tray. Each man took one and thanked the boy. Pudge bowed and retreated.

Spinelli took a careful sip. "I must say, the boy's getting better at coffee."

A tiny grin slipped into the corner of the captain mouth. "I know." He set his cup down and sat back, folding his hands in his lap. "I'm a little surprised."

"At what?"

"At myself. The feelings are different now; probably not all that unusual, but surely unexpected on my part. It began when we sighted the island, but it has grown greatly since we heard the scouting reports."

"And that is?"

Brewer took another drink. "The fear is gone, and I don't know why. All that's left is rage."

Spinelli set his cup down. "William, forgive me for asking, but do you believe your wife to be dead?"

"No, I don't think so. I don't know why, but I do not think so, and I am no longer distraught. All I feel now is anger."

Spinelli took a long, slow drink of his coffee, taking the time to study his host. His face was firm but not worried; in fact, he seemed resigned to some unknown fate. The doctor made a mental note to keep an eye on his friend.

Brewer drained his cup and set it down on the settee beside him. "I'm all right, Adam. I will do my duty. That's all I have right now." He leaned his head back and closed his eyes. "But I will say this, privately, to you, Adam. I honestly do not know what I will do if we find Elizabeth dead."

Although not normally a religious man, the doctor closed his eyes and offered a silent, fervent prayer that they would not have to find out.

* * * * *

Lieutenant Greene looked over his shoulder and saw a glow above the tree tops, announcing the coming sunrise, so he turned and signaled his men to stay low in their boats. He faced forward again and bent low himself. He was in the stern sheets of the lead boat, the others being commanded by Lieutenant Cromwell and Senior Midshipman Murdy. They had entered the channel single-file and successfully negotiated the first turn unnoticed. Now they approached the second turn, beyond which lay the bay and the pirate sloop.

Traveling silently down the center of the channel, the British made the second turn and headed for the bay. Greene sat up slightly and raised his telescope to his eye to survey the scene in front of him. The rising sunlight now at his back allowed him to see clearly. He saw no one on the shoreline and only two men moving about on the deck of the sloop. He held up one fist to signal which plan of attack they would use. Cromwell, in the second boat, altered course and headed to the shore to secure the beach end of the path to the village. Greene and Murdy would take their boats to the sloop, one on each side, to board and take over the ship as quickly as possible. Following the takeover, they too would head to the beach, to head for the village, taking care to capture all pirates fleeing in their direction.

Greene watched as Cromwell's boat surged ahead. He saw the men go ashore as his own men reached the sloop's side and swarmed up to the deck. By the time Greene stepped onto the deck, Murdy had secured the ship. The two sentries seen by Greene as they approached were indeed the only crew aboard. Greene immediately ordered both crews ashore.

Captain Brewer and his men had come ashore just after midnight. He was thankful for the small amount of moonlight available from the crescent moon. He allowed Captain Enfield and his scouts to lead the way through the jungle toward the pirate village. They arrived about two hours before dawn and halted while the scouts sneaked forward to survey the situation in the village. Brewer crouched behind a tree and forced himself to wait patiently for the scouts to return and report. Enfield soon approached him and reported a situation very similar to their previous visit. The only sentries seen were at the door of that same hut. Nothing else was seen moving. Clark guided Brewer to the village's edge to see for himself. The sergeant pointed to a small hut off to the left where the captain saw the two guards in front, the one of the left taking his turn to sleep while his partner kept watch. Brewer patted the sergeant on the shoulder, and the two retreated. The captain led his team around so they came up behind the hut.

"It's the one just ahead," he pointed at the small windowless structure. "The sentry who's awake is on our left. Alfred, he's yours; just make sure he doesn't raise an alarm. Sergeant, the sleeper's yours. Ready? Let's go."

They crept forward through the darkness with Sergeant Clark in the lead. Near the hut, he stopped and raised a fist, signaling the others to halt as well. He moved to the right side of the hut and waited for Alfred. The captain's servant edged forward and crouched. He drew his dagger and nodded to the sergeant. From his position, he could just see the sentry's left shoulder. Brewer watched as the little man squatted, dagger in his hand, rocked back and forth a couple times, then sprinted forward. He leapt on the guard's back, clamped his left hand over the unfortunate man's mouth while the right hand plunged the dagger into his neck. He pulled the dead man backward to the ground and dragged him behind the hut. A moment later, Clark appeared, dragging the body of his guard back as well. Brewer, Mac, and the doctor made their way quickly to the door.

"Mac!" Brewer whispered. The coxswain put his shoulder to the door and shoved it open as quietly as possible. Brewer looked around to see if the sound disturbed anyone, but no one appeared. He ducked into the hut with the doctor hard on his heels.

It took a minute for his eyes to adjust to the darkness. His heart melted when he saw the form of his wife lying on a mat on the floor, covered by a thin blanket. He stepped over and touched her shoulder, fearful that there would be no response. His heart leapt when her eyes fluttered open and looked around. Her eyes locked onto his dark form and she gasped. He heard her draw a deep breath and realized she was about to scream.

He clamped his hand on her mouth, and she began to fight him. "Elizabeth!" he hissed. "Elizabeth! It's me! William! It's me!"

She stopped fighting at the sound of his voice, and her eyes went wide. She slapped the hand from her mouth and wrapped both arms around his neck. He hesitated only a moment before pulling her tight.

"I knew you'd come," she whispered. He felt her tears on his neck.

"Are you well?" he asked her. She nodded. "Can you walk?" Another nod. He threw off the blanket and pulled her to her feet. "Come along, we've got to get you out of here."

They made their way to the door. He pulled her to a halt just inside—an idea hit him.

"Elizabeth," he whispered, "do you know which hut belongs to Black Rose?"

"Yes," she said. She stepped outside the door and pointed to a large hut on the other side of the well. "That one."

"Good," Brewer muttered. "Come, let's get you to safety."

They bent low and ran back toward their own forces. Once safely in the company of Captain Enfield and his forces, they paused by a tree.

"Elizabeth," he said, "you remember Doctor Spinelli, don't you? He will escort you to the rear. Wait for me there."

"What?" she stammered. "You're leaving me? Now?"

"Just for a while," he tried to reassure her. "Wait with the doctor."

"But, William..."

"I've got business to attend to," he said firmly. "Please, go with the doctor."

He turned to Spinelli. "Get her out of here. I'll be back as soon as I can."

He drew his sword and left them behind. Elizabeth stood there with tears flowing down her cheeks. The doctor stepped in front of her so as to get her attention quietly. "This way, if you please," he said, motioning her to the rear. He finally had to take her by the arm and steer her away from the village. She looked over her shoulder the whole time.

Brewer found Captain Enfield talking to Sergeant Carter, with Mac and Alfred standing nearby. "Are we ready to go in?" he asked.

"Yes, sir," Enfield said.

"Alfred, Mac, and I have a line on where Black Rose is," Brewer said. "We're heading for her hut."

Enfield made to protest, then thought better of it. "As you say, Captain. We'll keep the rest of them busy."

Brewer patted him on the arm. "Good man. Mac, Alfred, let's go."

The three of them made their way around the outside of the village to a point closer to the pirate queen's hut. When they were about halfway, they heard the shouts of British sailors and marines attacking. Brewer stopped and looked at his companions.

"No need for secrecy now," he said. "Let's go!"

They made their way into the village. Brewer broke down the first door they came to and found three pirates inside in various stages of dress and inebriation. Mac shot one in the chest as he stepped through the door. Another pulled a dagger and charged at the captain, but Brewer's sword was longer. He allowed the pirate to impale himself while he shot the third pirate in the head. They headed back out into the growing melee. Alfred went straight for Black Rose's hut. Brewer and Mac looked at each other and then ran to follow.

As they ran, Brewer glanced around to see how his men were doing. Two groups were fighting in the area of the hut where Elizabeth had been held, as though pirates had thought to check on their prisoner. He thought his men were holding their own, and from the corner of his eye, he saw Royal Marine reinforcements heading that way. To his right, he saw the first of Mr. Greene's men emerge from the jungle to seal off the village from that side. He looked ahead to see Mac kick in the door to Black Rose's hut so he and Alfred could enter. A moment later they reappeared. Mac shook his head.

"Empty, sir!"

Brewer frowned. "She's here somewhere! We can't let her escape! Mac, we know she's disguised herself as a man before, she may be doing so again. We need to stop anyone who's small—you know what I mean! Pass the word!"

"Aye, sir!" He ran off to pass on the captain's orders.

"Sir!"

Brewer spun to see Alfred pointing at a group of five pirates coming out of a hut. The captain saluted him with his sword. "Let's go!"

Alfred got there first and attacked low, slashing the first pirate across his abdomen as he slid past. The man screamed as he dropped his sword, then grabbed his stomach in an attempt to hold his guts in. Brewer brought his sword down on the man's neck and shoulder to put him out of his misery. He looked up to see Alfred parry a slash at his head. Brewer buried his dagger in the man's ribs as he ran past. He barely had time to raise his sword to defend against a thrust from the next pirate. Brewer sidestepped and slashed low, but this pirate was good. He blocked the blow and stepped inside to bring the hilt of his sword hard into Brewer's gut, catching him by surprise. The captain doubled and did his best to roll out of the way. He heard the *swoosh* of the blade missing him by inches and kicked out blindly. The pirate jumped back, giving Brewer room to regain his footing.

He could see Alfred was in the middle of his own battle, so he knew he was on his own. The pirate held his sword in front and circled to the left. Brewer remembered a trick he'd seen Lieutenant Cromwell use, but he knew he had to time it perfectly. So, he waited until the pirate raised his sword to strike, then he dropped to one knee and spun, kicking out with the other leg to sweep the pirate's legs out from under him. His foe was taken completely by surprise by the maneuver and went down hard on his back. Brewer rolled quickly and brought his elbow down savagely on the man's ribs, paralyzing him by knocking the breath out of him. Brewer jumped over the man and grabbed the man's sword, bringing it down as hard as he could across the man's neck. Blood flew when both arteries in the neck ruptured. The captain rolled away and got to one knee as he looked around for his sword. He saw it a couple steps away and went to retrieve it.

Lieutenant Cromwell had got the word from Captain Enfield that the captain was going after Black Rose, and he was to take his team into the village and cause as much mayhem as possible to provide cover. He led his men through three huts before they finally found some pirates to fight. He stayed outside while his men dealt with the enemy. That's where Mac found him and delivered the captain's warning that Black Rose was not in her hut and might attempt to escape disguised as a man. Mac left, and Cromwell took renewed interest in sizing up the pirates. He was about to follow his men into the next hut when a strange movement caught his eye. He stepped back to get a second look; sure enough, there was a short pirate with his face covered and a hat pulled down tight on his head, slipping past an empty hut. Cromwell decided to investigate, so he headed toward the little man. His rage grew when he saw the pirate hamstring one of the marines from behind and then run away. This guy seemed to be avoiding a straight-up fight with anyone. Cromwell followed him as he ducked in between two huts, heading for the jungle.

"Going somewhere?" he called out. The pirate turned and attacked without a word. Cromwell parried and stepped to the side. He jumped back to avoid a slash at his leg, then made a thrust that his enemy ducked, taking full advantage of his small size. Cromwell moved to his left and stepped in for a quick attack. His thrust was parried just in time, but he was able to follow it in until their swords were hilt-to-hilt. He brought his knee up into his enemy's gut. The pirate doubled over, and the lieutenant brought his fist hard to the side of his enemy's head, dropping him to the floor. He stood over the dazed form and kicked his sword away. The pirate rolled over, and his hat fell off, revealing long, dark hair. Cromwell pulled away the cloth covering the pirate's face— and found a woman's face looking up at him.

"Well, well," he said, as he lowered his sword point to within an inch of his enemy's neck. "Black Rose, I presume?" He could see from the hatred in her eyes that he was correct. "On your feet. My captain is anxious to meet you."

They found the captain, along with Mac and Alfred, standing outside Black Rose's hut. Brewer turned as Lieutenant Cromwell and his captive approached.

"What have we here?" Brewer asked.

"Captain," Cromwell said, "may I present to you Black Rose?"

"Just the person we were looking for," Mac remarked.

"The pleasure is all yours," Rose said.

"Be that as it may," Brewer said, "I would like to introduce a friend of mine. This is Alfred Thomas." Brewer indicated the small man standing beside Mac.

Rose's eyes narrowed, and hatred poured from her visage. She spat on the ground in his direction. She turned to Brewer.

"I presume you found your wife," she said, "and that she is safe now?"

"Yes," the captain said coldly, "but there will be a reckoning."

"I do not fear your hangman's noose."

"Who said anything about the hangman?"

Rose watched with a questioning look as the captain pulled his sword from its sheath and held out his empty hand. One of his men gave him a pistol. "Step into the hut." "What?" she asked.

He ignored her and turned to his officers. "Take whatever captives we have down to the bay. Keep a close watch on them. I'll join you there shortly."

He turned his back on them and stared at his prisoner as they slowly moved to obey his command. Rose held his eyes and was pleased somehow to know that the hate in the captain's eyes seemed to equal her own. Good. Whatever he had planned, she would not beg for her life. She would keep her pride.

But when the evacuation to the bay was completed, they were still not alone. Alfred remained standing in the same place.

"You, too, Alfred," Brewer said sternly.

"No, sir."

"Excuse me?" the captain said.

"Remember on the ship, sir?" Alfred stepped forward and spoke in a low voice, as though something were his fault and he alone had to atone for it. "When I said that Black Rose was mine? I'm here to collect. She is a coward, Captain. She didn't have the courage to seek me out herself. She had to kidnap an innocent woman and kill yet more innocent people, servants in your father-in-law's household, all because she wanted me. Well, here I am. We shall settle this, she and I."

"Alfred," Brewer said, "regardless of what I intend to do here, I cannot allow you to extract personal vengeance. One ruined career is enough."

"I concur, sir." Alfred walked up to him and put his hand on his captain's arm. "I believe your wife is calling you, sir. You'll find her at the bay."

Brewer looked into his servant's eyes. He surrendered. He turned and headed down the path to the bay without another word.

Rose looked at her sole remaining captor. "What now, little man?"

Alfred looked at her coldly. "Now I kill you as I did Cofresi. No, I take that back. He had the honor of dying in battle. You only deserve to slaughtered like a dog."

He pulled a pistol from his belt and shot Black Rose in the chest. She fell to the ground and did not move. He stepped up to her body and looked at it a moment, hoping his rage would ebb. Then he stepped into the hut and reappeared a moment later. He stood over her body.

"This is justice for the likes of you," he said. He dropped a black rose on the corpse and turned to walk down the path to the bay.

EPILOGUE

Captain William Brewer sat on the settee in his day cabin with his wife, Elizabeth, beside him. His arm was around her, holding her close to him. HMS *Phoebe* was on course to St. Kitts now, to reunite mother and father with daughter and grandfather. Their time at Port Royal had been mercifully short. Brewer had turned over the captives who survived the assault on Black Rose's camp, along with Flint and his men to the admiral's guards. Brewer promised to mention in his report that Flint had voluntarily surrendered the location of Black Rose's camp to him. Admiral Cartwright accepted his reports, both written and verbal, without comment, other than he would forward them to the Admiralty along with his own comments.

On his way out of the building, the admiral's aide had stopped him to present the admiral's orders. He'd opened them as soon as the man left and was surprised to find that Cartwright ordered him to take HMS *Phoebe* on a one-month patrol of the Lesser Antilles, to includes stops at St. Kitts to give the admiral's personal thanks and respects to the retiring governor there, and also Martinique to see if he could pick up new intelligence on French intentions in the Caribbean.

"Father will be leaving for England in two months," Elizabeth said. "Shall I still accompany him? Perhaps set up house for us in England? We never did come to a decision on that score, you know."

"I know," he said as he ran his fingers through her hair. "I think it would be wonderful to have a place to come home to."

She looked up at him and smiled. "I think so, too. Where shall we settle?"

"Smallbridge?"

Elizabeth wrinkled her nose at the suggestion, and the sight almost made him laugh out loud. "I don't think so," she said. "I love Lady Barbara, and I shall surely visit, but I have no desire to live in Smallbridge."

"As you wish," he said. "Will you look to the north country with your father?"

"I don't think so. I am leaning toward the outskirts of London, although I believe Mac mentioned that Cornwall was a lovely place."

Brewer chuckled. "I shall leave that choice entirely in your hands, my dear. I shall write you a letter to take with you. That, and the marriage license signed by Admiral Lord Hornblower, should be sufficient to grant you full access to my London accounts." He kissed her forehead and rose. "If you will excuse me, my dear, duty calls. I must take a turn around the deck. I shall return soon." He bowed and left the cabin.

Elizabeth watched him go, and then she laid her head back on the settee and closed her eyes. It had been nearly a month since her rescue, and she still began to shake every time he left her alone. She rose and walked out to the dining cabin to sit at the table.

Alfred appeared in the door of the pantry. "May I get you something, Madam?"

"I don't think so at the moment," she said, "but thank you. Please, Alfred, sit. I realize that I have not thanked you for your part in saving my life."

Alfred sat on the opposite side of the table and two chairs to the left, the closest chair to the pantry door. "No need for that, Madam, I assure you. It was on account of me that your life was threatened at all."

Elizabeth frowned and shook her head. "I don't see it that way at all, and I can assure you that my husband does not see it that way either. If anything, you were every bit the victim in all this, nearly as much as I myself. You acted in the King's service when you fought and killed the pirate Cofresi. What Black Rose did was the act of a madwoman, driven insane by grief. You had no control over that, nor do you bear any responsibility for it. I hope and pray that this incident will in no way impact your service to my husband and our family."

Alfred bowed. "No, Madam," he said sincerely. "Not while I have breath."

She rose, and he did the same. "Thank you, Alfred," she said. She made to return to the day cabin but stopped. "I also have not thanked you for saving my husband's life. I know from Mr. McCleary that you have done so many times."

Alfred nodded graciously, almost a half-bow. "Almost as many times as he has mine."

"I know," Elizabeth said, and disappeared aft.

Alfred watched the open doorway for some time, feeling his demons recede for the first time in a long time. He smiled and returned to the pantry. He looked forward to the future now.

THE END

ABOUT THE AUTHOR

JAMES KEFFER

James Keffer was born September 9, 1963, in Youngstown, Ohio, the son of a city policeman and a nurse. He grew up loving basketball, baseball, tennis, and books. He graduated high school in 1981 and began attending Youngstown State University to study mechanical engineering.

He left college in 1984 to enter the U.S. Air Force. After basic training, he was posted to the 2143rd Communications Squadron at Zweibruecken Air Base, West Germany. While he was stationed there, he met and married his wife, Christine, whose father was also assigned to the base. When the base was closed in 1991, James and Christine were transferred up the road to

Sembach Air Base, where he worked in communications for the 2134th Communications Squadron before becoming the LAN manager for HQ 17th Air Force.

James received an honorable discharge in 1995, and he and his wife moved to Jacksonville, Florida, to attend Trinity Baptist College. He graduated with honors in 1998, earning a Bachelor of Arts degree. James and Christine have three children.

If You Enjoyed This Book, please write a review.

This is important to the author and helps to get the word out to others Visit

PENMORE PRESS www.penmorepress.com

All Penmore Press books are available directly through our website and world wide distributors

BREWER'S LUCK

BY

JAMES KEFFER

After gaining valuable experience as an aide to Governor Lord Horatio Hornblower, William Brewer is rewarded with a posting as first lieutenant on the frigate HMS *Defiant*, bound for American waters. Early in their travels, it seems as though Brewer's greatest challenge will be evading the wrath of a tyrannical captain who has taken an active dislike to him. But when a hurricane sweeps away the captain, the young lieutenant is forced to assume command of the damaged ship, and a crew suffering from low morale.

Brewer reports their condition to Admiral Hornblower, who orders them into the Caribbean to destroy a nest of pirates hidden among the numerous islands. Luring the pirates out of their coastal lairs will be difficult enough; fighting them at sea could bring disaster to the entire operation. For the *Defiant* to succeed, Brewer must rely on his wits, his training, and his ability to shape a once-ragged crew into a coherent fighting force.

BREWER'S REVENGE
BY
JAMES KEFFER

Admiral Horatio Hornblower has given Commander William Brewer captaincy of the captured pirate sloop *El Dorado*. Now under sail as the HMS *Revenge*, its new name suits Brewer's frame of mind perfectly. He lost many of his best men in the engagement that seized the ship, and his new orders are to hunt down the pirates who have been ravaging the trade routes of the Caribbean sea.

But Brewer will face more than one challenge before he can confront the pirate known as El Diabolito. His best friend and ship's surgeon, Dr. Spinelli, is taking dangerous solace in alcohol as he wrestles with demons of his own. The new purser, Mr. Allen, may need a lesson in honest accounting. Worst of all, Hornblower has requested that Brewer take on a young ne'er-do-well, Noah Simmons, to remove him from a recent scandal at home. At twenty-three, Simmons is old to be a junior midshipman, and as a wealthy man's son he is unaccustomed to working, taking orders, or suffering privations.

William Brewer will need to muster all his resources to ready his crew for their confrontation with the Caribbean's most notorious pirate. In the process, he'll discover the true price of command.

PENMORE PRESS
www.penmorepress.com

BREWER
AND THE
BARBARY PIRATES

BY
JAMES KEFFER

It is said that a man is shaped by his past, and so it was with William Brewer. Before he took command of *HMS Defiant* in a hurricane, before he hunted pirates in *HMS Revenge*, Brewer endured a crucible of fire. Fresh from the tutelage of Napoleon Bonaparte on St. Helena, Brewer signs on for a cruise under Captain Bush in *HMS Lydia* to the Mediterranean to battle the Barbary Pirates. Here Brewer learns to fight, but he also learns what it means to command men in battle and what it takes to order men to their deaths. Their enemy is a Scottish renegade who is responsible for the deaths of dozens of his fellow sailors over the years and the selling of hundreds of Europeans into African slavery. Along the way, Brewer is introduced to new heroes and new devils. He also receives sage advice from no less than the Duke of Wellington himself. In the end, Brewer has to use all he's learned and going beyond to save *HMS Lydia* from destruction at the hands of pirates.

PENMORE PRESS
www.penmorepress.com

Brewer and the Portuguese Gold
By

James Keffer

The year is 1840. Twenty-three years ago, Horatio Lord Hornblower was governor of the island of St. Helena and hailer to its only prisoner, Napoleon Bonaparte. First mutual respect and later shared tragedy forged a clandestine friendship between the two men. Now King Louis Philippe of France has requested that the remains of the late emperor be returned, and Queen Victoria has granted that request. The French have also requested that the former-Governor Lord Hornblower attend the exhumation as the official British representative! Hornblower knows the situation is a veritable powder keg; the Ultra-Royalists, led by the ruthless Duke of Angouleme, will stop at nothing to prevent Bonaparte's remains from returning to France, while the Bonapartists, led by the late-emperor's nephew Louis-Napoleon, hope to use the return to stage a coup and establish a renewed French Empire. Hornblower must do his utmost to ensure the mortal remains reach French shores safely to pay a debt he has owed for over twenty years.

Penmore Press

Challenging, Intriguing, Adventurous, Historical and Imaginative

www.penmorepress.com